TRUE BLUE

Freya 'Free' Paterson has finally come back home. She's landed the job of her dreams working on an art project with the local school, but she hadn't planned on meeting the man of her dreams as well. With his irresistible Irish accent, Constable Finn Kelly is everything Free wants — genuine, kind . . . and handsome as hell. He's also everything Free isn't — stable and dependable. Yet despite the passion simmering between them, he just wants to be friends. What is he trying to hide? As Free throws herself into the challenges of her new job, fending off the unwelcome advances of a colleague and helping to save her beloved Herne River, Finn won't stay out of her way, or out of her heart.But just when she needs him the most, will Finn reveal his true colours?

SASHA WASLEY

TRUE BLUE

Complete and Unabridged

AURORA
Leicester

First published in 2018 by
Penguin Random House Australia

First Aurora Edition
published 2019
by arrangement with
Penguin Random House Australia

The moral right of the author has been asserted

A catalogue record for this book is available
from the British Library.

ISBN 978–1–78782–081–4

Published by
F. A. Thorpe (Publishing)
Anstey, Leicestershire

Set by Words & Graphics Ltd.
Anstey, Leicestershire
Printed and bound in Great Britain by
T. J. International Ltd., Padstow, Cornwall

This book is printed on acid-free paper

Dedicated to Trevor, my own clever, funny, kind Irishman.

1

That sky . . .

There was something about the colour of the Kimberley sky that gave Free a shiver of joy every time she drove home to Paterson Downs. It was a rare, extraordinary shade of blue. How could anything be so bright, pure and perfect? She memorised the hue, trying to lock it away in her mind so she could reproduce it on canvas. She'd never once succeeded, not in a decade of painting.

Below her ran the Herne River, rimmed with dark red like a sorrowful eye reflecting the world above. Free lined up her phone and snapped three photos, then swiped back to review them. Two were not particularly interesting, but the other had caught a flare of sunlight in the ripple of water over a rock — a strobe-flash on the river's blue surface. Free climbed the riverbank and hopped back into her car. She sat on the side of the road for a couple of minutes while she uploaded the photo to Instagram and tapped out a caption.

Day 197 of my #Herne365 project. The Herne River on a perfect Kimberley day, with a splash of sunshine. #NoFilter

She got back on the Herne River Road. *Oh, that sky!* Free gazed at it through the windscreen as she drove, losing herself in the vast, still, cloudless beauty of it above the burnished gorges.

Another blue caught her attention — blue lights flashing in the rear-view mirror.

'Ohhh,' said Free. 'Oh no.'

She checked her speed as she touched the brake. Ninety-seven, and the limit was a hundred along here. She had her seatbelt on — she'd been caught for that before. Not because she deliberately flouted the law; more because she tended to have a head full of things that didn't include buckling up. Or parking within the lines. She'd been reprimanded for that once, too.

Free pulled over and switched off the engine. She couldn't bear to sit waiting in the car so she swung open the door and stood on the side of the road, chewing her lip while the officer got out of the police vehicle. He drew nearer, sunglasses on, and it became apparent that, although young, he was enormous — broad-shouldered and of towering height. She shrank against her little white car.

'Um, hi,' she called as he came within earshot.

He didn't speak at first. He approached, coming right up close so she had to tilt her head back to look up at him, heart thumping.

Then he took off his sunglasses and there was a pair of friendly brown eyes. 'Good afternoon, Miss.' His voice was warm, and Free relaxed against the car.

'Did I do something wrong? I'm so sorry.'

'Not as such. We just noticed your boot's half-open. You lost something on the road back there.'

'Oh, crap! I was looking for my camera in the boot a minute ago so I could do a river photo for my Instagram, but then I realised I'd left it at home, so I had to use my phone anyway. I'm doing this picture-a-day project thingy about the river.'

The guy watched her in silence. *Oh God, I'm rambling.* Free dashed around to check the rear of the car. Sure enough, the boot was partially open, the lid still wobbling slightly. She pushed it wider, reviewing the contents.

'Oh no!'

He joined her. 'What is it?'

'The bride-to-be veil. And — *ugh* — the drinking straws are gone too.' She looked up. His caring expression made her feel somehow better again. 'Oh well. I guess I'll have to go back and see if I can find them.'

He examined her with those warm, intelligent eyes, and her pulse jumped back up a notch. How could she have failed to notice this guy in Mount Clair before now? Maybe he was from Roeburke, on secondment or whatever they called it.

'Want some help?' he asked.

She gave him a grateful smile. 'Would you? I can't believe I didn't shut the boot properly. I'm such a moron.'

'These things happen,' he said. 'I saw a couple of things fly out a few hundred metres back. Hop in the troopy and we'll see if we can find them.'

'You're a legend, Detective — ' She checked his name badge. 'Kelly.'

'Constable.' He grinned. 'Just call me Finn.'

'Finn!' Free was delighted. 'Like the benevolent Irish giant!'

His smile vanished. 'What?'

'You know, the legend of Finn McCool, the kindly Irish giant. I learned about him in Dublin. You're a giant, and you seem benevolent . . . '

Finn didn't speak and Free trailed off, hoping she hadn't offended him. They reached the police 4WD and Finn's passenger wound down his window.

'Freya Paterson. I should have known.'

'Briggsy!' Free looked between Finn and Sean Briggs, who was not in uniform. 'Oh! Are you on your way to Quintilla for Tom's buck's party?'

'Yep. Young Kelly here's my chauffeur, as I plan on responsibly enjoying a few beverages this evening.' Briggsy winked.

'Oh my God, this is so funny. I've been getting supplies for Willow's hen's party. It's a surprise. Willow didn't want a hen's, so we're springing it on her.' She hopped into the back seat. 'Finn said we could have a quick squiz for the stuff I lost.'

Briggsy rolled his eyes. 'Can't help yourself, can you, Kelly? Got to rescue a damsel in distress. Make it snappy. I don't want to be late.'

Finn turned the car around, tyres crunching as he moved back onto the long, straight road. 'What are we looking for, exactly?' he asked.

'A white veil attached to a plastic silver tiara with a Learner's *L* on it,' Free said. 'And some drinking straws shaped like . . . ' She stopped, realising what she'd been about to say.

Briggsy cast a knowing glance over his shoulder. 'Novelty drinking straws for a hen's night? I think I know what we're looking for.'

4

Free cringed inwardly, but Finn was trying not to smile.

The veil they found easily. It was caught on a barbed-wire fence, silver plastic glinting in the sunlight and tulle billowing in the strong breeze. Finn pulled over and Free jumped out to untangle it from the metal barbs. She inspected the netting. One big hole and another couple of snags.

'At least it got stuck on Paterson Downs fencing,' she said when she was back in the troopy. 'It's quite fitting, really. I might even be able to talk Willow into wearing it after I tell her the story.'

But there was no sign of the straws and after a few minutes' searching, they were obliged to give it up as a lost cause.

'Some truckie will probably find them stuck to his grille tomorrow,' said Finn.

'Oh good Lord, I hope not,' said Free. 'I hope they didn't go into the poor river. And I hope a child doesn't find them! They're tacky, but I wanted to make Willow laugh.'

'Just tell her you had a couple of coppers out searching for your willy straws,' was Briggsy's remark. 'That should make her crack a smile.'

Free broke into giggles. 'Thanks, guys.'

They brought her back to her car and Finn climbed out, walking with her to the driver's side.

'Hurry up, Kelly!' Briggsy called. 'I'm losing valuable drinking time.'

'Are you going to Tom's buck's party, too?' Free asked Finn.

'No, I'm just the driver.' He checked her face. 'You're a bridesmaid, then?'

She felt suddenly shy. His eyes — they were so wonderfully soft and kind, but with a spark in them that said quite plainly that he liked what he saw. And he was so damn *tall*.

She remembered to reply. 'Yeah, Willow's my sister.' She indicated the expanse of red and green beyond the fence line, cattle visible as specks in the distance. Paterson Downs late in the wet season. 'This is home.'

Finn followed her pointing hand, shading his eyes. 'Wow. That must be amazing. I'm a city boy, so I know nothing about station life.'

'You're here for a country stint, I guess. From Perth?'

Finn nodded.

'You must be desperate to get back to the city.'

His forehead creased. 'Why do you say that?'

'Well, it's kind of boring here, right?' she said. 'Mount Clair's criminal activity would be mostly pub brawls and street drinking. In the city, you'd have murders and organised crime, drug deals, corporate fraud. It would be more interesting, you know? More glamorous.'

Finn's lips curved. 'Mount Clair gets more interesting every day.'

Free gave him a proper once-over. When her eyes wandered back to his, he was red in the face. *Whoops.*

'How long have you been in town?' she asked, as though she hadn't been checking him out. 'Not long?'

'Since November.'

'Ah, that explains it.'

'What does it explain?' he asked.

'Well, I'm sure I would have noticed you around town if you'd been here a while. You're so tall and . . . ' Free stopped herself from saying *handsome*, but then couldn't think of anything else to call him. The word *hot* zipped around her head. 'Tall.'

His eyebrows shot up. 'Did you just say I'm tall and *tall*?'

'Well, you are quite tall.' She gave him a brave smile.

Finn burst out in a chuckle that was surprisingly boyish, given his size. She joined in.

'Kelly!' Briggsy hollered. 'Get your arse back here!'

'Coming, Sarge! Sorry — gotta go.' Still, Finn hovered. 'Maybe I'll see you again soon?'

'Yes! And thanks again for your help.'

He jogged back and ducked into his vehicle. Finn waved as they passed her and Free got back on the road, smiling. For all its small-town predictability, there was nothing quite like the generosity of people in Mount Clair. She was impressed with Constable Finn Kelly. Even if he hadn't been in town long, he already understood country kindness.

And he was so . . . tall.

She returned to the speed limit. The loss of the novelty straws wasn't a big deal, and Free could barely hold in her excitement as she drove the last couple of hundred metres to the homestead. She opened her car door. Willow would be so surprised —

7

The screen door banged. 'Where have you been?' Beth demanded, striding across the gravel driveway. 'Everyone else is already here.'

Free dashed around to the boot, flicking it open. She snatched up as many of the hen's party supplies as she could. 'Did I miss the surprise?'

'Of course you missed it.'

'Crap. Was Willow excited? I was making good time but I had some trouble on the drive here.'

She was going to tell Beth the willy straws story but her eldest sister had already collected her own armful of gear from the boot and was heading towards the house. Beth glanced back.

'You've left the boot open,' she called. Free went back to close it.

Inside, their father was refilling champagne glasses at the bench. He looked up when she arrived in the kitchen.

'How's my girl? I was starting to get worried!'

'Sorry, Dad. Had to stop to take a river photo.'

'Fair enough. This dam's getting beyond a joke. I was having a gasbag with Horrie Blackwell the other day. He reckons he saw a load of dead fish floating around in the water beyond the building site.'

'Oh no! What happened to them?'

'Stuffed if I know. It'll be the shit going into the water from the dam construction, I'd say.'

She groaned. 'Why won't anyone do something about it? It needs to be stopped.'

'Free!' Beth hissed, sticking her head around the corner. 'Are you coming or what?'

Free scurried into the lounge. There were a

couple of women from town sitting there with Willow. Free recognised Kate — the girlfriend of Sergeant Sean Briggs — and another two women she knew by face but not name.

'Free!'

Willow jumped up and came forward, and Free met her with a tight hug. She pulled back to inspect her sister. Free adored Willow's practical, hardworking soul and those slightly vulnerable dark eyes.

'I can't believe you and Beth did this.' Willow sounded a little tipsy already. She pulled Free towards the circle of women in the lounge room and they called out their welcomes. 'Do you know Kate, Karlia and Bee?'

Free hugged everyone. These women had become Willow's friends by default in recent months, because they were Tom's mates' girlfriends. Beth buzzed around, setting up the games and prizes Free had brought. Willow pushed a glass of bubbly towards Free as she sat down with the group.

'I ran into Briggsy on his way to Quintilla,' she told Kate.

Kate rolled her eyes. 'He'll be stuck into the Bundy in five minutes, and a sloppy affectionate mess by the time I see him later. Did he find someone to give him a lift out?'

'Yes, the new constable — Finn.' Free smiled at the memory of those kind brown eyes.

Karlia gave a whistle. 'Constable Finn Kelly. He can handcuff me and take me to the back of his paddy wagon anytime. You're single, Free — you should take a shot.'

9

'Yeah, get yourself a piece of the Finn action, girl,' Kate chimed in. 'He's not just hot, he's deadset the sweetest guy I've ever met. Hell, if I wasn't with Sean, I'd take a shot myself, age difference be damned.'

'I told Phoebe she should go for him,' said Karlia.

'Sean's already on it,' Kate told her. 'Mr Matchmaker has been plotting the Phoebe-Finn hook-up for weeks now. He's just gotta talk her into it. She got scared off his matchmaking services after the blind date with Tom.'

Both of them glanced at Willow. She was a little pink in the cheeks but she smiled.

'Yeah, I guess I messed that one up for Phoebe.'

Kate giggled once she saw that Willow wasn't huffy with them. 'I think it was Tom who messed that one up for her. It was pretty obvious Tom's thoughts were anywhere but on Phoebe that night.' She gave Willow's knee a little push. 'All turned out for the best, though. And maybe poor old Pheebs will have better luck with kind-hearted Constable Finn.'

The mention of Finn's kindness made Free remember the veil rescue, and she got up to grab it off the pile Beth was fussing over. She arranged it on Willow's head, deftly concealing the barbed-wire holes.

'How do I look?' Willow struck a demure pose and Free was startled by how beautiful and truly happy her sister looked, even with the goofy L on the tiara.

'Stunning,' she said, quite heartfelt. 'Beth,

come see. Doesn't Willow look stunning?'

Beth came to stand at Free's side, examining Willow. 'She does.'

'Are you two crying?' Willow demanded, her own eyes glistening.

Free was. And from what she could see, Beth was too. Then even Kate and the other girls were tearing up.

'Oh gawd,' groaned Willow, wiping her eyes. She grabbed her glass and took a big gulp. 'No tears! Please!'

'Imagine what we'll be like at the actual wedding,' Free choked.

'A game!' Beth brushed her arm across her eyes. 'That's what we need.'

She rallied the guests, organising everyone with their own little cardboard appendages to pin onto a poster of a sultry-looking male model she'd blu-tacked to the wall.

Free had to hand it to Beth. She knew how to salvage a party.

2

'Not bad,' said Beth, peering into the kitchen of Free's Mount Clair unit. 'Seems clean, anyway.' She opened the fridge. 'Mostly clean.'

'Look at this!' Free beckoned her into the second bedroom. 'This will be my studio.'

Beth nodded, shooting a dubious look at the carpeted floor. Suddenly, she jumped and gave a little shriek, but when Free scrambled to see what had scared her, it was just a tabby cat coming down the hall.

'Hello!' Free bent down to stroke its head and it purred loudly. 'He's adorable. I wonder whose he is.'

'A stray, maybe.' Beth stared at the cat with slight distaste. 'I hope he doesn't have fleas.'

'He looks clean and well-fed. The back door's open, so he must have let himself in.'

The tabby was a smoocher. He rubbed himself on Free's hand so ecstatically that she scooped him up, scratching his chin.

'What's your name?' she asked. The cat gave a meow that sounded remarkably like a word. 'Did you hear that? He said 'Max'!'

'Maybe he belongs to the people next door,' said Beth.

'It's possible. Or maybe he comes with the unit. It is fully furnished, after all.' Free grinned.

Beth eyed her. 'You know, you don't *have* to live here. You could live with me. I have room.

My place is bigger — and nicer.'

Free placed the cat on the ground. How could she tell Beth that she *wanted* to live in government accommodation — in this duplex — and not in her sister's pleasant house in the nice part of Mount Clair? The duplex was part of the job, part of the artist-in-residence contract with the high school, and it was special to Free. It represented the first real, important job she'd ever had. Beth, who'd been running her own medical practice in town almost since she graduated with a medical degree, wouldn't understand.

'It's all signed, sealed and delivered.' Free attempted a casual tone. 'And the duplex is so close to the school. I could walk if I wanted to. I'll try it out for a while and see how I like it.'

Beth shrugged. 'Please yourself. The offer stands.'

'Thanks, Beth.'

The cat made that cracked meow again and Free chuckled. 'I love that he says his own name. Will you stay, Max?'

The cat flopped on the carpet and commenced cleaning himself.

'I don't think he's going anywhere,' Beth said. 'Hopefully he's house-trained.'

Free was optimistic. 'Cats are always house-trained. It's their instinct.'

Willow had arranged a ute and two Paterson Downs station hands to help Free move in. Beth helped with unloading Free's gear, then they waved the guys off and Beth unpacked a box full of Paterson's cast-offs.

'You don't have any matching cutlery at all,' she called as Free heaved a box of art supplies into her new studio.

'Yeah, it's funky,' Free called back. 'Chic. The antique stores in Perth charge like wounded bulls for mismatched cutlery.'

'Yeah, but that stuff's stylish. Not Ikea and Kmart.'

Free shrugged inwardly. Who had matching cutlery at her age? She struggled with her large easel, pinning it open with her knee and one hand while she tightened the nut with the other. She transferred her latest work onto the easel, catching sight of a smudged corner as she did.

'Bugger,' she muttered.

It was still a little wet. It must have been bumped during the drive. She dug out a brush and used its hard wooden end to scratch texture back into the paint. *Hmm.* That wasn't quite right. She opened a tube of black and another of burnt umber and squeezed smidgens onto her metal palette, then worked into the corner again until the rock looked better. Not perfect, but better.

The sky was still wrong. Free stood back and frowned at it. No matter what she did, she couldn't recreate that particular blue. She unpacked jars of oil and turpentine, and squeezed out a lump of cerulean paint in among smaller splodges of whatever other colours she could put her hands on. Inhaling the hard, clean scent of linseed oil, Free blended the blue with white and green, adding a touch of ochre. Hey, that was looking good. More ochre? The tiniest

14

amount of silver, perhaps. Free tried the colour mix on the canvas and stood back, holding her breath.

Gah. Fail.

She sighed and plopped her brush into the turpentine jar just as Beth appeared. Her sister stopped short, her eyes going from Free's easel to the cat, still cleaning himself indolently on the carpet.

'Seriously, Free? You've been in your new place for half an hour, and you've already adopted a cat and started painting?' Beth edged behind Free and took her arms, steering her out of the studio. 'Priorities, girl. *Unpack*.'

'Oh yeah.'

'I have to go. I wanted to stay and help but my locum just called. He's got some kind of domestic emergency going on and needs to leave early.'

Free was relieved, which gave her a stab of guilt. 'It's okay, Bethie, you go. Thanks so much for helping me today.'

'At least your kitchen's done, so you should be able to make yourself some dinner. Willow threw in a bunch of cans and packets to start off your pantry.'

Free hugged her. 'My sisters are the best.'

'There are still some things outside, on that little table on your porch. Your printer and another box. Don't forget to bring them in.'

'I won't.'

'You should focus on your bathroom next,' Beth advised, collecting her handbag. She swiped away her long hair so she could sling the leather strap across her shoulder and studied Free. 'Are you sure you're going to be all right here?'

'Of course! I've trekked through mountain ranges in Nepal, Beth. I'm sure I can handle my first night in Mount Clair teacher's accommodation. And Max will keep me company.'

Beth departed, mumbling under her breath about stray cats and flea infestations. Free leaned against the railing that divided her porch from her neighbour's and waved as the Beast crunched out of the driveway. Then she went back to her studio. Max gave her a cracked meow greeting and she rubbed his ears, staring at the sky on her painting again. *Maybe a wee bit of yellow* . . .

The sun was dropping when she finally emerged from her painting reverie. Free stretched and put her brushes in the turpentine jar. Something had disturbed her. There was a noise, she realised — an unfamiliar sound coming through the wall. Was it music? A radio, perhaps. It stopped briefly, then started up again, louder and closer. *Singing*. Someone was singing right on the other side of the studio wall.

Of course — this was a duplex. There must be another teacher living next door, sharing a wall with her unit. Free picked up an empty jar and crept across the room, where she placed it ever so gently against the wall. She pushed her ear up to the glass, just like she'd seen in the movies, and the singing became a touch clearer. Her heart softened. Whoever it was had a lovely voice, and he was singing a song she thought

16

she'd heard in Dublin. Staying on the edge of Temple Bar, Free had stumbled into a local estate drinking hole, thinking it was a regular Irish city pub. At first they'd been unfriendly, but after she'd bought and drunk a couple of pints of Guinness, the barman finally cracked and they got chatting. Soon enough, half the people at the pub had introduced themselves, and included her in their gossip and songs.

As she listened and remembered, a warmth came over her — the same warmth she felt whenever she sat at the Paterson Downs kitchen table to drink tea with her father.

She smiled down at Max. *I think I'll like living here.*

★   ★   ★

'You don't need to be nervous at all.'

The head of the Mount Clair High School's art department was Jay Lincoln, a round, short woman with a mop of curly black and grey hair, upon which her glasses were permanently perched. She had beautiful big, dark eyes.

'The Year Tens and Elevens *want* to be studying art. They're not like the lower-school kids. Some of them would mess with you.'

Aidan, the other artist who'd been awarded a residency for the tile wall project, rubbed his sharp nose. 'They wouldn't want to mess with me.'

Jay smiled politely and Free hastened to break the tension.

'Hey, if I can survive the Mount Clair Muster

17

Festival beer tent, I can survive spitballs,' she said.

Jay guffawed. 'The infamous beer tent! Look, these are basically good kids. Some of them are incredibly talented, in fact. We've got a couple of kids who've picked up awards in the local shows and further afield. And anyway, by the time they get past Year Nine, they're doing art by choice. These are the interested ones.'

'Phew,' said Free. 'That's good because I wouldn't have a clue how to 'behaviour-manage' anyone.'

Aidan swept his gaze across the studio, spotless from its summer holiday clean-out. It was still deeply familiar to Free, even after nine years away.

'That's not what we're here for, anyway,' Aidan was saying. 'We're here to give these kids the benefit of our knowledge and skills. If there's any bullshit in my classes, they'll be out the door before they can say 'time-waster'.'

He smiled at her, but Free felt a little sorry for Aidan. He must have gone to a private school in the city, to have such a limited understanding of how Mount Clair teenagers worked.

'Maybe if someone's causing trouble, it's because he or she's got personal issues,' she ventured. 'Problems on the home front, or something.'

'Well, he or she can take his or her personal issues out of my studio,' Aidan said, with another of those cool smiles.

His confidence was astonishing. Jay gestured towards a thin woman with cropped grey hair, who was lugging a drying machine across the classroom. 'That's our assistant, Inga, who's been with us for years. She'll help you with materials, organising equipment, storing and moving stuff, setting up displays, that sort of thing. Inga!' She waved at the woman. 'This is Free Paterson and Aidan Hamilton, our two artists-in-residence for the tile wall project.'

They exchanged greetings and Jay moved them on, indicating a darkened doorway. 'The ceramics materials and kiln are in here.'

She led them inside, switching on the light. Free examined the equipment. A good-sized, newish kiln, and in a smaller storage room, slabs of plastic-wrapped clay and containers of glazing chemicals.

'It's two sessions per week, plus an after-school class, is that right, Jay?' Aidan was asking.

'Yes, two classes with either the Year Tens or the Elevens — I'll assign you one year each. And then one of you can do Tuesday afternoons, and the other Thursdays. That's your opportunity to make inroads with the tile work. The theory and design can happen during class-time. It dovetails nicely with the curriculum. But it might be easier to work on the practical stuff — moulding and glazing — in your after-school sessions.'

'Yeah, that'd be good.' Free poked through a box of paints. 'Hopefully, the students will be happy to stay beyond the hour we've been given, so we can get some of the more time-consuming stuff done.'

Jay had already nodded and stepped back out of the storeroom, but Aidan glanced Free's way.

He leaned in and spoke quietly.

'Our contracts only specify an hour per week for the after-school sessions, you realise?'

'Yeah, I know,' said Free. 'But if they're willing to stay a little longer, rather than leaving dead on the hour, we'll get through so much more. You know what it's like when you have to stop halfway through a job.'

'You'll only get paid for the hour. No overtime. Jay told me the grant is fully expended on our salaries and the equipment for the tiles.'

Free laughed. 'I wouldn't expect to be paid extra.'

Aidan's eyebrows rose and he ran his gaze over her but said nothing. Free stepped into the classroom after Jay.

'Tomorrow will be a good opportunity to familiarise yourselves with the equipment and set-up of the classrooms,' Jay said. 'Have you done the reading I sent you on learning outcomes?' They both nodded. 'Perfect. I'll be directing the content, but I'd like to hand over to you as much of the theory and skills work as possible. That's what you're here for, after all — to share your expertise. I'll spend some time with both of you individually tomorrow to run you through the term plans.' Jay paused. 'We're having a get-together at Mounties on Friday night. All the teaching staff. You should come, meet everyone socially before we start the term.'

Free nodded. 'Sounds good.'

Aidan pursed his lips. 'I'll see how I go. There's an art show I'm entering and I need to work on my entry piece. This week's been pretty full-on, with coming here today and again tomorrow, as well as settling into the unit.'

Jay wasn't particularly fazed. She cast Free a warm smile.

'Come along, straight after we finish here tomorrow. We're a good bunch when you get to know us.'

'I will,' said Free.

'I've finished the term plans now so I'll send them to you both,' Jay told them, and headed for the office.

Free ran her gaze over the classroom. This was where she'd spent her happiest moments of high school. Heart swelling, she took in the familiar deep troughs and laminated benchtops beneath paint-spattered windows. Outside, the blue sky cut through a bloom of white clouds. Breathtaking. Ultra blue and raw umber, maybe? Or cadmium —

'We should probably take the opportunity to compare notes on our teaching strategies for the term,' Aidan said. 'Are you free for a coffee when we're finished here?'

Free came back to the present. 'Um, okay, yeah. But I don't really have a strategy, as such. I was just going to do what Jay told me to.'

His mouth pulled up on one side. 'Perhaps we could just get to know one another a little better, then, since we'll be working together for the semester.'

Free was puzzled. 'Don't you need to work on your entry for the art show?'

Aidan chuckled. 'I can take an hour off.'

'Oh. Okay, if Jay doesn't need us here, we

21

could grab a quick coffee. But I need to spend as much time as possible going through the term plan. I can't help but worry I'll mess it all up.'

Free was hit with a wave of apprehension at the thought of teaching. She checked Aidan's face to see if he was showing any sign of nerves. *Hard to tell.* She was distracted by his stretched skin, thin lips and bulbous, pale eyes. It was almost as though his brown ponytail was pulling his face taut. If she released that ponytail, would his face relax into a normal, warm, friendly face? She itched to try it.

'Sounds like you definitely need a coffee,' he said, giving her a quick smile. 'You'll be fine, you know.'

'Hope so.'

'Let's head across to Marcel's Deli when we finish up,' he said.

'I'll shout you a brew.'

★ ★ ★

Free had walked to work, so Aidan drove them to Marcel's after Jay told them they were finished for the day. His car was spotless and brand-new, a dark silver in colour. It smelled expensive.

'I don't normally go to Marcel's,' she said.

Aidan indicated right, waiting for a red mud-coated 4WD to rumble past. 'Why's that?'

'Galileo's does fair trade beans, so I usually go there. I mean, since my sister taught me what that means.'

'Marcel's coffee is excellent,' he said.

'Oh, good. And they do fair trade beans?'

'I'd be amazed if they didn't.' Aidan braked suddenly and honked at a young Aboriginal woman crossing the road with two small children. She gave him the finger and Aidan sighed.

'Locals,' he muttered.

'It might be better to go a bit slower,' Free said. 'There's always lots of pedestrians on the main street.'

'Careless pedestrians,' he remarked. 'They'd get flattened in the city.'

He pulled in and parked outside Marcel's Deli.

'Oh, they're closing, I think,' Free said, seeing a young man lugging a sign inside the café.

'I'll check.' Aidan jumped out and approached him. They had a brief discussion, then Aidan gestured at Free to get out of the car.

'Are they still open?' she called.

Aidan beckoned again. 'Josh here says he'll make us a coffee.'

'You're not closing?' she asked the young man.

He shrugged. 'It's no trouble. Come in.'

'Why don't we just go to Galileo's, Aidan?' Free urged him. 'If Josh is trying to close up, we shouldn't delay him.'

'He's absolutely fine with it,' Aidan said, and his voice was so firm Free didn't feel like she could argue.

She climbed the step into the pink-and-brown-striped deli with its lit-up cabinets of croissants, quiches and pastries.

'Long black, topped up with lactose-free milk,'

Aidan called to Josh. He gave Free an inquiring look.

'Uh, flat white, please.'

'And a selection of macarons,' Aidan added.

They sat at a minuscule table on hard wooden chairs.

'So, what's your background?' Aidan asked.

'Oh, I'm a farm girl!' Free said. 'My family runs a cattle station on Herne River Road. I live with Dad and my sister Willow. We're going to organic certification.'

He raised his eyebrows. 'Really? Is that viable?'

'Yeah, well, I think so, anyway.' Free grimaced. 'I don't know, actually, but I don't think Dad would let Willow do it if it wasn't financially okay.'

Aidan already appeared to have lost interest in the topic. 'Actually, I meant your artistic background.'

'Oh! It's not very fabulous. I did visual arts at uni, then travelled a bit. Did some short courses with ceramics masters in Italy. I mainly do oil painting, charcoals and ceramics, you know?' She paused, hoping she didn't sound pretentious. 'What about you?'

'I studied VA at Notre Dame — '

'In France?' Free broke in, excited.

'The University of Notre Dame in Perth.'

'Oh — of course.'

'Then I won a grant to develop a piece of art for a corporate office in Perth. I've had two joint exhibitions and one solo. I do mainly sculpture and abstract pieces, and acrylics is my preferred medium.'

24

He stopped. Free was humbled.

'Wow. I've never had a solo exhibition. That is just amazing. It's so hard to be successful as an artist. I'm in awe.'

Josh brought them coffees and a gilt-edged tea plate loaded with macarons of various bright colours.

'Thank you!' She stared at the biscuits. 'How gorgeous!'

'Still think Galileo's is better than Marcel's?' Aidan asked with a smile.

Josh shot a surprised look at Free and she wanted to crawl under the teeny-weeny table. 'I never said that!' she said. 'I just meant that I'm in the habit of going there. But I'll definitely come back to Marcel's.' She attempted a smile at Josh and his face softened into a quick grin before he retreated.

'Try the purple one,' Aidan advised.

Free had been reaching for the one that looked like coconut but she hesitated.

'Go on,' he urged. 'It's the best.'

'Okay.' She picked it up and tasted it. *Licorice?* Yuck, she hated licorice.

'Blueberry.' Aidan looked satisfied.

'Um, it's licorice.'

He shook his head. 'Definitely blueberry. I had one the other day.'

Free wasn't sure what to do. It was certainly licorice, but Aidan was so adamant. And she couldn't finish it — it tasted disgusting. She put down the purple monstrosity and transferred her attention to her coffee, glancing longingly at that coconut macaron.

'It must have been amazing to have your own exhibition,' she said.

'Yes. A lot of hard work, but worth it.'

'Did you sell loads? That would be the best bit about an exhibition, I reckon — off-loading your art to make some space.'

He shrugged. 'Yes, I sold a few pieces. I was more interested in the exposure — you know, developing my brand — than worrying about selling anything. The market's dead at the moment, anyway, so it's more important to have a presence in the arts community than to sell work.'

'You think the art market's dead?' Free's heart dropped slightly. It was tough trying to make money from art at the best of times. She made a pittance selling her work. She hadn't noticed a decline in her sales through a local gallery or her online store, but maybe Aidan was right.

'Absolutely,' he said. 'Hopefully, it will pick up now the conservative government's back in power and the economy can recover.'

Free was speechless.

'I find that corporate purchasers are the best,' he went on. 'They understand that art is worth real dollars.'

'I don't think I've ever sold anything to a corporation,' she said. She sneaked the coconut macaron off the plate.

'They're great,' said Aidan, sipping coffee. 'Good payers, and they appreciate adventurous works.'

'Perhaps I'm not adventurous enough for corporate tastes,' Free said. She nibbled at the coconut macaron. *Oh, so much better!*

'Have you got any social media pages?' he asked. 'We should exchange details.'

'Yeah, you can find me under 'Free Paterson' on Instagram, Facebook, all the sites,' she said. 'Or just search for the hashtag *Herne365*.'

He frowned. 'What's that?'

'It's a project I'm doing. Posting a photo of the Herne River every day for a year.'

'Why?'

Free spoke around her mouthful of coconut macaron. 'I love the Herne.'

'A photo every day?' Aidan slurped his coffee. 'Doesn't that get a little — samey?'

'God, no! The river changes constantly. It's amazing. Check out my photos. You won't believe how much the river changes day by day.'

'I'll look you up.' Aidan pulled out his wallet and fished out a card. He handed it to Free. 'Here are my details so we can collaborate, or whatever.'

'Thanks!' said Free. Aidan seemed so accomplished. It was a relief to know she had his support. 'Tell me about this art show submission you mentioned. What are you working on?'

★　★　★

It was another hour of worrying about the poor barista before Free could get away. Aidan sipped coffee more slowly than anyone she'd ever met, telling her in fine detail about his latest acrylic on canvas. He talked about theme and colour, paradigm and juxtaposition. She knew all the words and concepts, but his explanation confused her. He must be super smart.

Free checked out his work online, and noted that he mainly worked on very large canvases, using jarring colours and aggressive streaks across a background of spatters. She struggled to relate to his paintings, but the guy was obviously successful. She looked forward to seeing the end result of this latest work he'd mentioned. Maybe he would incorporate some Kimberley colours or textures now that he was living in the region.

At home, Free pulled her car in to the single garage and heaved down the roller door. Beth had reminded her to be security conscious now she lived in town, saying it wasn't like Patersons, where nothing ever needed to be locked up. The tabby cat was waiting for her at the front door. He gave several of his funny little meows in his excitement to see her.

'Hello to you too, Max,' she cooed in reply. 'When I go shopping again, I'll get a cat litter tray so you can stay inside while I'm at work. Then you won't get hot. Come in and have some Snappy Tom.'

Max accepted her invitation and she sorted him out with a dish of food. Free banned herself from going into the studio, knowing her current canvas would distract her again. Instead, she lugged her printer inside from the porch and plugged it in. She wanted to print the term outline and make sure she knew back-to-front what was expected of her before school started next week. Jay had assured them several times that they didn't need to worry about the course content; that she would provide guidance. All Free and Aidan had to do was help develop certain skills in the students, and introduce the theory. Their main role was to lead the tile project. But Free couldn't help but worry. What if she stuffed up? What if she accidentally took the kids off track, or got them confused? It might affect their grades.

She pulled up the documents Jay had sent and hit print. The printer buzzed obediently into life, but before it even picked up a sheet of paper, suddenly made an unhealthy grinding noise and beeped at her.

'Oh, what now?' Free loathed technological problems and normally begged Willow to sort them out for her. She flipped open the front of the printer and saw something that made her suck in a frightened gasp.

Scales?

In an instant, she realised what had happened. Because she'd left her printer out on the porch for four days, a reptile of some description had crawled into it and made it home. Free stared at the patterned scales, momentarily paralysed with fear. Then she reached over to flip the cover closed. She ran to the kitchen and snatched up the pot holders Beth had hung from hooks. Barely breathing, and holding the printer as far as possible from her body, Free carried it back outside to the porch table. Then she dashed inside and closed the front door behind her with a shudder. Hopefully the snake would grow tired of its new accommodation and depart. In the meantime, she would have to do without a printer.

The ordeal made Free think a glass of wine might be a good idea. She rinsed out a glass and poured a generous portion of sauvignon blanc, dropping a couple of ice cubes in before she went to her studio. As soon as her hands were steady enough, she picked up a brush and immersed herself in her painting. It was the perfect way to calm down. That portion of rock was shaping up. Free squeezed some more blobs of paint onto her palette and moved on to the glimpse of dark-green river coming around the bottom of the gorge.

When the world outside grew dim, Free realised she was hungry. She put her brushes in the jar, picked up her half-full glass and went to seek out dinner. She hadn't shopped for a couple of days, so her pantry was in a sad state. Free boiled some fettuccine and stirred bottled pasta sauce through it. Her third pasta meal that week — she should get some frozen dinners. She hadn't posted her river photo of the day, she recalled, and it was too dark to get a new one. She scrolled back through her camera roll and found a recent picture of a delicate blue damsel fly perched on a piece of grass, the water a dark blur behind it.

A lonely damsel fly looking for a lover on Day 213 of #Herne365. #HerneRiver #NoFilter, she captioned it.

Someone had shared one of her older photos, she noticed with pleasure. Even better — they had used it to speak out against the diversion dam. It felt good to think people were using her photos to raise awareness of the danger of this dam project to their region's major river.

Free went back to her painting. She was so immersed that she didn't stop until after eleven, when a grumble of thunder brought her back to the present. No doubt, a storm was about to lash the town. Free put her brushes away, but at that moment, the sound of singing rose from next door. She grabbed her empty jar so she could listen at the wall. She didn't need it, really — the voice was louder this time. Free listened in breathless excitement, heart fluttering.

Abrupt silence.

Disappointed, Free headed for her bedroom. She was exhausted, she realised. She whipped off her clothes, shrugged into a comfortable T-shirt and dropped into bed. She was just starting to fall asleep when it started up again. Free caught her breath in the darkness, listening.

Ohh . . . The Pogues, 'Dirty Old Town'. Free softened inside, remembering that ride out of Dublin on a cheap tour bus to see an ancient battle ground and burial mound, a Pogues album playing on the coach's tinny speaker.

What a lovely voice this unknown neighbour had. Not pitch-perfect, but real and oddly heartfelt. She tried to imagine what subject he taught. Surely, he was a history teacher — a wild-eyed, dark-haired, whisky-drinking older man from the north of Ireland, perhaps even a freedom fighter in his youth. The song ended and Free sighed.

But he wasn't finished, after all. The gentle melody of a ballad rose, and although she didn't know it, the song tugged at her heart. She lost herself in the sound, drifting in and out of sleep. Even in her slightly strange new environment, the song somehow wrapped her in the warmth and comfort of home.

3

By midmorning on Friday, Free had worked herself into a fever of anxiety about starting classes the following week. To her utter amazement, Aidan left school at noon, declaring himself ready. He even invited her to join him for lunch. Free declined. She desperately needed more time.

Jay had assigned Aidan the Year Tens, and Free the Year Elevens. Perhaps that was half the problem. Why hadn't Jay given the Year Elevens to Aidan, who was clearly more confident than Free? Year Eleven was an important year — just one step before the challenging final year that included university entrance exams, or at least portfolio preparation for further education. Free would be working with Jay to ensure they covered everything in the curriculum, but it still felt like an enormous responsibility. Gazing at the lesson plans Jay had given her for Week One, Free felt sick.

Stop worrying, she ordered herself. Jay would lead the way. The head of the art department was sympathetic and smart. If it got too much and Free was screwing things up, Jay would take control. Free would rather give up the contract than wreck the kids' chances through crappy teaching.

Just before three, Jay stuck her head around the storeroom door. 'Hey, you want a lift to the pub this arvo, Free?'

'Yes, I walked this morning, so that'd be awesome. Thanks, Jay.'

'Meet you in the car park in five. Mine's the red Prado.'

Free pulled off her art shirt. She'd been checking the quality and range of materials so she was probably a bit of a mess. She scooted into the closest bathroom and checked her appearance. Her hair was never quite what she would call tidy — golden wisps and curls escaped no matter how severely she tried to smooth it back into a bun. She pulled it loose and adjusted her basic singlet top. She had accompanied the top with a light crocheted cardigan and a long skirt, uncertain of the dress code, but all the other teachers were wearing variations on shorts, cargo pants and capris, so Free made up her mind to follow suit in future. She bundled the cardigan into her bag. She was looking forward to drinks at Mounties with the staff.

Free headed out to the car park, wet season humidity warming her bare arms after several hours in the air conditioning. The sky was leaden but it wasn't quite raining. She reached the red Prado, smiling at another teacher who was also waiting for Jay. She'd seen him at lunch. He was an awkward-looking man, perhaps in his early thirties, with a balding head and excessively hairy legs.

'Hiya,' she greeted him.

'Coming to Mounties?' he asked.

Free nodded in reply. 'I'm Free Paterson.'

34

'Max Drummond.'

'Max!' Free looked at the man in delight. 'That's my cat's name!'

He gave her a shy smile. He had the thickest eyebrows Free had ever seen. Her fingers itched for a pencil and a sketchpad.

'What do you teach?' she asked.

'Science.'

'Oh, is Mr Caporn still here?' Free asked him. 'Chemistry?'

'Yes,' Max said. 'He's been here for over thirty years now.'

Jay appeared, crossing the car park to join them. 'Pile in!' she called. 'I'm gasping for a wine.'

'Mr Caporn was so patient with me,' Free said to Max as she climbed in to the back seat. 'I never understood the formulas.'

'How long's it been since you went to school here, Free?' Jay asked, backing out of her parking spot.

'Nine years. It feels like yesterday. I don't think I'll ever be able to call my teachers by their first names.'

'Did you get on well with them?' Jay wanted to know.

'Some of them. I think I had a reputation as kind of easily distracted.' Jay and Max laughed. 'I liked the teachers, generally. My favourite was Mrs Woodley. English.'

'Hilary's still here,' said Max.

'How long have you been working in Mount Clair, Jay?' Free asked. 'When I was at school, we had Mr Tunnidge heading up art. Ten-tunnidge, we used to call him.' She panicked as soon as the words left her lips. *Ack!* What an unprofessional thing to say — and it was such an unkind nickname.

However, Jay just chuckled. 'He was a big boy, all right. He was my predecessor, but he got offered a place in Perth. I'd already done my country service, but I jumped at the opportunity to be head of department. I ditched my job in Perth to come up here, not expecting to fall in love with the place.'

Free understood that. 'Isn't it amazing? The sky. The colours! The river. There's nowhere like it on the planet.'

'Oh, yes, absolutely. But I guess it's the people I love most. Everyone made me feel totally at home, like I'd lived here forever.'

Max murmured his agreement. 'The kids are gorgeous, too. I just love the earthy humour and genuine kindness in the Mount Clair community, even if the wildlife takes a bit of getting used to.'

Free told them the tale of the snake in her printer and Jay shrieked in sympathy.

'Might be a Children's python,' Max said in his soft voice.

'I don't know what it is. I just hope it leaves.'

'I'm a snake handler.' He said it so quietly, she almost didn't catch it.

'Are you? Do you think you could get it out of the printer for me? I'm at 17A Marlu Street.'

He gave a laugh, not exactly agreeing, but at that moment they arrived in the Mount Clair Hotel parking lot, so Free let it slide. Being

Friday afternoon, the pub was crowded, and it would only become more so as the night went on.

'Max, find out where the others are sitting,' Jay ordered him, leading the charge. 'I'll get the first bottle. Wine, Free? Oh, I know! Let's get bubbly, to celebrate your new job.'

Free followed her to the bar to help with glasses, waving to a few old schoolfriends. Willow's friend Kate was there, sitting at the bar with Phoebe Challis, a girl Free had met several times and liked. Free greeted them both, exchanging hugs. She would have introduced Jay but the woman was busy shouting her order across the noisy bar.

'You're here with the teachers, are you?' Kate asked. 'How's it going in the new job?'

'Good. They're really nice.' Free dropped her voice. 'I'm peeing my pants about next week, though.'

Phoebe nudged her. 'Why, Free? You'll be great!'

'New-job nerves.'

Phoebe started to ask for details but Kate had spotted Briggsy and a group of other blokes coming into the pub. She shouted and waved to them, and they headed over. The tall Constable Finn Kelly was with them, Free realised. Her heart leapt straight into an excited thudding.

'Here she is!' Briggsy's voice boomed. 'Miss Phoebe Challis, the most eligible young lady in Mount Clair!' Phoebe rolled her eyes and suffered a kiss on the cheek from Briggsy.

'Ouch,' she remarked, rubbing her face. 'Stubbly.'

Finn's eyes landed on Free and lit up. Damn, he was *hot*, with that big, strong body and clean-shaven jaw. She smiled back at him, that weird shyness suffusing her again.

'How'd you go without the willy straws, Free?' Briggsy asked, accepting a glass from Kate. 'Was the hen's do totally ruined?'

'We managed to drink just fine without them, thanks,' she answered. 'Turns out chicks don't need willies after all.'

He just about spat his drink and Kate and Phoebe howled with laughter. Finn grinned at her and tingles of excitement went to all the right places. *I wonder if I'll get a chance to talk to him tonight . . .*

Briggsy recovered himself. 'Well, I for one cannot wait for this wedding. I'm making a speech. I'm going to shred the hell out of Tom.'

Free grew alarmed. 'Oh, no, don't do that. Willow gets embarrassed so easily.' But Briggsy was already in a loud argument with Kate over whether he had any mortifying stories about Tom, and didn't hear.

'Don't worry.' Finn leaned down to say it quietly to Free. 'The sarge is all talk, but he's loyal. When it comes down to it, he wouldn't wreck anyone's big day.'

This close, Free could see his eyes clearly, and they were as bright and interesting as fresh water running over pebbles. She studied them. She could paint those eyes. Or a pebbly river. Finn smelt wonderfully fresh, too, as if he'd just

38

showered. Senses lighting up, her mind wandered towards the image of Finn stepping out of a shower . . .

'You thirsty?' he asked, breaking the spell. 'Can I get you something?'

'I'm already getting drinks with my crew.' She pointed, and at that moment Max appeared.

'I found the teachers' table,' Max said in his low, shy voice, so quiet that Free strained to hear it.

'Okay.' She smiled at Finn. 'It's great to see you again.'

He stepped back, nodding. 'Likewise. Have a good night!'

Um, nope. No, that wasn't going to be the end of their interaction tonight — not if Free had anything to say about it. She took the champagne glasses from Jay and followed Max. She could head back and hang out with Briggsy's group after the first drink, and hopefully get to know Finn a bit better.

The teachers were seated in the beer garden, where fans and spray-misters had been set up to keep hotel patrons cool. Jay poured the drinks and introduced Free around the table. Free snapped a group selfie with the champagne flutes and posted it on her Instagram account. She looked around to check on Finn several times but her line of sight was blocked by a bunch of blokes standing in the beer garden doorway.

Max lost some of his shyness and wouldn't stop talking about reptiles and snake handling. It got a little dull at times and Free tried to introduce a few different topics but he was persistent.

'Where's the other guy who got a residency?' one of the other teachers interrupted at last, and Free seized on the subject with relief.

'Aidan? He couldn't make it tonight.'

'I'm not sure about him,' Jay said.

'Why's that?' asked Free.

'Seems a bit up himself,' said Jay. The bubbly had obviously relaxed her. 'I mean, why isn't he here? Too good for us?'

Free had also been thinking he should have made more of an effort to fit in, but she didn't think it was fair to make accusations in his absence. 'He said he had to work on his piece for an art show.'

Jay chortled. 'Working on his *piece*, is he? Sounds about right.'

The others burst into laughter. Even Free had to smile, although she felt obliged to defend Aidan.

'He's a respected artist,' she said. 'He got this job, after all. I mean, I got it because I'm local, I guess. But Aidan's not local. He's super qualified. He's sold art to big companies in the city and had exhibitions and everything.'

Jay snorted. 'His exhibitions were funded by his family. Free, being local helped your case, but you got the contract because you're very talented and you had the experience and skills we were seeking. Plus, the YouthArts grant conditions specified that artists under thirty were preferred as a way of meeting the government's youth engagement targets. But

Aidan — he's thirty-five.' She paused. 'You know who his mum is, don't you?'

Free drew a blank. 'Umm . . . ?'

'Aidan Hamilton. It's not *Amanda* Hamilton, is it?' Max asked.

Jay nodded. 'The woman who owns the Buildplex conglomerate.'

Free gasped. 'No! Buildplex is the company working on the Herne River Dam.'

'That's her. One of the state's biggest businesswomen. Perhaps Aidan failed to mention this, but the company that commissioned some of his artworks for their corporate head office also happens to be Buildplex.'

Free was aghast. 'No. Really?'

'Buildplex are stepping on toes locally,' one of the other teachers threw in. 'It's not just the dam project. They've bought out some properties and small businesses, too. People are getting worried about how many fingers they have in pies in the region.'

Free pictured Aidan's self-satisfied expression as he'd told her about his corporate customers. How could he brag about that? It was cringeworthy. 'I'm totally opposed to the dam,' she said.

'You and half the town,' said Jay. 'Are you a member of that anti-dam group on Facebook?'

'Of course! And I've subscribed to the newsletter, and I sign and share all the petitions. I went to a protest at the construction site with my sister a few weeks ago.'

Jay lifted her eyebrows. 'Wow, you really are anti-dam.'

Another teacher leaned in. 'Why are you against it, Free? I thought this dam was supposed to save the local agricultural industry.'

'It's wrecking the river!' she said. 'They're going to divert the Herne so farmers can irrigate huge areas and grow crops like sugar cane and rice — thirsty crops.'

'Greenie groups are saying it'll interfere with the natural cycle of the river,' Max added.

'It's already happening,' Free said. 'My dad's friend spotted a load of dead fish downstream from the construction site.'

'It's certainly a contentious topic.' Jay lowered her voice. 'There are suspicions that the approval process was corrupt. *Corporate influences.*'

Free had also heard rumours about corruption, but she didn't know details. She waited, intrigued.

But another teacher snorted. 'Rubbish. The dam got approved by the government, based on the water needs in the region.'

Jay tipped her head. 'Maybe.'

'Didn't Amanda Hamilton send the office holders from the Mount Clair Chamber of Commerce on a trip to Japan to show them a similar project?' Max said.

Jay nodded. 'That's right. And several members of the chamber are also local government councillors, or work at the shire office. They *claimed* the Japan junket was allowed, as it was an educational trip — pro bono professional development, courtesy of the Amanda Hamilton Foundation. But it was an all-expenses-paid trip that lasted two weeks,

42

staying in the best hotels and playing golf on the world's most expensive course. And when they got back, they campaigned energetically for the dam to go ahead.'

'The chamber has been involved in the tile wall project, too, hasn't it?' Max asked.

'They have,' Jay said. 'They were pretty vocal in their support of the project as a tourist attraction and a statement of place for the town.'

Max was watching her. 'And you think Amanda Hamilton might've paved the way for Aidan to get the school residency, as well?'

Jay checked around them but the other teachers had lost interest. 'I don't know. YouthArts gave me first look at the applicants and he wasn't even on my *maybe* pile. And yet he got selected.'

Free fell speechless with horror for a few moments. It was bad enough that the dam approval process was dodgy — but now the residency as well?

'Wow,' she breathed at last, 'I thought it was a proper selection process.'

Jay shrugged. 'Perhaps it was. Maybe he earned the position fair and square . . . and maybe his mum is pulling a lot of strings in town since her company won the bid for a major construction project in north-west WA.' Jay sipped her wine, eyebrows raised.

Was this how things worked? Free thought about her own residency. Could her father — or perhaps Beth — have enough pull in the town to influence *her* selection? *No, of course not.* The

43

decision had been made jointly by the state government's YouthArts funding body and the local shire. Who would care what a local farmer or doctor wanted? With a tickle of doubt, she recalled that Beth was a member of the Chamber of Commerce. Her clinic had even won some chamber award last year.

'Oh well, at least we got you, Free,' Jay said. 'That's one good choice. You're not the daughter of a Buildplex executive too, are you?'

She clinked Free's glass, giggling at her own joke, but Free was glad when the conversation moved on from the integrity of her and Aidan's residencies.

The blokes had cleared out from the beer garden doorway by now and Free looked over at the bar to see if Finn was still there — and caught him glancing her way. His face immediately lit up with one of those beautiful smiles and Free returned it automatically. She hardly ever blushed but heat crept up her cheeks now, knowing this big, strong, *hot* guy was looking at her. She fidgeted with her glass for a few moments, then made up her mind to go to the bar for some water. She could just stand there, not far from Finn, and give him another smile if he looked her way. Maybe they would get chatting again . . .

But when she steeled her nerves and got up to fulfil her mission, Finn, Briggsy and their entire crowd had vanished.

Poop.

*   *   *

44

Free woke on her couch, the cat curled up and purring on her chest. She had a headache and a dry mouth. *Ugh.* Why had she gone and drunk so much? On her first social outing with her new colleagues, too.

Her disappointment over Finn leaving Mounties early floated through her mind and she cast the thought away. That had nothing to do with getting drunk.

Still, after discovering his departure, she had knocked back a glass of bubbly a little more quickly than she should have — and it was on an empty stomach. It had made her tipsy. Tipsy meant suggestible for Free, and Jay had suggested shots. Free knew she was a lightweight when it came to drinking, but before she had a chance to think the better of it, she, Jay and two other young teachers had shots lined up on the bar. Some of the staff had left around seven, but the singles and kid-less stayed on. Reptile-loving Max Drummond, who apparently didn't drink, drove everyone home in Jay's car around eleven, spilling Free in through her front door. Vaguely aware that she should eat something, she'd stuck a bowl of baked beans in the microwave and . . . that was the last thing she remembered.

The cat jumped onto the coffee table and gave her a pointed look. 'Max,' he said.

Free staggered over to the kitchen, where the microwave was intermittently beeping to let her know her baked beans were ready. She opened the door to stop the hellish beeping and held her breath, averting her eyes while she tipped the bowl into the bin, genuinely fearful for her

45

stomach. She put a piece of bread into the toaster. She could probably handle toast.

She gave Max some cat biscuits and let him outside, then flicked on the television and stared at a music video program, her thoughts slipping back to the night before. Good Lord, what if she'd embarrassed herself in front of everyone? But nothing awful came to mind. Jay had been drunk too, so she probably wouldn't have thought much of it even if Free had done something stupid. She relaxed slightly as she fetched her toast, then sat back down to nibble her breakfast and sip water.

She almost spilled her drink when her phone rang right beside her. *What the hell?* Ah — her handbag was hiding beneath a couch cushion. She dug out her phone and saw the caller ID: Beth.

Free tried to sound bright and coherent. 'Hiya!'

'Morning.' Beth's voice was as collected as ever. 'You ready?'

Free thought furiously. 'Ready for . . . ?'

There was a subtle pause and the hint of a sigh. 'Did you read your messages this morning? Or did you only just wake up?'

'No, I've been up for ages.' Free checked the clock: ten-thirty. 'I haven't looked at my phone this morning.'

'There's been a bridesmaid dress disaster. Willow emailed the online store to ask when the dresses we ordered were going to arrive and got a reply from a liquidator. The business has gone bust.'

Free dropped her toast. 'Our dresses?'

'Are no more,' said Beth. 'Willow's dress was through a different shop, thank God, but ours aren't coming. Willow's been messaging us all morning. She's on her way into town. We're going to try Pizzazz.'

'Oh, Beth — *Pizzazz*?'

'I know, but it's only a couple of weeks till the wedding,' said Beth. 'We're running out of options.'

'What time are we supposed to be meeting?'

'In ten minutes.'

Free thought fast. Surely she could get dressed and drive to the main street in town within about ten minutes. 'Okay, I'll be there.'

'I'm at yours, out the front. Should I come in or wait in the car?'

Dammit. Sprung. 'You'd better come in.'

Free dashed for the pile of clean washing on her coffee table. At least she could answer the door fully clothed and pretend she was almost ready. But suddenly Beth was in the doorway, having let herself inside. Hadn't she locked the door when she got home last night? *Whoops.*

'Morning, Sunshine.' Beth laughed as Free scrambled into a long sundress. 'At least you're out of bed.'

Free repressed a scowl. 'I'll be as quick as I can.'

Beth glanced around, taking in Free's last night's clothes abandoned on the floor and toast-and-water breakfast. She checked her phone. 'Willow's already in town, at Galileo's, ordering us coffees.'

'I'll be ready in two seconds.'

Beth shot her a sceptical look and tapped out a reply to Willow. 'Hurry up. I'll get her to order you a detox smoothie, shall I?'

Free fumed inwardly as she went into her bathroom. Bloody Beth and her relentless competence. She always knew best, was always on time, always knew when Free had screwed up. Free sprayed some deodorant and swept her tangled hair back into a hasty bun. Trying to ignore the dreadful things the taste of toothpaste did to her stomach, she cleaned her teeth and then grabbed a pair of big sunglasses. By the time she'd slipped her feet into sandals and returned to the lounge room, Beth had somehow found the time to helpfully fold her clean washing. It was stacked in neat piles on the coffee table.

The humiliation smarted like a slap. 'You shouldn't have done that. You don't need to do my housework for me.'

Beth gave a little shrug. 'I don't mind. I had nothing else to do. You ready? Let's go.'

It was lucky Beth was driving because Free wasn't even sure that she was fully sober yet. They met Willow inside the café on Main Street. Free inspected her sister's anxious face and hugged her.

'Don't worry about the dress thing,' she told Willow airily. 'I'm sure we'll find something gorgeous today.'

Unexpectedly, Willow turned her worry onto Free. 'Are you all right? You look tired.'

Beth fought a smile. 'Free had a big night last

48

night, didn't you, Free?'

'No! Well, I went to the pub.'

Beth laughed and Willow relaxed. 'Good time?'

'Yeah. I got to know the teaching staff a bit better.'

Her sisters wanted to know about her new job, so she described the set-up at the school and her upcoming teaching work as they sipped coffee. Free started to feel slightly better, and by the time they'd finished their drinks she was ready to face a morning of dress shopping.

There was only one store where a girl could find a formal gown in Mount Clair, and that was the forty-year-old Pizzazz Boutique on Main Street. It was the place where most women in Mount Clair had bought at least one high school ballgown, awards night frock, cocktail party dress or bridesmaid outfit.

Beth sighed, flicking through dresses on the rack marked *Weddings*. 'Nothing in the colour we chose. I suppose shimmer grey is too much to ask from Mount Clair,' she added under her breath. She pulled out an emerald green dress and gave it a critical examination. It was satin and slinky, with fine straps. 'This isn't bad. It would complement the guys' ties, too. What do you think?' She checked with Willow.

'That's pretty,' said Willow. 'But . . . '

Beth had already pulled out a second one and handed it to Free to try on.

'But?' Free prompted, putting a hand on Beth's arm to stop her sister from charging straight for the fitting room.

49

'Oh, it's really dumb, but Tom threatened to be a 'groom-zilla' when we first got engaged. He said he wanted pink bridesmaids, and I thought it would be funny if . . . '

'Oh my God, yes!' Free bounced on the spot. 'That would be the best.'

Beth's face was wary. 'Bright pink or soft pink?'

Willow shrugged but Free was already scanning the rack for pink dresses. If Willow wanted pink, pink she would have. They'd never even asked her what she wanted and Beth had pretty well chosen the shimmer-grey bridesmaid gowns for them from the online store. Free handed the long green one back to Beth, spotting a frothy baby-pink number.

'Look!' Free whipped it out. It was V-necked and fitted at the waist, with soft chiffon folds that fell to the knees. Willow looked delighted; Beth, appalled.

'There's only one,' Beth said hastily. 'We need three, remember?'

Free pushed the one she'd found at Beth and hunted more concertedly in the dress rack, but she only found lilac and pale blue in the same pattern.

'Hang on, this might work.' She forced Beth to hold the pink one up in front of her and then held the blue one in front of herself. 'And Tanya in the lilac.'

Beth was still frowning but Willow was thrilled. 'Yes! They look really cute together. And Tom will be so shocked,' she added, chuckling.

Under sufferance, Beth tried on the pink and

Free, secretly gleeful, the blue. She was right — they did work together, and Willow looked so excited that Beth relented, although she obviously hated the romantic chiffon dress. They fit, too, and the lilac was in the right size for Tanya, Willow's best friend from Perth.

'It's meant to be,' Free declared.

'They'll show every bit of red dirt,' Beth predicted and Free discerned a sour note in her voice.

'Who cares?' Dropping her voice, she added, 'They're what Willow wants.'

Beth gave an infinitesimal roll of her eyes but let it go. It was worth it when Willow hugged Free goodbye at the end of the shopping trip and whispered '*Thank* you' in her ear.

★   ★   ★

After Beth dropped her home, Free debated whether she should paint, drop in to the school to do some more prep work, or take a nap. *Me, teaching*, she thought, terror seizing her all over again. She envisioned how her first class would go on Monday: dozens of teenagers with hostile faces, watching as she fumbled with her pile of papers, searching desperately for her first lesson plan. *Hmm*. She should definitely go to the school to do more preparation. She could take her daily river photo on the way.

She dug her key to the school's art room out of her handbag, but a knock on the door interrupted her preparations to leave. Free answered it and stood in open-mouthed shock

51

when she found Constable Finn Kelly on her doorstep, rubbing Max's ears.

He lifted his eyes and looked as astonished as her. He was in uniform. Free caught her breath in panic — *Beth . . . Willow . . .*

But Finn broke into a smile. 'Free! You — you live *here?*'

'Um. Yes . . . '

So damn *tall*. And that hard, strong frame with those broad shoulders. Good Lord, he was stupidly hot, with those eyes like a Kimberley stream — all warm colours marbled with light. She forced herself to blink.

'Is everything okay?' she asked. 'Have I done something illegal?'

Finn seemed to recover from the surprise. 'No, it's all okay. It's not an official visit. I'm off-duty, actually — just finished my shift. It's just, I noticed the printer.' He indicated the porch table.

The snaky printer. Free hadn't touched the thing since Thursday. 'Oh, yeah.'

'Are you getting rid of it? Because the kids' literacy centre is asking for unwanted computer equipment and we take donations for them down at the station. I could take it for you, if you want.'

'Ah, gotcha. Well, I don't really want to give it away because it's quite a good one. Only, it's got a snake in it.'

His eyebrows shot up. 'Pardon?'

'A snake.'

Finn stared at the device. 'There's a *snake* in your printer?'

Free nodded, stepping out onto the porch. 'I know, right? I only left it out for a few days and a snake got in, somehow. I nearly peed my pants when I opened the cover and there it was.' She clutched her hands together, making a face. 'I'm too scared to open it and see if it's gone. I'll wait until someone else can deal with it for me.'

'Fair enough. Wildlife, huh?' Finn shook his head. 'It gets in everywhere. We've got a possum in the roof at work. Scared the hell out of me, thumping around when I was there by myself one night. I thought there was a break-in — either that or the place was haunted. And there are bats that hang in a tree out the front of the station.'

Free chuckled. 'That's the Kimberley for you.'

There was a silence. Would he make a move to go? Finn shifted his weight and hitched a hand in one pocket.

'Did you have a good time at the pub last night?'

'Yes, it was fun,' she said, her hope rising. 'I've got a job at the high school. The teachers wanted to go for a drink to celebrate the new school year.'

'Or drown their sorrows at the end of school holidays?'

She smiled. 'Maybe. I drank a little too much — but I wasn't driving or anything. Max drove us home.'

He didn't appear to be judging her. 'I would have liked to stay on at Mounties but Sarge said we were leaving. He'd caught a couple of barra earlier in the week. He cooked them up for us on

53

the barbecue back at his place.'

'Nice.' She bit her thumbnail. 'Do — do you want to come in? I could make you a cuppa.'

Finn's face lit up but he hesitated. 'Are you sure it's okay?'

In answer, she pushed open the screen door to let him in. He manoeuvred past her and accidentally brushed her arm with his, setting Free's heart racing in the process. Everything about this guy was big, warm and strong. She was tingling all over just from that one meaningless touch.

Finn's eye fell on her packing boxes. 'Not fully moved in yet?'

Free tried to focus on his words. 'No, only got here a couple of weeks ago. Sorry, I know it's a mess.'

'This isn't a mess. You should have seen my place when I first moved in.'

'I should unpack but I keep getting distracted.' She flicked on the kettle and rinsed out a couple of mugs.

'By what?'

'By a painting that I'm right in the middle of doing.'

'You paint?'

'Yeah, I'm an artist — well, aspiring artist. I'm doing a residency at the school. That's why I've got myself a government duplex to live in.'

'I'm always in awe of artistic people. I can't even draw a stick figure that looks like a stick figure.' Finn watched her drying the mugs. 'Could I see the painting?'

'Oh — um, okay. Yeah.'

She abandoned the tea-making and led Finn to the studio. It was always strange showing her art to people she didn't know very well, and Free hardly ever let anyone see her works in progress. She almost changed her mind halfway down the hall — but that would be crazy.

Free twitched the easel round to face Finn more fully and pretended to be busy tidying up brushes before steeling herself to check his reaction. He was gazing at her painting, a frown on his face. She waited. *He doesn't like it.* She tended towards abstract styles and some people didn't appreciate that sort of thing. The pause went on so long she eventually folded.

'It's a section of rock along the Herne River.'

'Talbot Gorge. I know it,' Finn said, his eyes locked on the canvas. 'Wow. It's amazing. The red of the rocks and the green of the water — perfect.'

Free was silenced. He recognised Talbot Gorge from her semi-completed impressionist painting?

'I know it's not finished, but the colour is . . . ' Finn bent right down close to the painting and then moved back. 'Amazing. I just — the light. How did you make it look like that? Like it's glowing off the canvas?'

Free had been overpraised by suitors in the past, but this was different. Finn was mesmerised. He was moving from side to side to catch her painting from all angles, almost as though he'd forgotten she was there. Free felt a wave of emotion. There was something deeply honest and real about this man. She watched as he admired her painting, and was speechless at the power of his response.

'You're incredibly talented,' he said, his eyes landing on hers so suddenly that her heart stuttered.

Free scrambled to recover. 'Rubbish. The sky's all wrong, as usual.'

He returned to the painting. 'Well, I like it — but I know what you mean. It's not quite the right blue.'

'Mount Clair's sky is distinctive. I've never been able to reproduce it.'

'It's close enough. I'd say you'll nail it one day. But it doesn't really matter because this is bloody extraordinary.' He glanced at the floor. 'Hey, the government housing people are pretty lenient, I've heard, but they could freak out if you get paint and turps all over the carpet. It might be an idea to lay a drop sheet down in here.'

Free looked down. He was right — there were spatters of paint and oily turpentine drips marking the carpet. 'Yeah, good idea. I will.'

He followed her back down the hall to the kitchen. She still felt trembly, but managed to make them cups of tea without spilling anything. He took three sugars in his tea, which made her laugh.

'I used to think people arbitrarily gave up sugar when they hit adulthood,' she said. 'I stopped taking sugar in tea and coffee when I turned eighteen, and spent the next year hating the taste of both before I finally got used to it.'

'I'm not planning on growing up,' he said.

'I don't think I could, even if I wanted to,' she

56

answered with a grin.

They sat at her little four-seater wooden table with their mugs, Free sweeping crumbs away with a hasty hand.

'How does your residency work?' he said.

'Well, the local government is putting a public artwork at the entry to the town — a tile wall. They wanted to involve Mount Clair kids, so they've contracted a couple of artists-in-residence for the high school. The idea is that we help the kids come up with a concept and design, and then oversee the actual creation of the tiles. I really wanted to take part when I heard about it. In fact, if I hadn't got a residency, I would have volunteered in some way. I was busting to be involved. I was lucky, though, and I got a contract. Aidan Hamilton is the other artist. He's a Perth guy. We've both done quite a bit of ceramic work and have other specialisations they want us to share with the students.'

'What are your specialisations?' he asked.

'Oils and charcoal for me. Sculpture and acrylics for Aidan.' She'd resisted up till now but her eyes wandered over his muscular shoulders.

Finn saw.

'Um, I was just looking at the badge thing on your shoulder,' she said hurriedly. 'Briggsy's is different, isn't it? What does it mean?'

'My epaulets? My rank is constable, so it's blank, no stripes. Briggsy's a senior sergeant so he's got the three stripes and a crown.'

'How long have you been a cop?'

'I just finished my probation not long ago, and applied for a few different country postings.

57

They offered me Mount Clair and I moved here in November.'

'You're from Perth, didn't you say?'

Finn gave a nod. 'I am, yep. My family lives there — well, my mum and dad do, anyway. My sister got married a couple of years ago and moved overseas to be with her husband.'

'You must miss them,' she said. 'How long do you think you'll be in Mount Clair?'

'I do miss them but I kind of like it here. The people are so welcoming. It feels like home already.'

'I've always wanted to know — is it interesting, police work?' Free asked. 'The TV shows seem to suggest it's loads of action, rolling around on the ground, tackling people, and shooting at cars and stuff. Either that or lots of boring paperwork.'

Her words made him laugh.

'Yep, sometimes exciting, sometimes boring. Sometimes rewarding and sometimes frustrating, but I like it. I can't imagine doing anything else.'

'What does your average day's work look like?' she asked.

He told her about some of the situations he'd attended in recent times and Free asked questions, intrigued. When he mentioned Briggsy, the conversation turned to their mutual friends. Free told Finn the story of Willow and Tom. He knew Tom through Briggsy, and had heard about Tom's helicopter crash, but was interested in hearing Free's version of events. What felt like a few minutes of talking was, in fact, two hours before Free noticed the time. She jumped up.

'Oh no! I was going to go down to the school and get some work done.'

He was on his feet immediately, apologising for taking up her time.

'No, don't be sorry,' she said with a rueful smile. 'It's me. I have no sense of time. That's what my sisters always say. If I'm enjoying myself, I'm even worse than usual.'

His warm eyes glowed. 'I enjoyed myself too.'

Free was suddenly very aware of his manly strength — the way his uniform shirt stretched across his chest and clearly visible biceps. This guy didn't look gym-ripped, either. He was simply naturally *built*. What did his chest look like under that shirt?

'Maybe I could just go into work tomorrow instead,' she said.

'No, don't let me stop you from what you need to do.' Finn pocketed his phone. 'Anyway, I've had a long day. I'd better go clean myself up and get some rest.'

He seemed clean to Free, but she could hardly argue with him needing rest. They stepped out onto the porch, where Max greeted them with his distinctive meow.

'It's such a coincidence that you live *here*,' Finn said.

'Yep, me and Maxie.' She nudged the cat and he rubbed himself against her skirt. 'Why do you say that? Because you happened to knock on my door?'

'No, because I live here too!' Finn pointed at

the door of the other unit in the duplex, just a few steps away. 'I'm in 17B.'

Free gaped. 'You *are*? You're my neighbour? That's amazing!'

Her spirits went into a mad dance to think she had this delightful man living right on her doorstep. *It's meant to be!* Finn stood looking at her for a few seconds, his eyes roaming over her face as though he wanted to say something else. Something like *When will I see you again?* Free's pulse accelerated and she waited, hardly breathing.

But Finn simply turned away with a light 'Well, see you around!'

He descended her porch stairs in one step and bounded up his own.

'Bye,' she called as he went inside.

It was only when she was in her car on the way to the school that she realised something incredible.

Finn must be her phantom next-door singer.

4

Jay finished recounting Free's artist biography and looked around at the Year Elevens.

'So, Miss Paterson will be sharing all of that expertise with you throughout the semester, and I'm sure I don't need to remind you what an opportunity this is for you all. Not only will you be working with a professional artist, you'll also have your names associated with a major public art installation in Mount Clair for decades — perhaps longer.'

The sixteen- and seventeen-year-olds — twelve of them in total — were duly impressed.

'Questions?' Jay added.

A hand shot up. 'Will we get paid for the public artwork, Miss?'

Jay chuckled. 'Sorry, Cameron, not this time. But all our materials are paid for.'

'Do we get to choose the topic that the wall's going to be about?' asked a girl.

'Yes. We want the theme to come from you, then our artists-in-residence will prepare a final concept and submit it to the project committee for approval.'

'But we get to have input, right?' Cameron pressed.

Free nodded. 'Definitely. I want you to have total ownership of the design.'

Jay interjected, more cautious. 'The design needs to be of a certain standard for the committee to approve it, which is why we have professional artists leading the way.'

A girl with straight, dark hair raised her hand. Jay nodded at her with a faint look of surprise. 'Tia?'

Tia turned to Free. 'How did you get the job at the Victoria and Albert?' she asked in a soft voice.

Free couldn't hide her grin. 'Oh, wow. Good question! I was dating this Brit dude, right? Nothing serious, but he was, like, a lord or something. Son of a lord, maybe. Honestly? The guy had a carrot up his bum, but he was nice-looking. Classic fair-haired English aristocracy. I reckon he was rebelling against Mummy and Daddy by dating an Aussie farm girl like me. Anyway, his aunty worked at the V-and-A, high up. Senior curator. They had an international exhibition coming to the gallery and she was hiring temp staff to manage bump-in, but one of the temps fell through on the day unpacking started, so Harold — that was the bum-carrot guy — he put *me* forward. It was the most amazing thing! I mean, the work itself wasn't amazing. We just had to unpack stuff, document it, wipe down the frames and glass, and make sure it got delivered to the right part of the exhibition. But going in every day, and being able to tell people I worked at the V-and-A? *That* was amazing!' She shook her head at the memory.

Jay stared, but the class, which had been giggling sporadically as Free spoke, burst into laughter. At length, Jay cracked a smile too.

62

'Well, at least we know we'll get honest answers from Miss Paterson,' she told the students.

Hmm, maybe she shouldn't have said that about Harold having a carrot up his bum . . .

Jay handed the class over and Free almost froze in terror, but breathed again when she saw that Jay was staying to assist. She told the students they would be building on their landscape skills in advance of some oil painting work planned for the first part of term, and took them outside with pencils and sketchpads, taking advantage of a break in the rain.

'Just find somewhere to sit and sketch what you see. Say, sixty to eighty degrees field of vision.' There were some puzzled looks so Free elaborated. 'If the world around you was a clock and you were sitting in the middle, you just want to draw about two hours — three o'clock to five o'clock, for instance.'

They understood that, and found spots to perch so they could get started. Free called out instructions, taking them through the steps she followed to sketch a landscape.

'Mark the boundaries of your scene with your eyes, and sketch the whole scene super fast. Then focus on one bit. A tree. A post. The footpath. Just try to get that one bit right.'

She walked around with her camera and got each student to photograph the scene they were sketching. Then, before the heat got too uncomfortable, Free took them back inside and used the smartboard to show them the work of seminal landscape artists in a slide show. She tried to stick to her script, which was based on curriculum materials provided by Jay — but couldn't help interjecting her own thoughts throughout.

'Turner! He's a *god* to me. See the light? Have any of you worked with oils much? No? Oils are so bloody hard to learn, but worth it, because I reckon it's the only medium that allows you to capture the light like this. Oh. My. *God*. Look at it. *Look*.' Some giggles rose and Free spun around to look at the students, half scandalised and half laughing. 'Seriously, you guys. *Turner*.'

Some of them were nodding, she was glad to see. They got it. Jay grinned at her from where she sat in the corner with a laptop.

The class concluded with a discussion of perspective and proportion — more of a refresher on what they'd already learned in previous years than anything else. As they packed up, Free encouraged them to start brainstorming for a tile wall theme.

'We've got about two weeks to smash out a concept before we move on to the design stage, so you need to get thinking. I'd love for the concept to come from one of *my* students.'

The kids went to lunch and Free looked at Jay apprehensively, but the woman wore a smile.

'Great session, Free. I love how you adapted the content to give it a more personal feel. And well done on getting Tia talking!'

'Who?'

'Dark-haired girl, Tia Kaneko. She hardly ever speaks, but she asked you a question straight up, and even contributed during the slide show.

Okay, she's Year Eleven now and she might finally be coming out of her shell, but I suspect it's more that you've put her at ease with your chilled-out teaching style. Nice work!'

Free waited for the sting in the tail of Jay's praise — but the woman was done.

'Catch you in the staffroom shortly,' was all she said, turning away to collect her papers.

In the staffroom, Free pulled out the apple and packet of crackers she'd shoved into her bag that morning. She gazed around the table enviously. Everyone else had such delicious-looking lunches. Mrs Woodley was tucking in to a piece of lasagne she'd reheated in its Tupperware container, and Max had a pie. Aidan joined Free, giving her one of his tight-faced smiles. The things that had been said about him on Friday night came into Free's head. *How does he sleep at night, knowing his career is a sham?* She shook herself. She mustn't assume anything without giving him a chance. Perhaps there was some mistake. Misinformation, or exaggeration in the rumours.

Aidan opened up his lunch — an exquisite collection of sushi pieces in a compartmentalised lunch box. He unscrewed a tiny vial of soy sauce and poured it over his lunch, glancing up at Free.

'You just had the Year Elevens, didn't you? How did it go?'

'Pretty good.' She bit into a cracker. 'You had the Year Tens first thing, yeah? How was that?'

'Not bad.' He munched sushi thoughtfully. He even had some of those snap-apart bamboo

65

chopsticks. 'The kids are quite giggly and unfocused, aren't they? I'd expected a little more maturity, I must confess.'

Free thought it over. 'I guess there's a difference even in one year. Mine were pretty good. I was probably the least mature of all of them.' She gave him a half-grin.

Aidan ate in silence for a moment. 'I suppose it's only natural that kids will find art theory a little dull. Oh, hey.' He brightened. 'I've thought up a great theme for the tile wall. Tell me what you think.' He leaned closer. 'River of Life.'

Free's love for the river surged at the idea. *See?* she told herself. *He's not like his mother at all.*

'That sounds amazing! Like, the story of the Waugal forming the river system, the wet and the dry seasons, the wildlife, the ecological heritage — a monument to our amazing river . . . '

He hesitated, chopsticks halfway to his mouth. Free eyed his sushi longingly.

'Oh, well — yes. I suppose it would be *politically correct* to include that stuff. I was referring to the agricultural side of things. Irrigation. The journey of the region from drought-stricken to irrigated by the new diversion dam. A celebration of the area's growing agricultural livelihood.'

For a moment, Free thought Aidan must be joking. As son and heir to the company constructing the Herne River Diversion Dam, this was far too sleazy a move to be genuine. Wasn't it?

It appeared he was serious. Aidan was waiting for her to reply, picking excess wasabi out of one of his sushi rolls.

Free spun her apple in her hands. 'I'm not sure that's such a good thing to celebrate. I mean, the dam's not even built yet. I don't think it's going to be good for the environment. If we use that theme for the tile wall, then we'll have a permanent monument to something that caused environmental devastation.'

She'd hoped she was being tactful but the look on his face told her she'd missed the mark by a mile. Aidan put down his avocado roll.

'*Devastation?* Seriously?' He gave his head a minuscule shake. 'You're a farmer's daughter, aren't you?'

'Um, yes. My family owns a cattle station.'

'You understand farming then, don't you?'

'Well — '

'See, this is why this sort of artwork matters. It educates people. It helps the everyday Joe understand what the Herne Dam will do for the town.'

Free blinked at his condescension. 'Aidan, I didn't mean to offend you. But with a permanent public artwork like this, maybe it's too early to focus it on the dam, since we don't even know if it will be completed. There are protests going on and calls for more environ-mental studies — '

'Of course it's going to be completed. And I'm not offended.' He smiled at her, his Adam's apple bobbing as he popped another piece of sushi into his mouth. 'I enjoy a robust discussion

— it's the best type of flirting. I'll discuss the concept with Jay and see what she thinks.'

Free was so rattled by the 'flirting' comment that she almost missed the way he'd completely ignored her opinion. What if Jay liked the River of Life idea too?

Free worried in silence about the fate of the project. Hopefully, the kids would come up with a better concept.

* * *

At the end of the day, Free headed home, stopping to snap her daily river photo. She had always heard that the mental work of teaching was exhausting, but she was so tired she almost couldn't be bothered closing the garage roller door. Beth's tales of Mount Clair break-ins and car thefts were the only thing that made her pull it down.

Her tabby cat was waiting for her on the porch railing. 'Max,' he said.

Free laughed. 'Hello, Max. You hungry?'

As she unlocked her front door, Finn stepped out onto his porch, a pair of scissors in his hand. Now this was something nice to come home to.

'Afternoon,' he said.

'Hi, Finn!'

She used scratching Max's ears as an excuse to dillydally, not taking her eyes off Finn. Every time she saw him she was surprised anew by how handsome he was, with that genuine smile.

And that *holy-mother-of-God* muscular body.

Stop, she snapped at herself. *Stop objectifying*

68

him! 'How was your day?' she asked, fixing her gaze on his face.

'Good. And yours?'

'Great! I mean, scary as hell, but it turned out okay.'

Finn's smile grew. 'I bet you were a hit with the kids.'

'They're lovely. They were really good to me. But I was still terrified.'

He leaned on the little balustrade dividing their porches. 'I remember my first day working in Mount Clair. I was petrified too. Senior Sergeant Briggs — let's just say he can be pretty intimidating.'

'Oh God, yes. I bet. The tatts. The facial hair.'

'It was more his pep talk,' said Finn. 'He pulled me into his office, sat me down opposite him and said, 'Right, Kelly, you're fresh out of your probation in Perth and this is your trial by fire. You might think Mount Clair's a harmless backwater, but the place is a hotbed of issues — issues that have been here since the whites got off the boat and decided they owned the joint.''

Free was impressed. 'Holy crap.'

'I got a half-hour lecture on the topic. 'Now, these issues aren't the be-all and end-all of the problems in Mount Clair, but they sure as hell act as a starter gun for a lot of them,' Briggsy said.'

Free's respect for Briggsy doubled. 'He's right. Transgenerational trauma. It's like a sore spot that gets worse and worse over time.'

'That's it, yeah.' Finn leaned down to a potted plant on the porch and clipped some leaves with his scissors. It was coriander, Free realised.

'You're cooking?'

'Yeah. Thai green curry.'

'Oh, *yum*.'

He hovered. 'You hungry? I've made too much.'

Free practically bounced on the spot. 'For real? I'd love some!'

'What about Max?'

'He'll be fine. I'll feed him later. Let me just dump my stuff. I'll be there in a sec.'

Free dashed inside and put her gear down. She changed into a fresh skirt and singlet before heading to the bathroom to brush her hair and apply lip gloss. *That's enough*, she told herself as she sprayed perfume. The poor guy was just inviting her over for a spontaneous neighbourly meal, and she was acting like it was a romantic dinner. She gave Max some biscuits, not wanting Finn to think she was a neglectful owner, grabbed a bottle of wine and headed next door.

Finn opened the door with a smile but it faltered when he swept a glance over her. Free almost panicked. Had she dressed inappropriately? But there was nothing negative in his face as he opened the door wider to welcome her inside. It smelled good in his house, like garlic, lemongrass and spices. She followed him to the kitchen, stomach rumbling.

'I'm crap at cooking,' she confessed. 'It must be so good to have culinary skills.'

'I wouldn't say I'm skilled.' He stirred the pot on the stove and moved across to rinse the coriander at the sink. 'I can do enough to get by.'

'That's still better than me. Wine?' she offered, unscrewing the bottle top.

'Yeah, okay. I don't generally drink wine but I'll give it a go.'

'More of a beer drinker?'

'Beer and cider.'

'That's so Dublin.'

Finn looked at her quickly. 'Sorry?'

'Or is it Northern Ireland? I'm not very good at picking the specific region from an accent.'

He forgot his stirring, eyes on her face. 'What do you mean?'

'Aren't you from Ireland?'

'How — how did you know that?'

Free relaxed. 'Phew, I thought I'd got it wrong for a second! It's your accent. It's very faint but I can hear it. And the way you look, I think. There's just something Irish about you. You're solid and strong, and you have a kindness in the way you talk.' She was about to mention his singing but stopped herself. If she let on that she could hear him, he might stop, and that was the last thing she wanted.

It took him a moment, but he eventually gave his head a slow shake. 'Impressive. You're spot-on.'

'When did you come to Australia?'

'I was twelve.'

Free tipped her head to the side. 'Really? That's weird. I'd have thought your accent would have been cemented by then, but it's barely detectable.'

Finn returned to stirring the curry. 'I made a conscious effort to lose my accent.'

'Why? Girls go nuts for an Irish accent!'

He choked on a laugh. 'Is that so! Well, I copped it, big time, whenever people realised I was Irish.' He poked at the rice in another pot. 'My first day of school in Australia, the teacher asked a maths question. Sixty-six and two-thirds times zero-point-five. I didn't want to be the stereotypical dumb Irishman, so I put my hand up. I figured I could show the other kids right from day dot that I was a smart guy, good at maths. She called on me. So, what'd I say? 'Tirty-tree and a turd, Miss'.'

She could just see it. Free couldn't help a burst of laughter.

'Oh no.'

'The other kids were rolling in the aisles,' he said. 'I never lived it down. From that day on, it was *Paddy* this and *Mick* that and 'Talk, Finn, do the accent', and 'Hey, Finn, how do you sink an Irish submarine?''

'How?' Free interrupted.

He stopped prodding the rice and turned to face her, his eyebrows tugged down. She waited.

'Knock on the hatch.'

Free thought about it for a moment, and then chuckled. 'Yeah, that's quite funny.'

Finn broke into a grin. 'Somehow it doesn't seem quite so bad, coming from you. Maybe I was being oversensitive.'

'No, I get it. It's hard when you get stuck with a particular identity you can't shake.' Despite Finn's big, strong body and his air of calm capability, he suddenly seemed a little vulnerable. She would have liked to take him into her

72

arms. He came closer, standing across the bench from Free so he could observe her face. Her heart rate switched into high gear again.

'Is that the voice of experience speaking?' he asked.

'Yeah, I suppose so. My eldest sister, Beth, she thinks I'm a ditz.'

'Why?'

'Well, I'm a bit forgetful. I get caught up in the moment, especially if I'm painting, and lose track of time. It always seems to happen when I'm supposed to be somewhere. And also, I travel. A lot.'

'How does travelling make you ditzy?'

'It doesn't.' Free tucked some hair behind her ear. 'Just, sometimes I decide I'm going somewhere — and I just go. I mean, why hang around? There's no point planning something months in advance, is there?'

'Not unless you've got prior commitments.'

'Exactly. I mean, why would *I* need to give people loads of notice if I want to travel somewhere? It's not like they're relying on me for anything. It's not like I'm booked to give a keynote speech, or run a company or whatever.'

Finn made an amused noise as he turned away and picked up the rice pot for draining. 'It sounds like you and your sister are playing out the classic eldest and youngest roles. You've got her pegged as the controlling bossy boots and she's got you pegged as the flighty, thoughtless baby of the family.'

He'd meant it in jest but Free experienced a little pang of pain. Finn was right. Why did it have to be that way between her and Beth? She wasn't overreacting, was she? If only Beth would show her a little respect. Free felt obliged to defend herself.

'Get this. Know what she did last year? My dad had a heart attack while I was in Italy. I was going to fly home but Beth told me it was really minor — no big deal, Dad was fine. She convinced me to stay in Europe. It was only when Willow came home to run the station that I realised how serious it was. Can you imagine if he'd died — how awful it would have been if I'd been overseas at the time? Beth had no right to hide the truth from me.'

Finn was gazing at her with concern and Free discovered she had tears in her eyes. She sniffed and wiped her eyes hastily, trying to laugh.

'Sorry. I cry way too easily. I'm like a leaky tap.'

'You wear your heart on your sleeve,' he said, those warm Kimberley-creek eyes on hers. 'It's — ' He stopped himself and turned back to the stove. 'It's a good thing.'

'You do too.'

Finn shot her a faux glare. 'Me! No, I don't.'

'You do so. I can read your face. You're very genuine.'

'Nah, that's just my disarming interview technique.'

'Well, it's very convincing.' Free twiddled a piece of her hair. 'I wouldn't want to be on the receiving end of an interview with you. I'd spill all my crimes before I realised what had hit me!'

'I wish all the perps were like that.' Finn took

the curry off the stove.

He served the meal and they sat at his spotless rectangular table to eat. Free glanced around for the first time while he fetched cutlery. His place was pleasant and welcoming, with cushions that matched the couch, and minimal mess. He'd hung a photo of his family on the wall and Free scoured it eagerly. Finn was taller than both his parents, and his mother and sister shared kindly round faces framed by bright-red hair. There were more photos on the cabinet. Free loved the laughing faces in all the photos of his family. The Kellys must laugh a lot if every single picture had captured it.

'You have a cool place,' she commented. 'You've settled in, huh? Made it your own.'

'Well, I'm here for at least a couple of years.'

'Why so long?' She tasted the curry. 'Oh wow, this is really good!'

'Thanks. As for why so long, I like Mount Clair. I feel sorta happy here.'

She smiled. 'Good! I wouldn't want to think you were stuck somewhere you didn't like for a couple of years.' Free's eyes wandered back to the photos. 'What's your sister's name?'

'Aislinn. She went back to Ireland a few years ago — was working and staying with family, but she met a bloke there and got married, so she stayed. She's having a baby. Next month, as a matter of fact. My mother and Aislinn are close. Mum video-calls with her every day.'

'Does she visit? Your sister, I mean.'

'Aislinn and her other half don't have much money, but Mum and Dad have already been to visit them twice since she moved last year. There's another visit happening shortly. It's an expensive habit my parents are developing.' Finn tried his wine. 'I'm taking a few days' leave at the end of the month, heading home to Perth to see Mum and Dad before they go to Ireland.' He locked his eyes on hers, sending another buzz of excitement through her. Did he even realise he could do that?

'So you've travelled a lot?' he prompted.

Free was grateful for a point of focus. 'Yes! I took a gap year across Asia and Europe, then while I was at uni I deferred my course for six months and lived in Melbourne. Then I did eighteen months in America and Canada, working at resorts in the ski seasons, and youth camps in summer. That was a blast. I usually find work when I'm overseas and that funds my stay. I was going to come home but got sidetracked and ended up in the UK for a while. So that was nearly two years away from home, all up. My last trip was only four months, though. It seems harder to make money than it used to be. Maybe I'm getting fussy in my old age about what jobs I'll do and where I'm willing to sleep.' She smiled at him. 'My friend who lives in Pisa, Flavia, she asked me to meet her in New Zealand in May, but I've got the contract at the school until July.'

'NZ will still be there when your contract's over, though,' he said. 'Plenty of time to visit.'

'Absolutely,' she agreed. 'What about you? Have you travelled much?'

'Not as much as you, but I've seen a bit of Australia. We've done some big road trips, including a Grand Final trek to Melbourne a few years back. We're footy fans. And we went back to visit my parents' family in Ireland once, but Mum and Dad aren't exactly loaded, so it's over eight years since we all did that together.'

'How old are you now?' she asked.

'Twenty-seven.'

'Same!' she exclaimed. 'Well, I'll be twenty-seven at the end of February.'

'I was twenty-seven on November twenty-ninth.'

'How bizarre! Mine is the twenty-ninth too.' Free calculated. 'So you're exactly three months older than me.'

'You're a leap baby?' He was smiling. 'Of course you are.'

Free frowned. 'What do you mean?'

'Your birthday's just like you. Uncommon,' he said, his eyes on hers.

Free's heart skittered out of control but Finn pulled his eyes away and dove back in to his meal.

'What do you mean by that?' she asked, willing him to lift those gorgeous eyes again.

He shrugged and passed her the chopped coriander, so she let his odd remark slide.

'I don't get a real birthday this year, since it's not a leap year.' She speared a piece of eggplant. 'But I still want to do something fun. I might organise a pub night here in Mount Clair. Keep the twenty-eighth free, okay?'

Finn nodded. 'Shall do, if possible. I have to

do a night shift once or twice a week — go out on patrol.'

'Why's that? Because you're big and strong?'

He spluttered his wine. 'No! Because I get rostered on like everyone else.'

'Oh, right. Of course. Police work must be heartbreaking,' she added, shaking her head. 'Road accidents and arresting people who've made mistakes. God, I'd be in tears all day long.' Free stirred coriander into her food with her fork. 'I mean, what do you do if someone's broken the law but it's because they were trying to do something good? Like, I was reading about this guy in Tassie the other day, and he'd chained himself up to an old tree in this ancient rainforest. The cops came and used boltcutters and dragged him away and arrested him — and the tree got cut down! It was so awful. I couldn't believe it. How could they let that happen? I mean, all he was doing was trying to save the tree. I was so mad at those cops.'

Finn grimaced. 'That's a tough one. It's not the officers' fault, though. I imagine the guy would have been trespassing or something, and they had to do their job. Yeah, it stinks sometimes, but in the end, it's our job to protect people by making sure everyone follows the law. We need to do it, or the justice system will fall down.' His brown eyes were so earnest, Free had no choice but to believe every word he said. 'If we make exceptions, then we're opening the door to corruption. Like, if I'm allowed to make an exception for someone chaining himself to a tree, then why can't some other officer make an

78

exception for a violent drug dealer?'

Free turned the idea over in her mind. 'Yes, I suppose so. But what about integrity? I mean, if you passionately wanted to save the tree, and you knew it would be cut down if you took the protester away, you'd just leave him, right?'

'It doesn't work that way.' Finn gave her a half-smile. 'I have a duty to arrest him if he's breaking the law, no matter how I feel about it. It's part of the job. That's what I do — I follow the procedures of the law.'

'Ohhhh.' Free sat in silence for a few moments, struggling to fathom it. 'I'd be hopeless in your job,' she declared at last.

Finn laughed. 'I'd be hopeless in yours. How's your painting coming along?'

They chatted about the Talbot Gorge piece and, since Finn wanted to know about her art career, she told him about the mural work she'd done for a chain of cafés in Melbourne and the unexpected invitation to take part in a group exhibition in London — and the even more unexpected emerging artist prize at a Perth art show. But those were just the highlights, so she also told him about some of her disappointments — the failure to be selected for several shows, and the time she overheard an art critic dismiss her painting as a 'presumptuous attempt, lacking in maturity'.

Finally, Finn checked the time. 'I'm so sorry, Free, but I have to get ready for work.'

Free stared at him in amazement. 'Oh wow, really?' She checked her phone and jumped up in dismay. 'Crap. Ten-thirty! I swore I'd change my habits and get to bed by ten during the week.'

Finn carried the serving dishes to the kitchen. 'Hey, there's loads left over. Do you want to take some curry for your lunch tomorrow?'

'Oh my God — yes! My lunch was so lame compared to everyone else's today.' She hesitated. 'But only if there's enough for you to have some too.'

'Yep. Plenty.' He pulled out a couple of lunch boxes and proceeded to load them up with rice and curry. 'Do you want extra for Max?'

Free repressed a giggle. Clearly, Finn had never owned a cat. 'No, he might get a sore tummy if I give him curry. It's probably best he sticks to his usual out-of-the-can cuisine.'

'Okay.' He closed a lid over the lunch box and passed it across the bench.

'Thank you so much,' she said. 'I'll think of you while I eat my lunch tomorrow.'

He laughed. 'No need.'

'I'm sure I'd think of you anyway.'

She said the words before she thought them through, and then wanted to slap herself, seeing how uncomfortable Finn looked. *Ugh, way to sound like a psycho, Free.* Where was her self-censor? On vacation, as usual.

'I'm sure I'll think of you, too,' he said, then clamped his mouth shut again, not meeting her eyes.

She hid a delighted grin, heart hitting gallop speed. 'Thanks again for dinner — and for your company. I hope you have a fun night at work.'

He recovered enough to smile at her choice of

80

words. 'Monday night. Should be quiet.' He opened his front door. 'I'll walk you home.'

'All three metres?'

True to his word, he walked the ten or so steps to her door.

'Bye, Free.'

She looked up at him. She would normally hug a friend goodbye. Were they friends? Of course they were. Free dove in. Their difference in height vanished when Finn leaned down into her embrace, circling her with his strong arms. For a few moments, they fitted together perfectly. He smelt wonderful — a trace of sunscreen, a hint of aftershave and a whole lot of big, strong man. She couldn't tell if the thumping between them was Finn's heart or her own. Free heated up, her thoughts sliding sideways to what it might be like to kiss Finn — but then her phone made a noise that meant someone was trying to open a chat with her. Finn pulled back in a hurry.

'I think you're wanted,' he said. 'Don't forget to lock up — there have been a few break-ins around town.'

She closed the door and locked it. Max sauntered out from the bedroom to greet her as Free deposited the curry in the fridge. A shower could wait until the morning. She discarded her clothes and fell into bed, reliving that delicious hug, imagining how it might have gone if they'd been braver. He would stroke a big, strong hand down her back and, when she lifted her face to meet his gaze, he would say what his eyes had already told her.

You're beautiful. I'd like to kiss you.

Free would curl her arms around his muscular neck and hold on, anticipating the touch of his warm lips, pressing herself close against his strong frame . . .

She spent several minutes contemplating how Finn would kiss her, before taking a detour into more sensuous territory. Then a soft sound caught her attention. He was singing as he got ready for work, all his suppressed Irish inflection coming through in the ballad. She strained to hear the words.

'And a kiss in the morning, early,' was all she could make out, but it still made her smile widely.

She fell asleep with the beautiful sound in her ears.

5

Tuesday was the day Free had been assigned to run after-school sessions with her art students. She printed A3 copies of their landscape photos and, when they arrived at the end of the school day, told them they had two options for the afternoon. They could work on their sketches or sit with Free for a walk-through of oils. A couple of kids were immersed in their sketching, but most chose to gather around Free as she dabbed paint onto a blank canvas. The quality of the school's oil paint collection left her less than impressed. She had some new paints on order from Bostons — her favourite art supplies store — and they were due to arrive any day now. She would bring them in to show her students how decent oil paints made all the difference.

'You can mix oils with so many different things, it's crazy,' she said. 'Leonardo da Vinci was the most incredible experimenter when it came to oils. You know about his scientific inventions, right? Well, he took the same approach with his painting. Like, he worked on canvas, paper, cloth, rock, plaster — wet plaster for murals — you name it. I mean, seriously, the guy tried just about everything to see what would get the most awesome results. And he mixed his oils with everything, too. Beeswax, egg whites, flaxseed oil, tobacco oil and loads more — I can't even remember them all. Google it. It's insane. He was a kind of nutty professor. Can't you just imagine him giggling away to himself while he used all that weird crap to create the best colours and consistency he could?'

The kids laughed with her.

'I bet it drove his wife nuts,' said Cameron.

'My mum hates it when I bring stuff inside to mix with my paint,' Tia added in her soft voice.

'What do you mix?' Free asked her, excited to find a fellow experimenter.

The girl shrank a little when the other kids turned their heads to look at her. 'Sand. Sawdust. Crushed shells.' Her voice had dropped to practically a whisper.

'With acrylic?' Free asked, and Tia nodded. 'That's awesome. I used mainly acrylics before oils stole my heart. I used to mix them with river mud and all kinds of stuff. My dad lost the plot when he caught me mixing blue paint with cattle minerals. Gotta say, it made a wicked purple *impasto*.'

Tia's confidence rose again. 'I used tapioca flour once. It made a smooth, thick texture.'

'Was that what you used on your pearling boat painting?' Cameron asked and Tia nodded. 'Tia won the Broome Art Show in our age group last year,' he told Free.

Free stared at the girl. 'That's amazing!'

'Yeah, she did this boat moored in the harbour with really chunky paint,' another girl said. 'It was atmospheric.'

'It was bad-ass.' Cameron nudged Tia, whose eyes had dropped to the floor. 'Your grandad's boat, right?'

'My great-uncle's.' Her voice had faded to whisper level again. 'He was a pearler.'

'Japanese pearler?' asked Free, remembering the girl's last name was Kaneko.

Tia nodded.

'My grandma was a servant to a Japanese pearler,' another girl offered. 'They say she was, like, his concubine.' She gave a crooked smile.

'My great-great-grandfather owned a station,' Cameron said. 'And my great-great-grandma was his servant. Jamadji.'

The discussion continued. Many of the kids in the group were able to contribute a story about immigrant or Aboriginal heritage, or a mixed ancestry. One girl told the story of why her family had emigrated from eastern Europe twenty years earlier, and a boy said his family had arrived as refugees on a boat. Free explained how her own great-great-grandfather had been a convict who'd earned his ticket of leave and had been given the Paterson Downs pastoral lease for a song.

'They're cool, these stories.' Cameron was bright-eyed and wearing a grin.

'You said it,' Free answered. 'Mount Clair kicks arse for diversity. Now, if you want to blend your colours, you can use a few different techniques.' She demonstrated so they weren't wasting their precious work time, but continued the topic of discussion as the kids watched her blend. 'The history of Mount Clair is so fascinating. Some of it's not pleasant. Some of it is horrific. It's like a conversation that needs to keep happening so we don't gloss over the pain

85

experienced by any one group. We have a whole bunch of amazing stories, and they made Mount Clair what it is.'

Tia said something so softly that Free couldn't hear it properly, but Cameron did. 'Yes!' he exclaimed. 'That'd be cool.'

Tia looked at Free, her eyes alight with hope.

'What did you say?' asked Free. 'I didn't quite catch it.'

Tia took a breath. 'I said that maybe our heritage stories would make a good theme for the tile wall.'

Cameron was thinking hard. 'We could do art styles from all the different cultures. Story tiles about the Dreaming, the invasion, pearling, farming — all that stuff.'

Several of the kids were nodding eagerly. Free was almost speechless.

'This is the best idea I've ever heard,' she breathed. 'It's so honest and *real*. Tia, you're a freakin' genius.'

The little smile that crept onto Tia's face was wonderful to witness. Free abandoned the canvas and snatched up a pen and paper, scribbling down ideas that poured from the students. The exciting thing was that they were unanimous in their enthusiasm for the concept. The class was immersed in the discussion and the allotted hour flew. Some of the kids had to leave at 4 p.m. but others text-messaged their parents or simply decided to stay on and take turns with the oils. Free told them about *sfumato* and they practised saying the word amid much giggling.

'Seriously, I can't wait to make a start on

the tile project with you guys as soon as the concept's approved. We're going to create the most amazing public artwork this town has ever seen!'

They all grinned or made jokes and Free thought about how lucky she was to get this group of kids. Finally, the cleaning staff descended and the class broke up.

'I'll see you guys Friday,' she called. 'Email me if you have any more tile ideas, okay?'

Fat raindrops fell on the windscreen as she drove home, threatening a torrent. She put her car away and dashed to the front door, checking on her way to see if Finn was home. *Hmm, inconclusive.* He didn't appear to own a car and she'd only seen him driving police vehicles. Maybe he walked to work? Or caught a lift. She should invite him around for a meal — return the favour. Free knew how to cook pasta. Oh, *yes* — that Pisan pesto dish Flavia had insisted on teaching her how to make! She could just imagine how impressed he would be as she whizzed pine nuts and basil with olive oil in her sparkling blender, smiling over at Finn's handsome face. He would sit at her kitchen table, sipping wine, while Free glided across her immaculate house in a chic apron like a blonde Nigella Lawson, Finn's admiring eyes fixed on her . . .

Whoops, she'd forgotten to lock the front door again. Free slipped through her unlocked door and the reality of her culinary — and housekeeping — abilities hit home. She wasn't going to wow Finn with a gorgeous meal. If he

87

came over now, all he would see was mess — a giant mess. Her clean clothes lay in heaps all over the coffee table and couch, abandoned there unfolded when she'd brought armfuls of washing inside before work that morning so it wouldn't get wet. Dishes, rinsed but unwashed, were piling up. Boxes of packed items still dotted the living area. The only space that was semi-organised in the entire house was the kitchen, which Beth had done. And possibly the studio, since Free had been forced to unpack all her art supplies when she couldn't find a tube of paint she was after.

Did she even own a blender?

Free flicked on the air conditioning and slumped onto the couch. *Damn.* She was too exhausted to clean or unpack. *Tomorrow*, she decided. She had two days off work now before taking the Year Elevens for double art on Friday. She would get the place properly sorted out.

A knock on the front door made her jump up in panic. Sure enough, it was Finn, looking tall, fresh and sexy in a T-shirt and shorts, those warm eyes sparkling down at her. Overwhelmed with a big dose of shame about her messy house, Free skipped out onto the porch and closed the door behind her.

'Hi!'

'Hi. How was your day?'

'Amazing! Awesome!'

His smile grew. 'Great! You'll have to tell me about it. I'm heading to work soon, but, um — I did something. I hope you don't mind. The postie came with a parcel for you but he needed you to sign for it and you weren't here so I, uh, well, I signed for it for you because I knew you might not get home in time to collect it from the post office and I wanted to save you the trouble . . . ' He took a breath at last and held out a package, slightly red in the face.

'Thanks! That was very cool of you.' She took the parcel and he visibly relaxed. 'It'll be my new paints. I'm stoked, because the oils at school are crap.'

She attempted to tear it open but it required scissors so Free pushed through the door and headed for the kitchen.

'Come in,' she threw over her shoulder.

She located a knife and sliced open the package while Finn closed the door behind him. 'I absolutely love my supplier.' She held up the paints to show him. 'Oh, look, they put in some prezzies! I'm a good customer,' she explained. 'I spend almost everything I earn with these guys, so they throw in freebies for me. I got a new spatula and some fine brushes this time.' She inspected her gifts.

'No art supplies shops in Mount Clair, I guess?'

'Nope. There's the newsagency. They've got a corner devoted to sketchpads, pencils and flimsy easels, but that's it. I have more luck down the hardware store.'

She smiled at Finn and caught him examining her kitchen. Free froze. *Oh good Lord*, she'd completely forgotten about hiding her pigsty of a house from him.

'Excuse the mess,' she added weakly.

He brought his gaze back to hers. 'Huh? Oh, I was just looking at your paintbrushes all lined up on the windowsill. It must be tough not having a proper studio.' He swept his gaze around the living area. 'Your place is almost the same layout as mine, just flipped. Except you have this half-wall here. What a shame they stuck it there, because this living room would be a much better place for you to paint — you know, with a sink nearby.'

He kept looking around, and even put his head around the corner to peer into the laundry. Free was silent. Was Finn seriously checking out her house, trying to work out a suitable studio arrangement for her? As though her art career was important . . . and her livelihood, her comfort, were his concerns? A peculiar quiet happiness stole over her.

'Hmm, there must be a good solution.' He glanced at her, suddenly self-conscious. 'Well, I'm sure you'll work something out. I'd better get going.' He turned for the door.

Free followed him, still lost for words. He'd made it to his front door before she found her voice again. 'Finn, wait.'

He turned.

'Can, um — can I cook for you?'

His eyebrows rose. 'I thought you didn't cook.'

'I don't, not really. But I could try.'

He chuckled. 'Sounds good, in a scary kind of way. When were you thinking of?'

'When are you free?'

'I'm working now till 2 a.m., then a day off tomorrow.'

'Me too. Lunch tomorrow?' she suggested, her voice trembling a little. *So weird.* She couldn't remember ever getting nervous around a guy like this before.

'Lunch would be good.' He hesitated. 'Just us two?'

'Um, yes.'

Something like caution crossed his face. But a moment later he straightened a little and threw her a quick smile. 'Yup, that's very neighbourly of you. See you then!' And he was gone.

Free went back inside. Her hands were still shaking and she shook her head at herself. All those holiday romances and whirlwind affairs with guys she'd met in exotic places — none of *them* had made her react like this. She realised what it was. None of those guys, for all their romance and seduction, had treated her quite like Finn did — with such natural consideration and respect, and deep, irrepressible kindness.

It was startling. And lovely.

Startlingly lovely.

★   ★   ★

Right. Unpacking. Cleaning.

Free stacked dishes in a sink full of soapy water while she munched breakfast cereal. She peered out the window at the long kikuyu grass growing in the red dirt of her backyard. Where was Max? She hadn't seen him since she'd let him out after breakfast. She went into the studio to collect her paintbrushes so she could wash them, too — and noticed a fix required on her

91

Talbot Gorge painting. *Oh good Lord*. How had she missed *that* before? She put down her bowl, opened her palette and seized a brush. She dabbed paint and it looked better almost immediately. This would only take five minutes.

A knock at her front door snapped her out of it. Free stretched and put down the brush. Maybe it was the postie. Hopefully not Beth, come to criticise and take up the time she needed to clean. She opened the door to Finn, sans uniform, a Powderfinger T-shirt stretched across his muscular body.

'Oh, hi!' She made a valiant effort not to stare at his chest. 'You're early!'

'Am I?' He checked his phone. 'Twelve-thirty?'

Free gaped at him. 'Twelve-thirty — *what?*' She grabbed his phone to verify and groaned. 'Finn, I'm so sorry. I was going to tidy up but I got caught up with my stupid painting.'

She cursed herself, but Finn brightened. 'The gorge painting? Can I see?'

She nodded and led him through her appalling mess, apologising all the way. Finn just laughed.

'Seriously, I don't care. I'm not here to see how tidy you keep your house.'

Free was silenced. They stopped in front of her painting and Finn locked his gaze on the canvas.

'Wow. *Wow.*' He leaned in close to look at it. 'Free, it's incredible.' He turned and those warm eyes shone into hers. '*You're* incredible.'

The wave of emotion that went through her almost made her catch her breath. She had to check in with her brain to make sure this was really happening — yes, Finn meant it. He believed what he'd just said and, in that moment, she believed him. Tears sprang to her eyes.

'What's wrong?' he asked, stepping closer and reaching for her arm. But he stopped before he touched her and pulled his hand back, watching her with an uncertain frown.

'Leaky eyes, remember?' she said, trying to laugh. 'Lunch,' she added, striding towards the kitchen to conceal the unsteadiness in her legs.

She yanked open the fridge and Finn found himself a seat at her round wooden table. He was asking about work and her painting but Free barely heard him because she was coming to a dreadful realisation that she had nothing to give him for lunch. Flavia's pesto involved fresh basil and pine nuts, olive oil and parmesan cheese . . . and the only thing she had on that list was the cheese.

'Hey, would you rather go out somewhere for lunch?' she interrupted Finn. 'A café or something? My shout.'

'No, I like it here. Please stop worrying about how tidy your house is, Free!'

'Oh, okay.' She gave him a weak smile. 'Well, do you mind waiting ten minutes while I nip out and get some stuff from the shop, then?'

He comprehended. 'You're short on supplies? I've got food at my place. What do you need?'

She checked the fridge again, fighting a blush. 'It depends what you want. Sandwiches? I've got plenty of jam and vegemite. But bread is optional.' A smile started at the corner of Finn's mouth and she groaned. 'Yes, I know. I've invited you around for lunch and now I've got nothing to give you. Lame.'

He couldn't hold in a laugh. 'Wait here. I'll get some things.'

Finn was back a minute later with fresh bread, ham, cheese, tomatoes and lettuce. Free accepted them gratefully and constructed sandwiches while they chatted about work. She tried to put the thought of how badly she'd managed lunch out of her head. *He doesn't care. He's not judging.*

'So, your sister's wedding,' he said as they ate. 'It's at the Forrests' station, yeah?'

Free picked ham off her plate. 'How did you know that?'

'Briggsy's asked me to drive him and Kate there, and home afterwards. They want to have a few drinks but they've got no transport.'

'Ah, right. You're always ferrying Briggsy around, it seems.'

'Not normally. He's not a big drinker but this is his best mate, so I guess the buck's night and the wedding day are special occasions for the sarge.'

Free nodded. 'It's a pretty low-key event, as weddings go. Willow wouldn't have it any other way. I think Tom's done well just to get her to agree to wear a dress and stop managing cattle for a day.'

Finn tipped his head. 'Paterson Downs is one of the big local beef producers, right? But *you're* not interested in farming life?'

'God, no. I hardly know one end of a cow

94

from the other. Willow's the expert, and that's just how Beth and I like it.'

'Did you like living on a station?'

Free nodded with energy. 'I loved it, but I especially love living in the *region*. This place — the Kimberley — is just . . . ' Words failed her but Finn's expression showed he understood. 'I'm not a farmer, though. I couldn't do what Willow's doing.'

'It'd be a hard life, cattle farming,' he agreed.

'Willow's doing amazing things with Paterson Downs. She's taking it to organic, did you know? She and Tom. She's the most incredible environmentalist.'

'And you are too, right? You're against the diversion dam.'

What kind of super detective was this guy? 'How did you know *that*?'

Finn gave a little shrug. 'Uh, not sure. Must've heard it somewhere.'

'Yes, I'm against the dam. The Herne runs alongside our property, so the dam project is significant for my family.'

'You spent a bit of time by the river growing up, I guess?'

'Yeah. I love that river. It means a lot to me. I can't quite explain it. And the dam is potentially disastrous for the river, not to mention the land clearing for farming, and the impact on our water quality. Nutrients, algae, salinity . . . ' Free stopped herself. 'Ugh, sorry. I sound like a pamphlet. Blame my sister.'

He smiled. 'No, it's interesting. It gives me a context for the protests against the project. I'm

95

learning more and more about the diversion dam every day. It's a worry.'

She relaxed. 'You should come along to one of the demonstrations or info sessions. There's still an opportunity to stop the work so more environmental research can happen.' Free paused. 'Are you allowed to go to rallies, being a cop?'

'Yes, of course. Just not in uniform or while on duty.'

'Oh, good!' She sipped her water. 'The more people who get involved, the better.'

'You must have a real connection to the land, being a farm girl.'

She laughed. 'I'm not a shining example of a farm girl, but living on a station is a unique experience! I wish I could show you Paterson Downs. Have you ever stayed on a cattle station?'

'No.'

'Oh, wow, you've got to try it,' Free said. 'It's amazing. You could come stay some time, if you like, to get a genuine feel for station life.'

She had asked casually but suddenly she liked the idea of showing him around her home. She was proud of Patersons, and would love to see his response to the vast property and its busy homestead. She had the feeling he'd love it. It would allow her to get to know him better, too — much better. He must understand, from this invitation, that she was interested in him. Free waited breathlessly, trying to gauge his reaction.

Finn focused on his sandwich. 'Sounds like a great experience.'

His tone could not have been more noncommittal, and Free cringed inwardly.

'Anyway.' She fought through the humiliation. 'Willow's wedding is at Quintilla rather than Patersons because they're better set up for entertaining. It's going to be a casual kind of thing, catered by the station kitchens, only a few people from town coming. Beth and I will go home on the Friday to have one last night with Willow before she becomes a missus. Not that she'll actually *be* a missus,' she recollected. 'She'll always be *Ms* Willow Paterson, unless she gets a doctorate and then she'll be Dr Paterson, just like Beth . . . ' She trailed off, aware she was digging herself into a hole of incoherent ramblings.

Finn remained fixated on his sandwich. 'Did you start that picture of Talbot Gorge while you were out there — at the gorge, I mean?'

Now he was trying to change the subject. This couldn't be worse.

Free played along. '*En plein air?* No. I took photos and then used one as a reference.' She watched Finn sadly. Clearly, she had come on too strong. *Maybe* . . . Free had a sudden thought. 'Oh! Have you recently been through a bad break-up?' she asked.

Finn choked on his mouthful of food and was obliged to take a drink of water.

'Why do you ask?' he managed at last.

'Just a vibe.'

Finn had gone red in the face, although that might just have been from the choking. Free examined him, her own lunch forgotten.

He cleared his throat. 'I split up with my ex-girlfriend back in October.'

Aha! 'So, just before you left to come live in Mount Clair?' Free asked. 'Makes sense. Long-distance relationships suck. It must have been painful, though.'

'No, it wasn't quite like that . . . ' Finn trailed off, but because she was still waiting, he resumed. 'It *was* kind of messy. Elyse — well, it wasn't about the long-distance thing.'

'What was it about?'

He toyed with a fork. 'I haven't really talked to anyone about this.' Free nodded, still waiting, and Finn gave an unexpected laugh. 'You're not going to let me off the hook, are you?'

She realised what he meant. 'Oh, you don't want to talk about it?'

He shrugged. 'Not really. But I will anyway.' Finn settled his gaze on hers. 'Elyse and I met about a year ago. We got introduced by a mutual acquaintance. She was popular; loads of friends. Nice-looking, I guess.'

'Can I see her?' Free interrupted.

'Huh?'

'Have you got a photo or something?'

Finn's brow creased. 'You want to see a picture of Elyse?'

'I'm visual. I need to get a picture of anyone I'm talking about. I've seen the photos of your family, so I know who you mean when you talk about them. It would be good to see a photo of Elyse too.'

He shrugged and unlocked his phone. He scrolled back through his camera roll — a long way back — until he found a photo to show her.

'This was at an outdoor concert last year, just before we split.'

Free took the phone and inspected the picture. It was a selfie of Finn and Elyse, sitting on a picnic blanket with crowds of people on the rolling green lawn behind them. She zoomed in on their faces, first Elyse, who had dead-straight honey-brown hair and flawless makeup, her lips held just right to maximise the height of her cheekbones and give her big, smoky eyes.

'She's extremely beautiful, but she looks a little disconnected from you,' Free commented. She switched her attention to the five-month-old image of Finn and softened inside. 'Maybe I'm just comparing her to you, though. You have such a gorgeous, genuine smile.'

Free slid his phone back across the table and discovered Finn staring at her with his mouth slightly ajar. *Ack*, had she offended him? He recovered himself, red-cheeked once more.

'Uh, thanks. Anyway, Elyse was in HR. She had a good job with a big company in the CBD, but she knew I was planning to go country at least for a while when I finished my probation. I applied for a couple of positions, including one in Mount Clair.'

Free nodded. Elyse had baulked at the distance when Finn took the job in Mount Clair, she guessed. The girl didn't want a part-time relationship. Or maybe she *had* wanted to come up to the Kimberley with Finn, and he hadn't been able to live with the idea of cutting her career aspirations short —

99

'Then a mate took me out for a beer and let me know she was cheating on me with a friend.'

'What?' Free gasped. 'Oh *no*. No way. How could she? Are you sure it was true?' She snatched the phone off him and peered at Elyse again. *Oh — yes.* It was obvious now that Free knew the truth. The girl was cold and narcissistic.

Free was outraged. 'Why the hell would she cheat on *you*? You're so kind and warm-hearted. You'd never neglect a girlfriend — you're not capable of neglecting *anyone*. You just need to look into my eyes and I can see how *giving* you are. Plus, you're hot! I mean, look at you. Big, hot and muscly. And you have the most interesting eyes I think I've ever seen. I can't imagine ever getting tired of looking into them.' Free shook her head, increasingly annoyed with this *Elyse* girl. 'Was she nuts? She must have been insecure or something, to need extra male attention. You didn't deserve that.'

Finn's gaze locked on hers. His eyes were full of something resembling gratitude — and longing. Her skin tingled in response to it and, despite his rejection just minutes earlier, Free knew with utter conviction that he wanted her. Felt something. She pushed his phone back towards him, her pulse racing. The honesty between them was like a hot-coal walk — agonising but exhilarating. She wanted it to end, and yet never wanted it to end.

It ended.

'You're right.' Finn got to his feet. 'It hurt like hell and no-one deserves that. Free, thank you

100

for lunch, but I'd better let you get on with your day.'

She jumped up. 'Oh. Okay.'

Finn pocketed his phone, took his plate into the kitchen and emptied the scraps into the bin before placing his plate on the sink. She followed him to the front door, bewildered. *Was I too pushy?*

Finn turned to face her. 'Thanks again.'

Free nodded. Finn hovered for a moment. Maybe he could see the hurt in her expression.

'You're . . . ' Finn glanced away and back to her face. 'You're really sweet.'

He took off down her steps and up his, then through his front door without looking back. Free closed her own door and wandered back to the table, staring at Finn's spot, crumb-free and cleared of dishes.

Such a good guest.

Such a confusing man.

6

The next time Free got a lunchbreak with both Jay and Aidan, she told them that Tia had contributed an idea for the tile wall.

Jay interrupted before she'd even heard the idea, her face bright with pleasure. 'It's so good to see Tia responding to you like this, Free. She's always been such a mouse. It's obvious you've clicked with her as a mentor, and hopefully that will keep drawing her out of her shell the more the semester goes on.' Jay scooped some chickpea and couscous salad onto her fork. 'Tia's a real innovator. She has huge dedication to the skills-acquisition side of things, too — not to mention bucketloads of talent.'

Free nodded in agreement. 'So, her concept is this. Cultural heritage. A no-bullshit, honest story of the multicultural history of Mount Clair and the Kimberley more generally.'

'Sounds very *right-on*,' Aidan said, making a wry face.

Free gazed at him in dismay. 'Oh *no* — I don't want it to be like that. Not some empty statement about diversity. I was thinking it could be a real, genuine acknowledgement — true stories of the area's history. No whitewashing. It might not always be pretty, but the truth has its own beauty, you know?'

His eyebrows crept up. 'True stories? Like?'

Huge question. Free waved her arms around,

trying to express herself. 'Like, stories of the traditional owners, colonisation, settlement, farming, immigration, asylum seekers, mixed ancestry, the subjugation of certain groups, languages, adaptation ... ' She paused for breath. 'Tia's grandfather, he was a Japanese pearler in Broome, and Cameron's great-grandmother was a Jamadji domestic servant — '

'Sounds like a left-wing protest,' Aidan said with that same tight smile. 'Very topical but kind of dull and depressing, like so many earnest, misguided public artworks.'

She drew back, smarting over his negativity. But before Free could answer, Jay swallowed her mouthful and burst out, 'I love it! Did the kids honestly come up with it themselves?'

'Absolutely.' Free recounted the conversation she'd had with the kids in her after-school session.

Jay shook her head, impressed. 'Could you write this down for me, Free?' she asked. 'Scope it up? I'd like to take it to the principal, and if he likes it we can send it on to the committee.'

'I'm not sure the Year Tens will be on board,' said Aidan. 'They've been getting quite excited about the *River of Life* idea.'

'I'll run it by them on Monday,' said Jay. 'I think if it's presented to them properly, they'll like it too. After all, every single kid can contribute something of themselves to this.' There was something cool in Jay's manner to Aidan. The department head paused, rubbing her chin. 'We should think up a good name. *Diversity Wall? Unity in Diversity?*'

103

Free instantly disliked both of these suggestions. 'My sisters are good with words. I'm seeing them this weekend. I might ask them for some ideas for a title, and then I'll put them in the scope for you to consider.'

Jay agreed and went to get a cup of tea. Aidan ate his Vietnamese rice paper rolls in disgruntled silence. *Awkward.* Free picked at her extremely boring Vegemite sandwich and tried to think of a way to appease him.

'Um, maybe the *River of Life* concept could be incorporated, Aidan. After all, the agricultural history of Mount Clair is a big part — '

'Oh, let's not sully your concept by trying to blend it with another.' He gave her one of his patented tight-cheeked smiles. 'I'm not fazed in the least.'

His body language said the opposite to his words. Free wasn't sure which to trust. Aidan flicked a gaze from her face down to her chest and Free froze. Had she really seen that?

'Listen,' he said. 'There's an outdoor movie night this Friday, at the foreshore. Are you available?'

Free's jaw dropped. 'Me?'

He chuckled. 'Yes, you. Why are you so surprised?'

'Um, I just thought maybe our, um, political views weren't very compatible. On stuff like environment and society . . . '

His eyebrows rose. 'Why would that matter?'

'It matters a lot,' she said, her voice firm. This was the one thing she knew about relationships.

He shrugged. 'We haven't had much of a

chance to discover whether we're *compatible* or not. This could be an opportunity.' He waited.

Spending a Friday night with Aidan did not appeal. With a gasp of relief, she recalled that she was otherwise committed.

'I'm sorry, Aidan. It's my sister's wedding this Saturday and I'm tied up for the whole weekend.'

'Ah, okay. I'll work out another date, then.' He dipped his rice paper roll into a pot of chilli sauce. 'Watch this space.'

★ ★ ★

Beth collected Free for the drive to Paterson Downs on Friday afternoon, bridesmaid dresses hanging from the window hooks in the back seat of the Beast.

'How's work?' Beth asked as they turned onto Herne River Road.

'It's fantastic. I love it.'

'That's great.' Beth switched on the head-lights. 'I thought you'd be good at the job. The kids like you, yes?'

'It's a pretty special bunch they've given me,' said Free. 'I'm lucky.'

'It's only one extra year at uni to do a diploma of teaching, you know,' Beth said. 'That'd be a good fallback if you find it hard to make an income from your art.'

'I don't make much,' Free admitted. 'But if I can pick up the odd contract like this, then I'll make enough to scrape by. And Dad says he doesn't care if I never earn a cent because I'll

105

always be welcome at Patersons.'

A smile touched her sister's lips. 'I bet he does. I just meant, you know, if you wanted more financial independence.'

Free twisted her mouth, considering it. 'I'm not sure I'd want to be a schoolteacher. I enjoy the job so far, but it's really hard work, teaching. Curriculum and all that. You've got kids' futures in your hands.'

Beth shrugged. 'Okay. Just a thought. Keep your mind open. You might be better suited than you think.'

'Maybe. Hey, what shoes are you wearing tomorrow?' Free asked.

Beth shot her a frown. 'Silver sandals, of course. That's what we all agreed.' Free went into a momentary panic. When the hell had they agreed on *that*? 'You were in that chat, I know it,' said Beth.

Free thought furiously. 'Oh, yes. I saw a chat happening during the week. Tanya suggested nude heels, right?'

'Yes, but Willow thought silver sandals would be better. She didn't want us attempting heels in the dirt.'

Free hadn't read that far into the chat. She contemplated the shoes she'd brought along. White pumps from Perth, natural leather sandals she'd picked up in Rio, or sequined thongs from Delhi. Oh, why had she left her gorgeous strappy silver sandals back at the unit? The thongs were silver, she recalled. Maybe she could get away with that?

She shook herself. What the hell was she

thinking? You didn't wear thongs to a wedding. 'Um — '

'Free, please tell me you brought silver sandals of some description to wear in the bridal party at your sister's wedding,' Beth said, a sigh in her voice.

'Of course I did,' Free snapped.

Beth raised her eyebrows but said nothing. They lapsed into silence as Free wondered what on earth she was going to do about shoes for the next day.

By the time they'd arrived at Paterson Downs, she was no closer to a solution. Free kissed Willow and her father, then hid in her bedroom to panic in privacy. She had silver acrylic paint, she realised, catching sight of the surplus art supplies she'd left at Patersons.

And a pair of brown leather sandals.

Half an hour later, she left the newly silvered sandals to dry on her windowsill. She went out through the yard to say hello to Devi, her closest friend at the station. Devi was a dorm assistant but could usually be found helping Jean in the station kitchen.

Free joined her family on the patio. 'Are the Forrests coming over tonight?' she asked. 'And where's Tanya?'

'They'll all get here soon,' Willow told her. 'Tom's collecting Tanya from the airport as we speak, and the Forrests are coming for dinner. It's just a barbie.'

'I really hope that dress fits Tanya.' Beth sounded a little fretful, which wasn't like her.

'Did you hide the dresses?' Willow asked. 'I

107

want them to be a surprise for Tom.'

'They're all hanging in my room, door shut.' Beth was still chagrined about the dresses, Free noted, with a flicker of mischievous glee. But her amusement vanished when Beth leaned close to Free's ear and said, 'Tanya and I both got gifts for Willow. You could give her the horseshoe in the morning, when we give her our presents.'

Crap! Free had been tasked with buying a little satin horseshoe for Willow to carry down the aisle, but in the craziness of starting work that week — and other stuff — she'd forgotten. *Good Lord.* First the sandals, now the horseshoe. And there was nowhere Free could get one, either. The only horseshoes around Patersons were the iron ones in the tack room. She was such a damn screw-up. And she couldn't fix this by painting something.

Wait.

Free thought about the row of ancient, rusted horseshoes that lined the Patersons' tack room shelf. She excused herself and slunk with utmost stealth into the relative gloom of the stables. The stable-hand, Kira, was filling hay nets, the air thick with the scent of chaff and manure.

'Hi, Free,' the girl said, noticing her. 'Do you need something?'

'Uh, yeah.' Free made her odd request and Kira only stared a little bit before she showed Free her options. Free selected the smallest, lightest-weight horseshoe on the shelf and dashed back to her bedroom. She rubbed it down and opened the silver paint again. Minutes later, a shining silver horseshoe rested on the windowsill next to her sandals.

This might just work.

★　★　★

Tanya was full of excitement and wanted to open the champagne as soon as she arrived at Paterson Downs. They all drank a glass on the patio and tucked in to the delicious thick steaks and field mushrooms Tom had cooked, but tiredness hit everyone soon after dinner. The Forrests made a move to leave, so the Paterson household went out the front to say goodbye.

It took some effort to get Tom into the car since he'd suddenly decided he had private things to say to Willow before they tied the knot the next day. He took her a little way down the driveway to murmur with her, until his father gave a particularly long blast of the horn. Tom jogged back and scrambled into the rear of the vehicle, grinning like he'd won the lottery. Willow returned to join them on the porch, trying to conceal a smile, and Free glowed inside. It filled her with joy to see Willow looking so loved and blissful after all those years of being tense and serious. Her thoughts drifted sidewards to Finn saying, 'You're really sweet.' She'd hardly seen him since that lunch. Hopefully, she'd randomly bump into him again on Monday. If not, she'd arrange things so she did.

They tidied up and carried cups of tea out onto the patio.

'Oh, I need to pick your brains, girls,' Free

109

said as they settled back into the old cane chairs with their father. 'We need a title for our tile wall project.' She told them about Tia's cultural heritage concept.

'I *love* that idea,' said Willow. 'What about *Land of Colour?*'

Free tapped it into the memo app on her phone. 'Good one. I need a few suggestions.'

'Um, how about *Cultural Kaleidoscope?*' offered Beth. '*Diverse-City?* Like a play on words.'

'*Kimberley Rainbow,*' Tanya broke in.

Free kept tapping and they threw out a few more suggestions. 'I'd love to use something that really captures the idea of putting down roots in Mount Clair. You know, how everyone's from different backgrounds but we've joined together and become part of the place. Some of us were already here, some came as part of colonisation, and others are still arriving, you know? Something that captures that.'

'Right, I see,' her father said musingly. 'Something that says born and bred.'

Free stared at him. 'Dad! That's awesome! *Born and Bred.* It's short, snappy, and says exactly what I want it to say. You're brilliant!'

He chuckled in surprise but her sisters agreed that it was just right.

'You're a bush poet, Barry,' Tanya declared. 'You've got a way with words.'

'Bullshit,' he said, but he looked pleased.

'This time tomorrow, Willow will be married,' Beth announced. She caught Willow's eye. 'We're going to make sure tomorrow's perfect for you.'

'Perfect?' Willow gave a laugh. 'I'll settle for pretty good. It's just a ceremony and a party. Ultimately, it doesn't make any difference, does it?'

'Gawd, you're so unromantic,' Tanya groaned. 'It's not just a party. It's an opportunity to be the princess for the day, look beautiful and have all eyes on you.'

Dismay crossed Willow's face and Beth snorted a laugh. 'I don't think you're selling it to her, Tan!' She got to her feet. 'Well, I don't want bags under my eyes so I'd better get to bed. I'm wearing a dress that looks like I'm going to my Year Ten formal tomorrow, so I'm going to need a youthful complexion to pull it off.'

Free glanced anxiously at Willow, hoping she wasn't hurt by Beth's barb. 'Oh, Beth, you look great in the dress,' she said. 'Hot. It shows off your legs.'

'Whatever,' said Beth, but she had a half-smile that showed she was joking. 'Goodnight, all.'

★　★　★

Free set an alarm for seven, and the minute she woke up she checked the state of the silver sandals and the horseshoe. They were completely dry.

'Hallelujah for that,' she muttered.

Willow was outside working with the cows and Free could hear that Beth was up, chatting with Tanya in the kitchen as they clanged about with dishes and breakfast. She dug in among her textile scraps and found a piece of natural leather

111

string left over from when she'd gone through a jewellery-making craze. She looped it through the topmost nail holes in the silver horseshoe. Next, she used a silver texta to pen *Willow and Tom* with the date on a little piece of white card, hole-punched it and threaded that on too, then tied off the ends of the string. She wrapped the whole thing in tissue paper and joined the others for breakfast.

It was midmorning when Willow finally stopped working and came inside to shower. Upon the arrival of the hairdresser they'd booked to work on their hairstyles, Barry declared it a 'bloody danger zone' of women running around, semi-dressed, and shut himself in his bedroom. Tanya painted Willow's nails while she sat in the kitchen with hot rollers in her hair. Free watched the process, updating her Instagram with her latest river photo. It came from her trusty store of favourite pictures in case of days like this, when she couldn't get out there to take a new one. The photo had captured the red riverbed, just starting to peep out from under the wet season's gradually diminishing flow. She tapped out a caption.

The Herne's water levels are just beginning to recede as the end of the wet season comes into sight. Always full circle. #Herne365 #Natures Wisdom #NoFilter

'That stuff dries your nails super fast,' Tanya told Willow. 'Touch them. They're fine.'

Willow tested her nails' dryness. 'Oh, good. I don't have the patience to wait for nail polish to dry.'

'If they're dry enough,' Beth said, 'then I think it's bubbly time!'

She poured the drinks and they chorused a *cheers*, clinking glasses.

'While you're held captive in the hairdressing chair, Willow, we'll give you our wedding-day prezzies,' Beth informed their sister. 'You go first, Free.'

Free went to her room for the tissue-paper package, returning a moment later to thrust it into Willow's hands. Willow protested that they shouldn't have bought presents, but when it was unwrapped, she gazed at the horseshoe in delight.

'Free, where on earth did you find this? I didn't even want one of those poncy bridal horseshoes but this — this is gorgeous! Did you get it custom-made?'

Free could not have been more pleased with Willow's response. 'I made it. It's one of our horseshoes from the stables.'

Willow peered at it more closely. 'Oh my *God*. I think it's one of Tuffie's!'

'It was the smallest one I could find.'

'Then it's definitely Tuffie's.' Willow's eyes shone. 'Free, how did you even think of this?'

Beth glanced at Free with a grin. 'I knew I could smell fresh paint last night. Necessity is the mother of invention, hey, Free?'

You don't know the half of it, Free thought, remembering her silver sandals.

Beth presented Willow with a pair of little stud earrings that were almost an exact match for the old willow-tree pendant their sister always wore

— originally a gift from their mother. Free had often wished she had something like that necklace to remember their mother by. Beth must have searched high and low to find such a gift.

'I couldn't let you wear your boring sleepers to your own wedding,' she said when Willow thanked her, her face glowing.

'You girls know me so well,' she said with a chuckle that had a bit of sadness beneath it. Free blinked back her own tears, avoiding Beth's eye.

Thankfully, Tanya didn't notice they were having an emotional moment, and pushed in to give Willow her gift.

'It's for your trousseau,' she said with a wink.

'My what?' Willow asked, but when she opened the box and found an impossibly tiny white lace G-string and matching teddy, she understood.

Willow was a blusher, and this made her blush. Free giggled wickedly. 'Ply her with champagne, Tan. If we give her enough throughout today, she might even wear that for Tom tonight.'

Tanya took the hint and they all toasted Willow, sipping bubbly as they did their makeup and took their turns in the hair-styling chair. The hairdresser took advantage of Free's natural curls to create soft tendrils around her hairline, twisting the rest of her hair up high on her head. When she was done, Free went and changed.

'I know you always believed you were a fairy,' Beth said when Free emerged in the powder-blue dress, 'but dressing like one as an adult is beyond a joke.'

114

'Shush, Willow will hear you,' Free answered, but she couldn't help a giggle. It truly was a hilarious little fairy frock. Pretty, but certainly not dignified.

Tanya appeared, smoothing down the front of her lilac dress, her face rapturous. 'It's gorgeous! I never thought Willow would choose something like this. I'm going to wear it to my family's Easter party in April.'

Beth lifted an eyebrow and Free tried not to laugh again. The dress looked adorable on Tanya, and Free told her so. 'Come on, Beth, where's yours?'

Beth rolled her eyes and begrudgingly donned her pink dress. She looked beautiful, Free thought, although it wasn't at all her usual style. But then, Beth would look stunning in just about anything.

They helped Willow into her sleek white gown, modelled on their mother's wedding dress. It was a perfect style for her — simple and elegant. Thanking the universe for waterproof mascara, Free took dozens of photos while Beth fitted the veil.

At last they were all ready and Barry came cautiously out into the living area in his best pants and shirt, his shoes polished to a high sheen. He inspected them.

'What do you think, Dad?' Free asked. 'Willow's doing a pretty good Audrey Hepburn impression in that dress, don't you reckon?'

'Free, Bethie, Tanya — you girls look bloody lovely,' he said, 'but I'm sorry to say not one of you is a patch on Willow today.'

They all laughed as Willow denied it, but Beth scoffed. 'Take it, Willow. That's how it should be on your wedding day.'

Willow had been unable to handle the idea of arriving with a fanfare and had settled with Tom that the bridal party and their partners would assemble at Quintilla before the rest of the guests turned up. Patersons' staff had cleaned out two of the farm vehicles, and now ferried them over to the neighbouring station.

Tom came outside to greet them with one of his groomsmen and Willow sent her bridesmaids out of the car first, laughing at his astonishment.

'You wanted pink!' she called from the car.

'You've gone above and beyond,' he called back. 'They're like marshmallows!'

But when Willow climbed out, Tom went absolutely quiet. Free had never seen him lost for words before and she nudged Beth and Tanya to draw their attention. Tom pulled Willow close and wrapped her up in his arms for a kiss.

Beth groaned. 'He'll wreck her lipstick before the ceremony.'

Briggsy and some others pulled in to the Quintilla parking area at that moment — Finn at the wheel as chauffeur. Free's pulse jumped. She'd forgotten he was playing taxi for Briggsy. If only he were staying. Briggsy, plainly stressed, had just got off work. He hightailed it into the house to change into his best-man suit. Finn helped Kate and another woman out of the car. There were the customary hugs, kisses and ravings about how beautiful everyone looked. From the corner of her eye, Free saw Finn had

116

his gaze locked on her, his expression dumb-struck. So he *did* like her, she thought, spirits soaring. Then why had he clammed up like that on their lunch date? Was he just super shy? She crossed to him and put her arms out as though presenting herself for his appraisal.

'Finn the benevolent giant, bow before the fairy-floss queen.'

He attempted a laugh but his colour had deepened and he looked unbearably awkward, his eyes darting around the group as though he was seeking a rescuer. Everyone was chatting excitedly and no-one came to his aid. Although this reaction was as confusing as ever, Free leaned in for a quick hug of greeting, breathing in that yummy Finn-branded scent that was becoming so pleasantly familiar.

It was like hugging a plank of wood.

'Are you all right?' she asked, drawing back.

'Yeah, fine. How are you?'

'I'm fine.'

He glanced at her face and looked hastily away but a moment later his eyes wandered back and examined her, from her hair down to her painted silver sandals. It was as though he couldn't drag his gaze away — and it was electrifying. As she took in his mesmerised expression and red cheeks, Free's hope rose again. He either *really* liked what he saw — or he was suffering from heat stroke.

'Come on inside, Finn,' Tom invited as they all headed for the house. 'You look like you need a beer.'

Finn snapped out of his reverie. 'Oh, no,

117

thanks, mate. I'll be off. Have a great day. What time do you want your pick-up, Kate?' he called after her.

Kate didn't even hear, and Tom raised his eyebrows. 'You're going back to Mount Clair, only to turn around and drive all the way back out here later tonight?' he asked. 'Why aren't you staying for the wedding?'

'Uh . . . '

Free comprehended what had happened. Tom had only got to know Finn since the wedding invitations were sent. Finn hadn't been asked, but Tom had forgotten that. She stepped closer again, taking Finn's warm, strong arm.

'Come on,' she said. 'Stay. I think you've just been invited.'

'No way,' he said quietly, standing his ground. 'I'm not gatecrashing a wedding I wasn't even invited to.'

Willow either caught some of what was said or worked out the situation. She broke from Tom and crossed to Finn. 'Please stay,' she said with a warm smile. 'It can be a bit hard for us to keep up out here on the station, but you're part of the crew now.'

Finn still hesitated. Tom shouted to him. 'Getting you a beer. Right now.' He headed into the house and Willow followed, Beth fussing over the wedding dress's hem.

Free looked up at Finn. 'Please?'

The indecision faded and he nodded. She restrained a wriggle of delight.

'I'm skipper, so no beer, though,' he added.

'Not even one?'

118

He shook his head. 'Nah. I'll stay on the softies.'

Finn was swept up in Briggsy's crowd during the wedding itself and Free was far too busy with the ceremony and the photos to seek him out. However, the energy between them ran hot. Every time she looked his way, he was watching her. She was so excited she could barely focus on the celebrant's words. It felt like she and Finn were locked in their own little secret world of mutual desire and she longed for a chance to speak to him again. Scratch 'speaking'. She wanted to kiss that sexy mouth and look into those warm eyes at close — very close — range. Unluckily, her bridesmaid duties kept her at the bridal table for much of the evening.

At last, late in the night, the formalities ended. Tom and Willow took to the hired dance floor, snuggled up close together as they danced to a U2 song. Free knew Willow had been dreading the bridal dance, but as far as she could tell, her sister barely even knew anyone else existed in that moment. Her Audrey Hepburn dress streaked with red dust, Willow had her arms around Tom's neck and her eyes on his, the two of them deep in conversation.

'What's the bet they're discussing cattle?' Beth murmured to Free, which made her burst into laughter.

Best man Briggsy came to claim chief bridesmaid Beth for the dance, so Free looked for her own bridal party partner. But Tom's mate Hendo had shirked his duty and was dancing with his girlfriend. Finn passed by at that moment so Free grabbed her opportunity — and his hand.

'Hey! I've got no partner — will you dance with me?' she asked, smiling up at him.

He nodded immediately and they moved onto the dance floor. Free reached up to put her arms around his neck but he caught her hand on the way and they ended up in a more conservative, formal pose, her hand clasped in his; the other one on his shoulder. *His big, strong shoulder,* she thought, resisting the temptation to squeeze the hard muscle. Maybe he didn't want to get too close to her in front of her family. Fair call. She didn't want to get tongues wagging at her sister's wedding, either.

'Nice ceremony,' he said a little gruffly.

'It was. I'm so happy for Tom.' Free watched her sister dancing for a moment. 'Know what he told me after they got engaged? He admitted he's been in love with Willow, like, forever. Hundred per cent, head-over-heels in love. It was only when he nearly died in the chopper crash that she realised she felt the same.' She grinned up at Finn. 'If anyone deserves Willow, it's Tom. And vice versa.'

'They spent a long time apart, though, right? Didn't your sister only come home last year?'

'Yeah. He never stopped loving her, though. No matter what.'

Finn was silent, his face remote, and Free felt a sudden pang. Was his ex-girlfriend on his mind?

'Where's Max tonight?' he asked from out of the blue.

'Max . . . ' *Huh?* Maybe talking about inane things was Finn's comfort zone. 'At home, doing his thing, I guess. He's an independent spirit. I left him something to eat.'

He nodded. 'The sarge is acting a bit funny,' he remarked, glancing towards Briggsy.

'Is he?' Free hadn't noticed anything out of the ordinary, but she turned to stare. Briggsy looked normal to her, chatting with Beth as they danced.

'Yeah. I can't quite explain it. He's almost a bit *too* jolly.'

'Maybe he's just emotional,' Free suggested. 'Lots of *feels* today.'

Finn shrugged and she felt his shoulder muscle move beneath her hand. *Holy crap. This guy is just . . .* She pressed slightly closer almost without thinking. Finn stopped moving abruptly. He released her hand and stepped back.

'Thanks for the dance,' he said. 'I'd better go — I was supposed to be getting Kate a drink.'

He walked away, leaving Free gazing after him in dismay.

Clearly, Finn did not want to dance with her.

But those looks he's been giving me all night, from the moment he first saw me . . .

Free sat down on a spare plastic chair, frustrated. She'd never had so many mixed signals in her life — or maybe she'd never had any patience with decoding mixed signals before. Finn liked her, she was sure of it.

So what's his problem?

121

7

'Thanks again for the lift home.' Free studied Finn's profile in the darkness. Maybe if she stared long enough, she'd see right through into his brain. 'I could have got a ride with Beth tomorrow afternoon, but I really need to work on a scoping document for Jay before Monday.'

He nodded, hands on the wheel, and her frustration rose again. Finn was focused on the road ahead and wouldn't even look her way. Briggsy was singing Bruno Mars's 'Just the Way You Are' to Kate in the back seat.

'God, Sean,' Kate groaned. 'Would you please shut up?'

'Beautiful wedding,' he said, his words a little slurred. 'When *you* gonna marry *me*, Katie? Been waiting for years.'

'I'm not having this conversation.'

'Why not?' Briggsy raised his voice to include Free and Finn. 'Don'tcha reckon Katie should marry me, Miss Free? Kelly? We've been together since we were practically kids!'

'Stop it,' Kate hissed.

The argument startled Free. She'd always thought of Briggsy and Kate as happily and permanently de facto.

'What's this scope you need to do?' Finn asked.

Free realised he was trying to act as though there was no argument happening in the back seat. She scrambled to join in. 'Oh, well, it's kind of a statement of concept, giving the reasons behind the theme of the tile wall and an idea of what it might look like.'

'Am I not your *Mr Right*, Katie?' Briggsy was asking, his voice dropping. 'Am I just *Mr Right Now?*'

'That's enough, Sean.'

'Come here, beautiful.'

'Keep your bloody hands to yourself!'

Free had to stop herself from twisting around to stare.

Briggsy sounded hurt this time. 'I just tried to hold your hand, for Chrissake. No need to act like that.'

Her voice was hard and cold. 'You're drunk. Just cut it out.'

'Kate.' Briggsy attempted to lower his voice to a murmur, but he was so drunk it carried. 'Why are you acting like this lately? What have I done?'

'I'm joining the local footy team,' Finn said in an unusually loud tone.

By now, Free just wanted to hear what was going on with Briggsy and Kate, so she merely mumbled an acknowledgement in reply, but Finn kept on talking in that booming voice over the top of their murmuring. 'Yeah, I'm a bit out of practice, but the fellas assure me that's not an issue round these parts. They say the game's played in fun. I don't know, though. They're probably more competitive than they let on.'

'Stop comparing us to Tom and Willow,' Kate was saying in a low, tense voice. 'We're not them.'

'I don't want to be them. But why won't you commit to me? I just want you. We've been together for years. I'm happy with you, Katie. Aren't you happy with me? Every time I mention marriage, you shut me down. Isn't this, what we have, isn't it serious for you?'

'I don't *want* serious.' Kate sounded close to tears. 'God. I knew we shouldn't have bought a house together.'

Briggsy sucked in a breath. '*What?*'

'I wasn't ready. I don't need this pressure.'

Their voices had grown louder and Finn made another attempt to distract Free.

'Your painting of Talbot Gorge, will you sell it?' he asked.

'Um, I don't know. I guess if someone liked it and offered a fair sum, I would.'

'How do you decide what to charge for a painting?'

'There's a calculation you can use. Materials plus time. I don't use that method, though, because I'm either horribly slow or stupidly fast when I produce something.' The voices in the back seat had dropped away to angry mutters once more.

'I wouldn't mind buying it,' Finn said.

Free whipped her head round. 'Huh? My painting?'

He made a slight movement with his shoulders. 'Yeah. It's really good. And the track out to Talbot Gorge is where I first learned to four-wheel drive. It means something to me. That's why I wanted to know the asking price.' He didn't appear to be kidding.

'I was going to put it in the Broome Art Show, if it turns out okay.'

'Well, do that. But if you don't sell it there, maybe we could talk about a price.'

She glanced into the back. The argument had reached a stalemate. Briggsy and Kate were sitting far apart, staring out of their own windows.

She turned back to Finn. An idea had popped into her head. 'Are you working in the morning?'

'No. Tomorrow arvo.'

'Oh, right.'

He glanced her way. 'Why do you ask?'

'Well, I was going to see if you'd like to come with me out to Talbot Gorge, especially since you know how to four-wheel drive and I'm not great at it. And because you like it there. That photo I'm using — I took it a couple of years ago now, and I wouldn't mind having another look at the place. I'm a bit stuck on one section of rock and seeing it in real life again might unstick me.'

'Ah, right. Sorry, but . . . yeah. Work.'

'We don't have a vehicle to use, anyway.' Free hesitated. 'But maybe we could borrow one and go next weekend?' She waited breathlessly.

'Where are we going?' Briggsy broke in, leaning forward.

'Talbot Gorge,' Finn answered.

Free was torn. She didn't especially want Briggsy crashing in on the date — but it might be a good way to put Finn at ease. Although Finn's honest eyes said he was interested, he hadn't been receptive to any of her gentle moves. *We've only known each other a couple of weeks,*

125

she reminded herself. Perhaps he was simply cautious. If they hung out in a group, he might feel more confident about her.

'Next weekend,' she said to Briggsy. 'Want to come along?'

'Hell, yeah.'

'Are you and Kate free next Sunday?' she asked. 'And do you have a four-wheel drive, Briggsy?'

'I am,' said Briggsy. 'And I do. The one you're sitting in right now. I think you've got next Sunday off too, haven't you, Kelly?' Finn gave a sound of acquiescence and Briggsy sat back again. 'I bloody love Talbot Gorge. We'll go for a swim. Remember when you and I went swimming there, Kate?'

She maintained a frosty silence and Briggsy slumped against the seat. He resumed staring moodily out of the window.

Finn turned up the radio to fill the silence for the last half-hour of the drive. Free was immensely glad when they dropped Briggsy and Kate home at the residential estate a couple of minutes out of town.

'Do you need your car in the morning?' Finn asked his boss. 'If not, I'll pick you up for work after lunch, yeah?'

Briggsy waved him away, declaring he planned on sleeping in and definitely wouldn't need his vehicle back.

'Wow, that was intense,' Free said after they'd called their goodbyes and pulled away from the kerb. 'Did you ever see any of that stuff before tonight?'

Finn hesitated before shrugging. 'Not really.'

'You're a terrible liar,' Free said with a giggle. 'It's okay. I don't gossip.'

He relented. 'I've noticed a bit of tension between the sarge and Kate before, but tonight was the worst I've seen. I think he's keen for kids, getting married, the whole bit. She's not. He makes the odd throwaway joke about it but there's an undercurrent. Kate — well, she's not interested in settling down.' He paused. 'What he said back there, about being *Mr Right Now* for her? I think he nailed it.'

'Oh, that's sad.' Free's heart ached for Briggsy — but also for Kate. 'I guess if he wants the family life, children, marriage and so on — and she wants her freedom — then that's a pretty fundamental mismatch. Still, she might change her mind. She's only, what, late twenties?'

'He's thirty. She's thirty-two.' Finn stopped at a red light and rowdy pub-goers crossed the road in front of them. 'I don't know. I'm not sure she'll change. If she doesn't want that life with him now, why would a year or two make any difference?'

'People change all the time.'

'Not really.'

Free glanced his way. 'Seriously? You don't think people can change?'

'Not fundamentally. They can change their behaviour and outlook — to an extent. But not the things deep inside that make them who they are.' The light went green and he moved the car forward.

'I've seen people change,' Free said stoutly.

'It's cynical to say they can't.'

He chuckled. 'You're very trusting.'

'So are you.'

He laughed more, a note of surprise coming through. 'I just told you I don't believe leopards can change their spots and yet somehow I'm *trusting*?'

'I don't think you're as cynical as you make out, Finn. You have this thing where you just radiate positivity. I saw it when you pulled me over on Herne River Road before Willow's hen's party. I felt better as soon as you spoke to me. You're kind and decent, and you expect other people to be kind and decent, and I'd be willing to bet that, more often than not, they naturally rise to your expectations. There's nothing like someone thinking you're great to make you want to be great.' Finn didn't answer and she rested her head on the window, tiredness hitting. 'You should work with young people, with a gift like that.'

Finn scoffed. 'A gift!'

'It's a *gift*,' she repeated. 'I look into your eyes and I see myself amplified, reflected back much smarter, better — more reliable, more talented, than I actually am.' She had to stop herself from adding 'prettier'. 'That's a *gift*. Imagine if you made kids feel like that about themselves.'

'I look at you and I see what I see,' he said. The discomfort had returned to his voice. 'I don't need to amplify anything to see how smart or talented you are.' He clamped his mouth shut but her heart jumped, a smile coming to her lips.

'Thank you, Finn,' she said. 'And that's

exactly what I mean. That's how you make me feel.'

'That's how you *should* feel.' Finn's eyes were on the road but, in the streetlight, she detected a faint crease above his eyebrows.

'If anyone makes you feel less than you are, less than amazing, you should . . . ' He stopped and scratched the back of his neck as though second-guessing himself. But then he went on, blurting out the words. 'Then you should let them know that hurts you. And if they still don't realise how amazing you are, you should consider . . . moving on from them.'

Was he talking about Beth? How could she move on from her own sister? Whatever he meant, she appreciated his words and leaned over to put her hand on his where it rested on the gearstick. He tensed and she thought for a moment he would pull away. He didn't. He released the gearstick and squeezed her hand. Free went hot all over in an instant, her heart rate leaping into a wild, irregular thump.

They were almost home. What would happen when they stopped?

They arrived, and Finn pulled the car in to his carport, climbing out straight away. *Okay, no car kiss then.* She gathered her gear and clambered out after him. Finn bounded up onto his porch and she paused at the foot of his steps, watching him as the security light flicked on. His T-shirt was stretching over his hard shoulders as he dug for his house key.

She took a breath. 'Do . . . do you reckon I could come in for . . . for a coffee?'

He stopped dead, key in the lock, and turned to catch her eye.

'I don't think that's a good idea.'

She dropped her gaze. 'Oh.'

'Where's Max?' he asked.

Deflecting again. She gave him a sad half-smile. 'Probably snoring on my bed.'

Finn unlocked his door. 'Goodnight, Free.'

He shut the door before she could even reply.

★　★　★

In bed, in the darkness, Free realised what it must be. The wave of comprehension was so powerful it made her catch her breath. Max even stopped purr-snoring for a moment, alarmed by her gasp.

Of course.

Finn wasn't rejecting *her*. Not specifically her. He did like her, just as his face always blatantly showed. But he'd been so wrecked by his ex-girlfriend's infidelity that he'd lost all his trust in women. He wasn't ready for love — for dating again. He wasn't even ready for the night of impulsive passion Free had just offered him. Finn had been too badly burnt.

The gravity of it brought tears to her eyes. *The poor guy.* His heart had been ravaged — devastated by what that woman did. She got angry at Elyse again. Okay, she didn't know what had happened in Elyse's life, and sometimes things went wrong enough to make people stray — but to do it to someone like Finn? Elyse must be a cold person to have knowingly hurt such a

130

beautiful soul. If she could just show Finn that not all women hurt men. Not all women cheated. Some women would cherish his beautiful, innate goodness like it should be cherished, and not hurt him or leave him . . .

Whoa. Where had *this* come from? All she'd wanted from Finn was for him to admit what she saw in his eyes: that he wanted her too. How had she made the leap from *that* to suddenly imagining she was the key to his happiness? She'd only just met him. She didn't know how to heal him or be his happily-ever-after. And Finn truly deserved a woman he could trust.

And yet that vision of being Finn's one-and-only — of being adored, trusted, and giving Finn happiness — persisted.

A faint sound alerted her. Finn was singing. Free folded her pillow over her exposed ear to muffle the noise, a little alarmed by her thoughts of the past few minutes. But curiosity won. What was he singing this time?

She didn't know the song, but it was certainly a more mournful tune than she'd heard from him before. It was as though Finn was pouring that sadness deep in his heart out through the melancholy ballad. For a few minutes, it brought those damn tears back to her eyes.

Then it became a comfort and lulled her to sleep.

★ ★ ★

Thunder woke her at nine in the morning, which was lucky because Free had forgotten to set an

131

alarm. She needed to work on the scoping document for Jay, not to mention create a PowerPoint slide show on gridding for her Year Elevens. As far as possible, she put the thought of Finn out of her head.

She ate cereal as she drafted the scoping document, typing *Born and Bred* as the proposed title for the tile wall. Thank goodness Jay preferred this theme to Aidan's horrible *River of Life* idea. Free could not have worked on that theme. The thought of Aidan brought his tight face and unpleasant proposition back into her mind. Ugh, hopefully he would forget about his threat to ask her on another date.

Max interrupted her work, demanding to be let outside. He did his usual disappearing act for the daylight hours. Weird cat: he liked to snuggle up in the air conditioning during the night but was happy to spend the day outside in the stifling wet-season humidity. He was obviously perfectly adapted to Mount Clair's climate.

Free was still in her pyjamas when a knock sounded at the front door just before noon. She threw on a kimono and answered it. The hairy-legged biology teacher, Max, was there examining her printer, which was still sitting on the porch table.

'Max!'

He looked up and gave her a shy smile. 'Good morning. It's definitely a Children's python.' He indicated his bike, resting against the porch railing. 'I was passing by and noticed your printer was still outside. I thought you might want me to get the snake out for you.'

132

'Oh! Yes, please!'

'This species is very shy. They like to steer clear of humans but the dam construction work has scared them into the township lately,' he said.

'That bloody dam.' Free sighed.

'There's an info night coming up about its impact on the local wildlife,' he told her. 'You might like to go.'

'Yeah, I saw that in my emails. Are you anti-dam, Max?' she asked, but he was poking at the printer, completely focused on the snake.

'It was probably chasing a gecko or a frog and followed it into the cartridge holder. It's wedged in there pretty tightly, but I should be able to ease it out.'

'Please do!' she said.

Max went to his bike and unzipped a strapped-on carry pack to pull out a rectangle of fabric.

'What's that?' Free asked.

'It's my snake bag.'

She goggled. 'You keep that on your bike?'

'I like to take one everywhere. You just never know when you might need a snake bag.'

He had to dismantle the printer slightly to extract the little python. Max showed it to her once it was out, explaining the markings and its anatomical structure. It was quite cute now she knew it wasn't dangerous.

'This one's a bit worse for wear after being stuck in the printer for a couple of weeks,' he said, his thick eyebrows tugging down in concern as he inspected the reptile. 'Dehydrated and a little malnourished. I might take it down to Kev.'

'Kev?'

'He's got Reptile Rescue. You know it? On Flametree Avenue?'

'I can't say I've noticed it before.'

'Well, Kev's a true expert. They're endangered, you see, these pythons. Since they've been scared off the riverbed, they're getting killed on the roads more. But Kev'll rehabilitate this little guy for a couple of weeks before releasing him, to give him the best chance.'

'That's awesome. And you'll take it over to the rescue place for me?'

'Yes, it's no trouble.'

Finn's front door opened and he stepped out onto the porch in his uniform. Free's heart jumped from first to fifth gear and her mind raced with all those confusing thoughts from the night before.

'Good morning,' he said, noticing them.

'Hi, Finn. Look what Max has just done! He's liberated the python from the printer. Or the printer from the python. Not sure which.' She stopped rambling and giggled weakly.

Max held the snake up to show Finn, who leaned over the divider railing to take a closer look.

'He's a good-looking little bloke. Not venomous, I'm guessing?'

'Not at all.' Max inspected the python's scales. 'And quite young, I'd say, judging from the colour of his markings.'

'Max is taking it to a local reptile carer,' she told Finn. 'Hopefully, they can make him nice and fat and healthy again before he's released.'

Finn smiled and then nodded at Max in a friendly manner. 'Well, you have a good day. I'm off to work.'

They called out their goodbyes and Free watched as Finn departed with his wall of self-protection intact. Max stuck around for a few more minutes, explaining the habitat, diet and hunting habits of Children's pythons in painstaking detail. At last Free pointed out that she still needed to get dressed and Max left her alone, waving as he rode off on his bike with a bag full of snake.

8

Jay was delighted with Free's work on the scoping document.

'Free, this is fantastic,' she said, scrolling through it on-screen. 'The title is great. The examples you've drawn up of how some of the tiles might look — awesome. And putting in comparable projects around the world? What a stroke of genius. It'll blow the committee's mind to think Mount Clair could be like New York City! I'm just going to beef up the learning outcomes section a little, including some values-based benefits. Promoting harmony, building multicultural awareness, creating a sense of shared journeys and togetherness, giving voices to marginalised groups . . . '

'Ooh!' Free gazed at Jay with admiration. 'You've got all the best words.'

'You've done a brilliant job to get it this far. Aidan, do you want to take a look?'

He barely glanced up from the slide show he was creating. Free could see him typing a convoluted explanation of minimalism. 'No, I trust you,' he said.

Jay shot Free a sidewards look. 'No worries. I'll finish this up and show it to the principal during lunch. I might even be able to drop it off to the committee today. They said they'd only need a week or so to consider any concepts. We all have to sign it before it's submitted, so don't

136

go home without ducking your head in the door this arvo, okay?'

Free nodded and Aidan grunted something like acknowledgement. The bell rang a minute later, so Free went to the classroom to meet her Year Elevens. She'd brought her new paints in to show them, and jumped straight into it. Jay joined them just as the students began to experiment with the oils on their own canvases.

'Wow, these are so much better,' Tia said when Free passed by her desk.

Free stopped to watch the girl run the brush back and forth along the canvas to create a grey undercoat, and Jay came to stand beside them.

'The brushes are better too,' said Tia. She looked up and saw Jay. 'Can we get some of Miss Paterson's paints and brushes, Ms Lincoln?'

Jay came closer, inspecting the materials Free had brought in. 'Are these your personal supplies?' she asked Free.

'Yes. I wanted the kids to see how the quality can vary from brand to brand.'

'Only the best for Miss Patz's class,' Cameron put in with his big grin.

Jay smiled at him. 'Well, we use student quality, whereas Miss Paterson uses professional artists' quality.'

'Is there a big price difference?' Tia asked.

'There is,' said Jay.

The invoice was still in the parcel in which Free had brought her paints, so she pulled it out to show them. Jay paused over it, eyebrows pulling together above her dark eyes.

'Hmm. That's very cost-effective, for

professional-quality paints. We pay almost as much for student quality through our supplier. And fixed-price shipping,' she added, noticing the line at the bottom of the invoice. 'Bostons. I might have to investigate switching suppliers.'

'They're the best,' said Free. 'It's all online, no paper catalogues. Once you get through the wholesale purchaser registration, it's so easy. You just shop and pay with credit card or PayPal. They ship within forty-eight hours and they've never once stuffed up my order. And they send me freebies because I spend a lot with them!' She winked.

Jay's face fell. 'Online payment? Bugger. They probably won't take cheques, will they? The school uses a purchase order and cheque system.'

Free was appalled at the thought of such an outdated purchasing system but tried to conceal it. 'Yeah, I don't think Bostons will take cheques. It says credit card or Paypal only on the site — but maybe they'd be willing to work something out, seeing as it's a school. Perhaps register as a wholesale buyer and put a note on the form asking if they will consider it?'

'What does wholesale mean?' Cameron asked.

'When you're registered as a business or organisation, you can access lower prices,' Jay explained. 'The idea is that you buy in bulk — wholesale — and then when you sell them, you make a profit by charging more. You charge a retail price.'

'And *you* count as a wholesale buyer?' Cameron asked Free.

'Because I'm an artist selling goods and services, I've got an ABN — an Australian Business Number,' said Free. 'Schools have them too.'

'Can't Miss Patz sell stuff she orders from Bostons to the school then?' Cameron suggested. 'She might be willing to take cheques.'

Free laughed but Jay eyed her thoughtfully. 'Would you do that for us?'

Free considered. 'Why not? If you let me know what you want, I'll order it and then you can reimburse me with a cheque.'

'Great!' Jay scribbled a note on her clipboard. 'I'll get the office to set you up as a supplier. Charge the shipping to us and you could even put a little margin on for your trouble.'

'No way,' said Free. 'I wouldn't add anything on.'

Jay tipped her head. 'You should add in a percentage. The costs seem low enough through Bostons that it won't much affect our overall spend, even if you charge a distributor fee. Can you spare *these* paints, Free, if we were to buy them off you? These oils? I'd like to keep them for the kids to use now.'

'Oh!' Free thought it over. 'Yeah, I probably can. I can reorder some for me. I don't think I'm desperately low yet.'

'Lovely. You can put an order for the school through at the same time.' Jay took the invoice out of Free's hand. 'I'll get a purchase order made up for this one so we can raise a cheque. You'll need to give us an invoice.' She moved away to see what some of the rowdier students were doing on the other side of the classroom.

'You're a tycoon, Miss Patz,' Cameron told her. 'Except you totally should have added a cut for yourself.'

'Get on with your work,' she told him with a grin.

Free did the rounds, stopping to watch them all work for a few minutes. Seeing Tia's dark head bent over her canvas, Free was struck with a sense of recognition. Tia was so far inside her work, she'd lost all sense of where she was. Beside her, Cameron fidgeted, chatted with his classmates, and checked on Tia's progress every couple of minutes, but Tia was deeply immersed in that soft grey undercoat. That was how Free painted, too — losing all sense of time, the world fading to invisibility. The buzzer went off, indicating it was clean-up time, and Tia looked up in shock before an expression of disappointment crossed her face. She dropped her paintbrush reluctantly into a jar of turpentine reluctantly and caught Free's eye.

Free nodded at her canvas. '*Sfumato*,' she said with a smile.

Tia returned the smile. 'I wish I could take it home to work on it, but Mum would freak out.'

'The smell?'

'The mess, the smell, everything.'

Free could sympathise. Her father and sisters were forever making comments about her paints. 'Hey, I have a place to paint. You're welcome to come around, if you like.'

Tia's eyes lit up but, a moment later, doubt crossed her face.

'Me too?' Cameron asked.

'Of course,' said Free. 'Anyone who needs a place to paint can come to mine. 17A Marlu Street.'

Cameron looked at Tia. 'Cool! When?'

Free thought about it. 'Anytime, really. After school or on weekends. If I'm not there, you're out of luck, but if I'm there, you can come in and paint. BYO easel, canvas and materials. I've got plenty of jars, turps, brushes and stuff. Just don't come too early on weekends,' she added. 'I sleep in until at least nine.'

'Hell yeah. Me too,' Cameron said.

Tia was still watching Free, hope bright in her eyes. Why did she look so torn? After they'd cleaned up and the bell went, she found out. She overheard Cameron trying to talk Tia into going to her unit to paint on the weekend. The quiet girl was noncommittal. Tia went to her next class and Cameron heaved a sigh, looking at Free.

'Don't you think she'll come?'

He grimaced. 'Dunno, Miss.'

'Why not? I thought she wanted a space to paint.'

'Too shy, I reckon.'

'Ohh.' Free's heart twinged for poor Tia, with that crippling shyness. 'Do me a favour, Cameron. Tell her I'm expecting her on Saturday.'

His colour deepened. 'Uh . . . '

'Oh — don't worry if it's a big deal.'

'No, it's okay. I can do it.'

He departed and Free was reminded of why she'd been glad when she finished high school.

That complex emotional interplay, secrets, mean people and mysteries . . . University was infinitely better. There, she'd met people she could relate to — people with more transparency. Her mind wandered to Finn. Again.

'Hey, when you place the school's order with Bostons, could you get some stuff for me?' Jay said, appearing from the storeroom. 'I need a few things for my home studio, too — spatulas, sponges, *impasto*. I'll put them on my shopping list, but make sure you order them separately so the school doesn't get invoiced for my personal stuff.'

'Why don't you just create your own account?' Free asked. 'You'd have an ABN as an artist, wouldn't you?'

'Never bothered with that, and I *hate* online shopping. I'd much rather get you to do it for me, if you don't mind?'

'Of course not.'

Free went for lunch — another crappy lunch of crackers and an apple — and spent the afternoon preparing for her next lesson. After school, Jay printed the amended *Born and Bred* scoping document and they both signed it.

'The principal thought it was excellent too,' Jay said, fishing in her stationery drawer for a document wallet. 'Hopefully, Aidan hasn't forgotten to stick his head in the door. If he signs it now, I can drop it into the shire office on my way home.'

But Aidan didn't appear, and when Free finally checked the car park, she found his car was gone.

'Bloody hell.' Jay's eyes flashed with anger when Free returned and broke the news. 'Tomorrow and Wednesday are days off for him, too — so I won't be able to get this into the shire office until at least Thursday. Son of a bitch.'

Free was a little startled by Jay's reaction and, seeing this, Jay sighed.

'Sorry. I just reckon this is a dick move on Aidan's part.'

'I'm sure he'll feel really bad as soon as he realises,' Free said.

Jay studied her face. 'Sometimes I'm not sure whether you're highly diplomatic or honestly naive, Free!'

Free puzzled over this for a moment, before gasping. 'You think Aidan did this *deliberately*? To delay concept approval?'

'Well, he wanted his little *River of Life* concept, didn't he?' Jay said, collecting her handbag and switching off the art office light.

Free trailed after Jay, turning the idea over in her mind. Would Aidan honestly stoop so low? Would he do something that petty, just to inconvenience Jay — just to get a little revenge because they hadn't supported his dodgy concept? That kind of thing could cause setbacks in the progress of the tile wall project, so it wasn't in anyone's interests, including Aidan's. She couldn't quite believe it of him.

At home, the cat was waiting to be let inside. She flicked on the air conditioning and made her way to the studio to stare at her painting. It needed something. The blue of the sky nagged at her but trying to fix that was pointless. She had to accept she couldn't get it just right.

'Max,' said Max, appearing at her feet.

Free crouched down to give his chin a good rub. This close to the floor, she noticed the carpet. *Oh heck!* She'd wrecked the floor covering under her easel. Why the hell hadn't she put down a drop sheet when Finn suggested it a couple of weeks ago? Thinking about him made a lonely wind blow through her. She hadn't seen him at all since yesterday morning. If anything she'd avoided him, increasingly embarrassed about her clumsy pass at him after the wedding.

As if he'd heard her thinking about him, Finn made a noise in his unit. He must have just arrived home and was banging around and humming as he settled in after work. Free steeled herself. She had to get back on the horse — face him again before it became too awkward. Apologise for making him uncomfortable, and show him she was willing to simply be his friend. *For now.* She almost went out the front immediately to knock on his door, but lost courage. A text message, maybe? Dammit, she didn't even have his number. She looked him up and found Finn Kelly on Facebook.

The profile photo showed Finn holding a baby freshwater crocodile. She knew exactly where that had been taken. Snapper Gooding's Herne River Cruises — the guy did twilight jaunts along the river and occasionally jumped into the water to snaffle a little croc so the tourists could pose with it. Free zoomed in as far as she could. As always, Finn's eyes were full of warmth and fun. That familiar sense of happiness washed through her and she wanted to kick herself. Why couldn't she just take no for an answer with this guy?

Maybe she should friend him. *Screw it, what's the worst that could happen?* She hit 'Add Friend' and within moments a notification popped up to say he'd accepted. Free sent him a direct message.

Hi, Finn. I just wanted to say thanks again for the lift home on Saturday night, and thanks for putting up with my crazy family forcing you to stay for the wedding.

He began typing a reply. She waited, sipping water and biting her thumbnail.

Anytime. Sorry about the backseat drama. And I enjoyed the wedding.

There was a long pause while he wrote something else, as though he were typing something longwinded — but when it was over, only four words appeared.

You guys looked amazing.

Thank you! And don't be sorry — you had no control over backseat drama. Free took a breath. *I suspect it wasn't the only thing that made you uncomfortable that night.*

Another long typing pause while she munched peanuts feverishly and listened to her pulse hammer in her ears.

Nah, it was all fine. Things can be confusing sometimes, huh?

You said it, she wrote back, relieved.

Briggsy's set on going to Talbot Gorge Sunday. You still interested?

Of course!

He sent her a smiley face. *We'll ALL go, yeah?*

He must be inviting some others, too. Good plan: approach with caution. He could get to know her among friends.

Sounds great, she replied. *BYO bathers and towel!*

Done.

Okay, I'd better go. I just realised I have totally mucked up the carpet in my studio. I'm going to look up some old-fashioned carpet cleaning remedies.

Hey — on that, I have the best news for you, Finn wrote back. *Can I come around for a minute?*

Of course! she answered.

Free jumped up to open the door and found Finn stepping out of his door at the same moment. His ever-present smile grew as he bounded up the porch steps to join her.

'Are you here by yourself?'

Her heart jumped up and attempted to block her windpipe. 'Yes . . . '

'Come with me.'

He made for her studio and Free scurried after him. Once there, he knelt down beside the patch of ruined carpet and felt around in the loop pile as though searching for something tiny he'd lost. But a moment later, he wedged his nails in and lifted a whole piece of carpet up. Free gasped and Finn looked up at her with a grin of triumph.

'They're tiles. Carpet tiles! I noticed it at my place and remembered you have the same carpet here.'

'Oh my God, Finn! You're a freakin' genius!'

He laughed. 'Just a random discovery. Pretty handy, though, don't you reckon?'

She nodded wildly. 'I can replace them!'

Finn looked doubtful. 'Well, maybe. New ones might not match because these are already a bit worn and faded. But we can switch them round, put the bad ones in a wardrobe or under some furniture. That way, the housing mob might go easier on you, or not even worry about it when you vacate.'

She caught his eye. 'This is the best news I've had all week.'

He shrugged off her gratitude. 'Now, let's do something about protecting the floor in here. Would you object to working on a lino mat?'

'Pardon?'

'Wait here.'

She waited, increasingly amazed by his kindness — and even after her unwelcome come-on. When Finn returned, he was carrying a roll of linoleum, around two metres wide, and some tape.

'This is a cast-off from work. They're renovating the station kitchen.'

He went into action, carefully placing her easel in a corner, moving her roller trolley and shuffling her tubs and toolboxes full of paints and supplies to the back wall. Then he unrolled the lino — scratched and worn but clean — and taped down the edges so they would lie flat, before replacing everything where it had been. Free watched the process in open-mouthed astonishment.

Finn turned to her. 'What do you think? Could you live with that?'

Approach with caution? Screw that. She threw herself at him, hugging him hard.

'Thank you!' she managed.

'Oh no — are you crying again?' Finn extricated himself, laughing uncertainly.

'Leaky eyes.' She wiped them and looked up to find him watching her with a slightly crooked smile. 'That's one of the kindest things anyone's ever done for me.'

'Bullshit.' But his smile widened.

'You're a special guy, you know that?'

He looked away. 'You've gotta finish that painting now. That's the trade-off.'

'It's yours when it's done.'

'I'll buy it,' he said quickly.

'No way!' She shot him a faux glare. 'It's a thankyou. You've really looked after me since we met. You've cooked for me, chauffeured me and even saved me from myself with this lino mat.'

He set his gaze on the painting. 'I'd love to have it,' he said, his face softening.

The power of the feeling that wound up inside Free almost took her breath away. Watching Finn gaze admiringly at her painting, after he'd just done something incredibly thoughtful for her — and standing there being so damn *tall* . . . it made a wave of intense emotion sweep through her. She turned away in confusion.

'Um, want a drink?'

He paused. 'No, thanks. I won't stay. I've got stuff to do — and you've got a painting to work on.'

She was glad of his light tone, even if she was disappointed by his answer. 'Thanks again, Finn. You're the best. Truly.'

He dismissed her thanks with a wave of his hand. 'See you later.'

She saw him out the door and sat at the table, thinking about Finn. Trying not to think about Finn.

Crap.

★ ★ ★

Jay was right about the delay. Aidan didn't sign the scoping document until Thursday, which meant that Jay, who played badminton on Thursday afternoons, couldn't get it to the shire office until Friday afternoon. They'd lost a whole week because of his oversight — which Jay considered a malicious move.

On Saturday morning, Free woke to a banging at her front door. She pulled on her kimono and went to answer it, searching for an accurate clock as she went. She still hadn't set the microwave clock, and only God knew where her phone was. She reached the front door. *Whoops* — not locked again.

Cameron and Tia stood on her porch.

'You still in bed, Miss Patz?' Cameron said with a grin.

'I told you we shouldn't have come,' Tia murmured, colouring.

'Oh, hey, you two! You're here to paint? Come in!'

Free checked if they needed drinks and then

led them to her studio, breathing a sigh of relief that kids didn't generally judge you on cleanliness.

'Okay, got your canvases? Did you bring easels?'

'Nah, we rode our bikes here,' said Cameron. 'We can just work on the table.'

She set up a card table and found a desk easel for Tia — Cameron said he was happy working flat on the table — and gave them a pile of rags and a jar of turpentine. Tia set up her materials in a row.

'Ooh, new paints?' Free asked.

Tia nodded. 'My dad was in Perth last week. He got some oils for me, since I've been talking about them so much. Same ones as yours.'

'Tia said I could borrow them,' Cameron added. 'She didn't want me bludging off you.'

Free chuckled. 'That's pretty cool of you, Tia. Look, there's more turps over here, and spatulas, palettes, scrapers, pokers, pointers, prodders and anything else you can think of, all in a big fat mess in this toolbox. Help yourself to any of them. I'll get myself dressed and have some breakfast, and then I'll join you.'

'I like your floor,' said Tia, seeing the lino. 'I'm going to tell my mum. She might be able to get some second-hand lino from somewhere.'

'It's clever, isn't it?' Free agreed.

She left them to paint and went for her shower. It was eleven already, she discovered when she dug her phone out of the bedclothes. She must have fallen asleep while messaging with international friends last night. Then it was

150

music videos with toast and coffee, so it was a good forty minutes before Free joined the kids. Cameron had barely touched his canvas but Tia had made strong progress. Tia was silent while Free got set up, but when Cameron came to peer over Free's shoulder, curiosity won. She joined them.

'Is that a local place?' Tia asked, staring at the scene.

'Yes, Talbot Gorge.'

'I know that place,' said Cameron. 'Good fishing, especially now the Herne's been buggered up by the dam.'

Free made a face. 'I went to a rally to stop the dam in December, but it's starting to look like it will all go ahead, no matter what we do. Breaks my heart.'

'You went to that Save the River thing, did ya?' Cameron looked impressed. 'I wanted to go, but Mum said no. She's paranoid I'll get in trouble.'

'What do you mean, in trouble?' Tia asked.

'With the cops. My older brothers, they've both done time.' Cameron looked self-conscious. 'Mum's deadset on keeping me outta trouble. Her brother, my uncle — he died in jail. Y'know. Suicide.'

'Oh, Cam, I'm so sorry,' Free said.

'One of my brothers is much better now. Settled down. But the other one's into all kinds of bad shit. Mum swore she'd keep me safe and out of prison, or die trying.'

'I understand,' said Free. 'But there's no reason why you'd get into trouble at a peaceful protest. Save the River got loud, but never

151

violent. Going to demonstrations is so important. I went to the most amazing rally in the States, at a university. It was about marriage equality. We sang songs, and linked arms and lit candles, all while conservatives and fundamentalists shouted at us. I never felt more inspired.'

Their two young faces were also bright with inspiration. Free smiled at them, filling with pleasure to see their honest energy. *Changemakers in training*, she thought.

Tia turned her attention back to Free's painting. 'This is amazing. I wish I could paint like you. How do you get the rocks to look so liney? Kind of streaked . . . '

'Striated?'

Free demonstrated the technique on some scrap paper, and then several more that might help Tia. The girl returned to her little easel, and Free came to stand at her shoulder, giving suggestions while Tia tried the new techniques on her canvas. Free was impressed. Tia learned lightning-fast, and had plenty of natural understanding of light and shade.

Cameron was a different matter. Oils were not his comfort zone and he fidgeted around, doing anything other than getting stuck in to his painting. Why had Cameron been so keen to come along? He was more interested in inspecting the studio, hovering around Tia while she tried to paint, and telling them stories about fishing and swimming at Talbot Gorge. He didn't seem to mind that Free and Tia were both too immersed in their work to reply with more than the occasional grunt of acknowledgement.

It was after four when Tia finally finished up. She looked startled by the lateness and apologised to Free, who waved a casual hand.

'Seriously, it was great! Come back any time. I got loads done on my painting, too. It was fun to have you here.'

Tia left her painting at Free's place to dry and Free promised to bring it to school for her. Cameron's was still dry enough to transport, so he shoved it rather carelessly into his bag and they rode off together on their bikes.

She'd enjoyed their company. Maybe she should join a local artist's group so she could paint among others. The last time she'd been in a group, there was a touchy-feely older bloke there who'd given her the absolute creeps. He kept trying to come over and show her how to do things. After two sessions, she'd opted not to go back.

Maybe she could just hold her own little open studio sessions on weekends and invite people to come paint? She could even offer classes for school students. She had a brief vision of herself supervising a room full of kids happily painting, while she offered help and advice. Free filed the idea away for the future, when she had her own place and grew out of being unreliable.

She tidied the studio, then went to her wardrobe, where she spent an inordinate amount of time planning an outfit for tomorrow's trip to Talbot Gorge.

9

Sunday morning was overcast but dry. Free clambered over the divider onto Finn's porch and banged on the door. He answered a moment later.

'Ready?' she asked, bouncing a little with excitement.

'Yep.' He scanned beyond her, perhaps checking the sky for impending rain. 'Is it just us?'

'Yeah — and Briggsy and Kate, right? Don't forget your bathers. I'll bring the car out.'

She dashed for the garage. Finn met her on the road and climbed into the passenger side of her little car. When he was seated beside her, Free burst into laughter.

'What?' he said, a smile starting at the corners of his mouth.

'You! Look at you!'

He looked down at his own knees, sitting well above the level of his hips. He was holding his elbows in tight as well, and his head brushed the ceiling of the car.

'Yeah, I don't always fit so well into little Matchbox cars like this.'

She scoffed. 'It's the car's issue, not yours, right? You're not a benevolent giant.'

'Of course not.'

They headed to Briggsy's place and parked on the verge. Finn went to knock on the door while

154

Free loaded her camera, bathers and towel into a backpack. When she climbed out, slapping a hat onto her head, Finn came back towards her, a set of car keys in his hand. His brow was furrowed.

'What's wrong?'

He indicated Briggsy's vehicle with his head and she went for the back seat but Finn climbed into the driver's seat. She deposited her backpack and joined him in the front.

'What's going on?'

'Sarge wants us to go to the gorge without them. He said they've realised they've got a few things to do today.' He caught her eye and dropped his voice. 'I think there's trouble going down.'

'Oh no.' But Free couldn't help a little flicker of delight. She would have Finn all to herself for the trip. 'What a shame. You don't mind still going, just us?'

'Of course not.'

They discussed their work weeks as they drove the forty minutes out of town towards Talbot Gorge. Finn seemed to relax as they chatted, and even made a noise of excitement when she told him about the art-supplies ordering she'd be doing for the school and Jay.

'That could be a nice little income stream,' he said. 'Becoming a local distributor for Bostons, I mean.'

'Yeah, I suppose it could. I might look into it after my contract at the school ends.'

They reached an unsealed road that led into increasingly rocky terrain. Free was filled with admiration for Finn's four-wheel-driving skills.

155

There was water everywhere but he navigated the mud and streams like a pro.

'You've certainly picked this up quickly. Hey, look up ahead. The river crossing is underwater.'

Finn pulled up and Free jumped out, snatching her camera off the back seat. She crouched at the edge of the water and snapped a series of photos of the red water swirling through rocks and furrows. Currents, flux, stirred-up sediment. It was like blood pumping through veins. Free adjusted her lens and tried to capture the waterline, fluid sucking at the dried edges of the red clay.

Finn spoke. 'You really love the river, don't you?'

She looked up from her task. 'Who doesn't?'

'You seem to have a special connection.'

Free snapped a couple more shots and stood. 'Yes. I don't know what it is. It just makes me feel . . . ' She stopped, unable to find the words.

Finn waited.

'Like there's more to the world than meets the eye,' she said at last, knowing it was hopelessly inadequate as an explanation.

He didn't answer and she felt a little stupid. She sneaked a glance and found him gazing at the water. Free took heart. Finn's face showed he understood.

She headed back to the vehicle, placing her camera on the back seat. 'Are you going to be okay with crossing, do you think?'

Finn checked the water gauge at the side of the creek. 'Yes, this is pretty shallow. I might just wade through it first to make sure there are no surprises. I wouldn't want to wreck Briggsy's car.' He looked at his shoes.

Free spied what appeared to be a brand-new pair of thongs in the back. 'Here.' She reached in and grabbed them for him. 'You can break them in for Briggsy, save your sneakers.'

He nodded and changed footwear, leaving her beside the car while he waded out into the knee-high water. *What a view*, she thought, scanning the red-brown mud and the flat sheets of rock surrounding the tumbling water, beneath the glare of an overcast sky. The sun broke through for a few moments, making the water sparkle so sharply it hurt her eyes. Free shifted her admiration to Finn's broad shoulders and tight bum as he pulled off his sunglasses and bent over to peer into the water. *Ohhhh, my goodness.*

She couldn't wait to swim with him.

'All seem okay?' she asked as he returned to the car and climbed back in.

'Yes, looks nice and simple.'

He adjusted some settings in the vehicle and they moved steadily through the creek. Free gave him a little cheer when they bumped up the other side and Finn couldn't conceal a smile. It wasn't far to Talbot Gorge from that point, and within minutes they'd reached the vacant parking area perched at the top of the gorge.

'No-one else here today,' Free said as they climbed out of the vehicle.

'We should have organised a group,' he said.

Inside her head, Free disagreed. 'It's been a while, but I think the trail into the gorge starts

157

over there.' She pointed.

Finn was applying sunscreen. 'That's right. Just round that boab.'

He tossed her the bottle and she coated her face and other exposed bits before handing it back to him. He locked up Briggsy's 4WD, and when he turned back towards Free, she saw a big white blob of sunscreen beside his nose. She reached up to wipe it off, smiling. He ducked away.

Free recoiled, pulling her hand back. 'You've just got some sunscreen next to your nose.' She turned away, pretending to inspect the low scrub and hiding her hurt in the process. Did she smell bad or something?

He's not ready, she reminded herself.

They walked along the trail into the gorge in silence, Free carrying her backpack and Finn carrying his own drawstring-style pack. When they came to the section of rocks she was painting, Free stopped and snapped some photos. She tried to memorise the scene, stepping close to examine the rock walls: their outline and corrugations, the smooth burnished glow of the ore-rich red rock. Free touched it. It was warm under her hand, but not too hot since the sun was hiding behind cloud today.

She looked for Finn when she'd completed her investigation and found him seated nearby, watching her.

'Shall we keep moving?' she asked. 'It's stifling. I'm dying for a swim.'

Finn led the way, following a path flattened by countless other visitors. Together, they made the easy descent into the gorge, skipping quickly over sections of the trail where ants swarmed. The water looked a deep, mysterious green at the bottom and there were wild seasonal waterfalls gushing down the rocks. Thousands of litres of white water spilled over cliff faces, churning the darkness at the bottom into a bubble bath before fanning out into those inviting green pools. They stopped at the biggest pool and Free dropped her backpack in the shade, relieved.

'I'm going straight in,' she called above the waterfall's noise, unbuttoning her shorts.

At first, Finn glanced her way but then turned resolutely to look at the waterfall. *Huh.* If he was that uncomfortable with seeing her legs, wait until she pulled off her T-shirt and he got a load of her white bikini.

But Finn wouldn't even look her way. She splashed into the pool, exclaiming at the breathtaking thrill of coolness. The fury of the fall made a fine mist in the air above the waterhole. Free steered clear of the fall, paddling around the edge.

'It's so good!' she cried. 'It cools you right down, instantly!'

But when she checked on him, she discovered Finn sitting on a rock at the water's edge, admiring the fall. His grey T-shirt was stuck to his chest, sweat visible down his front.

'Can't you swim?' she called.

He finally looked her way. 'Of course I can. You need your bronze to get into the academy.'

'What are you doing, then? Get in!'

'No, I might just . . . '

'Finn, are you serious? It's like, a million humid degrees out there.'

He only hesitated for a moment longer before he stood, kicked off his shoes and peeled off his T-shirt. *Holy shamole!* Free had to stop herself from gaping. His chest was all natural muscle definition and gleaming, tanned skin, with a hint of hair between his pecs and a smooth abdomen angling down into low-slung boardies . . .

He jumped in with a mighty splash and resurfaced in the centre of the pool. Then he made straight for the waterfall and dove underneath. For a couple of minutes, he was only visible in brief glimpses through the rushing torrent. At last he emerged, smiling.

'Best I've felt all day,' he called.

'Getting into water is the only thing that truly cools you down up here.' She hardly knew what she said, she was still so flummoxed by the sight of Finn in nothing but shorts.

'You should go through the waterfall too,' he replied, swimming around the pool aimlessly. 'Feels amazing.'

He was still being cautious. He only glanced her way every so often, and stayed well out of her reach. She sighed inwardly.

'No, I've been scared of waterfalls ever since I saw a giant lizard come down one,' she said. 'It almost crushed Willow.'

'Holy crap! Okay, fair call. What was it? A Mertens' water monitor?'

Free shrugged. 'I don't know. It was huge. Probably a Komodo dragon, or maybe a velociraptor.'

He chuckled, relaxing slightly. Free pulled herself up on the side of the pool and climbed onto a rock, preparing to jump in. Finn was doing that thing again. Looking at her, pretending not to look, looking again. In an instant, she lost all patience. *Damn him*. He *would* look. She would make him look. She stood on the rock, dripping from her white bikini, staring hard at Finn until he finally gave in and looked. Triumph surged along with heat into every nerve ending. There was Finn's real face. His real feelings.

Deep, raw desire.

She did a shallow dive and emerged right in front of him, moving in close. Ignoring the pounding in her chest, Free trod water just inches from his face, her eyes locked on his. At this proximity, she could feel the water beneath the surface swirling around her bare skin from Finn's movements. They were so close — almost touching. The friendly, pebbly warmth of his irises had gone dark — hungry — and for a moment, Free was certain he would reach for her.

He dropped his gaze to the water. 'Free, please don't. I really want to stay friends with you.'

What . . . ?

It couldn't have been more humiliating if he'd physically pushed her away. Tears sprang to Free's eyes and she turned to swim the other way, clambering up onto the rocks. She reached for her towel. The rejection was as hard and real as a stubbed toe and her eyes were watering enough to prove it.

Finn climbed out and stopped near her on the rocks. She sensed him standing behind her, watching her.

'Free — '

'I'd like to go home,' she said, holding her voice steady.

He was silent for a minute. 'Okay.'

She pulled her clothes over her damp bikini and got back on the trail to the car park. The walk was good. It forced her to focus on where she was putting her feet instead of the mortification that was making her face burn and giving rise to a sick feeling in her gut. Her mind kept going back to the look on his face as he'd gazed up at her standing on the edge of the pool. The fierce buzz of heat between them when she came close. Hadn't she seen desire? Longing? How could she have mistaken that look in his eyes? Free yanked her thoughts back. She'd thought Finn was someone she understood, but she'd misread him, so badly.

She wasn't intending to sit in sulky silence for the entire drive back to the Mount Clair township, but Free didn't trust her voice. In any case, her heart was so heavy, she could think of nothing to say that wouldn't sound forced. Finn was quiet too. The only noise he made was an exclamation of surprise when a kangaroo jumped out onto the road in front of them. Luckily, he had time to brake, so the animal bounded safely off into the scrub.

When they got back to Briggsy's house, the senior sergeant was watering pot plants on his front verandah. He waved, looking more cheerful

162

than she'd expected. Free put on a smile.

'You two weren't gone long,' he remarked as Finn approached to hand back the keys.

'Bloody hot out there,' Finn said, and it seemed to suffice as an explanation.

'I bet. You coming in for a beer, Kelly?'

Finn checked Free's face and she pulled her eyes away. 'Yeah, why not?' he said to his boss.

'Free? Fancy a coldy?'

'No, thanks, Briggsy.' She collected her gear. 'I've got a bit of work to do at home.'

'Shame. Well, I'll make sure this bloke gets a ride home later, one way or another.'

Free said goodbye and slunk to the sanctuary of her car to drive home alone. When she got there, although she attempted to work on her lessons for the week, that moment of Finn's rejection kept surfacing. The humiliation hit fresh every time. Ugh, why'd she come on so bloody strong? What an idiot she'd been, practically throwing herself at him. And after the wedding, when she'd asked to go inside with him . . . The heat rose in her cheeks as she thought of it. She had not a scrap of dignity to call her own, she decided, giving up on work.

She checked the clock. Five-fifteen. Free went to the fridge for a bottle of wine and, when she had a healthy glassful in her hand, sat down with her phone and messaged Beth.

Hi Bethie.

Beth replied immediately. *What's up?*

Nothing. What are you up to?

About to go for a jog. You okay?

Just had a crappy day. Free debated whether

163

she should tell the truth. Would Beth judge her? *Why?*

People are confusing.

Beth called. Free swiped to answer.

'Tell me what happened,' said Beth. 'Who's being a dick to my sister?'

That was all she needed. Free wouldn't admit exactly *who* she was talking about but she indulged in a satisfying long diatribe about men who gave mixed signals, and thought it was fun to string girls along, and waited until a girl was practically begging for a kiss before announcing he wasn't interested. She punctuated her unburdening with gulps of wine and handfuls of slightly stale chips she'd found in her pantry.

Beth made sympathetic noises. 'Men!'

'What sucks the most is that I want to hate him but I can't. If I'm completely honest with myself, it's me who screwed this up. He wasn't responding the way I wanted so I kept pushing until he had to be brutally clear with me. Gah! I'm such a loser.'

'Stop that,' said Beth. 'He's the loser, not you.'

'No, the poor guy just wanted a friendship and here I was trying to impress and seduce him. I don't know.' Free sighed. 'I guess I'm not his type.'

'Maybe we can find you a cattle farmer. They're loyal as all hell and don't know how to be duplicitous.'

'No, thanks. No men for me for a while. I'll be laying very low until this blows over. Hiding inside, curtains drawn all day long.'

Beth disappeared for a moment and Free

heard voices. 'Who's that, Beth?'

'It's Carolyn, my running partner. She's here for our jog.'

'Okay, I'll let you go.' Free sagged on her chair, loneliness hitting again.

'Do you feel better?'

'Yes, thanks, Bethie,' she lied.

Free farewelled her sister and sniffed, staring absently at the chip packet and the empty wineglass.

Time to paint.

★ ★ ★

Free's plan was to avoid Finn and attempt to forget about the disaster that was their trip to Talbot Gorge. It seemed he had the same idea. She didn't see him once. On Thursday it sounded like Finn was going to be home all day, so Free went to the school, even though it wasn't her usual work day. She did lesson planning and marking, sitting at her laptop in the art department office. Aidan was teaching his after-school session as she prepared to go home, but before she could leave, he cornered her in the art office. He had his phone in his hand.

'I've got a call from a corporate client,' he said in a low voice. 'It's important that I take it. I don't suppose you could look after the Year Tens for a few minutes?'

'Of course,' she said.

He stepped outside to take his call and she went in to sit with the Year Tens. They were copying notes off a screen, but chatting and fidgeting in their teacher's absence. Free was startled to see he had them writing out his slide show. Was she supposed to do things like that? She mostly did practical work with her students.

'Hi, guys,' she said. 'Mr Hamilton needs to take a call, so I'll hang out with you while you do your work.'

'Again?' someone muttered. 'He needs his phone surgically removed from his ear.'

There were a few giggles. It looked like she would have to refocus them on their work.

'What are you learning about?' she asked, reading through the slide.

'Boring shit,' a kid called.

'No way!' she exclaimed, comprehending the topic. 'Expressionism rocks. What's your favourite expressionist painting?' she asked a girl at the front.

The girl shrugged. 'We haven't really looked at any art yet. We're doing background stuff.'

Free sat down at the laptop connected to the projector. She minimised the slide show and opened a browser.

'I'll just show you a couple of pieces, if you don't mind,' she said. 'Edvard Munch is my favourite. *The Scream*. You'd know it — it's so famous. See? It's like a mental breakdown moment. I always feel like I can hear death metal playing when I look at it.'

There was some laughter.

'I like Dali,' the girl at the front offered. 'Melting clocks.'

'Oh God, me too — but that's surrealism.' Free was hit with a brainwave. 'Let me show you something. I found it on Youtube. It's like a musical run-down of all the schools of art throughout the nineteenth and twentieth centuries. It's hilarious.'

She located the video and played it for the kids. Free loved the way their faces lit up with amusement as they watched. She'd almost forgotten about this video — she would have to play it for the Year Elevens too.

'I totally get the difference between impressionism and expressionism now.' The girl who said this sounded relieved. 'That's in the test next week, Ms Lincoln said.'

'It's just a bit of fun, but nice and memorable,' Free agreed. 'That guy's done a whole series of silly art theory vids. Surprisingly useful. I could hear them singing in my head when I was doing exams at uni. I swear that's the only reason I passed.'

'My neighbour's in your class,' the girl at the front said. 'Tia. She reckons you're doing loads of art with the Year Elevens. Painting, clay, sketching. How come they don't have to do any theory and we do?'

Free didn't know how to answer. She thought she'd achieved a good balance between theory and practical work with her students but maybe Aidan had it right. Suspicion nagged at her. Could it be that Aidan had it wrong? Perhaps he was too focused on the theory component.

'Ms Lincoln might be the person to ask about that,' she said. 'It might just be that the curriculum is quite different for Year Ten and Eleven — or perhaps Mr Hamilton wants to get

167

the theory out the way first so he can focus more on the practical for Term Two.'

The girl still looked a little hard done by. Free explained some features of expressionist art and got them to try one of them on art paper. Before she knew it, one or two were packing up — it was four o'clock. She waved the Year Tens off and tidied the classroom. At last, twenty minutes later, Aidan sauntered back in.

He grimaced. 'Thanks, you're a lifesaver. When someone who's paying you ten grand for a sculpture wants to chat, you chat. Don't tell Jay, will you?' He winked. 'I owe you one.'

What the hell? Free gritted her teeth.

'No worries.' She made a move to leave.

'Don't rush off,' he said, coming to stand in front of her. 'I was going to ask, do you know the Sawmill restaurant?'

'Yeah, it's good.'

'Are you free to go for dinner with me?'

He did that thing again where his eyes dropped to her chest. Free's skin crawled and she lifted her hand, outwardly to play with her big gemstone pendant but actually to hide her breasts from this perve.

'I can't really afford it,' she said. 'It's pretty pricey.'

Aidan smiled. 'My shout.'

'Oh, thank you, but I've got a lot of work to catch up on. Might have to take a raincheck.' She gave him a vague smile.

He tipped his head. 'How about on the weekend?'

She groaned inwardly. 'Um, Aidan, I don't

think we should, you know, go on dates. It might be frowned upon by the school.'

'Is that all you're worried about?' He touched her arm playfully and she stiffened. 'There's nothing in our contracts that says we can't, you know, *fraternise*.'

He was looking at her with a sparkle in his eye, a slow smile spreading up his tight-skinned face. Suddenly, Free felt deeply unsettled. She stepped back.

'I don't think we share the same values,' she blurted.

Aidan's thin eyebrows knitted. 'Values?'

'Yes. I'm passionately opposed to the dam your family's company is building. I respect you and I'm honoured to be working with a successful artist, but I'd like to keep things professional, please.'

The frown remained. Then, unexpectedly, Aidan laughed.

'Maybe you're right. I didn't realise how strongly you felt. I'm not sure I want to be seen out to dinner with an eco-Nazi.' He swept a gaze down over her again. 'Pity. That cuteness is kinda wasted on you.' He shot her a smile to show he was joking. She knew he wasn't.

Cheeks burning with anger, stomach sick with disgust, Free turned and left. When she got home, Finn's front door was open, a light shining through the screen door. She would have liked to vent about Aidan's unpleasantness to him, but that was impossible. Instead, she went inside her unit and tried Beth's phone. It went to voicemail. Free hung up, sighing, and set to work making dinner. Maybe she could do a stir-fry? Or a curry? *Dammit*. Not enough vegetables — and no spices. Free groaned. Pasta, yet again. She could hear Finn humming and singing, and the sound made her heart ache.

Seemed she could attract the worst sort of guy, while repelling the best ones.

★ ★ ★

After that Thursday, Aidan's unpleasant overtures ended, transforming into contempt and sarcasm. He only spoke to Free to disagree with her opinion or make a smart-arse remark about greenies. Or feminists. Or hippies. Nothing she said was correct, or even worth his attention. If he wasn't ignoring her altogether, he was smirking to show how stupid he considered her opinion. It was a relief to go to work on Tuesday knowing it was Aidan's day off.

At least Free's students continued to remind her how much she loved her job. Cameron was so confident that the *Born and Bred* theme would get approved, he'd already started planning his tile. He had spoken to his grandmother about Jamadji art techniques he might be able to use. His nanna wasn't an artist, but she directed him to a local gallery that dealt exclusively in authentic Aboriginal art, and Cameron asked Free if they could visit as a class.

'Absolutely,' she said. 'I know Olly, the owner, from local art events. Exhibitions and so on. I wonder if we could take an excursion after school this week. Who else would like to come?'

170

A number of the other Year Elevens were willing, so Free asked Jay if the outing was allowed. Jay gave Free permission slips the kids' parents could sign and Free arranged a Friday afternoon visit with Olly.

She succeeded in avoiding Finn for yet another week — until Friday morning. Free was on her way to school when blue and red flashing lights once again appeared in her rear-view mirror.

'Ohhh no,' she murmured, checking her speed as she pulled over on the quiet residential street. She looked down to see if she had a seatbelt on — she did. As an afterthought, she twisted around to check her boot was properly closed. Looked okay. *Crap*. What had she done this time?

She climbed out and waited, gazing at the cop car. *Oh good Lord*. That was Finn in the vehicle with another police officer. They appeared to be having a heated discussion, and the female driver, at least a decade Finn's senior, finally pointed at his door, her face stern.

Reluctantly, Finn climbed out and approached Free's car, sunglasses on. Free shrank against her car door a little, just like she had the first time she met him. Before he'd showed her his warm, wonderful eyes.

Finn kept his sunglasses on. 'Hi, Free. Didn't mean to spook you. It's just, well . . . '

He gestured at her car and for the first time she noticed what was on the roof. Her handbag and a travel mug of coffee.

'Oh!' Free gave a slightly strangled giggle. 'I'm

171

so sorry! I'm such a moron.'

He reached for the coffee and she went for her handbag, tossing it into the car. Their fingers touched briefly as Finn passed her the coffee cup and Free went hot with embarrassment.

'Will I get a fine?' she managed.

'No, of course not,' he said. 'I just didn't want you to lose your gear.'

'Thanks.'

He nodded and headed back to join his partner in the car. After a few steps, he paused and turned back to her.

'And you're *not* a moron.'

He went on his way.

Free got back into her car and sipped her lukewarm coffee, hands shaking as tears started to prick her eyes. *Damn him.* Why did he have to be so infernally sweet — and yet not fancy her?

Not bloody fair.

10

Jay poked her head around the art-room door. 'Free, we're going to Mounties after work. You coming?'

Free was balancing cleaned brushes in jars, bristles up. 'I've got the excursion to the gallery but I'll pop in for a drink afterwards, okay?'

Jay gave her a thumbs up and Free resumed tidying the classroom. She loaded the oil-paint box onto a shelf in the art storeroom and the art assistant, Inga, edged past Free to place a box of lino-cutting tools on another shelf.

'Hey, Inga, are you coming to Mounties?'

'No, I think a quiet night's in order for me.' The older woman smiled. 'A glass of wine and a nice dinner at home.'

'Fair enough.' Free looked over the school's collection of ceramic stains and glazes. 'Are these all the glazes we have?'

Inga glanced down. 'Yep, as far as I know. It's a decent range of underglaze colours. You're not using oxides, I don't think?'

'No. And clear glaze?'

Inga nudged a tin with her shoe. 'Right here. Almost full. Most of the kids learned how to apply glaze suspension with an airbrush in Year Nine.'

Free bent down to inspect the ceramic glazes more closely. She levered open a half-used bottle of underglaze and found it sitting in a stodgy mass at the bottom of the container.

'Doesn't look too good,' Inga remarked.

'No. That's nasty.'

Free opened each of the others until she unscrewed the white and was hit with the stench of sulphur. Free fumbled to get the lid back on, blinking, and Inga coughed.

'That's turned,' she said.

Free flapped a hand to clear the air. 'Yeah. Most of these haven't even been opened, but they're old.'

She paused to read the composition chart on the tin of clear glaze suspension. Aidan stepped into the storeroom, bumping past Free as though she were an unexpected obstacle. Inga manoeuvred her way out.

'Causing a traffic jam,' Aidan commented to no-one in particular.

'What do you think about this glaze, Aidan?' Free asked.

He looked at the tin she was indicating. 'It's a clear glaze. It's used to varnish ceramics.'

She attempted to ignore his sarcasm. 'I don't have much respect for that brand.'

'One brand's much the same as another when it comes to glazing suspensions,' he said. 'I didn't pick you as a brand snob. That's not very egalitarian, is it?' Aidan's mouth pulled up on one side. He'd amused himself, it seemed.

Free gave up on the discussion and resolved to do further research when she got home. She met her students as the final bell rang and herded them into the centre of town for their gallery visit. Olly, the owner, was a man in his fifties. A

174

smile lit up his weathered face when he saw her, and Free leaned in for a hug.

'Hey, Olly! Long time no see. Thanks for letting me bring this bunch here to visit you today.'

'No problem.' Olly examined her students. 'You want to learn more about Aboriginal art, I hear.'

'They've been introduced to the topic,' Free told him. 'Jay invited a visiting Whadjuk Noongar artist, Marjorie Crump, to come in and show them a few things in Year Ten.'

'Oh yeah, I know Marj. Her art's a bit different to our local Jamadji art, though.'

Free nodded. 'And now we're doing the tile wall project on heritage — hopefully. So Cameron and maybe some others want to explore ways to tell their families' stories. Right, Cam?'

Cameron looked at Olly. 'I'm Jamadji. My great-great-nanna was a servant on a cattle station and she had a baby to the station owner. Her daughter, my great-nan, she got taken away. Stolen generation.'

Sadness tightened Free's throat. 'I didn't know that, Cam.'

He gave half a shrug. 'Yeah. My nan told me herself. She's one of the organisers for the Sorry Day march in Mount Clair every year. But her mum, and her mum's mum, they didn't like to talk about it. Great-Nan was five when they took her away, so she remembered it happening and everything. They stuck her in a home down south and she didn't get to see her mum again

175

until she was nearly thirty.'

One of the other girls in the class had a similar story. Something crossed Olly's face that made Free think he had his own story, but he just indicated his gallery.

'Some of these paintings tell stolen-generation stories. Come for a walk around with me.'

He took them on a tour of the artworks, explaining some of the imagery, then let them have a go with the painting materials he kept in a large studio at the rear of the gallery. Olly took Cameron under his wing and talked him through the differences between male and female artistic styles used by the local nation so Cameron wouldn't misrepresent the Jamadji tradition.

'What about if I work on my tile designs *with* my nan, so that the women's stories get told, too?' Cameron asked. 'Would that be against the rules?'

'I reckon that might be okay, actually,' Olly said. 'As long as you're not trying to tell people's stories for them, or without permission, you know what I'm saying?'

Free assisted the other students and tried out some of the techniques herself. They finished up around five.

'You've cleaned me out,' Olly said with a chuckle, checking his paint supplies as the kids were tidying up.

Free felt dreadful. 'I'll replace them!' she said hastily. 'I can get acrylics just like that.'

'I was only kidding,' Olly assured her. 'I'm almost out of lots of colours. We do workshops for aspiring indigenous artists in here, so we get

176

through a lot of paint.'

'Miss Patz has the best paints,' Cameron chimed in.

'Is that so?' Olly eyed Free. 'Where do you get your paints from?'

'Online, from Bostons. You?'

'I order most of mine in from the Carrolls catalogue but the range is bloody awful. And I have to use three separate wholesalers for ordering, so the shipping's ridiculous.'

'You should use Bostons,' Free told him. 'They sell everything in one place. I'll drop by and show you the paints. You won't believe the quality. And the cost — so cheap.'

'Come in and show me. I'm here tomorrow if you're not busy.'

Free nodded. 'I will.'

'Miss Patz is getting in paints for the school now,' Cameron added.

'Are you going into distribution, Free?' Olly asked with interest. 'I'd love to have someone come around once a month to check what we're low on and order it for us. I hate doing that job, and I'm shithouse at it.'

'Oh!' Free considered it. 'I could probably do that.'

'Good stuff! Let's talk about it tomorrow. Now, I've gotta close up, so you mob'll have to get out.'

The kids called their thanks and piled outside onto the pavement. Free farewelled a couple of students who were going straight home, and walked the remaining three back to the school to wait for their lifts. When everyone had gone, Free hopped into her car and headed for Mounties. She would just have one drink and a short chat tonight, she decided, and then head home. She was knackered.

Inside, she wound her way through the crowded hotel. A bunch of people she'd gone to school with were there, and they called out greetings. Free stopped and chatted for a couple of minutes but declined when they invited her to join them.

'I'm going to sit with my teacher friends,' she told them with a grin. 'I've officially joined the dark side!'

She found Jay, Max and several other staff members in the beer garden. Jay made room for her and whispered in Free's ear. 'Look who's graced us with his presence tonight.' She nodded across the table and Free saw Aidan, chatting with the sports teacher.

Free pulled her gaze away before he could catch her looking. 'I'm glad he's trying a bit harder to fit in now.'

'How did your gallery excursion go?' Jay asked.

'Great! Olly was fantastic. He let us try some of the techniques in his workshop space, and really helped Cameron a lot. I just hope the *Born and Bred* concept gets approved so they can actually use what they learned.'

Jay finished off her wine with a shrug. 'The kids'll be able to use it no matter what.'

'That's true.' Free munched peanuts from the bowl on the table. 'Olly's the best. Oh, Jay — Olly asked me about managing *his* art-supply ordering using Bostons, too! I might have to open a shopfront soon.' She laughed.

'Do you sell art supplies, Free?' another teacher asked.

'I've got an account with an online wholesaler, that's all.'

'Oh, right,' she said. 'It's just, I've got a couple of friends who run market stalls, selling their own crafts. They buy a lot of artsy stuff.'

'If they want to order through me, they can,' said Free. 'But they could just do it directly.'

'Cool, I'll let them know.'

Jay watched Free thoughtfully. 'You know, we've got a busy arts community up here. This town needs an art store. Maybe you should look into that.'

The other teacher looked appalled. 'Art store! God, no, Jay. Online's the way to go. Free could just have a web store and avoid the overheads of renting a business premises and all that crap.'

'I think I'd prefer that,' Free confessed, shooting Jay an apologetic look. 'I could probably handle placing orders through Bostons and posting or delivering stuff to people. But I'm not reliable enough to turn up and open a shop every morning.'

Jay shook her head with a half-smile. 'You've been reliable enough to turn up to work every day for us.'

Free remembered being pulled over before school and laughed weakly. 'I almost didn't this morning!' She told them the story and her audience guffawed.

'I did that with a full shopping bag once,' said

Jay. 'But I wasn't as lucky — I lost my cargo. I only realised what had happened when I went to get something I'd bought and noticed a whole bag was missing. Some lucky Mount Clair pedestrian scored some cornflakes, vegemite and tampons that day.'

'Glad I'm not the only scatterbrain in town,' Free told her, giggling.

'You having a drink, Free?' Jay asked. 'I'm ready for another.'

'I'll get it for you.' Free rose. 'My shout.'

But Jay pressed money firmly into her hand. Free headed for the heaving queue at the bar.

'Free!'

It came from behind her and Free twisted around, scanning the crowd until the call was repeated and she spotted Phoebe Challis standing a few bodies away. She manoeuvred her way through the throng to give Phoebe a hug.

'You look pretty. I love your skirt,' said Phoebe. 'God, Mounties is packed tonight, isn't it?'

'You said it. You look nice too. Cute romper. I haven't seen you for weeks. How's things?'

'Good! Crazy week at work. They keep gradually reducing the number of tellers, but the problem is it's getting busier in Mount Clair with all the diversion dam workers flying in. It's embarrassing how long the wait times are some days.' Phoebe made a face. 'Hello, angry customers.'

'Ugh. I hate that banks don't provide human service any more,' Free sighed. 'They seem to forget that sometimes people need to talk to someone about their money stuff.'

'Highly automated banking doesn't suit small towns,' Phoebe agreed. 'Come sit with us, Free?'

'I'm here with the teachers but I might join you for a chat before I leave. Where are you sitting?'

Phoebe pointed out the table and Free saw Kate, Hendo — and Finn. She turned back to the bar, an unpleasant warmth creeping up her neck and cheeks.

'Briggsy not here tonight?' she said, trying to sound carefree.

'No, he's working.' Phoebe leaned in conspiratorially. 'I finally gave in to his latest matchmaking strategy. I'm on a date with Finn Kelly tonight. You know him, I think? The new constable.'

Free's stomach flipped itself into a knot. 'Yeah, I've met him.' She hesitated, but made herself ask. 'How's the date going?'

Phoebe shrugged, a small frown touching her face. 'Good, I think. Who knows? I'm not great at dating, to be honest. My track record with relationships is piss-poor. But Finn's being sweet and attentive, and he hasn't walked out in disgust yet, so it seems to be going well.' She laughed. 'Briggsy says Finn was falling all over himself to go on a date with me, so I figured, what the hell?'

'Cool,' Free said through a tight throat.

The barman was ready to serve her at that moment, and she had to force her thoughts back into coherence so she could remember Jay's request. She got herself a soft drink. Phoebe kept

181

chatting brightly while Free waited for her drinks. When the barman finally handed her the order, she made an escape, keeping her eyes resolutely on the beer garden doorway. No way would she look at Finn . . . Finn, who was *falling all over himself* to date Phoebe. Bitter jealousy rose inside her as she thought about him telling her that he wanted to be 'friends'. No wonder. He'd already met someone else.

Well, that solves the big mystery.

'You okay?' Jay asked as she arrived back at their table, handing over the drink and Jay's change.

'Yep!'

'You look a bit hot and bothered.'

'It's hot. Bloody hot. And that bothers me.' Free forced a smile and Jay chuckled.

Free's phone buzzed and she checked it, finding a message from Beth.

You home tonight? I got takeaway and have SO MUCH Indian food. Want to come over and share?

Free could have wept with gratitude for Beth. Yes, she wanted to go and eat takeaway with her big sister and get away from the train-wreck this night had become! She downed her lemon squash in three gulps and jumped up.

'My sister just reminded me I'm supposed to be somewhere else,' she said. 'I'm going to love you and leave you. Sorry, everyone!'

There was general outcry and then some hugs, blown kisses and goodbyes. Aidan watched, expressionless. Free made for the closest exit, keeping her eyes carefully away from Phoebe's

182

group. Hopefully, she could sneak out unnoticed.

She'd almost made it. Nearly there. Just four more steps and she'd be out in the warm, damp night air —

'Free!'

Her heart plummeted. It was *him*. She turned.

'Hi, Finn. Just on my way out.'

He looked as uncomfortable as she felt. 'Oh, right. I didn't even realise you were here till now.'

'Flying visit.'

Finn hesitated. 'Sorry about giving you a fright this morning,' he blurted. 'My colleague, she switched on the lights before I could stop her.'

Free shuffled her feet and met his eyes swiftly. 'It's okay. I need to be less of a forgetful dummy.' His eyebrows knitted and she glanced towards the door. 'I'd better get going.'

'You don't want to, uh, come join us for a bit? Just hang out with us?'

Free was so outraged she forgot to be embarrassed. 'Come join you and Phoebe on your *date?* No, thanks,' she shot at him.

Finn blinked at her. He opened his mouth to say something but changed his mind. He dropped his eyes to the floor, his lips pressed together, and gave his head a brief shake.

'Goodnight, Finn,' she said as coolly as she knew how, and walked away.

★   ★   ★

Beth saw evidence of tears as soon as Free arrived.

'What's wrong?' she asked, her voice low with concern. 'Come inside. What's happened? Tell me.' She pulled Free into a hug.

'Oh, gawd, it's so stupid, Beth. Seriously. It's not even worth talking about.'

'Don't give me that crap.' Beth steered Free to the suede couch and sat her down. 'Wait here.'

She went into the kitchen for a minute and came back carrying a plate heaped high with curry and rice, and a giant glass of wine. She gave them to Free. 'Eat. And talk.'

'Get yours first,' Free gulped.

Beth fetched her own dinner and curled up on the couch opposite. 'Well?'

At times like this, Free didn't mind Beth's bossy ways. She didn't hesitate to spill the story. Beth listened, silent except for the odd sympathetic noise, until Free had finished.

'Oh, Free. That *jerk*. So Finn is the mystery guy you told me about a couple of weeks back?'

Free confessed he was.

Beth shook her head. 'I thought it might have been him. It sounds like Finn's a total mess. I agree with you — he'd be screwed up from that bad relationship with his ex. He's probably scared of meeting a girl he might really like.'

Free forgot her dinner, staring at Beth. 'You think?'

'Yes, but that doesn't mean you should give him another chance if he changes his mind. Like I said, he's a mess. He's got warning signs all over him.' Beth put her plate down on the glass coffee table and fixed Free with a serious gaze. 'What you've just described — the mixed signals

— those are not the actions of a guy you can trust. He's not in a good place, by the sound of it. *Avoid*. Danger, danger, and not in a sexy way.'

'I live next door to him,' Free reminded her, taking a gulp of wine. 'Difficult to avoid.'

'Well, you need to have strength, then, Free. Look, I saw how he looked at you at the wedding. It's perfectly clear he's attracted to you. But he will just continue to mess with you. It's his MO — his pattern. Deep down, he's still angry over the ex's betrayal. If you let him in, he'll play you. He's looking to punish someone. He might even seek revenge on his ex by cheating on *you*. Or he wouldn't be able to trust you, so he'd be all over you, always wanting to know who you're with and what you're doing.'

Logically, Beth's words made sense, but Free struggled to visualise Finn as a bitter, brooding cad who would string her along and cheat on her.

'He's not interested, anyway,' she said. 'You got that bit wrong.'

Beth's smooth forehead creased in the lamplight. 'Are you sure?'

Free nodded. 'I gave him plenty of opportunities. He never bit, not once. It's just so much worse now because I was telling myself it was all because his trust had been damaged — but it turned out he was interested in another girl altogether, and that's why he didn't want to know about *me*.'

'Well, then he's thick as well as screwy,' Beth declared. 'And he'd better not come near my baby sister because I've got access to some

185

highly toxic pharmaceutical substances.'

Free felt loved and smiled gratefully. Beth would always look out for her. Unexpectedly, the memory of that discussion about how Aidan Hamilton got his residency contract surfaced. How far would Beth go to look out for her? Far enough to influence a decision about an artist residency at the local school?

'He's sneaky.' Beth broke into her thoughts. 'I thought Finn seemed genuine, too. When you wouldn't tell me his name last week, I thought it could be him, or maybe someone from work. That other resident artist.'

Free wrinkled her nose. 'Ew. No way. Aidan's a creep. And he's dodgy as. His mum runs the dam construction company, did you know? And he was pushing to make the tile wall a monument to the project. *River of Life*. Can you believe that? That dam's *wrecking* the river.' She sniffed, wiped her eyes and drank her wine. 'Oh, yeah, I was going to tell you — there's an information night coming up soon about the threat to wildlife from the dam. Do you want to come with me?'

'You're still involved in the anti-dam movement?' Beth's eyebrows crept upwards.

'Well, yeah. It's important. What?' Free added when she caught Beth's bemused expression.

'I'm impressed, that's all. I don't think I've ever seen you commit to a cause like this before.'

'I've been involved in other causes.'

'Yes, you told me about that protest you went to in the US but you were just in the right place at the right time and happened to agree with the protest, right? This is different. You're educating yourself, taking a stand, attending events and even inviting others to get involved.' Beth studied Free as though she had presented with a particularly intriguing medical condition. 'Maybe you're changing.'

Free wiggled her hair tie loose and rubbed her hands through her hair. Could Beth be any more patronising? With an effort, she refrained from responding and ate her curry.

After their meal, they settled in to watch a movie on Beth's huge flat-screen. The wine made Free sleepy and she woke in the middle of the night to find that Beth had draped a light blanket over her on the couch and gone to bed. Free rolled over and spotted her phone where it sat blinking with low charge on the coffee table. She needed to go home. Max would be wondering when he could get inside to have his dinner and go to bed. But it was so comfy on Beth's couch . . .

Free sighed and pushed back the blanket. She couldn't just leave her poor little cat outside without an evening meal. Free groped for her bag and let herself out of Beth's place, locking the door behind her. She drove home in the quiet 2 a.m. darkness. Max was nowhere to be found when she got home. All her shaking of the cat biscuits and calling were in vain. She got settled in bed but, just as she was drifting off, heard a piteous cracked meowing from the front porch. Free jumped up and let the tabby cat inside.

'Where were you, Max?' she whispered. 'You must be starving.'

Max answered by rubbing against her legs. He was really filling out these days, what with getting two square meals a day, plus plenty of love and care. Free gave him some food and Max nibbled at it. When the house was still and dark once more, he finally decided he was ready for sleep, and jumped up to join her on the bed. She reached down and rubbed his head.

All was quiet from the house next door. *That's good*, Free decided. She had to get on with having inner strength and holding her head high. She had to enjoy being independent, living with her cat, teaching an awesome bunch of kids and working on a major public art project.

⋆ ⋆ ⋆

Free was woken at ten by Cameron and Tia, who'd arrived for their Saturday morning painting session. Free enjoyed their company while she worked on her own landscape. Later in the morning they were joined by two more of her students — Ethan and Jorja. After sharing lunch with her students — boiled spaghetti, stirred through with broccoli and cheese — Free remembered she was supposed to be showing the Bostons paints to Olly.

'Oh, crap,' she cried, jumping up. 'Are you kids okay here for half an hour? I need to go catch Olly at the gallery.'

'We'll leave,' Tia said immediately, getting to her feet.

'There's no need to go, if you're not ready,' Free assured her. 'You guys can stay as long as you like.'

The students were happy with that. 'We won't trash your place, Miss Patz, promise,' Cameron said with a grin. 'No wild parties.'

Free scrambled into her car and made a mad dash for the gallery.

'I'm so sorry, Olly!' she said when she arrived in his shop, sweating and puffing.

He just laughed. 'It's okay, we're open till three.'

'Jeez, really? I almost busted an artery trying to get here.'

The gallery was quiet so they went into the workshop, where Free showed Olly her paints and equipment using a little spare canvas board. He was as impressed as Jay had been. Free couldn't wait to demonstrate how easy it was to use the Bostons system. She logged in to the web store on Olly's desktop computer and spent some time showing him the search and ordering processes. He watched but the look on his face had become sceptical.

'Yeah, okay, okay, Free. I could do it,' he said at last. 'But I'll bloody hate doing it. That's why I want you to do it for me. Check my gear, make the order and charge me for the stuff and your labour. What d'you reckon? How long would it take you to check the supplies and make an order for us?'

'Maybe half an hour, an hour?' Free hazarded.

'Great. Go for it.'

She stared. 'Right now?'

'You're not busy, are ya?'

'Well, no, but . . . '

'What's your percentage for service?'

'I couldn't charge you, Olly.'

'Like fun you couldn't!' He eyed her. 'What's fair for a job like that? Fifteen per cent on sales? Eighteen?'

'No, Olly . . . '

He gave a sharp nod. 'Twenty it is. You drive a hard bargain.' She opened her mouth. 'Don't argue,' he warned. 'Or I'll have to make it thirty. Now get to work.'

Olly went out the front to chat to the tourists browsing the gallery. Free wandered along the shelves of his beautiful workshop. She noted any empty or near-empty paints, solvents and mixers, and counted his paintbrushes. Whenever she spotted a damaged one, she put it aside and marked down the size.

'This is adding up,' she called when the tourists left with a couple of painting purchases. 'I've just entered the order and it's almost four hundred.'

'That's not bad,' he said, putting his head around the door. 'You haven't scared me yet. I need some canvases and paper, too.'

They discussed types and sizes and Free completed the ordering process. 'Six hundred and thirty-seven dollars.' She checked Olly's face, a little apprehensive.

He considered. 'So that makes it about eight hundred, with your percentage. Seems reasonable. That's about what I'd normally spend and the quality's bloody topnotch. Plus I reckon you've done a better job noticing what's low or missing than I would've.' Olly stuck out his hand with a smile. 'Nice doing business with you, Free.'

She laughed with delight and shook hands. Free finished up the order, opting for fourteen-day payment terms, and Olly wrote a cheque to Free then and there. She left, promising to deliver his materials as soon as they arrived. While she drove, her spirits danced at the thought that she'd helped Olly. And all while ordering art supplies, which was practically her favourite thing in the world. *Wow.* Could she do this sort of thing to make a living?

Ethan and Jorja had left by the time she got home, but Tia was still immersed in her work. The girl's landscape was looking amazing. Free raved about it and asked Cameron what the heck he'd been doing all day if he hadn't even touched his painting. He grinned sheepishly and muttered that he couldn't just leave Tia on her own.

'My clouds look stupid,' Tia sighed.

Free inspected them and made a couple of suggestions, assuring her that clouds were one of the hardest things to paint. Tia murmured something while Free tidied up the mess Jorja and Ethan had left. Cameron agreed, looking at Free for a response.

'What was that?' asked Free.

'Tia reckons you should do private art classes. You're a really good teacher, Miss Patz.'

'Thanks.' Free chuckled. Everyone had career ideas for her, it seemed.

'Seriously,' said Tia, going pink. 'You're so good at explaining things. Ms Lincoln, she sometimes takes a brush and works on your painting to show you a technique or whatever. I don't like it when someone else paints on my painting. But *you* never do that.'

Free tried to hide her horror. 'Oh, yeah, I couldn't do that. I'd freak if someone did it to me, too.'

'So, you should give classes. Run, like, a painting group where you help people.'

'Isn't that what we're doing here?'

'Yeah, but you could make a buck out of it, Miss Patz,' Cameron said. 'I mean, don't charge us, 'cause we're your students already.' He shot her a grin. 'But you could charge other people.'

Free smiled. 'It *would* be fun. Maybe I'll think about it after my contract's finished at the school.'

'I wish you could stay on as our teacher,' Tia said unexpectedly, and hid her face, pretending to closely examine her painting.

Free was touched. 'I do too,' she said. 'But when I'm finished, I'll still drop in at school from time to time to see how you're going.'

The kids finally set off at four-thirty, leaving Free alone with her thoughts. The thoughts weren't good ones. Finn popped straight back to the forefront of her mind — specifically, Finn and Phoebe. She hadn't heard or seen him all day and that was a good thing. She didn't want to see him. Not now . . . maybe not ever. Was he out with Phoebe right now? Holding hands — kissing? Maybe they'd even gone to bed. Oh good Lord, what if he was next door in bed with Phoebe at this very moment? A call came in and she seized her phone gratefully. Willow's name was on the screen.

'Hi, Will!' Free tried to sound positive. 'How's married life?'

'Much the same as unmarried life, except I seem to get asked that question a lot more,' Willow said.

'How's Tom?'

'He's good. He's currently transferring the entire contents of Dad's video collection to digital storage so we can finally get rid of the VHS.'

Free giggled. 'Lucky Tom. Welcome to the Paterson clan.'

Willow chuckled in agreement. 'And what about you? How's your week been?'

'Good,' Free lied.

'That's great. You seem to be enjoying the contract.'

'Yes, it's awesome.'

'Are you still okay to come and stay with Dad for the long weekend?'

Free had to think about it for a moment before she remembered what she'd promised. 'Oh, yes! Of course.' Willow's honeymoon in Bali.

'Are you sure you don't mind coming home for the whole weekend? Even on your birthday?'

'Of course not!' Free had already abandoned her idea for a pub catch-up on her birthday. *I mean, what if I bump into Finn and Phoebe being all lovey-dovey while I'm there trying to celebrate my birthday?* She was better off at home with Dad.

'Thanks.' Willow sounded relieved. 'We fly out on Friday morning and get home Wednesday afternoon, so if you're here on the weekend, Dad'll only be on his own Monday and Tuesday nights.'

Free thought about it. 'Well, actually, I can probably stay Monday night too, since it's a public holiday. I'm not technically needed until my after-school session on Tuesday. I usually work all Tuesday, but I'll ask Jay if I can just come for the afternoon session and then switch my full day to Wednesday.'

'Oh, that'd be great,' said Willow. 'Then Dad's only got one night on his own. He insists he's fine and I believe him, but still . . . '

'Yeah, I get it,' said Free. 'I'll sort it out so I can be there till Tuesday morning. Where are you staying in Bali?'

'Nusa Dua,' said Willow.

'Oh, it's gorgeous there,' Free exclaimed. 'The beach is heavenly. Are you going on any tours?'

'Yes, some kind of volcano and temple tour, I think.'

Free's wanderlust reared up. 'Awesome. I'm so jealous.'

'Tom wants us to get tattoos,' Willow said. 'I said no chance.'

Free burst out laughing. 'Maybe the Patersons cattle brand for you, huh?'

'Now there's a thought.'

They laughed together over tattoo ideas for Willow and when the call ended, Free felt

194

brighter . . . until Finn popped back into her head. She sighed. Why couldn't she just forget about him?

There was nothing else for it. She'd have to paint until bedtime.

11

Notification that the *Born and Bred* tile wall concept had been approved arrived in Jay's inbox on Monday. Free's class was as thrilled as she was, and chattered excitedly about their ideas for the tiles. Free stayed back on Monday afternoon to take stock of all the ceramics materials, and Jay and Aidan put their heads in to observe her toils before going home.

'It's a pretty good stock of glazes,' Aidan remarked. 'Brand notwithstanding.'

Free summoned her inner fortitude. 'I'm a bit worried about them,' she said to Jay. 'This clear glaze, I'm not sure it's a good fit for the clay you've selected.'

Jay checked Free's face. 'What do you mean?'

'You know, crazing.' Jay still looked blank, so Free explained. 'Fine cracking in the glaze.'

Jay laughed. 'I know what crazing is. But why do you think we might have a problem with it?'

'It can happen when the glaze doesn't suit the clay. You know how the glaze and the clay both shrink during firing? Well, they can shrink to different degrees.' Free hunted for a way to explain it. 'Just imagine you're the clay, and the glaze is a pair of jeans. If the glaze isn't a good fit for the clay, it can become too tight. Glazes have enough strength to handle a bit of tension, just like jeans do. But if there's too much tension, it'll literally pull itself apart. It's like you're bending

196

over and your jeans rip. And also, these underglazes are old. Look at this one. It's sort of gone *off*.' She opened a bottle she'd inspected the previous week and showed Jay how the product was sitting in a congealed lump.

'Off?' Aidan's voice was heavy with scorn. 'These are *glazes* we're talking about — chemicals, not baking ingredients. They don't go *off*. The underglaze just needs a good stir and a bit of water added. And that clear glaze will be a good match for the clay Jay's ordered, in my opinion.'

'No, I don't think it will,' Free told him, keeping her voice calm. 'I was visiting with this ceramic artist in Italy, right? She didn't speak much English, but I managed to understand what she said about the glaze being a match for the — '

Aidan laughed. 'Sounds like it might have got lost in translation. That's completely wrong.'

Free was silenced. For a moment, she doubted herself. But no — she knew this stuff. Giacoma had shown her the severe crazing on the pots she'd made using a combination just like the one they were contemplating.

'I'm worried about the durability of the tiles if we use this glaze,' she said.

Jay looked between Free and Aidan. 'We'd be looking at significant costs to replace it all, Free. I didn't budget for this, because I figured we had everything we needed except the clay. There's a small contingency fund which should almost cover it, but that will use every cent we have for the project.' She tipped her head to one side,

197

studying Free. 'Are you sure it's going to be a problem?'

'I really don't think it is,' Aidan drawled.

Jay ignored him, keeping her gaze on Free.

'I honestly believe it's going to be a problem,' Free told her. 'I'll do some more research to make sure, but I think we'd be better off spending the money, unfortunately.'

Jay nodded. 'You'd better go ahead and make the order, then.'

Aidan stood still for a moment, his eyebrows raised. Free thought he might lash out at her — or even Jay — for flouting his opinion. She waited, her shoulders tight with anticipation. But in the end, he just turned and strolled away like he didn't give a damn.

Free stayed at school, using the art office computer to research clay and glazes until the cleaning staff came in and started vacuuming around her. By the time she left, however, she was confident she was right. Ordering new materials was much smarter than taking a chance on the old stuff. Imagine the kids' disappointment if their tiles ended up damaged or ruined within a couple of years because they couldn't stand up to the Kimberley weather.

She drove home, tiredness hitting. It had been an emotional weekend and a busy day. She put the car in the garage but couldn't be bothered closing the roller door. She apologised silently to Beth. *Too knackered.*

That night, Free felt lonely. It was windy out and there were cracks, snaps and odd noises all through the house. Free wished she was home at

198

Patersons as she lay in bed with Max snuggled up at her side. Despite her exhaustion, it took a long time to get to sleep.

She woke in daylight to an ungodly stench. Free pushed back her hair and traced the odour to the bathroom. There was a cat turd in the bathtub.

'Oh, Jesus, Max. Really?' She shot him an accusing look. 'You've got a litter box!'

Max barely graced her with a glance. He just yowled his broken meow and tried to get her to follow him to the kitchen to make his breakfast.

How the hell was she going to deal with this stinky mess? If it touched her hand, she'd freak out. She might even vomit. She remembered a box of disposable latex gloves she'd bought for when she worked with chemicals — they were still in the car. Throwing on her kimono, Free opened her front door to make the dash across the damp lawn, clicking open the boot with her key as she ran.

'Ow!' She'd stepped on something sharp. A doublegee? Free lifted her foot to check and was alarmed to see bright red oozing from a cut between her first two toes. That was a chunk of glass, not a prickle. In fact, there was broken glass all over the ground.

Then she saw it. Her car had a smashed window. Free sucked in a breath and picked her way around the side to get a better view. A door was ajar, too. There was glass all over the front seat and the glove box hung open. Her old CD collection was scattered across the passenger seat, and all the spare change from her centre console was gone. Even the lucky crystal cat from Flavia — the one she kept blu-tacked to her dashboard — was missing. Free stepped back, her gut clenching. She half hopped, half ran back to the house but instead of going inside, she climbed Finn's porch steps and banged on his door, trembling.

It took an age for him to answer. He was still pulling a T-shirt down over his stomach as he opened the door.

'Free?' He saw something was wrong immediately. 'What is it?'

'My car got broken into.'

'Oh, shit. Are you all right?' He reached for her but stopped halfway, stepping outside instead. 'Let's have a look.'

She led the way to the garage but stopped a distance from the shattered glass, wrapping her arms around herself while he went closer and bent down to peer inside the car.

He emerged a minute later and crossed the yard to where she stood. 'They've made a bit of a mess. Is anything missing?'

Free shrugged. 'Just spare change and a couple of other little things. My phone and bag were inside the house with me.'

'Where's Max?'

Um, what? Maybe Finn thought the thieves had hurt Max. She'd heard of people doing awful things to pets during break-ins.

'He's inside, waiting for his breakfast. He's fine.'

Finn watched her worriedly. 'You look upset.'

She sucked in a breath and dissolved in tears.

This time when Finn reached for her, he didn't stop himself. He pulled her close and hugged her, stroking her hair.

'I know,' he said, his voice soft. 'It feels horrible when someone does this kind of thing. It's okay. We'll call the station and make a report. The forensics guys will come out and take a look. If it's any consolation, it was probably just kids ransacking your car for spare change.'

'I think I heard them last night,' she said through her sobs. 'I hate that they were out here going through my car while I was alone inside. What if they'd tried to break into the house? What if it *wasn't* kids?'

He ran his hand over her hair again, pulling her in even tighter. 'I get it. It's not like you're here all by yourself, though. You've got Max.'

'Finn! This isn't funny. What good would Max be if someone broke in? He couldn't protect me. He'd just hide under the bed.'

Finn was silent but he kept her close. Breathing in his warmth, she gripped his waist and buried her face in his T-shirt, comforted by the steady thud of his heart. At last she broke from the embrace and looked up at him. His warm brown eyes were full of concern for her — but there was something else in his face. Something deeply troubled.

'Can I come over while I make the report?' she asked, not wanting to be anywhere but near Finn in that moment.

He nodded. As they headed back to the house, she slipped her hand into his. It felt natural. She didn't even care if he didn't like her romantically, or was freaking out, or was dating Phoebe, or anything else — because in that moment she simply needed him to hold her hand. Whatever he felt, he didn't push her away. Max had slipped out onto the porch, and was sitting patiently on the divider rail.

'You get your phone and your bag,' Finn said. He noticed her foot. 'Holy crap. What happened there?'

'Oh, don't worry, I just trod on a piece of glass. I'll grab some tissues.' She stepped inside, Finn following her, and the cat turd smell hit her again. She groaned, dropping Finn's hand. 'You might want to wait for me outside. I need to fix something quickly. Max pooped in the bathtub.'

Finn whipped his head around to look at her so quickly she wouldn't have been surprised if he'd hurt himself. 'I beg your pardon?'

'I guess his litter tray wasn't pristine enough for him.' She rolled her eyes and attempted a laugh. 'I should give him some bickies, too.'

'Oh wow, I thought you meant . . . ' He trailed off. 'So you have a *cat* called Max?'

It was Free's turn to be surprised. 'Of course I do. You know that.' She indicated the expectant tabby cat.

Finn's mouth fell open. 'That's *my* cat. He lives with me.'

They watched each other in bewildered silence. 'Hang on,' Free said at length. 'Are you saying Max also lives with *you?* Are you sure? It's not his — I don't know, his twin, or doppelganger, or whatever?'

'This tabby cat right here, the one with the weird meow, is definitely living with me. He has been since I moved in here back in November. He even sleeps with me during the day when I'm on night shift.'

'And with me at night. Max, you little player!' she scolded the cat. 'I guess you're eating four meals a day, too. No wonder you're getting so chubby.'

'I call him Donald. Because he sounds like he's quacking.'

Free gave a shaky laugh. 'I call him Max because I swear that's what he says. This is too weird.'

'Hey, don't worry about the cat poop right now,' Finn urged her. 'It's not going anywhere. Clean it up later. Just grab your stuff and come over.'

She nodded, and ducked inside for her phone and handbag before shooting back out and locking the door behind her.

Finn appeared outraged. 'Max isn't coming?'

She looked down at the cat, who was still gazing at them in contented silence.

'Not Max the cat. Max your boyfriend,' Finn said.

'My boyfriend!' Free's mouth fell open. 'What boyfriend?'

'Max. Your boyfriend.'

She remained utterly baffled.

'Glasses, thick eyebrows. Likes snakes. Lives here.' Finn was watching her in concern. 'Are you sure you're okay, Free? Did you hit your head? Maybe you're in shock.'

'Are you talking about Max the biology teacher? The snake catcher? He doesn't live here. And he is not my boyfriend!'

Finn was silent. It wasn't until Free descended the steps and made for his porch that he regained the power of speech. 'Wow, I'm sorry,' he said, following her slowly. 'You said you lived here with Max, and I assumed . . . '

She shook her head vehemently. 'That guy is not my boyfriend. He's just a friend from work.'

'So . . . your boyfriend is a different Max altogether?'

'My *boyfriend?* I only know two Maxes — my cat and my colleague. I don't even have a boyfriend.'

Finn's face changed entirely in an instant. He reddened, right to the tips of his ears. He opened his mouth to speak but lost his words and closed it again. After a few moments, he drew himself up and released a slow breath.

'Come on,' he said, pushing his door open. 'Let's go make this phone call.'

Inside, Finn became his normal self. Free tended to her foot, washing it in his bathroom basin and then stopping the blood with a handful of tissues. Finn called the station so she could report the break-in and made her a cup of tea. When Free finished making her report, she phoned Jay.

'Oh no, sweetie,' said Jay when Free told her what had happened. 'Are you okay? Did they take anything of value?'

'No, nothing important,' she answered,

although the thought of Flavia's crystal cat gave her a pang.

'Do you need to take the day off?'

'No, I'll come in,' Free said. 'I'll just sort out a few things. I'll be late, but I'll be there well before our after-school session starts.'

'It's all right. Don't stress. Just come in when you can.'

As she rang off, Finn knelt down in front of her and picked up her foot in his big, warm hand. He gently removed the tissues and inspected the cut.

'It looks okay,' he said. 'I don't think you'll need stitches, but you should probably get a tetanus shot.' He replaced the tissues, tucking them carefully between her toes.

'I had a booster only last year,' she said. 'It's not serious. I think a bandaid should do the trick.'

He caught her eye and stared at her for a few moments. Free's heart rate bumped up again. Why was he looking at her like that? Like he'd never seen her before. She became acutely aware that she was sitting there with just a light satin kimono over her singlet and knickers — no bra or anything. He let go of her foot.

Finn stood up and moved to the other side of the table, where he sat down. 'They're not busy, so they're sending someone out this morning.'

'Huh?'

'Forensics.'

'Oh.' Free bit her thumbnail, staring at her phone in her hands. She should tell Beth. Beth might know what to do about the car. She tapped out a message.

My car got broken into. They smashed the window. I won't be able to use it until it gets fixed. She finished with crying- and terrified-face emojis.

Beth called immediately. 'Are you all right?'

'Yes, I'm fine.'

'Where are you?'

'I'm fine, Beth. I'm at Finn's place. He's looking after me.' She smiled at Finn and he smiled back.

Beth *hmm-ed*, a distinct note of disapproval in her voice. 'Where was the car?'

'In the garage — '

'Locked up?'

Free hesitated. 'The car was locked.'

'But not the garage?'

'I was really tired . . . '

Beth sighed. 'Free, I told you to lock your garage every time!'

'I'm sorry. It was only once.'

'Once too often.' Beth sounded annoyed and Free regretted contacting her. 'Call your insurer. They'll authorise a repair for you. I use Fonti's Automotive on Lillypilly Street. Then call Willow and ask if someone from Patersons or Quintilla can come into town today. Get them to send a vehicle for you to use while yours gets repaired.'

Free's regret vanished. Beth was so wonderfully competent.

'Okay,' she said in a small voice.

'Are you sure you're all right?'

'Yeah, I'm okay. Thanks, Beth.'

'I can come around after work . . . '

'No, I'll be fine,' Free assured her.

She ended the call and rang her insurer. The sympathetic woman told Free that she could indeed use Fonti's for repairs and advised her to clean up the glass carefully before driving it to the repairer. Finn caught wind of what was being discussed, and after she hung up he offered to help her sort out the glass as soon as the forensics team had been. Free called Willow next, and found out a Quintilla staff member was doing a grocery run that day. Willow promised to send an extra vehicle with a station hand. Free silently thanked Beth for always knowing just what to do.

Finn's colleague from the Forensic Section arrived soon after — a jolly blonde woman of about fifty, named Jo.

'We've had a spate of car break-ins,' she told Free brightly. 'You're one of three in the past week, so don't feel special.' She gave a gravelly laugh. 'They've left a few prints at the other scenes, but no matches on the database as yet.'

Free unlocked her house and went for a dustpan and the vacuum cleaner. As soon as Jo was finished, she and Finn set to work tidying up the mess. Finn brought plastic bags to collect the glass chunks, and grabbed an extension cord from his own place so he could vacuum. When it was done, he used antibacterial wipes to clean down the doors and the interior.

'I can't see anything disgusting, but I'd want to clean my car if it happened to me,' he said.

Free thanked Finn and went inside for a shower. *Oh wow*. He had even removed Max's turd from the bathtub. Her mind flew back to Finn's absurd mistake: that the Max she lived with was her boyfriend. Her *cat*, for goodness sake! But it made sense. He'd had no idea she had a cat. He'd thought her cat was his cat. She burst into laughter in the shower. He must have been labouring under that misapprehension for weeks — ever since Max the biology teacher had come around to help with the snake. Maybe even before that.

All of a sudden her body froze, even with warm water running over her back.

Was this . . . could *this* be why he'd refused to make a move? Why he'd never responded to any of her moves? Because he thought she was trying to hook up with him while she had a *boyfriend?*

Oh. My. *God.*

No *way.*

But he was dating Phoebe, she recalled. Maybe he genuinely wasn't interested, and had liked Phoebe from the start. He'd been 'falling all over himself' to go on a date with Phoebe, after all. Her spirits sank again — but not all the way.

A warm little flicker of hope remained.

★   ★   ★

Free was provided with a battered blue farm ute for the duration of her car repairs. It was comforting to be in a station vehicle after the break-in. She would trade in her car for a four-wheel drive as soon as she had a consistent income, Free decided. It was the best kind of vehicle for Mount Clair. Anyway, she didn't even want her little car now that some stranger had broken into it and stolen her stuff. The thought of the little lucky crystal cat from Flavia saddened her every time she remembered it.

All through her waking hours, thoughts of Finn intruded. She kept coming back to that crazy misunderstanding between them. How could he honestly have thought the Max she lived with was the biology teacher at school? She was dying to discuss it with him, but Finn's work hours seemed to coincide with her home hours. She needed to thank him for his help, too. By Wednesday evening, Free couldn't let it go on any longer and sent him a direct message.

Thank you so much for helping me yesterday morning! I would have completely freaked out if you hadn't been there. And Max/ Donald says thank you for taking care of his disgraceful lapse in manners.

Obviously at work, Finn took a couple of hours to reply. *Any time! You looked so upset, my heart went out to you. And Donald/Max has more than just a crap in the bathtub to answer for. Little con man!*

Free chuckled. *I'm glad he has a second owner. I'm going home to Patersons for the long weekend, and now I don't have to worry about him.*

Finn responded. *Uh-oh. I'm going home too. Mum and Dad leave for Ireland next week to be there when Aislinn's baby comes, so I'm going to Perth from Friday till Tuesday. I was going to ask YOU to feed Donald!*

It's okay, Free replied. *I already bought one of those electronic timed biscuit dispensers for Willow's wedding weekend. I'll put that out for him and he can sleep on the porch.*

Phew! Finn finished with a smiley face.

She badly wanted to keep the conversation going but forced herself to stop. He was dating Phoebe. *Curse my mythical boyfriend.* She sighed.

To her surprise, Finn was the one to keep it going. *When will your car be fixed?*

Friday, Fonti's reckons.

Good to hear. I'm at work so I'd better go before Briggsy catches me messaging you. Make sure you lock up, all right?

I've been incredibly diligent about locking up since yesterday morning! Free replied.

She went back to the Bostons website to finish her online order for the new glazes Jay had asked her to source. She still had Jay's cheque in her handbag, she recalled, as well as one from the school, and another one from Olly for gallery supplies. She'd better get to the bank tomorrow and put those cheques in, because she would have to pay her Bostons account within a week.

Free went to bed, rubbing the purring Max's ears. She thought about the cat sleeping with Finn during the day and coming back to sleep with her at night-time. Time-sharing them. It made her smile in the darkness. She wished Finn were home. She would have liked to hear him singing tonight.

12

When Free arrived at the bank late morning, only two tellers were on. She had to queue for over half an hour among irate old-age pensioners. She hoped she wouldn't get served by Phoebe. She liked the girl but she couldn't help that jealousy swelling in her heart whenever she looked at Phoebe's sweet face. *Bloody bad luck*, she thought miserably. If only Finn hadn't got things so arse-about, he might be dating Free now instead of Phoebe Challis.

Of course, when it was Free's turn, she was called to Phoebe's counter. The girl's dark-blue eyes brightened when she saw her.

'Hi, Free! How are you?'

'I'm good. You?'

'Good, thanks. What can I do for you today?'

Free fished in her bag. 'I've got some cheques to bank.'

Phoebe nodded and got to work entering cheque details on her computer. She appeared a touch more serious than usual. Maybe she was in work mode.

'How's the art project coming along?' Phoebe asked, tapping on her keyboard.

'Great! We've had theme approval, so we can finally get started on tile designs. The kids are *so* into it.'

Phoebe smiled. 'How sweet.'

'But I had a rough start to the week. My car got broken into.'

Phoebe's eyes widened. 'Oh no!'

'Yeah. At home.'

Free's thoughts drifted to Finn looking after her when she discovered the break-in. How big and strong he'd felt when he held her in his arms — and how tender his hands had been when he checked her bleeding foot. With a jolt, she remembered Phoebe was dating Finn, and felt horribly guilty for thinking of him in that way.

'Um, maybe Finn told you already . . . ' she said.

Phoebe shot her a quick look. 'Uh, Finn — he and I — we're not together.' Free was stunned into silence and Phoebe smiled at her tightly. 'We agreed there was no spark.'

'Oh!'

Phoebe sighed and stamped one of Free's cheques in a disgruntled manner.

'Um, do you want to talk about it?' Free ventured.

Phoebe checked her computer's clock. 'Yeah, that'd be good. I'm on lunchbreak in ten. Can you wait for me?'

'Of course. Meet you at Galileo's?'

Phoebe nodded and handed over a receipt. Free left the bank and made for the coffee shop, heart racing. Finn and Phoebe were *over*? She tried to feel sorry for Phoebe and failed abjectly.

Maybe . . . Now that there was no imaginary boyfriend in the way . . .

Free reined in her thoughts. She must not go *there*. She might just be setting herself up for disappointment again and, anyway, what kind of friend was she to rejoice in Phoebe's misfortune? She stepped into the cool air of the café and sat in a booth to wait, fidgeting with her hair, thoughts spinning.

What if . . . ?

No! Stop it, she scolded herself.

Within minutes, Phoebe appeared in the doorway, searching the tables. Free waved until she caught Phoebe's eye.

'Hey.' Phoebe plumped herself down opposite, and gave Free a look of heartfelt gratitude. 'Thanks. Sometimes it's easier to talk to someone who's not in the circle, you know? I mean, you're in the circle, but not *in* the circle. Not *super* in.'

Free nodded. 'Yep. I know what you mean.'

Phoebe looked relieved. They agreed to order first, then talk, so they queued up at the counter to select Turkish rolls and drinks.

'It was weird, the thing with Finn,' Phoebe said when they were seated once more. 'I mean, I told him I agreed that there was no spark between us — but honestly, what else can you say to someone when they're breaking up with you? Not that we were even *together*, not really. It was just two dates. But I actually thought it was going quite well. I mean, he seemed a bit shy. A bit slow to make a move, you know? He hadn't even tried to kiss me. But I figured he might be working up to it — being a gentleman.'

A secret part of Free was deeply glad that Finn had not kissed Phoebe. She stomped on the thought and focused on Phoebe's words.

Phoebe rested her chin in her hands, elbows on the table, and gazed at Free. 'But then on Tuesday afternoon, he showed up at my place after work and said he wanted to talk. He said he'd been doing some thinking and realised we'd be better as friends. You know, the usual crap. 'I really value your friendship, Phoebe. You and I work so well as friends, and I'm just not getting a romantic vibe, *blah-blah-blah*.'' Phoebe attempted a laugh but it died quickly and tears came to her eyes. 'Sorry. It's not really *him* I'm upset about, specifically. It's the whole dating game. Sometimes I think there must be something wrong with me.'

Free's own eyes filled in response. 'Are you *crazy*? You're fun, cool, beautiful and altogether lovely! Any guy would be lucky to have you.'

That just made Phoebe gulp a sob. 'Then why can't I just meet someone? This isn't the first time Briggsy's tried to set me up with a guy, you know. It never works out.'

'I know he sent you on a date with Tom, but sheesh, Pheebs. Tom was a lost cause.'

She sniffed. 'I know. Briggsy told me how Tom had been after Willow forever. He always tries to make me feel better when it's another bust. I'm up to five.'

'Five what?'

'Five failed set-ups.'

Free's mouth fell open. '*What?*'

Phoebe nodded again, colouring. 'I told you, there's something wrong with me. I'm cursed.'

'They can't all have knocked you back. They'd have to be blind *and* stupid.'

214

Phoebe laughed gratefully. 'Well, there was Mick. He moved down to Perth for work after two weeks. Alex. He wanted to take me 'roo shooting for our second date. Not my scene. Then Tom. He was in love with your sister. Then Ty. He seemed like a nice guy. Decent job, good sense of humour, and not in love with anyone else — but then Briggsy caught him selling pot to his workmates, and banned him from seeing me. And now Finn. Good-looking and sweet but apparently we have no *spark*.' She grimaced.

Free was growing more and more horrified. 'Are you saying Briggsy set you up with all these guys?' Phoebe shrugged. 'What the *hell*? How can you be expected to meet a guy you like if you've got some interfering, big-brother type — the local sergeant, for God's sake — hovering over your shoulder, trying to force you into a relationship? That's not how it works! Love is random. Accidental. You just live your life and then one day it'll hit you with the right person.'

Free realised with shock that she was giving relationship advice. She cringed inwardly. *What a fraud.* But Phoebe was gazing at her with a peculiar expression of hope. She sat back and shook her dark head.

'I don't know, Free. It's so hard to meet a nice guy. If Sean does the vetting for me . . . '

'*Vetting!* What is this, a bloody cattle show?' Free was forced to pause while the waiter served their lunch. As soon as he left, she burst out once more. 'Phoebe, it's really wrong of Briggsy to mess with your love-life like this. Who does he think he is? Maybe he should try to fix his own screwed-up relationship before he interferes in anyone else's!'

Phoebe was startled. 'What do you mean?'

'You know, the stuff with Kate. The commitment stuff.' Phoebe waited and, too late, Free realised she'd spilled a secret. 'Forget I said anything. I've probably got the wrong end of the stick.' Free steered them back to the topic at hand. 'Anyway, your love-life is *yours*. Tell Briggsy to butt the hell out, or I'll tell him for you.'

Phoebe burst into laughter. 'Okay, Free. Maybe you're right.' She wiped her eyes and chuckled again. 'I can just imagine you shouting down big, burly Sergeant Sean Briggs.'

They discussed work and friends while they ate their lunch. Free asked Phoebe to come along to the Herne River wildlife talk, and Phoebe looked much brighter when they hugged goodbye.

Free headed for her ute in the bank car park. It was so hot inside that she burnt her hand on the seatbelt buckle. The air conditioning had barely kicked in by the time she arrived home, and her dress was stuck to her skin.

Her mind kept wandering back to Phoebe's story. So Finn had shut things down with her on Tuesday evening? Tuesday morning was when he'd discovered Free was single. But she could be making a connection where there wasn't one. Maybe he'd already been planning to end the dating trial with Phoebe. It was probably just a coincidence. Free packed a bag for her weekend at Patersons, since she wouldn't be coming home after work the next day, but her thoughts crept back to the night Finn had driven her home from the station after the wedding. The night she'd asked to go inside with him. *Where's Max?* Finn had asked her. *Where's your boyfriend?* He'd been reminding her that she was otherwise committed — at least in his head. What would have happened if he'd known then that the only Max she lived with was a greedy tabby cat?

She forced her thoughts back to the present. Finn wasn't home, as far as she could tell. Probably working. Free paced her house, practically bursting to know the truth. Had all her first instincts about him been correct? She didn't hear the telltale noises of Finn arriving home until it was so late she couldn't casually visit any more. She snatched up her phone and, seizing on the easiest opener she could think of, messaged him.

Hey, Finn, any word on the car break-ins? Any suspects?

He replied a couple of minutes later. *Hi, Free. Nothing yet, sorry. Probably not worth holding your breath.*

Free garnered her courage and typed. *Can I pop around for a minute?*

There was a pause. *Now's not a great time. Can we take a raincheck?*

She frowned. *I just wanted to ask you something.*

Ask away.

Uh, nope. She wasn't going to do this via direct message. She ignored his raincheck request and grabbed her house key, locking the door behind her and scrambling over the divider railing. She knocked.

When Finn opened the door, he looked like a different man altogether. His face was pale and strained, and those pebbly-creek eyes were shadowed, as though a storm cloud hung overhead.

'Finn!' she said, shocked. 'What's wrong?'

He paused, indecisive for a moment, then moved aside and indicated she should come in.

'Do you want a coffee, or . . . '

'Finn.' She grabbed his arms and forced him to look at her. 'What's happened?'

He sagged slightly. 'I just spoke to my dad. Mum had to fly to Ireland early because Aislinn went into labour. It's a boy. I'm an uncle.'

Free released him. 'Is your sister okay? The baby?'

'Yeah, they're both fine.'

'Well, congratulations.'

'Thanks.' He sank into a chair and Free hovered nearby. 'It's just, Dad told me something. They were going to wait until I visited this weekend to break the news but because Mum had to fly out, Dad decided to come straight out and tell me.' His gaze stayed on the floor. 'They're going back. For good.'

'Back — to Ireland?'

'Yeah. They want to be close to Aislinn and the baby. And future grandkids, I suppose.'

'Oh wow.' Free was left almost breathless with the brutality of it. 'What about *you*?'

Finn shrugged. 'Mum and Aislinn have always been really close. I guess I was a bit more independent than Aislinn. They're encouraging me to consider moving back too, but they know that I love Australia. My friends and my career. My life. They're all *here*.'

Tears ran down her cheeks, and when Finn noticed, he reached a hand out to take hers. 'Don't, Free. Don't cry.'

'Sorry. Your heart must be breaking. I can't stand it.'

The darkness lifted from his eyes momentarily, and his expression softened. But then his mouth became tight and he dropped his gaze again.

'Dad's leaving for Ireland tomorrow. He's coming back in a month or two to pack everything up and get the house ready to sell. I've cancelled my trip back to Perth this weekend. Lucky I got travel insurance, huh?' He gave a half-hearted smile. 'Briggsy'll be pleased. He was spewing about having to work this long weekend, but I might as well take his shifts now.'

Looking at him sitting there in pain, she just wanted to take all his sadness away. Free stepped forward and put her arms around him, pulling him close so his head was resting against her chest. She couldn't stop her tears. After a tense moment, Finn relaxed and slipped his arms around her, holding on in silence.

At last he pulled away, getting up to put the kettle on. She thought she saw him brush an arm across his eyes, and her own tears continued to fall unabated.

'Tea? Coffee?' he said.

She shook her head. 'No, thanks.'

219

'What did you want to ask me about?'

'Um, I forget.'

He glanced back at her, and seeing her tears, grabbed a handful of tissues and passed them to her. 'I don't think I've ever met anyone as empathetic as you, Free Paterson.'

She caught her breath and seized the moment. 'Finn, don't cancel your leave. I'm not letting you stay here to be miserable all by yourself. Come with me to Paterson Downs for the weekend.'

He smiled and opened his mouth to argue, but she kept her eyes on his, willing him simply to agree. The words died on his lips.

'I'll be looking after my dad because Willow and Tom are on their honeymoon,' she added, knowing he would only agree if she pretended *she* was the one in need. 'Will you come? Help me out and keep me company?'

All Finn's awful pain was in his eyes. She wanted to pull him close and sob against him but kept her gaze locked on his, silently pleading with him to let her help.

At last, Finn gave a half-shrug. 'Sounds good. I'm in.'

★ ★ ★

Finn drove the farm ute behind Free in her newly repaired car. The only reminder of the break-in was that her car was unusually clean inside, and there were no mint wrappers or spare change in the centre console — or crystal cat blu-tacked to the dash. Her heart thumped every time she glanced in the rear-view mirror and saw Finn in the blue ute.

A whole long weekend with him.

She wouldn't be so insensitive as to have *the talk* about their potential relationship this weekend. That could wait. The poor guy was grieving. He was losing his whole family in one hit. She could hardly believe his parents would do it to him. But then, she understood it a little bit, too. They had to choose: the daughter with their new grandchild, and the added bonus of returning to their extended family back in Ireland — or their more recent life in Australia, and the son who had moved thousands of kilometres away from home for work. She couldn't blame them, but she still hated seeing Finn's pain.

So no — she wouldn't raise the Phoebe issue or the boyfriend mistake yet. She would just give Finn the best time she could, and be there for him if he wanted to talk. She would be his friend. That was what he'd always wanted, even when she was offering him more. 'I just want to stay friends with you,' he'd said at Talbot Gorge while she was treading water just inches from his body. She melted a little inside. He was so honourable.

She pulled over at a floodway and Finn pulled in behind her. Free hopped out and he called through the open window, 'Everything okay?'

'Do you mind if I just stop to grab a photo?'

He smiled. 'Of course not.'

She reached into the passenger seat for her camera and scrambled down the bank of the

Herne. It was still flowing, but it was smooth and slow rather than the hedonistic rush of the month before. Free crouched beside a piece of dried, cracked mud that was lifting at the edges like bark. She took a photo then peeled the mud back with one finger, and her heart jumped when a red, worm-like larva came into view. *Gross.* But amazing. She focused the lens and snapped several shots, trying to capture its vivid scarlet against the browner red of the sticky mud. *Glorious.* Free replaced the dinner plate of dried mud and stood up. She snapped another couple of photos of the gently moving surface of the river and made her way back to the car, waving at Finn. He waved back and they got on the road again.

She was tempted to stop for more photos at the floodway closest to home but didn't want to inconvenience him so she continued until they reached the stone and wood sign that read *Paterson Downs.* That familiar sense of comfort washed over her. As they approached the homestead, she tried to look at it through Finn's eyes, knowing it was the first time he'd ever seen the place. It was an unfashionable house, she realised, giggling a little. Mission-brown brickwork and lichen-encrusted orange roof tiles. Those seventies-style arches. Lacy curtains over copper venetian blinds.

But beyond the house were massive sheds, busy cattle yards and the Herne River snaking through thousands of kilometres of red and green land beneath a vast azure sky.

Free parked, pointed Finn towards a spot and

222

popped her boot. He arrived beside her and picked up their bags before she could, and they looked so light and easy to carry in Finn's hands that it would have been silly to offer her help. She led him towards the house, almost skipping with excitement.

'I can't wait to show you around the station. Excuse our house. It's super daggy, I know. Apparently, there was an old cottage farmhouse here once, but they knocked it down and rebuilt when Dad was a young bloke. I'm sure you can appreciate how in vogue this design was in the 1970s. Hi, Jazz!' Free greeted a farm dog, whose tongue lolled in a welcoming grin. 'She's the friendliest of our dogs. The others are real workaholics. Look — there's Willow's pony, Tuffie. He's too old to ride nowadays, but he's got the best possie, in the yard that overlooks the house. Willow insists on him having that spot. It's got good shade and he's kind of a pet, so she likes having him close to the house. See this?' She pulled open the screen door and paused to tap the dragon-embellished brass bell missing a clapper. 'This was Mum's bell. I used to think that if you rang the bell, you'd summon the dragon.' She pushed through the dust-coated wooden door. 'Dad! We're home!'

'In here!' came Barry's voice.

Free led Finn to the kitchen. She bent down to hug and kiss her father where he sat at the kitchen table working on a jigsaw puzzle of watery canals. She'd bought it for him in Venice.

'Happy birthday, sweetheart.'

'Thanks, Dad.' She indicated Finn. 'This is

223

Finn Kelly. Do you remember him from the wedding? He's a constable in Mount Clair, and also my neighbour. He's been so good to me, especially when my car got broken into.'

'Yep, I remember ya, Finn.' Barry stood, shaking Finn's hand. 'Free told me she was bringing a mate along for the weekend. Thanks for looking out for her. Things can be a bit rough in town, crime-wise, and we're not used to having to lock up.'

'I did lock the car, Dad,' Free put in.

'Is that right?' Barry looked surprised. 'Bethie said you'd left it unlocked.'

'No, that was the garage door.' Free couldn't help a flicker of annoyance at Beth for dobbing her in to their father. 'Anyway, it's all fixed now. Car's as good as new, and the farm ute's back here, thanks to Finn. Come on, I'll show you where you'll be sleeping,' she said to Finn.

'Dinner in the station kitchen tonight,' Barry called after them. 'Six-thirty.'

'Got it,' she called back.

She showed Finn the guest room, glad that Willow had cleared it out for Tanya's recent stay. The boxes of old art gear were back in Free's paint-wrecked room.

'We've got an hour before dinner,' she said. 'Want to come for a ride around the farm?'

'A ride!' Finn rubbed his jaw uncertainly. 'I don't know how to ride a horse. Or did you mean something else?'

She hadn't meant horses or anything like that, but maybe he wanted a farm-style ride. 'We could take the quads.' Free recalled her last

224

attempt on a quad bike. 'Except I might crash mine. I suck at anything but cars. I can drive the farm ute around the tracks, though.'

Finn looked relieved. 'The ute sounds good.'

'Cool! First, I'll introduce you to everyone.'

She took Finn out to the station kitchen, where Jean made raucous jokes about Finn's height and Devi just stared in silent amazement. Free rattled off the names of the string of station hands, domestic staff and the couple of stockmen who'd arrived in preparation for mustering season.

'And this is Vern, our assistant manager,' she finished, presenting Finn to the quietly spoken man Willow trusted more than anyone else at Patersons. 'There's no-one who knows more than Vern about cattle.'

Finn shook the older man's hand. 'I'm in awe of you guys who can ride horses and muster cattle,' he confessed. 'All I mastered in my lifetime was a skateboard.'

Vern thought that was hilarious. 'You'll wanna be around tomorrow, then,' he said. 'Some of the boys thought they might have a barrel race.'

Free's eyebrows shot up. 'Does Willow know about this?'

'Yeah, she knows,' Vern said. 'She just didn't wanna be here while it happened.'

Free practically danced out to the ute. 'You are in for such a treat, Finn! I haven't seen a barrel race out here for years.'

'What the heck is a barrel race? I'm thinking, you've gotta chase a cow around a barrel . . . '

Free shrieked with laughter. 'Wrong! The *cow*

225

chases *you* around the barrel.'

He groaned but cracked a real smile for the first time that afternoon. 'I guess I'll have to wait and see.'

'That's right. Now, let's go for a bash round the farm.'

She stopped by the kitchen before they headed out, and asked Vern for a farm job. He helped them load up some bales of hay to take out to a paddock on the western side of the station, where foraging pasture was scarce for the small herd that had taken up residence there. Free drove through some yards and paddocks until they hit the western track in the dying sunlight.

'Now, in a minute,' she said, 'you can get onto the back of the ute and toss the bales out to the cattle.'

'Me?' Finn was smiling. 'How about I drive and *you* throw the bales?'

'Not a chance,' she said firmly. 'I'm an artist and have delicate fingers. You're a copper and you have brute strength. You're throwing hay bales, not me.'

He laughed but consented. She bumped through the pasture gate and the cattle came running. Finn jumped onto the tray and tossed out hay like he'd done it his whole life. Free watched him in the side mirror, marvelling at his strength.

Hot damn. She could watch him do that all day.

'Oops,' he said, when one of his bales flew too far and half of the hay landed on the wrong side of the fence.

Before Free could stop him, he'd jumped down to the ground and was crouching down, reaching through the fence to recover the hay.

'Finn, no!' she cried, but it was too late. An impatient cow had shoved past him to stick its massive head through the wires, sending Finn sprawling in the process. Finn lay half through the fence, coughing in the red dust, face in the dirt. Free yanked on the handbrake and scrambled out to help him. He heaved himself back through the fence and they both made a mad dash for the ute tray in advance of the arrival of the rest of the herd. Safe on the tray, Free giggled helplessly.

'Holy shit!' Finn gazed at the cattle, chest heaving. 'What happened?'

'You turned your back!' she managed through her panting. 'And you got in between a cow and its tucker.'

Finn watched as the herd arrived in earnest, shaking the hay bales apart and grumbling at each another. 'I always thought cows were docile.'

'Yeah, people think that.'

'Big, soft-eyed, calm, kinda stupid . . . '

'Not at all stupid.' Free slapped his arm, which made dust rise from his shirt. 'They may be big and soft-eyed, but they're also curious and surprising.'

He grinned at her, then the grin faded slightly. 'That explains you, then. Raised on a cattle station. Curious and surprising.'

She was startled into silence, but Finn edged closer to the rear of the ute to look at the cows.

He kicked the last bit of hay off the tray, in among the herd.

'I think they're distracted. Should we make a break for it?'

'Go!'

They both jumped down and scrambled into the cab of the ute.

'Phew,' said Free. 'Gotta say, cows scare the hell out of me.'

'I think they scare me now too.'

'Next time, stay on the ute.'

'Oh, I will.'

Free got the ute moving again, bumping along the track back home.

'If you head west along here, you get to the Herne River. That's the boundary of our property. I'd take you out there, but it's getting a bit dark. Maybe tomorrow?'

'Sounds good,' he said. 'How far is it?'

'Only about forty-five minutes from the homestead.'

He laughed. 'I love it. 'Only' forty-five minutes, she says. Most people can walk from one end of their property to the other in forty-five seconds.'

Pride brought a smile to Free's face. 'Not up here. To get to the southernmost point of Patersons, you'd have to drive for a couple of days.'

He shook his head. 'Incredible. I wonder how you'd cope in the city.'

'I lived in a tiny apartment in Stockholm once. I mean *tiny*. It was okay, but it never really felt like a home — like someplace I could stay. I think I feel like that about all cities. It was pretty cool being able to go downstairs to the cake shop right underneath us, though.'

'Us? You lived with someone?'

Loaded question? 'Majken, yeah.' Finn was watching her, she could feel it. 'She was a student,' Free added casually, just so he'd know.

'Ah, right.' Was that relief in his voice?

'You hungry?' she asked.

'Starving.'

'Awesome. It's almost dinnertime.'

13

The station dining hall wasn't at full capacity but it was still buzzing with a Friday night atmosphere. Since it was Free's birthday, Devi had got involved in cooking the meal. She knew how much Free loved authentic Malaysian food, and had made mee goreng and nasi dagang. Free was in ecstasy.

'I need to do an apprenticeship with you,' she told Devi. 'You're the dagang master.'

Finn devoured his own meal, Free was delighted to see, and was listening to the small crew of stockmen who loved telling tales of their daring and mastery to any newcomer. She was glad Finn had left the sadness of his family's news behind for the night. He caught her eye and shot her a smile, but one of the stockmen asked him a question about his work so he focused on the conversation again. He was a special guy, she thought. The men liked him, but he didn't get caught up in the alpha-male contests she was used to from blokes who worked in high-risk jobs like droving. *His* job was high-risk too — and yet Finn didn't carry that around like a trophy. He wasn't in police work to fight criminals. He was simply into helping people, and he expected goodness from them in return. She sighed. What a beautiful inner spirit Finn had.

And his exterior was pretty darn fine as well.

After dinner, her father ordered the lights turned low, and Devi brought a cake out from the kitchen, burning with twenty-seven candles.

'Here's my Freya, twenty-seven years of age,' Barry announced when the cake was sitting before her, candles melting all over the chocolate. 'Still our little fairy, flying across the world and making bloody beautiful creations. I don't pretend to understand you, sweetheart, but I love the hell outta you and couldn't be a prouder dad.'

His speech made her cry so hard she could barely blow out the candles. The cake — a croquembouche-style wonder Jean and Devi had concocted — was a hit. The social chatter continued into the evening but farm hours were rarely late hours, so the staff began to wander off to the dormitories by nine. Free and Finn returned to the house and Barry presented Free with a voucher to spend at Bostons online.

'How did you know?' she gasped.

'A little birdie told me,' her father said.

'You're the best, Dad.'

They worked with Barry on his jigsaw puzzle for a while, but soon enough, her father wished them goodnight and went off to bed.

'Do you want one last cup of tea?' Free asked Finn when it was just the two of them.

'That'd be good.'

'Listen,' she said, pausing as she went for the kettle. 'It's raining. Hear that, the rain on the patio roof? That's my favourite sound in the whole world.'

'Let's go and sit out on the patio with our tea, then,' said Finn.

He went outside to sort out somewhere to sit, loading up the double wicker couch with cushions and arranging the ancient bamboo coffee table so they could rest their feet on it. He'd pushed it right up to the edge of the patio so they could hear the rain and watch the lightning flicker on the horizon. Free placed their teacups on the table and settled down beside him.

'My dad'll be flying out in a few hours,' he said. 'It feels bloody weird knowing I'll be the only one of the Kelly clan left in the country. Permanently, too.'

'Are you totally sure you don't want to go with them?' she asked, although she didn't like the thought of him leaving one bit.

To her relief, he nodded. 'I'm sure. I remember Ireland well, especially how cold, grey and wet it was. I love Australia. There's no way I could go back. It's happened, it's all decided. I just need to deal with it.'

Free glanced his way. 'Doesn't mean you can't feel sad about it, at least for a while.'

'No point wallowing in misery.'

Free was a little puzzled by this. If it were her, she'd be in floods of tears. 'I guess not.'

He paused. 'You lost your mum when you were young, didn't you?'

She nodded. 'How did you know that?'

'Briggsy mentioned it. I was bloody sorry to hear about it.'

'Thanks. She died of breast cancer. I was

232

eleven — not exactly a little kid, but it feels like a lifetime ago that Mum was around.'

'So around the same time I was moving to Australia, you lost your mother. Big life changes for both of us. Not that mine compares to what you went through, even remotely, but . . . '

'No, I know what you're saying,' she said. 'Formative moments.'

'It must have been so hard for you to understand at just eleven.'

'Yes.' Free reflected. 'Sometimes I wonder if I've blocked out bits of that time from my memory. It all feels vague and surreal. I hardly remember any details, especially about how I felt. I remember everyone being really sad and quiet for a long time, but that's about all. I don't even remember much of what it was like having Mum around. I struggle even to remember what her eyes looked like.'

'Maybe it's a coping mechanism?' he ventured. 'I mean, you may have shut down a little when she passed away. Perhaps that's why you can't remember much about it.'

'Yeah, it's possible.' Free watched the lightning for a few moments. 'I saw Dad cry, and that scared me. I thought he never cried. Willow was barely holding it together, and Beth totally changed. She turned into Bossy Beth overnight, always telling me what to do and forcing me to go to bed on time, stuff like that. Trying to parent me, I suppose. But she vanished halfway through Year Twelve and went to stay at a boarding house in town. And then she went off to uni for years and years.'

233

'I can't even imagine what it was like.' His voice was full of sympathy. 'I suppose it must have brought you closer with your sisters, in a way.'

She dropped her eyes to her teacup and bit her thumbnail. 'Sort of,' she blurted, almost involuntarily. 'Just, I can't help but feel like they were luckier than me. They got more time with Mum.' Oh dear Lord, had she said that out loud? She'd never told *anyone* that — and she wasn't even drunk. How immature and selfish —

'Yeah, I'd feel the same way.' Finn sighed. 'With my parents leaving, I'm trying to rise above being petty, but I can't help resenting Aislinn for settling over there. This wouldn't even be an issue if she still lived in Perth.'

Free exhaled, overjoyed that he hadn't judged her admission. 'I know Beth has a letter from Mum, and Willow has her pendant. I have nothing. I try not to be jealous, but . . . ' Free trailed off and looked at Finn. 'But it's probably not useful to dwell on it — for you, either.' He made a noise of agreement. 'What was it like, where you lived in Ireland?' she asked.

Finn took a sip of tea. 'We had an old terrace house on a busy road, so there was a lot of traffic flying past. Mum never let us go out the front because she was terrified we'd get hit by a car. We had a lane behind the row of houses that led to a sports field, though, so we would run down there to hang out with our friends. I played a lot of soccer.'

'What about school?'

'School was walking distance from home, so

234

we walked every day, rain, hail, shine or snow.' Finn laughed suddenly. 'I remember, just before we emigrated, my teacher called me up the front and announced that Finn Kelly was moving to Australia. She assumed I knew all about the country we were moving to, and told the other kids they could ask me questions. She didn't know I was as ignorant as any of them. They were all asking questions like, did I need to get immunised against snake bites before I left; what language did they speak in Australia; would I be getting a pet kangaroo — that sort of thing.'

Free grinned. 'What did you say?'

'I did my best.' He slapped a mosquito. 'No, I hadn't been immunised against snake bites but I would probably take a course of antivenom. They speak Aussie in Australia, which is like a dialect of English. And, yes — hell yes, I'd be getting a pet kangaroo *and* a pet koala.'

She giggled. 'Awesome. Your family, what are they like?' she asked. 'Tell me more about them.'

'Dad's tall, like me, although I ended up taller. He's car-mad. He was a mechanic when he was younger, but these days he works in the workshop at a service centre, doing parts-ordering and stuff. I'm sure he thinks I'm subnormal, not owning a car. He used to spend hours looking for good deals on a motor for me but I never quite got around to buying anything. It drove him nuts. He's got an eye for a bargain, you see, and had no comprehension of me not caring about cars. When I was . . . ' Finn broke off and half glanced at Free in the darkness, but continued awkwardly. 'When I was with Elyse, we shared her car. Then I found out I was coming up to Mount Clair, so I figured I'd buy something locally. But I haven't urgently needed a car, not so far. I can walk to work or get a lift, and Briggsy lets me use his vehicle if I ever need it. And the rest of the time we use the troopies.'

'I didn't have a car for ages, either,' Free said, nodding. 'Beth found me the one I've got now. One of her patients, a little old lady, had to give up driving. Beth pretty much forced me to buy the woman's car.' She laughed, feeling ridiculous. 'I'm a bit of a pushover when it comes to my big sister.' She sipped her tea. 'What about Aislinn? Is she older or younger than you?'

'Older. She's thirty.' He dug for his phone. 'I was going to show you before, but got distracted by cow-feeding. Get a load of this. She sent me pictures of my new nephew. They're calling him Henry.' He showed her a couple of photos of a red-faced baby with tiny dark slits for eyes. He was held by Aislinn, a sturdy-looking young woman with a round, smiling face and red hair.

'He's adorable!' Free studied the photo. 'You don't look much like your sister. Except for your smile.'

'She's more like Mum,' he said, putting his phone away. 'Short and round.' He shook his head. 'I can't believe Aislinn's a mother now. I hope she's nicer to little Henry than she was to me.'

'What do you mean? She was mean to you?'

'Nothing out of the ordinary,' he assured her. 'Just your typical brother-sister nastiness. She would dob me in for wrecking something, so I'd

236

hide in her wardrobe to scare her, that kind of thing.'

'And your mum's like her?'

'Yes, in looks. And I suppose Aislinn's turned out like Mum in personality, too. Mum's got a good heart — always trying to make people feel better, helping out if someone's in a tough situation. She's a hard worker, that's for sure.'

'Does she work, like, in a paid job, too?'

'Yeah, she works in admin. Bookkeeping, secretarial services, that kind of thing.'

Free considered Finn's family. She pictured a tall, careworn father with grease-stained knuckles, poring over an *Auto Trader* magazine, calling out to Finn whenever he spotted a good deal. A little plump mother, her auburn hair going grey now, baking a chocolate cake for a family whose child was in hospital. That was where Finn got his deep, innate kindness, Free decided. And Aislinn — she would be cheerful and red-haired, helping her mum with the baking but simultaneously dobbing on Finn for pilfering the cooking chocolate.

'I wish I could meet them,' she said.

'That's pretty unlikely now,' he said flatly.

Ack. Free wanted to suggest he make a plan to go see them in Ireland, but she got the vibe Finn wasn't ready to problem-solve. She wouldn't be, either.

'What would you like to do tomorrow?' she asked in an attempt to brighten the mood.

'Aside from the mysterious barrel race? I'm not sure. Are there any more jobs that need doing?'

'You want to do farm jobs?'

Finn shrugged. 'Yep. Or whatever you want to do. What would you normally do, being home for the weekend?'

Free winced. 'Uh . . . sleep in. Paint. Do jigsaw puzzles with Dad.'

He chuckled. 'Sleeping in — I don't do that very often, but I'm willing to give it a shot. Painting? I can paint, if it's walls or doors. Jigsaw puzzles, now that's something I could genuinely get into.'

'I promise I won't sleep in very long tomorrow. I'll find us some farm jobs and then, when we're too hot and tired to work, we'll help Dad with his puzzle again. And at some point, you'll see a barrel race.' She checked his face. 'Does that sound okay?'

'Sounds fantastic.'

They drank their tea and watched the distant storm in silence for a few minutes, then Finn put his cup on the table and rose from his chair.

'Wait here,' he told her.

She waited. He was back in moments, and dropped a small parcel into her lap.

'What's this?'

'A birthday present.'

'Finn! You didn't have to — '

'I totally did,' he interrupted. 'It's your birthday. Plus, you invited me here to your home for the weekend, which was . . . ' He stopped for an instant but resumed quickly. 'Which was really kind of you. Anyway, this barely qualifies as a present, it's so small.'

He had so many good reasons, she didn't try

to argue any more. She unwrapped a glossy green cardboard box. When she manoeuvred the lid off, she found a little tabby cat figurine. Free held it up in the light from the kitchen window.

'Finn, this is so cool! It's a tiny Max!'

'Donald,' he corrected with a grin.

'Is it ceramic?'

'Yeah, china.'

'He's so *cute*! Do you know, I had a little cat in my car but it got stolen. This can take its place!'

'I'd noticed your crystal cat and figured it must have been stolen,' Finn said. 'This one's totally different, but — '

'No, I like it that way. The other one was from a friend, so I couldn't replace it even if I tried. But this is perfect, because it's different. This can be my new lucky car cat.' She turned it over in her fingers, inspecting it, thrilled with Finn's thoughtfulness.

'I knew you'd like it. I went to the shops to pick out something for you this morning — just some chocolates or wine or something. But then I saw this and had to buy it for you.'

'You really *get* me,' she said, smiling at him.

'You're easy to *get* because you're just yourself.'

'Thank you!' Free paused. 'I think that was a compliment.'

'Of course it was. You're just like one of your paintings — all light and colour, nothing artificial.' Finn held her gaze and Free's heart kicked into overdrive. For a second she thought he might move closer but then a dog barked out in the yard, startling them both. Free stood up to check what the ruckus was, but as far as she could tell in the dim light, nothing was amiss. Finn stood up beside her.

'What is it?' he asked.

'Just a random night-time bark, I think.'

He stretched. 'Bedtime.'

'Yep.' Free grabbed the cups and went inside, depositing them in the sink. 'Towels in the bathroom cabinet — help yourself. If I'm not up by nine tomorrow, throw something at me.'

He cracked up. 'I couldn't do that to you.'

'No, seriously, do. If you don't, I might stay there all day.'

'Okay,' he said, following her down the hall. 'You asked for it.'

She stopped outside her bedroom door. 'Goodnight, Finn.'

'Goodnight, Free.'

She stepped in for a hug, and it was amazing — tight, but somehow gentle. He smelt faintly of aftershave, with a pleasant blend of sunscreen and hay. A series of heatwaves started in various parts of her body. It would be so easy to slip a hand up to the back of his neck and stretch up for a kiss . . .

Free kept her hands where they were. She *would not* take advantage of him in a vulnerable moment. He was hurting, shell-shocked by his family's decision — and laying a snog on him would only confuse him more. She would give him time to deal with his sadness before she hinted that she was still interested.

She moved out of the hug and opened her

bedroom door. 'See you in the morning.'

In bed, she still had his scent with her. It made it hard to get to sleep.

14

Free woke at 8 a.m., glad she hadn't shamed herself with a ridiculously long lie-in. She scrambled into some shorts and a T-shirt and went in search of Finn. A glance through the open door into his room revealed it was neat and empty. Neither he nor her father could be found in the house.

Free let herself out the back door into the sunlight. The ground was dark russet, damp from overnight rainfall, but the sky was clear and vivid blue. She caught sight of Finn at last, standing with Barry by a horse yard. They were nattering together as they leaned on the fence rail.

'Young Finn here's signed you both up for plenty of hard work, Free,' Barry called as she approached. 'Starting with cleaning the cow pats out of the handling yards.'

'What the hell?' Free stared at Finn. 'Are you insane?'

The two men laughed together and she realised her father had been joking. Free rolled her eyes at them.

'Your dad's been explaining the cattle count,' Finn told her. 'It's a pity we're here at the wrong time, so we won't get to see it.'

'Well . . . ' Free was dubious. 'It gets pretty noisy and dusty. And it stinks. I guess you *could* call it interesting, but it's not exactly fun.'

'I can only imagine how hard the work is, but seeing it all — the counting, drafting, branding and so on? It sounds amazing.'

'We don't iron-brand the cows at Patersons any more,' she said. 'Willow switched us to freeze-branding. It's so much nicer for the cows.'

'Yeah, Barry was saying. I'd never even heard of that before. It's gotta be better than a red-hot iron on your backside, though, right?'

'You said it!' Free glanced at her father. 'Have we got any cattle-handling jobs for Finn this weekend, Dad?'

'The boys are preg-checking some heifers.'

Finn frowned blankly and Free shot him a wide-eyed look. 'Don't ask. You really don't want to know what that involves. Best we just stay out of the way.'

They pottered around the homestead for the day. Finn helped Barry with a couple of repair jobs in the house, and played a board game with Free when he was finished. After lunch, Free checked with Vern to see if they could help with anything, and he sent them on another stockfeed run. They would have gone on to the river but heavy storm clouds were gathering and Free didn't like the thought of being stuck in a ute almost an hour from the homestead while a thunderstorm was taking place. When they got back, preparation had commenced for the barrel races. Her father came outside with his hat on and leaned against the yard railing to watch the team set up, his eyes gleaming with pleasure.

'Dad was a rodeo rider once,' Free told Finn where they stood at another section of fence.

Finn's eyebrows shot up. 'Was he? Those guys are crazy, I've heard.'

Thunder grumbled in the distance as the stockmen rolled metal barrels out into a roughly triangular configuration in the closest stockyard. The younger team members hovered in nervous anticipation, while the older, more experienced drovers laughed and ribbed each other as they headed into the stables to saddle up. A high-pitched whinny arose nearby and Free noticed the old pony Tuffie watching the barrels, ears pricked up with interest.

'Oh wow, look at him,' she exclaimed, grabbing Finn's arm and pointing. 'He was a rodeo pony before Willow got him. He knows exactly what's happening!' Finn chuckled but Free suddenly realised how tight a hold she had on him. She relinquished his arm, trying not to think about how amazingly hard and muscled it was. *Good Lord.* It was getting more and more difficult not to touch him.

Once the barrels were in place, the stockmen rode out of the stable on their chosen mounts amid cheering from the spectating staff. Free could only imagine the arguments that had gone on in the stables over who would claim Linger and Ketsu, renowned as the quickest, most responsive mounts in the Patersons stable. Barry was asked to do the timing, and Nico — always a solid horseman — went first. Free knew he would set the bar high.

Si swung open the gate and Nico burst through, Ketsu leaping straight into a gallop. Their head stockman steered the young gelding

244

to the barrel on the right, whipping around it sharply before riding hard for the one on the far left of the gate. That one he navigated even faster, dust flying as Ketsu leaned deep into the turn. They bore down on the barrel at the top of the course and Free gasped as Ketsu seemed to almost turn on the spot.

'Holy crap!' Finn exclaimed beside her.

Barry hit the button on his stopwatch theatrically as Nico and Ketsu galloped back through the gate. 'Seventeen point three!' he roared.

Everyone whistled and cheered. Free sprang up onto the railing to get comfortable while she watched, Finn resting his elbows on the rail beside her.

'That was amazing,' he said. 'How the hell does anyone even stay on a horse moving that fast? Motorbikes, I get. They're predictable.'

Free disagreed. 'I'm not great on either, but at least I have a hope when I'm on a horse. They're coordinated and know when they've got a numpty on board. Machines — they rely on me to drive properly, and that's when things go south.'

Next was Paul, and then Vern. They performed respectably but not in Nico's league. Si did better, coming in at 19.6 seconds on Linger. Even Devi was cheering when he flew back through the gate.

'You gonna have a go, constable?' Si grinned as he brought his prancing mount round near the gate.

Finn broke into a smile. 'Could I?'

Uh-oh. This could end badly. Free watched in apprehension as they brought Patersons' largest horse over for Finn to have a turn. He was too tall to ride any of the mounts except for the great big bay named Hans.

'Better get him a helmet,' Barry called. 'I don't think he's done much riding, have ya, mate?'

'Definitely not,' said Finn, attempting to mount the solid gelding they'd brought him. Si took pity and held Hans still while Finn clambered up. Kira trotted over with a helmet for Finn and led his mount to the starter gate. Free heard the girl giving Finn a rapid induction in horseriding, explaining the reins and stirrups, and how to urge a horse forward. Free was torn. As far as she knew, Finn had never even been on a horse. What if he fell and got hurt? He might fly off as they rounded a barrel — he might even hit the barrel and split his beautiful face open . . .

She was just about to intervene when Barry shouted 'Go!' and Finn was off. Free clapped a hand over her mouth to stop the shriek of protest she'd almost emitted — but Hans was simply trotting casually towards the first barrel, Finn bouncing around on the saddle like a kid on a space hopper. She burst out laughing instead. Then, when he rounded the first barrel, Hans turned more quickly than Finn expected and — despite the slow pace — he slipped off into the dirt. He jumped up, laughing and red-faced, and managed to scramble back on. He didn't fall off again, but it was all Finn could do to steer the patient Hans around the barrels in the right order. He got an enormous cheer when he and Hans finally trotted back through the gate.

'Two minutes thirteen!' Barry shouted, grinning from ear to ear, and the cheers and laughter rose again as Finn slid off Hans. Several stockmen clapped Finn on the shoulder as though he'd ridden the best race they'd ever seen. Brushing dust off his backside, Finn rejoined Free.

'Well,' he said, tipping his head with a wink, 'are you impressed yet?'

Free laughed so hard she couldn't speak and Finn gave her a gentle push. 'Hey! That's enough. My pride's already in tatters.'

'You might still win,' she managed through her giggles.

'Yeah, if everyone else gets disqualified or struck by lightning, maybe.'

There were three more riders before the impending storm forced them to call an end to the barrel race — but at the last moment, Kira trotted out on Willow's preferred muster horse, the compact palomino known as Peanut.

'Am I too late?' she asked Barry.

'Not at all! You go for it, Kira,' he nodded.

Kira was unbelievable. She pushed Peanut through the gate and they flew around the first barrel, turning so tightly it made Free catch her breath. Free scrambled for her phone and managed to hit the *record video* button just as Kira reached the final barrel, scooting around it as though Peanut had wheels. The girl zipped back through the gate and Barry hit the stopwatch button.

'*Sixteen bloody seconds point six!*' he yelled at the top of his lungs.

Everyone went wild for Kira, even Nico, whom she'd outridden. Barry declared their nineteen-year-old stablehand the winner and the race was over, station hands rolling the barrels away as the stockmen took their horses back to the stable for unsaddling. Free and Finn headed for the house, laughing over the race highlights.

'I'm cooking for us tonight,' Free said, remembering, 'so you might want to send up a prayer.'

'Stop that,' he said. 'What can I do to help?'

She got him started on preparing vegetables on the opposite side of the kitchen bench. It would be a steak dinner, since Barry wanted to take advantage of Willow's absence to eat as much meat as possible. Her father disappeared to watch the news.

'Have you spoken to your sister today?' Free asked Finn.

'Yep, we had a quick text chat.'

'How is she?'

'She's sore and tired.' Finn smiled. 'She made that very clear.'

'I can only imagine! I hope her husband is a supportive kind of guy.'

Finn considered. 'He's okay. I've only met him a handful of times, but he seems like a decent bloke. I don't know if he'll be up for Husband of the Year. But he's better than some.'

Free peeled a garlic clove, thinking about his words. 'That's a shame. I'd struggle if I thought either of my sisters was with anyone less than completely deserving.'

Finn shrugged. 'What can you do, though? You can't exactly tell someone they could do better. Or that they're with someone who will never be as good to them as you want.' He fell silent, and when he spoke again his voice held trepidation. 'I have to admit, I thought that about *you*.'

She attempted a carefree laugh, although her heart rate bumped up. 'Stop judging my imaginary boyfriend, would you? He's amazing. Cooks, cleans, buys me flowers.'

Finn's smile returned. 'I honestly believed you were seeing that Max guy. Not just seeing him — living with him!'

She shook her head. 'Finn. Really? I mean — really?'

'Really. Okay, I figured he was punching way — *way* — above his weight, and I thought you might be suffering from low self-esteem or something, to be seeing a guy who was so incredibly inferior to you, but — '

'Hey!' she protested. 'Be nice. Max Drummond is a good guy. I'm not interested in the *least*, but he's a nice man. He saved my wonderful printer from that creepy snake, and he saved that poor little endangered snake from my nasty printer.'

Finn pushed the chopped carrots to one side and started on the cauliflower. 'I'm sure he is a nice guy. It's not that he seemed evil or abusive. It's just, you were so . . . unsettled. I assumed the relationship was a mess and that's why you were . . . ' He stopped.

'That's why I was cheating on the mythical

boyfriend with you? Or at least trying to?' Free said it without thinking and then caught her breath.

His chopping ceased and Finn didn't speak. For a tense few seconds she thought she'd upset him, but then he lifted his eyes to hers and they were still warm and full of light, just like always. She started breathing again.

Finn sank onto a kitchen stool. 'Obviously, I've got a negative view of infidelity. After what happened with Elyse, having been on the receiving end of cheating, I wouldn't wish it on anyone.'

He wasn't finished but Free broke in. 'I *get* that you thought I was being unfaithful to the imaginary boyfriend, but believe me, I wouldn't cheat on anyone. I mean, it's easy to say that, but I honestly don't think I would. I couldn't even get to the point where I was contemplating playing around, because if I was that unhappy I'd just damn well say something, straight up.' She grimaced. 'I try to be tactful but I end up blurting out exactly what I'm thinking most of the time. Beth's always telling me off for that.'

Was she making sense? Finn didn't look angry or hurt.

'Your break-up with Elyse, that must have been terrible for you,' she said.

Finn rearranged the pile of chopped carrots. 'I won't lie to you. It sucked. I thought Jeremy was my friend, after all — and I had no idea she was keen on him. Or that she'd lost interest in me. Apparently it started when they were drunk one night and then they hooked up a few times afterwards. I don't think they're together now. Funny thing is, after I got over the initial shock, I wasn't as devastated as you'd expect. I kind of just got on with things.' Finn gave Free a crooked smile. 'I kept expecting to fall in a heap and start mourning, but I never did. There was even this weird feeling deep inside me — like relief. I guess I knew Elyse and I weren't meant to be — that we weren't one another's *forever*. Maybe if she didn't cheat on me and we didn't break up, we might have got stuck together in a more permanent way. Got married or whatever. What happened was humiliating, but in a strange way I'm sort of grateful. It sure made me think more carefully about who I'm with.'

She couldn't think of anything to say. Finn pulled the chopping board closer and resumed slicing. He was silent, so Free focused on mixing up a garlic and herb rub for the steak. She washed her hands and dug for a vegetable steamer pot in the cupboard. She'd need an extra-large pan to do three steaks at once. What had happened to that non-stick one they used to have . . . ?

'Free,' Finn burst out, as though he'd been holding his words inside. 'Can I be honest with you?'

Free straightened, blinking. 'Of course.'

He was on his feet before she'd finished, and came around the bench so he was standing right in front of her. He was so close she could feel his body warmth against her skin. She stared up at him, her heart skittering out of control.

Finn's Kimberley-creek eyes searched her

face. 'I feel like there's something between us. You and me. Even while I thought you had a boyfriend. I knew I should back off because you weren't single, and I wasn't about to get involved with someone who was already in a relationship — but . . . ' He took a breath. 'But I had a lot of trouble backing off. I wanted to be in your life, even just as a friend.'

Free went warm and soft inside, although her heart didn't slow one bit. 'I thought there was something between us too.' Her voice was little more than a whisper. She cleared her throat and made an effort to speak properly. 'But you kept friend-zoning me. It didn't make any sense, because I really thought you liked me. Like, at Willow's wedding, and then swimming at Talbot Gorge. I saw you trying not to check me out, and failing.'

Finn reddened. 'You're so damn honest.'

'Are you — ' Free hesitated. 'Finn, are you a . . . '

She took his arm and stepped nearer to examine the side of his head, just above his ear. He made a small noise of surprise but she paid no attention. She was discovering something extremely interesting about Finn. The close-shorn hair that grew on his head was clearly a dark *auburn*. She inspected the very faint freckles beneath his tan, the warm colours in his startled eyes, and returned to the pindan-hue of his half-centimetre growth, only detectable at close range beneath the powerful fluorescent kitchen light.

'Finn, I do believe you're a ranga.'

252

'What?'

'A redhead. A ginger. A bluey. But you're pretending you're not, aren't you? It's the Irish thing, right? You don't want to admit you're an Irish bluey!' She reached up a hand to touch his hair. 'But it's beautiful. It's so perfectly *you*. Why would you hide that?'

Finn slipped an arm around her waist, his eyes urgent. 'I haven't been able to stop thinking about you since the moment we met.'

His big, strong frame was tantalisingly close, his hand warm on her back. Locked in place, Free caught her breath as his eyes dropped to her lips —

'What a load of bullshit!' Barry's voice blasted from the living room, and Finn released her instantly. 'Have you seen this crap, sweetheart?'

Free cursed inwardly. 'What's that, Dad?'

'About the diversion dam. Bloody wankers at the shire, letting that Hamilton piece of work wreck our river. Come and look at this.'

Finn shot her a rueful look and returned to the other side of the bench. Free went to watch her father's news story.

⋆ ⋆ ⋆

Free couldn't quite remember how she got through cooking a meal. Her father claimed to enjoy it, but she didn't know what vegetables she served or whether the steak was rare or well done; she was too fixated on the joy of Finn's confession. That one brief moment, with Finn's hand on her lower back, the fluoro light glaring

253

overhead in the daggy Patersons kitchen, had surpassed all her most romantic, sexy memories. Forget that Dutch guy in the field of tulips, vast windmills turning in the summer sunlight. Forget Andre by the fire at the snowed-in ski lodge in Canada. Forget Paulo and that moonlit walk along Ipanema Beach. This moment with Finn, his eyes showing everything he'd tried so hard to hide, exploring her face like he was starved of the sight of her —

'The new season of *I Gotta Sing* starts tonight.' Barry was smiling across the table at Free. 'I've been looking forward to it, sweetheart.'

'Oh yeah. Cool,' she said.

She fidgeted through the reality show and then through a conversation about the *Born and Bred* project, wishing her father would just go to bed and leave them alone. But Barry was buzzing with sociability after the afternoon's barrel race. He chatted on and on, telling old stories about his rodeo-riding days. Free prayed for patience every time he started a new one, and began to despair of getting any time at all alone with Finn that night.

At last Barry got to his feet. 'Well, I'm off. See you two in the morning. Make sure you switch off the lights, Free.'

Her spirits rose. 'Will do, Dad. Night-night.'

'G'night, Barry,' said Finn.

Free barely waited until her father was out of the room before she jumped up from the single recliner and crossed to where Finn sat on the double couch. They had so much more to discuss. And she was dying for his kiss. Finn's face lit up with answering happiness as she sank down beside him.

'I promised, *promised* myself that I wouldn't bring up the question of *us* this weekend,' he said. 'If it went badly, it would make our weekend kind of awkward.'

She gasped at the synchronicity of it. 'Me too! I wanted to give you a fun weekend — just be good company for you after what happened with your parents last week.'

'And I wanted to rewind, take us back to the start so I could get it right this time.'

'It wasn't your fault. Just a mix-up. That damned imaginary boyfriend!' She shook her fist.

Finn narrowed his eyes, although his smile remained. 'I did *not* like your imaginary boyfriend. Not just because I was jealous, but because I suspected he was talking down to you.'

'Why did you think that?'

'Because of the way you always put yourself down. I figured you must have picked that up somewhere.'

Free stared. 'I don't put myself down!'

'You do! You're always calling yourself flaky, a moron, a loser . . . '

Did she do that? Enough that Finn would assume some nasty boyfriend was verbally abusing her? But Finn had also believed she was trying to start an affair with him, she recalled. That must have coloured his view of the mythical boyfriend.

'Ugh, I hate to imagine what you must have

thought of me,' she said. 'I mean, as far as you knew, I was living with a man, but I practically begged to come and stay the night after the wedding. You must have been disgusted with my morals.'

'I wasn't. I just thought you were lonely — that things weren't great with you and Max. And that he was the luckiest bastard who ever lived but he didn't seem to know or care what you were getting up to.'

'You were way too generous to me,' she admonished. 'You would have been within your rights to give me the cold shoulder, but instead you tried to be my friend.'

'Yeah, sort of. Except I kept catching myself doing things *friends* aren't supposed to do. Thinking about you all day, coming out onto the porch when I heard you get home so I could see you. Hoping you'd split up with your boyfriend so I could ask you out.'

Free just about squirmed with delight. 'That's so sweet!'

'It was only after our Talbot Gorge trip that I knew I had to do something — anything — to move on.'

She winced at the memory. 'Because of my oh-so-subtle attempt to seduce you?'

He shot her a smile. 'When you stood up on the rock, giving me that — that *challenging* look, and then swam right up close to me . . . holy crap. That was hottest thing I've ever experienced. I knew I was going to be stuck in the pool for a while, waiting for, uh, my reaction to subside.'

She drew a sharp breath and stared while Finn went red. Free had to forcibly restrain herself from glancing down at his lap, the heat in her own body rising.

'Uh, yeah.' His face was scarlet by now. 'Lucky you got upset with me. That killed the mood.' Free was thrilled, and Finn's blush faded when he saw her smile. 'That vision of you in your bikini is burned into my brain. I knew that day I had to somehow take control of my attraction to you, or I'd give in to temptation — boyfriend or not.'

'So you dated Phoebe?'

He inclined his head.

'And then I got mad at you.' Free chuckled, shaking her head. 'What a gigantic balls-up it's all been.'

'I wanted to like Phoebe. I do like her — but not like I like *you*. Briggsy had been pushing me to go out with her for weeks but I couldn't get you out of my head.'

'Huh, really? Phoebe heard that you were super keen to go on a date with her,' Free said, remembering.

His eyebrows shot up. 'Where'd she hear that?'

'Briggsy — '

Finn gave a short laugh. 'Briggsy told me *she* was 'super keen' for a date, so I figured I might as well test the waters. I was desperate to distract myself from *you*.'

Free rolled her eyes. 'Briggsy the matchmaker.' She smiled. 'You know what? I'm *so* glad we talked about us this weekend after all.'

'Me too.' Finn caught her hand. 'It's been a

bloody confusing few weeks, falling for you and having to act like I hadn't.'

He was looking at her in a way that made her think she might get her kiss at last. She waited breathlessly, but instead of leaning closer, he lifted her hand and pressed his lips to it. Free's mouth fell open at the simple, tender gesture.

'Thank you for inviting me to stay with you this weekend,' he said. 'I love your station and being able to spend all this time with you.'

Finn paused, listening, while Free's pulse hammered in her ears and she floundered for something to say.

'It's raining again,' he said. 'Want to go sit outside on the patio?'

Kiss me — I can't wait another moment! Free nodded dumbly and Finn jumped up, helping her to her feet. But when he went to move towards the back door, she tugged on his hand and he turned to her. Free gave up trying to form words. She reached up, wound her arms around his neck and hung on tight. Once again, there was that wonderful moment when he curled down over her, and the discrepancy in their height vanished — but this time he met her lips in the middle. *Finally*, he was kissing her. She clung to his shoulders and he slipped a hand up under her tangle of hair. For such a big, strong guy, he kissed so gently that it was simultaneously heavenly and unbearable, and Free wanted more. She squeezed him as close as she could, throwing herself into the kiss.

He broke the embrace to look deep into her eyes in the lounge-room lamplight, breathing heavily. 'I've never met anyone like you. You're incredible.'

Words still eluded Free, but the hit of emotion she felt was wondrous. *Perfect.* And utterly overwhelming.

They sat outside in the darkness for hours, talking, kissing, listening to the rain. When Free drifted off to sleep against his shoulder, Finn squeezed her gently to wake her.

'Bedtime,' he whispered, and she longed to be at their home in Mount Clair so they could have 'bedtime' together.

There were several more kisses before she went to bed, and then Free lay there thinking for a long time. This pull to Finn was more powerful than anything she'd felt before. Other guys faded into washed-out insignificance beside Finn. She thought back over some of her holiday romances. Those guys were like two-dimensional line drawings of men. Finn didn't romance or seduce women — he was just himself, and that on its own was incredibly, desperately romantic. Finn showed his true spirit: he was kind, caring, trusting. Compared to her string of holiday romances, Finn was vivid and multidimensional. *Real.*

And somehow, through all the confusion and misunderstandings, a connection had managed to form between them. The intensity of it made her quiver and flutter as though her insides were constructed of feathers.

In the morning, she would make pancakes, Free decided. With berries. She would cook breakfast for them, and then she and Finn could go for a walk and find somewhere private to talk and kiss and enjoy that connection between them — a connection so real, so big, it took her breath away.

★ ★ ★

When Free got up in the morning, she found Finn reading a newspaper at the kitchen table, smelling shower-fresh. She checked on her father. Barry was out of sight, with the *Cattle Chat* talkback radio show blaring in the lounge room. She stood by Finn's chair and slipped her arms around his neck. How did he always smell so good? The happiness in his face erased every last vestige of shyness. She dropped her face to kiss him.

'I'm making you pancakes for breakfast,' she said, bouncing a little on the spot.

'Will you still make them if I tell you I had a bowl of cereal for breakfast an hour ago?'

'Aw.' Free was disappointed. 'I should have set an alarm. Are you even hungry?'

'I'm always hungry when it involves pancakes.'

'Good. We'll call it brunch for you and Dad, breakfast for me.'

When she grabbed her phone to look up the ingredients required for pancakes, Free discovered several missed calls from Beth.

'Uh-oh,' she said. 'I'd better call Beth first. Back in two minutes.'

She went onto the patio and dialled Beth. Her sister answered immediately, sounding cross and flustered.

'What's wrong?' Free asked.

'What's *wrong*!' spluttered Beth. 'I'll tell you what's wrong. I called Dad this morning and he told me Finn Kelly is spending the weekend with you at Paterson Downs.'

Free was silent, processing Beth's anger.

'Free?' Beth spoke sharply. 'Is this the same guy we talked about? The one who screwed you over, pretending to be interested, and then fobbed you off for another girl?'

'Beth, *no*. Well, yes, it's the same guy, but I had it wrong.'

Beth's voice was sceptical. 'How so?'

Nerves rising, Free launched into an explanation. 'I thought Finn liked me, and he thought that I liked him too, only he also thought I was with Max — the teacher Max, not my cat — and he thought I was unhappy with Max. Not my cat, the other Max — but it turned out my cat Max is also Donald! *His* cat! But when the car got broken into, he was just so nice. He thought Max didn't even care that my car had been broken into, but of course I thought he meant my cat Max, aka his cat Donald. It was so confusing. But we sorted it all out and we both understand now. Straight away he told Phoebe that it was over. He's such a sweet guy, Beth, you will love him. His family are going home to Ireland so he was sad, so I asked him home for the weekend. I couldn't just leave him there, all miserable. He even brought the ute home for me. And you should have seen him in the barrel race! It was hilarious. He was chopping vegetables last night

261

and he told me how he felt about me. We could finally be honest. And Beth, Dad really likes him. He was even helping Dad fix the shower screen yesterday. And right now I'm trying to make him pancakes.'

There was a long, increasingly ominous silence. 'Freya Paterson, you don't just invite random men back to our family station for long weekends. I don't care how attracted to him you are. We discussed this. You understood exactly how bad for you this guy would be.'

Free's temper flared. 'I never said anything like that. It was you who insisted he was bad for me, and you don't get what happened.'

'Can you blame me? What you just told me doesn't make any sense.'

'It makes perfect sense. You just need to listen. He thought I had a *boyfriend*.'

'So he thought you had a boyfriend while he was leading you on?' Beth huffed. 'Oh well, that makes it so much better.'

'No, Beth! Listen to me. He didn't lead me on.' Free sighed. 'It's a bit complicated. I'll explain it when I get back to town. I'm trying to make breakfast right now.'

'Free, do *not* get involved with this guy,' Beth warned. 'I've met his type before. He might seem nice now, but he'll mess with you again, guaranteed.'

Free was furious but gave up. 'I've got to go. Come over this week and I'll explain everything. See ya!' She hung up before Beth could reply and then switched her phone to silent because a stream of texts followed, all dire warnings about men who don't respect boundaries and know how to play you so you feel special, but will — without a doubt — hurt you in the end. Free searched for a simple pancake recipe, attempting to ignore the messages.

The pancakes were more like crepe-pikelet hybrids, small and thin. But drenched in honey and with sliced banana — since there were no berries — they tasted okay. Barry and Finn both said they enjoyed them. Afterwards, they sat in the lounge room to play a game of Scrabble, Barry joining in. Free didn't mind that her father was there this time. She would have plenty of chances to get Finn alone when they got back to Mount Clair. It was good simply to spend time with Finn, and she loved the ease with which he got along with Barry.

Sitting there waiting for her father to play his turn, Free reviewed the video of Kira barrel-racing on her phone, pausing it at the moment Kira rounded the last barrel. She caught her breath. *What a fabulous still.* She took a screenshot and went for her sketchpad and charcoal, sketching in between taking turns at placing Scrabble tiles. The sketch came together beautifully, the motion and drama of Kira and Peanut mid-turn building with every stroke of the charcoal. Finally, she held it at arm's length, examining it critically.

'That's bloody good, sweetheart,' said her father.

'It's amazing,' Finn added quietly, staring at the page.

Free went warm inside. 'Should I give it to

her, do you think? To Kira?'

'I reckon she'll bloody love it,' said Barry. 'It's your turn, Free.'

15

They drove home in Free's little car on Tuesday morning, her new china cat blu-tacked onto the dashboard.

'Bummer it rained all yesterday,' she said. 'I really wanted to take you out to the river.'

'Never mind. Next time.' Finn paused. 'I think you've found a fan in Kira.'

Free smiled, remembering Kira's reaction when she'd received the charcoal sketch, finalised and sealed that morning. The nineteen-year-old had called it the 'most amazing' drawing she'd ever seen, and immediately photographed it, shared it on all her social networks, and then stuck it up on the dorm wall above her bunk.

Free honked to scare a flock of cockatoos off the road and they rose in a squawking flurry of white. 'It was lovely of Kira to be so positive,' she said.

'You've got so much talent, Free. I'm just waiting for you to take the world by storm and your art sales to skyrocket.'

'Hah. I'd need to be a reliable producer of quality art for that to happen. I'm erratic. Sometimes I produce nothing for a month and other times I'll do ten pieces. And of those ten, I'm happy with maybe one of them.'

'You're way too hard on yourself,' said Finn.

'You've only seen, like — what? Two of my artworks?'

'Two!' He gave a derisive hoot. 'Talbot Gorge, which is my favourite, plus the one you did for Kira yesterday, right? But you forget that there are three of your paintings hanging in the guest room at Paterson Downs, as well as your hand-painted tiles in the meals area, and the water tower sketch in the lounge. Not to mention the one I saw at Quintilla a couple of weeks back, at the wedding.'

'At Quintilla?'

'A painting of a horse.'

'Oh my God,' she said slowly. 'That's right. I painted King for Tom, years ago. He kept that?'

'It's in the guest bathroom. How could you not have noticed that your neighbours have your painting in their bathroom?'

She tried to picture the painting of Tom's big horse in the Forrests' guest bathroom. She gave up. 'I don't know. Sometimes I don't look past the end of my own nose.'

'And then there's the tiles and pottery you sell on Etsy, and the drawings and paintings you've posted on your artist page on Facebook . . . '

Free glanced at Finn, stunned. 'How do you know all this?'

He paused. 'Because maybe I've been a tiny bit obsessed with Free Paterson.' He gave a self-conscious laugh but Free's stomach flipped.

'You've been looking at my social pages and Etsy store?'

'Maybe once or twice.'

Free grinned. 'You are so sweet.'

'Phew,' he said. '*Sweet*, not a stalker. I love your Herne 365 Instagram project, by the way.

Your photos are stunning. And I crack up every time I see the hashtag 'no filter'. That's you all over.'

She groaned. 'I know, I know. Talk first, regret later.'

'No, it's beautiful.'

The warmth rose in her cheeks and she tried to curb her sheer, stupid happiness. 'Well, I can't wait to finish the Talbot Gorge painting for you. I feel like I've been working on it forever. I need to start something new.'

'What's next?' he asked.

She considered. 'I'm not sure. I took some photos at the station this weekend that I could use, or I might paint the Herne River. I should try to capture it while it's still in its natural state.' Free sighed. 'Do you want to come along to the next Save the River info session?'

'Is this a date or are you recruiting?'

She burst into laughter. 'Both.'

'Yeah, I'll come along. There have been protesters down at the construction site lately. We've been called in to move them along — several times.'

'Oh no! Why? Aren't they protesting peacefully?'

'Yes, but they're trespassing, and the site manager asked us to clear them out.'

The signs of town had started to appear: the craggy red knoll that gave the town its name, with its ugly metal antenna on top; the information board and the rest stop. Free frowned, thinking on Finn's words.

'But they're just there, not doing any harm,'

she said. 'They have the right to protest against the project, don't they?'

'Of course,' said Finn. 'But they aren't allowed to trespass on the worksite. If nothing else, it's a safety issue.'

'But you need to understand, the dam might wreck the river's ecosystem altogether. For good.' They turned onto the main street through town and rolled past shops, cafés and the pub. Free glanced at Finn. 'Haven't you seen the information coming out from the environmental agencies?'

'Yeah, I have. It doesn't look good at all. I can't understand why the project got approved when it has such a bank of evidence against it.'

'So why are you clearing the protesters out?' she asked.

Finn grimaced. 'I have to. If they've broken the law, I have to sort it out.'

'But they feel like a law has been violated, too,' she attempted. 'There's no cops to stand up for the river — '

'Uh-oh,' Finn interrupted her suddenly. 'Pull over, Free.'

Startled, Free obeyed. She followed his gaze and spotted what he'd seen — two men were in one another's faces, getting aggressive on the pavement outside the bottle shop across the street. A small crowd, presumably their buddies, had gathered to watch the show. The young bloke who worked in the drive-through was on his phone, looking anxious. There was some egging on from the crowd and then a cheer went up when one of the men made the first move

— a shove in the chest. Free gasped.

'Wait here,' Finn said, fumbling with the door handle.

'What? No!' Free grabbed his arm. 'They're drunk, Finn! They won't listen to reason!'

He only paused to shoot her a slightly quizzical look. 'This is my job.'

She might as well have been an insect on his arm for all the power she had to hold him there. He was out of the car door in an instant, stopping only to call 'Lock the car!' back at Free before he crossed the intersection.

By now the two men were swinging punches. Free watched, too frightened even to cry. Finn spoke into his phone as he ran, then crammed it into his back pocket and dived into the fray. Back muscles flexing, he grabbed one bloke by the shirt collar and swung him away, using his shoulder to fend off an attack from the other guy. The crowd booed and someone threw a bottle. It bounced off Finn's arm and smashed on the street. Free screamed and scrabbled for her phone, willing her trembling fingers to behave so she could dial triple-0. But pub security had joined Finn by now, and the two bouncers restrained one guy while Finn clutched the other man by his collar.

She stopped trying to dial. Finn was gesturing, talking to the bouncers while the crowd receded, perhaps wary of getting busted for being involved. Moments later, a police car rolled to a stop out the front of Mounties Drive-Thru Liquor. A female officer ambled over to Finn, smiling a greeting. There was a conversation between the cops and the bouncers, then the guy Finn had been restraining was helped into the rear of the police car. Another police vehicle arrived. Finn exchanged a few cheerful words with the other officers, then jogged back to Free and joined her in the front seat.

Free's mouth hung open.

'Sorry about that,' he said, as if he'd inconvenienced her with a pit stop.

She managed to form words. 'You could have been killed!'

'Nah,' Finn said. 'Those two were just drunk and disorderly. No knives or anything.'

'But . . . ' Free searched for her scattered wits. 'Is that what you do all day at work?'

'No, that's a tiny part of what I do. Unless it's a weekend nighttime patrol,' he added as an afterthought.

'Weren't you scared?'

'I was being cautious, watching them carefully. I've dealt with one of them before — several times, in fact. He's almost always involved in a bit of biffo at the pub on Friday nights. Sarge says it's a tradition.'

'Do you have to make a report or anything?' This was so far out of the realm of anything she'd ever seen a boyfriend do, Free could hardly process it. The image of Finn effortlessly dragging the two men apart was still looping in her head.

'It's okay, my colleagues will take care of that. I'll add my two cents when I'm in later. Those two will just go into the lockup to get sober. Drinking on a Tuesday morning,' he added with

270

a sigh. He brought expectant eyes back to hers. 'We can go now.'

She started the car, letting out a long, shaky breath. 'That was so scary. But . . . ' She thought of his biceps flexing under his shirt sleeves. 'It is wrong that I'm quite attracted to you right now?'

Finn broke into a laugh. 'Not in my book!'

They were home in Marlu Street within minutes. Free had to prepare for her after-school session with the Year Elevens, and Finn needed to rest, since he would be working an evening shift. They said goodbye at the bottom of the porch steps, but several minutes of Finn's kisses got her all heated up again.

'Go,' she said, pushing him away at last. 'I can't have you tired at work, not if you're having to break up scary street fights like that.'

Finn reluctantly let her go. 'I'm rostered on tonight and again tomorrow afternoon. When can I see you again?'

'Any time you like. I'm right next door.'

He grinned and pulled her close for a final kiss. Free went inside and fired up her laptop to check her objectives for today's session with the students — then Finn started to sing.

She couldn't resist. She dashed to the studio and held the jar up to the wall, thankful he didn't know she could hear him. It was a new song — she didn't know it — and he was singing with such beautiful joy that she couldn't hold in her smile. He was so breathtakingly real, with those Kimberley-creek eyes, singing songs that told his heart's story. Free's eyes filled with tears.

271

She had never understood another person like she understood Finn.

★ ★ ★

'Okay, so this one's from Linda, this one's from Colin, and this one's from Enza.' Jay pressed each bundle of paper into Free's hands. 'They all agreed to give you a ten per cent cut and pay the shipping charges.'

Free could hardly believe it. 'Why don't they just create their own accounts with Bostons? Seriously. It's so easy. And cheaper without my percentage.'

Jay chuckled. 'They don't care, Free. They just want you to take their pain away. They want to scribble down a list of wants and hand it to someone who will do the web ordering for them.'

'But — '

'Free.' Jay gave her an even look. 'Some of us hate online shopping. Some of us didn't grow up with it like you have, and don't feel as comfortable with it. Some of us don't feel okay with making online purchases because we don't have PayPal or don't use credit cards over the net. That's where you come in. Please, just do the orders for us and take our money.'

Free found herself nodding obediently. This awesome authority was why Jay was a successful head of a high school art department, she realised.

'You'd better keep track of all this,' Jay advised, turning back to her work. 'Come tax time, you'll need to declare your earnings.'

Free's thoughts flew to Willow. She was good at that sort of stuff. She should ask Willow when she got back from Bali — or maybe even Beth. *Ugh*. Beth. She still had to call her sister back to explain the thing with Finn.

The thought of Finn fired happiness into her heart and dispersed all her worries. Roll on tomorrow, so she could see him again . . .

'We'll start ceramics work this week, and make some practice tiles,' said Jay. 'Make sure the kids get their tile designs nailed over the next couple of weeks.'

'Okay, shall do.'

Aidan came in to the office just before Free went to her after-school session.

'Oh, hi. What are you doing here?' she asked.

'Marking assignments.' Aidan's tone was chagrined.

The tin of old glaze was still sitting on the office bench and he paused to inspect it, making a hmm-ing sound. She braced herself for a critical comment, thinking how his tight face seemed even tighter since she'd knocked him back.

'I still think this glaze would have been fine,' he told her, lifting his eyebrows above those cold, pale eyes.

A bolt of dislike went through Free. 'I did a lot of research on the topic. I'm sure the new glaze will match the clay better. I truly felt a bit wobbly about the old glaze.'

He gave a vague shrug that somehow conveyed deep scorn. 'Expensive way to feel a *bit wobbly* about something.'

Doubt crept in. *Crap*. If he was right, she'd

wasted hundreds of the school's dollars on glazes. But no — *she* was right, she was sure of it. *Remember what Giacoma said about the crazing from the glaze-clay mismatch?* Free turned away and headed to her classroom so Aidan wouldn't see the uncertainty in her face.

Most of the kids already had a clear vision for their tiles. There were a few students who were struggling to settle on a design, so Free sat with them and brainstormed. Focused on the subject and among friends, their ideas flowed. She was impressed with the creativity of the concepts these kids were coming up with. Within twenty minutes she was able to leave them to it, their pencils scratching as they sketched their designs. She checked in with Tia, who had reluctantly relinquished her oil painting to work on her tile design this week.

'Tell me about your design,' she said, peering at the 3D cross-sections Tia was sketching.

Tia flushed her usual pink but complied. 'I'm using my family's pearling history as inspiration. I want to do my tile as the inside of an oyster shell, with a pearl forming. I want it to be really multidimensional, with uneven texture like an oyster shell all around the outside, and the lump of pearl here, and then I'm going to glaze it with luminous colours so it's just like the inside of a shell.'

Free gasped. 'Oh my gosh, that sounds brilliant! It will be challenging to achieve the colours but you're very capable. Watch the tile thickness, yeah? We'll go through some techniques to minimise the chances of cracking during firing.'

Tia nodded, giving Free a shy smile. Free moved on to Cameron, who'd come up with three ideas for tile designs in collaboration with his grandmother, and was slowly getting them on paper. Cameron had the potential to produce something special, but he was a little unfocused. Hopefully, Tia's influence would rub off on him.

Several of the students asked about dropping in to work at Free's place on the weekend. It was odd that so many of them needed somewhere to paint. Didn't their parents support their artistic endeavours at home? She'd been lucky, Free realised, to have the backing and admiration of her father while she'd explored her avenues as an artist.

'You're *all* welcome to come and paint or draw at my place,' she told the group. 'We had four last time, but we can make room for more, no problem.'

Free worked at the school on Wednesday to make up for her Tuesday morning off, planning the coming week's lessons and sourcing a good video on tile-making to show the students. When she got home, she sent Finn a message to say he should come over when he finished work, then sat down to drink a cup of tea and catch up on her social profiles before she did the Bostons ordering. Flavia had updated, and Free knew enough Italian to know her friend was bitching about her job. Devi had posted a video of Si bottle-feeding a new poddy calf. Tom had posted a photo of cocktails by the pool in Nusa Dua, and complained that his 'extremely hot wife' wouldn't let him share a photo of her in bathers.

He and Willow must be home by now. A text message from Beth beeped through on her phone.

Are you back in town?

Free sighed and replied. *I am. Want to catch up?*

I'll be over just after six.

Hmph. So much for having time with Finn tonight. And she would have to re-explain the whole imaginary-boyfriend debacle to Beth. Free went into the studio and escaped into her work. The Talbot Gorge painting was all but done. She still wasn't completely happy with the sky. She frowned over it, dabbing paint here and there. She succeeded in making the sky a little richer but couldn't get the blue quite right. She forced herself to stop in the end. If she didn't stop now, she might ruin it. She stood back and tried to see it as one scene instead of a thousand strokes. If she squinted, she could just imagine it looked like Talbot Gorge.

Free put her brush into the jar of turpentine and wiped her hands on an old towel. It was either perfect, or it sucked. She wasn't sure which. The canvas would need a good month to dry before she finished it off with varnish. She placed it securely on the windowsill. Time to bid that piece of art farewell.

Finn messaged her to say he would be home from work around 8 p.m., and Beth arrived at a few minutes past six. Free poured glasses of wine. She'd need one to get through this conversation.

Beth accepted the glass and said a somewhat

grim 'Cheers'. She sipped and eyed Free. 'Well?'

Free struggled to keep her temper. 'Beth, you do realise I'm an adult, don't you?'

Beth raised her eyebrows. 'I just want to be sure you're not making a big mistake. I care about you,' she added.

Although it sounded slightly defensive, Free could see the sincerity in her sister's dark eyes. Free weakened. 'I know you do. But honestly, I'm okay. Trust me.'

'So, what's the deal with Finn, then?'

Once again, Free launched into the explanation. She was obliged to tell the story twice because Beth didn't understand.

'What about Phoebe?' Beth said when Free was finished. 'I thought you were friends.'

'We are. I hope we are.' She shot Beth a helpless look. 'I don't know. I *really* like him.'

'You'd choose Finn over Phoebe, even though you've been friends with her a couple of years and only known him — what? A month or so?'

Put that way, it sounded dreadfully cold-hearted. 'Finn and Phoebe didn't get very far. They only went on a couple of dates. They never even kissed. Maybe she won't mind that I'm with him now.' It didn't ring true as she said it and Free sighed. 'Look, I don't want to lose Phoebe's friendship, but this thing with Finn . . . '

Beth waited.

'He really *gets* me,' Free attempted. 'And I get him. I feel like I'm inside Finn's head sometimes. Everything he thinks is right there in his face.'

'I know you struggle to deal with people who

lack integrity, or aren't authentic about their feelings,' said Beth, to Free's surprise. 'So I can understand how enticing it would be to meet someone who seems really genuine, but how can you be so sure about him? Some guys — some people — are bloody good at playing a part.'

Beth looked so worried, so serious and sad, that Free wondered for the first time if Beth had ever been stung by such a person. Someone who'd played a part. Was that why Beth was adamant that Finn was out to trick Free?

She made up her mind in an instant.

'I want you to meet him.'

Beth tipped her head. 'Okay. When?'

'Tonight.'

'What, right now?'

'No, but he'll be home from work in . . . ' Free checked the time on her phone. 'An hour and a half. Stay for dinner and you can meet him later.'

Beth hesitated. 'I've got a Chamber of Commerce networking meeting tonight. It starts at seven.'

Free's mind wandered to that unpleasant place — the place where Beth was *close* with the chamber, in the same way Aidan Hamilton's mother was close with the chamber and pulling strings for her son. She forced her attention back to the present. 'Come back when you're finished, then.'

'No,' said Beth. 'These networking things can go on for a few hours. I'll meet him another time. Soon — this week.'

Free nodded. 'Yep. And then you'll see exactly what I mean.'

Fifteen minutes later, Beth departed. Free fidgeted around the house, waiting for Finn to get home. Why did Beth have to fill her head with problems? Free just wanted to enjoy Finn. Anyway, Beth couldn't possibly be right about this. Finn wasn't a player. But Beth was right about so many things in life . . .

The moment she heard a car pull up, she raced out onto the porch. In the darkness of the street, Finn was saying goodbye to someone through the window of a police vehicle, a backpack clutched in his hand. When he turned and saw her, a smile broke across his face. Thank God for him being so readable. Free jumped down the porch steps and bounded into his arms, landing a solid kiss on his lips. Finn dropped his backpack and pulled her in tight, kissing her with just as much energy. He only drew back to examine her and stroke her hair away from her cheek.

'I've been thinking about this all day,' he said.

Every last doubt evaporated. Behind him, Briggsy was staring from the driver's seat of the vehicle. Free waved at the sergeant and turned back to the house, keeping hold of Finn's hand as they climbed his porch steps.

'Want to share dinner?' he asked, unlocking the door.

'Yes. I've got . . . ' She thought. 'I've got eggs. And cheese. A quiche, maybe?'

'I've got spinach, mushrooms and puff pastry.'

'Perfect.'

In fact, it turned out she only had a couple of eggs, but Finn had half a dozen more, so quiche was still a viable meal. She sighed as he sliced mushrooms in his kitchen, a little envious.

'How are you so organised?' she asked.

'What do you mean?'

'With your shopping. You always seem to have so much stuff in your fridge.'

Finn was amused. 'I just go to the supermarket once a week.'

'Once a week?' Free shook her head. 'I'm there every second day, and I still manage to forget half of what I need. Every single time.'

'Do you use a list?'

'*Pfft*. Of course not.'

Finn cracked up. 'Well, then, yeah, you'll forget stuff.'

'I should have been born during the Great Depression. Rationing. I can make amazing meals with just two or three ingredients.'

'Yeah?'

'Yeah. Well, not always amazing. Sometimes pretty horrible, in fact. But still, I've survived this long.' She gave him a proud nod, reaching over to pull the bowl of eggs and cream towards herself. She whisked it with a fork, trying to dispel her worries about what Beth thought.

'My sister wants to meet you.' The words spilled out of her mouth before she could stop them.

Finn stopped slicing to look at her. 'Which one?'

'Beth.'

'The doctor?'

'Yes.'

Finn resumed slicing. 'Cool. That'd be good.'

He looked at her again and then put his knife down. 'Are *you* okay about it?'

Free stared down into the bowl of eggs, asking herself the same question. 'Well, the thing is, when I bumped into you when you were on that date with Phoebe, it upset me. I went to Beth for support. Now she thinks you're a scoundrel.' It was a relief to admit the truth. She peeked at Finn's face.

His expression was somewhere between dismayed and entertained. 'A scoundrel!'

'Yeah. She's been warning me off you.'

Finn couldn't help a laugh. 'I don't think I've ever had that sort of reputation before. This could be fun.' But his laughter disappeared and he caught her eye. 'You were really *that* sad when you thought I was into another girl?'

She gave a lopsided shrug. Finn came around to her side of the bench to fold her in his arms. 'I'm sorry. I hate that I hurt you.'

'We both had our wires crossed. We've uncrossed them. All good now.' She gave him a quick smile.

'Yeah, but it still hurt you. I hope you know it hurt me too. All I wanted from the moment I met you was to be with you. But 'Max' was in the way. I was in hell over it, Free. And the fact that your boyfriend turned out to be imaginary doesn't make the hell I was in any less real. It doesn't make what *you* felt any less painful, either. It's been a rocky road so far, this relationship.'

His words made her heart get warm and tight again. 'You're right,' she said, pressing her cheek to his chest. 'But it's also stranger than fiction.

I've explained it all to Beth but I'm not sure she even believes me.'

'With all due respect to your sister,' said Finn, pulling away, 'it's not about her. Do *you* want this? Do *you* think it's real — I mean, as real as it is for me?'

Free nodded vigorously. 'It's just, I haven't had this kind of relationship before.' He clearly didn't understand, so she elaborated. 'Like, one where I felt *this* way about a guy.'

Finn remained silent, his colour deepening. She pulled herself up onto the kitchen stool and fiddled with a pen lying on the bench.

'The other guys were, well — I could take 'em or leave 'em. You know? They were good fun. Hot-looking dudes, and romantic, I guess — but I didn't *feel* it. Not really. Not like this. This is a first for me.'

He released a long breath. 'I love your honesty.'

She grimaced, not quite sure why her words were having such an impact. 'Yeah, my brain-to-mouth circuit has no breaker.'

'So what do you want to do about Beth?'

'My plan is to introduce you properly so she'll realise how far off the mark she is to suspect your motives.'

'And if that doesn't work?'

Free frowned. 'As soon as she meets you, she'll see she's been wrong.'

Finn went back around to his side of the bench and resumed chopping, his face pensive. 'I hope so, but if she doesn't come to that conclusion, then what?'

Free bit her thumbnail. 'I don't know. I'll just have to tell her to butt out, I suppose.' Did she honestly have the courage to do such a thing?

'I don't want to come between you and your sister,' Finn said.

Free shoved her concerns away, whisking concertedly. 'Look, we don't even need to worry about this, because as soon as she gets to know you, Beth will see how wonderful and genuine you are, and she'll *loathe* herself for ever doubting me.'

'When am I meeting her, then?'

'Whenever you're ready,' said Free. 'Do you have any evenings available this week? Or maybe Saturday morning?'

'I can do Saturday morning.' Finn paused to grab the pen off the bench and scrawled *Meet Free's sister* on the coming Saturday of his calendar. Free looked on, shaking her head in admiration.

'You really are organised. You're, like, a total adult.'

Finn thought that was hilarious. 'I'm buying you a calendar,' he said. 'It will change your life.'

She watched as he finished chopping mushrooms and moved on to rinsing spinach leaves. *Look at him, cooking. Look at those intriguing eyes, that gorgeous smile. Look at that incredible body, those big shoulders, that strong back . . .*

'Finn.'

He looked up. 'Yes?'

She pushed the bowl of eggs and cream back across the bench. 'How hungry are you?'

'Pretty hungry. Why?'

'Because I was thinking maybe we could go to bed.'

His eyes grew round.

'Could you wait till later for your dinner?' she asked, glancing over the ingredients spread across his kitchen bench. 'Because if you can, there's nothing in our way any more. No imaginary boyfriend, no girl you're dating. It's just you and me, and the front door's locked, and if you're able to wait till later for dinner, then we could just go right now . . . ' She waited hopefully.

'I'm not hungry.' His voice was hoarse. 'Not at all hungry any more.' He came around to her side of the bench.

'Are you sure?' she asked.

Finn stopped just centimetres from Free to give her an incredulous stare. 'Are you for *real*? Of course I'm bloody sure!'

He'd scooped her off the stool and taken her into the bedroom within moments.

'You're really strong, aren't you?' she breathed when she found herself on the bed, looking up at him with wide eyes.

He lay down beside Free, his face close to hers. 'I'm gentle when it's needed.'

She bit her lip. 'You don't — y'know — have to be *too* gentle.'

His mouth tugged up at the corner and he closed the distance between them, his hand sliding up over her hip, his warm, soft lips pressing into her neck.

He was gentle, achingly gentle, until Free begged him not to be gentle any more.

16

Finn woke Free by stroking her shoulder, the morning sunlight peeping through his blind.

'I didn't think you could get more beautiful,' he said when she squinted an eye open and smiled at him. 'Then I saw you naked.'

'Mmm,' was all she could manage in reply. It was far too soon after waking up to speak.

'I need to go to work but I didn't want to leave without saying goodbye.'

Free groaned. 'Nooo. Don't want you to go.' Eyes still closed, she fumbled upwards and slipped an arm around his neck, attempting to hold him there.

He chuckled, his breath warm on her skin. 'I don't want to go, either. I don't chuck sickies but I have never been more tempted to take one than right now.'

'Good idea,' she mumbled. 'You're far too sick to work. You need to stay in bed *all* day.'

'I wish.' Finn came close to brush his lips against her cheek, then broke gently from her hold. 'You stay here as long as you like. Just lock the door after you when you go home. Donald's here and he's had some breakfast. He'll keep you company.' She murmured and Finn hesitated at the door. 'What'd you say?'

'Not Donald. *Max*,' she repeated, unable to keep her eyes open.

He made a noise of amusement and left her to sleep.

She woke properly just after ten, Max curled up against her back. For a while, Free simply lay in Finn's bed and smiled, thinking about the night before. Finn was everything she'd imagined and a hell of a lot more. Reliving the way he'd touched her, the sight of him above her, beneath her, and all kinds of other ways, got her so heated up she wasn't sure she'd make it through the day. He could not get home soon enough.

However, having skipped dinner, Free's stomach came to the rescue, reminding her it was time to eat. She got dressed and went to the kitchen. She could tidy up as a surprise for Finn — they'd left everything out on the kitchen bench when they headed for the bedroom last night. But when she got there, it was already tidy. She peeked into the fridge and saw he'd put all the prepared food in there, neatly covered with cling wrap. Even the bowl of whisked eggs.

Impressive.

Free let herself and Max out just as the postie was coming up her porch steps with a box in his arms.

'Oh, awesome, my stuff!' she said, locking Finn's door behind her.

'There're two more boxes in the van,' he told her.

Ah — of course. She had Olly's order as well. The postie helped her cart it all inside. Free made a coffee, forcing herself to hold off unpacking the goodies until she'd eaten a piece of toast. Then she dived in to explore her order.

There was nothing quite like the unpacking of new art supplies. She didn't want Olly to experience any disappointment, so she went through his entire order, ticking it all off. Bostons had never screwed up her deliveries before, but then, she didn't normally order quite so much. She needn't have worried. Everything was there, and they'd thrown in some freebies, as usual. She packed Olly's stuff back up, dropping the bonus brushes and box of pastels into a carton. A quick shower later, she loaded the boxes into her car, gave her lucky china cat a stroke, and headed into town.

Olly was busy with customers when she arrived at the gallery, so she took the boxes out the back and unloaded them all. She was struck by the set-up in his workshop once again: tubs screwed to the walls, huge shelving units and rows of hooks over troughs for hanging brushes and anything else wet. Even foldaway artwork drying racks. She eyed it all with envy as she unpacked. One day she would set up her own art space like this.

Olly came in as she finished up. 'Free, you bewdy,' he exclaimed. 'You put it all away for me, too?'

She grinned. 'I love your workshop, Olly. This is my idea of heaven.'

He was wandering along his shelves and tubs, peering at his new supplies.

'This is magic,' he declared. 'It's like the bloody art fairies came.'

Free gave a laugh of delight. 'I loved doing

this. Any time, seriously.'

'Book it in, then,' he answered. 'Once a month. You come in, take stock, reorder, then deliver and restock my shelves.'

'Really?'

'Bloody oath, chick.'

Free felt like she floated all the way home. This ordering work was brilliant. But more importantly, she had spent a heavenly night in bed with a man so wonderful she had never even imagined he might exist. Could life get any more perfect?

She did some lesson planning, then browsed her phone gallery, reviewing photos from the weekend at the station, looking for a good one of the Herne River. She stumbled across one with a close shot of some horsehair stuck on barbed wire in sharp focus against a background of blurry green and red, the river a blue streak in the distance. Free couldn't resist, and before she knew it, she'd started a new painting. This one was big — a landscape canvas over a metre wide that she'd had sitting there for months.

She heard Finn get home at four in the afternoon. Free shoved her brushes in the turpentine jar and ran over to his place.

Finn's tired face brightened when he opened his door to her. 'I was going to come over to see *you*. I just wanted to get changed first.'

'I couldn't wait that long.'

She stepped inside, Max trotting at her feet. Finn closed her in his arms, giving her a long kiss that wandered from her lips, down her cheeks and neck. Free hung from his powerful shoulders, glorying in the sensation.

'Hey,' she said. 'We have the easiest dinner ever tonight. Everything's whisked and chopped in your fridge, ready to go.'

'Yeah, I rescued it all last night after you went to sleep.'

'I know. You're the best.'

She told him about her delivery to Olly, lingering over the fabulous workshop set-up.

'He said it was like the art fairies had been after I'd unpacked everything,' she finished, grinning at the memory.

'This is a great opportunity,' Finn said. 'You could build your own business on this. You could even call it The Art Fairy. Have you set up a schedule?'

'Hmm?'

He elaborated. 'Have you scheduled a regular visit to Olly's gallery?'

'Yes, I told him I'd come every month.'

'So, you'll go see him this time next month? On the . . . ' Finn checked his phone for the date. 'On the seventh of each month, or the first Thursday, or whatever?'

She considered it. 'Yeah, the first Thursday makes sense.' An idea occurred to her. 'Hey, I should set up a monthly reminder in my phone. Just in case I forget.'

'If it was me, I'd definitely need a reminder of some sort,' he said.

Free pulled out her phone and set up a recurring reminder. 'You don't even need to buy me a calendar,' she said, feeling rather smug. 'Check me out, setting up a reminder. Beth would be so proud.'

Finn laughed and got himself a can of cider, offering Free one as well. She accepted, although she wasn't a fan of sweet drinks. She sipped, examining Finn as he put his phone and wallet away, then he disappeared into his bedroom for a few minutes. He reappeared in a T-shirt and shorts. Was he a little quieter than usual? He dropped onto the couch beside her and grabbed his cider off the coffee table, taking a swig.

'Are you okay?' she asked.

He gave her a big smile. 'I spent last night with the most amazing, beautiful woman in the world. How could I not be okay?'

'It's just, you're not quite . . . yourself.' She studied him. No, he was certainly not himself. Those Kimberley-creek eyes were not sparkling like they normally did. They were troubled.

'I'm just tired. I stayed up pretty late last night.' He caught her eye and winked.

'Because you were tidying the kitchen?'

Finn dissolved into laughter. 'Yeah, okay. I did get up to tidy the kitchen. You'd been asleep for a while.'

That was probably true. 'Why weren't you asleep?' she asked.

Finn stretched out, propping his feet up on the coffee table, and put out an arm so she could curl up against him.

'I watched you sleep,' he said. 'The hall light was coming through the door, shining over you. You looked like an angel, lying there. I couldn't get over it.' Finn stopped.

Free hoped he wouldn't look at her face. Tears

had filled her eyes and were threatening to spill over.

'It was good,' he added. 'All good feelings.'

There was more to it. Free was sure. 'What happened today?'

She felt his sigh, rather than hearing it. 'Not a great day. I attended a family violence situation. Repeat offenders.'

'What happened?'

'Parents not looking after their kids properly. It was their last chance. They'll probably lose the kids for good now, and I don't know how to feel about it. I don't want those kids to suffer in that household, but they didn't want to go with the child services worker. They love their mum and dad — and that shitty environment is just what they know. It's what they're used to. It's a bloody horrible situation. They all love each other but they're a mess as a family.'

'Oh no. Can't someone work with the parents to help them do better?'

'That's been tried. Social worker visits, an order to attend parenting classes — they never turned up — even temporary foster care. But those kids are getting exposed to drugs and violence on a daily basis — and God knows what else.'

'Oh wow,' Free breathed. 'I didn't realise it was that bad. The kids need to be made safe.'

'Exactly.' Finn gazed at his hands. 'It sucks that they're being split up, though. The kids were screaming and crying, 'Mummy, Mummy'. They didn't care about the problems — they just wanted to be with their mum and dad. The parents were screaming too. It . . . it rattled me.'

Her heart was at war with itself. Her first instinct was to see the children safe — but how could anyone split up a family like that?

'I don't know how you did it,' she said. 'I couldn't have.'

He shook his head. 'I had to. We had a court order from Child Protection.'

Free stayed still against Finn, deeply unsettled by the story. She felt another inaudible sigh from him and the weight of his sadness hit her. Her tears dripped onto his arm.

'Free?'

Finn's finger touched her chin and he lifted her face so he could see her better.

'Leaky eyes,' she said quickly, wiping her cheeks.

His sorrow seemed to fade and he kissed her softly. 'Holy shit, you're special.'

Beth was going to be mortified when she realised how wrong she'd been about Finn.

★ ★ ★

Beth arrived at Free's place promptly at eleven on Saturday morning. Free messaged Finn to come over and join them, but before she even hit send, she had another knock at her door.

'Will! Dad!' Free stared at them both. 'What are you doing here?'

Willow gave her a hug. 'Dad and I went to the wildlife impact session about the dam. I thought you were coming too, Free?'

'Was that this morning?' Free slapped her

292

forehead. 'Good Lord, I'm such a moron! I completely forgot.'

'Never mind. It was a good session, though. There's another public protest coming up — I'll flick you the details. Tom's gone to visit Briggsy this morning, so Dad and I thought we'd swing by to check out your place while we're here.'

'Thought I'd better make sure you're not living in some shithole, sweetheart,' their father added.

Free stepped back to let them inside and Willow went over to kiss Beth on the cheek. 'I saw the Beast out the front. How's work?'

'Busy,' said Beth. 'As always.'

'Well, well!' Barry was looking around. 'It's a pretty smart place you've got here. Good aircon, isn't it?'

'Yes! It's great,' said Free.

'And good security?' By now he'd kissed Beth as well, and was inspecting the screen door. 'Is this lock working?'

'Yep.' *When I remember to lock it!* she thought guiltily — although she hadn't forgotten since the car break-in. 'Come and see my studio, Dad.'

Her father was full of praise for the lino mat Finn had laid down and Willow admired Free's latest painting — the horsehair one — for several minutes.

'You just keep getting better, Free,' she said, as Barry and Beth went back to the kitchen. 'I love this. Even the photo you're working from is amazing. Did you take it?'

'Yeah, at the station on the weekend.'

Willow shot her a cheeky smile. 'Speaking of

the weekend, will a certain lonely constable be joining us for a cuppa this morning?'

Free rolled her eyes. 'Good news travels fast around here. Did Dad tell you about Finn staying with us on the weekend?'

'Of course he did. And Beth's been in my ear. She has a few reservations about him . . . '

Free sighed. 'She was the wrong person to spill my guts to when Finn and I had our wires crossed.'

'She just cares about you.'

Yep. Beth cared about her in the same way a parent hovered over a toddler with a cup of juice, just waiting for it to spill.

'You know she'd do anything to see you happy,' Willow added.

That brought back Free's uneasy feelings about Beth's influence on her residency contract. She exorcised the thought, leading the way out to the kitchen.

'How was Bali?' she asked.

'Really good. Fascinating place. The scenery was incredible.'

'Did you visit Kintamani?'

'Are you out of teabags, Free?' Beth was checking the pantry shelves as they arrived in the kitchen.

Crap. 'Hold on.' Free zipped out the front door and met Finn just as he was emerging from his place. 'Teabags?' she said breathlessly.

He nodded and went back in. He returned a moment later with a box of teabags and a packet of biscuits. Free seized him for a hasty kiss.

'Um, Finn . . . Dad and Willow are here too.'

To her astonishment, Finn looked unfazed. 'Cool,' he said, following her inside.

Barry greeted him in a friendly manner. There was silence while her sisters both carried out a not-so-furtive examination.

Free cringed. 'Willow, you know Finn, and Beth, I think you met him at the wedding.'

'Yes, briefly.' Beth gave him a composed smile. 'You live next door, I believe?'

'That's right, in 17B. Free's place was vacant for a couple of months, but when she moved in I knew it'd be either another copper, a teacher or a nurse.'

'And instead you got Free.' Willow said.

'None of the above,' Free joked.

Her voice sounded tight in her own ears. She glanced at Beth, but could read nothing from her sister's polite making-acquaintances face. *Gah.* She busied herself with the kettle and cups, horribly conscious of the unwashed dishes in her sink. *Jesus.* She really needed to grow up.

'Sorry about the mess,' she said as she placed cups of tea on the table for Beth and her father. 'Willow, you probably want a coffee, right?'

'Yes, but I can do it.' Willow headed for the kitchen, which left Free with nothing to do except join them at the table.

'Finn, you don't drink tea or coffee?' Beth inquired.

Shit! In her nervousness, Free had forgotten to ask him. But Finn — thank heavens — was shaking his head. 'Not right now. I just had a coffee. I might have a bickie, though.' He tore

295

open the packet and offered biscuits to Barry and Beth.

'How long have you been a police officer?' Beth asked.

'About two and a half years. I did my probation in Perth.' He shot a small smile at Free and she tried to relax. *He's perfectly capable of impressing my family.* 'Then I came to Mount Clair last November. Fantastic town.'

'Free says your family are moving overseas,' said Beth. 'That must be hard.'

Free frowned at Beth to let her know this was not a good topic for discussion. Beth ignored her.

'Yeah.' Finn glanced down. 'Yeah, it's not great. Life goes on, though, I suppose.'

'Ireland, didn't you say, sweetheart?' Barry addressed this to Free. She nodded. 'Are they emigrating?' he asked Finn.

'Returning.'

Barry grinned. 'You're a Paddy, are you, mate?'

Free jumped up. 'Willow, Beth, Dad, come see the backyard. I forgot to show you.'

Her father rose obediently but Beth just flicked her a look. 'I've seen it.'

'I'll have my coffee first,' Willow said.

Barry thought that was a good idea and sat back down. Free sank into her chair. This could not be worse. Beth was asking Finn painful questions and her father was teasing him about being Irish. She had never thought her family would embarrass her in front of a boyfriend but here they were, mastering it like they'd been in training for years. The sudden arrival of footsteps and voices on the porch was a welcome reprieve.

'Who's this now?' she gasped, scrambling up again.

It was Tom and Briggsy.

'Hey, Free.' Tom gave her a hug. 'Cool place! I went round to see *this* bloke' — he indicated Briggsy — 'but Kate had her girlfriends over for some sort of party-plan thing, so we made an escape.'

'How're you going, Free?' Briggsy landed a scratchy, bearded kiss on her cheek.

'Good! Come in. Cuppa?'

'Morning, Kelly,' Briggsy addressed Finn. 'Fancy meeting you here.'

Finn nodded, his cheeks reddening a little. 'Sarge. Tom.'

'You got any coffee, Free?' Tom asked.

There was no more room at the table, so the couch filled up and the party instantly became much more relaxed. Tom was full of stories about Bali, and Willow interjected with occasional corrections when he became inclined to embellish. Briggsy could talk too, and Barry was giving them both a run for their money.

'Oh.' Tom sat up suddenly, putting his coffee cup on the table. 'Check it out, Free.' He pulled up his T-shirt sleeve and revealed a fresh tattoo, still red around the edges.

'Oh wow, you did it!' Free went over to inspect it more closely. It was a little blue shape, only a few centimetres long. 'Is that . . . ' She squinted, trying to work it out. 'Is it a sitar?'

'A *sitar?*' Tom looked scandalised and Willow burst into laughter.

'I told you,' she said to him.

'Don't worry, Tom,' Beth called from the table. 'I can see what it's supposed to be. A soup ladle, right?'

He scowled at her but his eyes were twinkling. 'Ha-ha. You all know perfectly well it's a banjo.'

'Ohhh,' said Free, recognising it now. 'Oh yeah, I see it! That's super cute.'

'He should have got *you* to design it,' Willow said to her. 'I told him it wasn't a good idea when the tattooist didn't even know what a banjo was, and Tom had to google it to show him.'

Tom was attempting to peer at his own shoulder. 'You lot are bloody blind. It looks just like what it is.'

'It's such a sweet gesture,' Free told him, but she couldn't help giggling a little.

'I know a good tattoo artist in town,' Briggsy informed Tom. 'Let me know when you're ready to get it touched up so it resembles what it's supposed to.'

Tom muttered balefully as he retrieved his coffee. Free noticed Briggsy had Kate's name tattooed on his forearm. *Hmm, not good, considering the stress in their relationship. He might have to get it removed or covered if they split . . .*

She was brought back to the present by yet another knock at the door.

'Jesus H Christ, Free,' said her father. 'It's like bloody Hay Street in here.'

This time it was Cameron, Tia and Jorja. 'Oh, hi, guys,' she said, pulling the door open.

'She's got visitors, see?' Tia murmured to Cameron, her cheeks flushed.

'Want us to bugger off, Miss Patz?' Cameron asked.

'Of course not! Come in. Cam, just set up the card table in the studio, will you? You know where everything is, right?'

They did. They passed through the crowded living room, Tia still pink-cheeked, her eyes glued to the floor.

'Who are they?' Beth asked Free, dropping her voice.

'Students. They come around to paint on the weekends sometimes.'

'Why?'

Free shrugged, but couldn't think of one simple answer. 'Why not?'

'That's so *you*, Free,' Willow said, smiling, and Beth was chuckling too.

'So, when's the dam protest?' Free asked Willow.

'Thursday afternoon.'

Briggsy's eyebrows shot up. 'You lot aren't getting involved in *that*, are you?' He looked at Tom. 'It's been a bit fraught.'

'What do you mean?' asked Willow.

'We've had to clear the protesters off the site a few times,' he said. 'Getting rough and rowdy.'

'Some of them have targeted the workers,' Finn put in. 'Chucking bottles at them and things like that.'

'Oh no,' said Free. 'That can't be right. I went

299

to the last protest and it was completely peaceful. We just chanted and sang and held up signs, and the woman in charge spoke to the ABC news people. It was awesome.'

'Well, there are some protesters down there every day now, and they're misbehaving,' Briggsy told her.

'Bugger,' said Willow. 'That's not going to do the cause any favours.'

'Maybe the construction company is reporting that kind of thing to the police because they want to get rid of the protesters,' Free said with sudden horror. 'Making up lies about them to get them moved out!'

Briggsy was sceptical. 'There are some known troublemakers involved.'

Free found it difficult to believe. Briggsy was such a hardened cop, she thought, he probably tended to think the worst about people.

Her guests hung around for a while longer, but it ticked past lunchtime and Barry said he felt like a pub meal. He also wanted to go to the hardware shop for some 'garden choppers' before they did the drive back to Patersons. Everyone left, even Beth. Free waved them off, standing on the porch with Finn.

Beth was so damn hard to read. Did she like Finn or not? Was she convinced now?

'Your family's a really good bunch,' Finn said, leaning against the porch railing as the last car pulled away. 'Beth is nice. She didn't seem to have a problem with me after all — don't you reckon?'

'Yeah, I think so. I mean, not. I think not. I

don't think she had a problem.'

Finn tilted his head. 'Right. So . . . maybe she did?'

'Why would she?' Free flicked a dead beetle off her porch rail. 'She'd have to be insane not to like you.'

Finn looked at her with those honest eyes, which had only ever said exactly what he thought.

Free cast all doubt out of her heart. 'Anyway, who cares? She'll have to get used to you, no matter what.' She stretched up on her toes to kiss his lips.

'Miss Patz.' Cameron's voice broke the moment. 'Have you got some kitchen towel or something? We, uh, kinda spilled something.'

She ran to assist. Finn joined them a moment later with some Chux wipes to help sop up the turpentine that had tipped onto the table and the lino mat.

Cameron stared at Finn. 'You're a copper, aren't you?'

'Yeah, I am.'

'I saw you at the youth centre talk the other day.'

'Oh yeah.' Finn smiled at him. 'What did you think?'

Cameron shrugged, his face distrustful. 'We've heard it all before.'

Finn nodded. 'I think we need a new approach to drugs ed. What do you reckon would work?'

Cameron had clearly been raised to consider police the enemy. He shrugged again, but it wouldn't be Cameron if he stayed silent for long, and within moments he was talking.

'You gotta get to the kids younger. I'm sixteen. I'd seen more stuff than you guys talked about by the time I was twelve. You can't shock us. If you wanna educate the kids before they start, you gotta be talking to the six-, seven-, eight-year-olds.'

Finn paused in his cleaning. 'There's been talk about an early intervention program with primary kids, with older kids as mentors. We're looking for teens who keep themselves out of trouble to work with the little kids. Do you know anyone like that?'

When Cameron didn't answer straight away, Tia nudged him.

'I've stayed out of trouble,' he admitted.

'What do you reckon? Do you get along with younger kids?'

'You'd be perfect for that, Cam,' Tia said.

Cameron shrugged again, but there was a sheen in his eyes that told Free he was flattered — and interested. She smiled at Finn.

They left the students to it and went back to their coffees, where Free quietly filled Finn in on Cameron's background — his brothers' troubles and his mother's determination to keep him on the straight and narrow. Finn's face became bright.

'He's exactly the sort of kid we need for this new program. I'll tell Narelle about him — she's our community officer putting together the program. She'll be stoked.'

'I'm so glad you're here in Mount Clair,' Free told him. 'Apart from being hot, you're the kind of cop who'll make a real difference.'

He grinned. 'But mostly because I'm hot, right?'

'Definitely.'

17

To Free's dismay, Briggsy was right. The dam protesters were garnering more news coverage every day — and not because of what the project was doing to the river ecosystem. They had been caught trying to climb fences to get into the machinery lot, vandalising signage and even throwing rotten food at the workers. Each morning she read about it on her phone before work. Why didn't the protesters understand that they could hurt the anti-dam movement with this kind of behaviour?

She did the drive to the construction zone for Thursday's rally and spotted Tom's 4WD parked on the side of the road. Free pulled in behind it. Even at a distance, it was plain that this protest was more vocal than the one she'd been to before. She approached the ringlock fence around the site, where earthmovers and diggers were parked for the night in the red mud beyond. The crowd waved signs and chanted, their energy high.

Save the Herne!

Irrigation today — Devastation tomorrow!

Think future not dollars

Buildplex = Land Rapists

Hamilton OUT!

'What do we want?' a woman was shouting.

'Buildplex out!' screamed the crowd.

'When do we want it?'

'NOW!'

Wow. Free scoured the crowd for her sister and spotted her at last, standing with Tom beside the fence, a slight distance from the main crowd. Free made a dash through the throng to join them, hugging them both in greeting.

'This is pretty wild,' she said over the noise.

'Yeah, it's ramping up.' Tom's eyes were bright with interest. 'Good to see people getting behind the cause.'

'They should be focusing on the river, though.' Willow chewed a nail, her dark eyes worried. 'Not screaming about Buildplex. If Buildplex weren't doing it, some other company would be. It's the Department of Infrastructure we should be trying to get through to.'

'In the end, I suppose it doesn't really matter who they're screaming about,' Tom said. 'If it gets on the news, it raises awareness.'

'Look.' Free had spotted cameras and microphones. 'That's the ABC radio woman. And there's the local newspaper guy.'

The protest's spokeswoman made a speech to the media about corruption in the government planning department and then went into a rant about the Buildplex construction company's lack of ethics. The crowd cheered each statement of condemnation and shouted 'Shame!' whenever the Hamilton name was mentioned. Willow and Free exchanged glances.

'What the hell are we even demonstrating against here?' Willow murmured.

Tom wore a frown too. 'The protest's angle has certainly shifted,' was his remark.

305

To their relief, an environmental scientist was in the crowd, and the ABC reporter interviewed him as well. That moved the protest back onto the ecological issues. But there were still a number of people in the crowd shouting angrily about Buildplex and Amanda Hamilton. As soon as the reporters left, Willow tugged on Free's hand.

'Let's go,' she said. 'I don't like listening to that woman squawking on about Buildplex. Yeah, they've got a bit to answer for, but they're not the main problem. Let's get out of here before the police arrive.'

'Okay,' Free agreed.

Finn was rostered on right now, she recalled. Hopefully, he wouldn't be called out to deal with the more rambunctious protesters. As a supporter of the anti-dam movement, he would surely be torn between his job and his conscience. She followed her sister and Tom back to the cars, where they said their goodbyes.

'I'm going to write a post in the Save the River group tonight,' Willow said, her mouth set in a line. 'We need to stay focused on the real issue here, and not turn into a lynch mob.'

'Yeah!' Free gazed at Willow with heartfelt admiration. 'You'll say it so brilliantly, Will.'

She waved them off and headed home, wishing she had some way to help. Realistically, all she could do was share Willow's post. Articulating cogent arguments on political issues was not exactly Free's forte.

Oh — of course! She could share the post on her artist profile! She had over two thousand followers on there. That would be a great way to raise awareness. And there was her Herne 365 project on Instagram. She could use social media to show the Herne in all its glory — the hard, cracking beds in the dry season, and the gushing fury during a flood. She could share her photos along with Willow's words — and then she could *pay* to boost the post so that more people saw it.

Free spent the evening picking photos to create a powerful collection that showed off the beauty of the Herne River and its ecosystem. As soon as she spotted Willow's post, Free shared her photos and her sister's inspirational words about staying true to the essence of the movement — to call the government to account over the Herne River ecosystem — and not to slam the bland corporation which had won the rights to complete the dam project. Free immediately got a slew of likes and comments, so she paid twenty dollars to boost the post.

Waiting for Finn to get home from work, she watched her post's visibility skyrocket. Some of her students were liking and sharing, too — she saw Cameron's name, and Jorja's, then Tia's. Cameron had commented, *I want to go to the next protest!*

Free smiled. Okay, she might only be a little cog in the machine, but this was one way she could use her skills make a difference.

⋆ ⋆ ⋆

Free loved her students' engagement with the ceramics art form. She introduced them to more advanced techniques than they'd tried before, and they made practice tiles to experiment with drying and bisquing. Free tried to make sure they learned from their failures and successes.

'You know how you kept picking it up while you were working on it?' she said to Cameron when his practice tile emerged warped from the drying process. 'That's called overhandling.'

He looked at it critically. 'It's kind of cool, though, the way it's shaped. Twisted like a piece of bacon.'

'It is cool,' she agreed. 'If it was a sculpture, it would be *so cool*! But it's a tile, and it won't stick to the wall properly unless it's flat, so maybe next time try to stop yourself from picking it up, okay?'

'Yeah, all right,' he sighed. 'It's just easier if I can move it around while I do the relief.'

'Believe me, I know exactly what you mean,' she commiserated. 'Choose a smaller piece of gyprock to work on next time, so you can turn it more easily.'

'What about mine?' asked Petra. 'I didn't overhandle, and it still bent.'

'Yeah, but I think I remember seeing you using a lot of water, is that right?'

'Yeah, to make it smooth.'

'It's just, if there's too much water in the clay, it will dry slowly in certain parts of the tile, so you'll get warping. It's like when you get drips of water on paper — the wet bits shrink as they dry, which pulls the whole piece of paper into a funny shape. You need your clay to be pretty dry when you're making tiles.'

Petra stared at her warped tile, her mouth turned down in vexation.

'Guys, it's okay,' Free told them. 'These are practice tiles. This is why we're making them — to make sure our final tiles come out exactly how we want them.'

'Mine's got some fluffy crap stuck to it,' said Ethan.

Free examined his tile, which had dried beautifully flat, but did have, as he'd said, fibres caught in the clay. 'I think they might be gyprock fibres from the edges of your board. Remember how I said to tape the edges? That's why.'

'Huh. I heard you say tape it, but I thought you were just being paranoid and didn't want us to scratch ourselves on the edges.' He grinned.

She smiled back at him. 'No, there's method to my madness.'

They made another batch of tiles and dried them. These were better, with minimal warping. Free got them to make yet another batch and then, when the first ones were almost leather-hard, they used them to practice with underglazes. They had to make use of the school's existing underglaze collection, since the new ones had not yet arrived. Free taught them to wipe the clay dust away with a damp cloth and score in a design with a needle tool. Then they painted in their designs and worked with fettling tools to reiterate the lines. While they were working with the glazes on a Monday morning, she got a hit of the dreadful sulphur odour.

'Who let Polly off the perch?' Cameron held

his hand over his nose.

Free laughed. 'Is someone using the white underglaze?'

'That's gross,' said Jorja, holding her nose.

'Open a window!' Free called to Tia, who was the pink-faced culprit with the offending bottle.

Tia did so. 'Sorry! I really need the white.'

'How we suffer for our art,' said Free. 'I can't wait for the new glazes to arrive.'

'I'd rather change my design colours than smell *that* again,' Jorja mumbled.

But it was abundantly clear that Aidan still thought the new glazes were an extravagance.

'I've had the Year Tens using the existing supply of underglazes on our practice tiles,' he remarked over lunch one morning.

He stirred his chia pudding with a teaspoon and kept his eyes on Free until she weakened.

'How are they going with it?' she asked.

'Excellent. They're really coming along. It's amazing what a solid drilling in art theory can do for an amateur.' He dipped his teaspoon into the grey pudding. 'There's a lot of the school's glaze store still remaining. I hope these new ones you've ordered don't go to waste.'

'Haven't you noticed any issues with the glaze-clay match?' she asked with a pang of self-doubt.

'Not yet,' he said, his tone careless. 'We haven't done any clear-glazing yet, of course. But so far, so good.'

Free bit her thumbnail and stared down at her Cruskits. *Hell.* What if he was right about the old glazes being fine for the clay? Had she wasted the school's money?

'Don't worry.' Aidan gave her that tight-cheeked smile, his pale eyes bright with amusement. He dropped his voice and touched her hand. *Ugh.* His touch was as clammy as a cadaver's. 'I won't mention anything to Jay. It can be our little secret.'

The knot in her stomach tightened. 'I'm pretty sure we really did need those new glazes.'

He lifted his eyebrows with a we-shall-see expression and popped the spoon in his mouth. He used his upper lip to smooth the pudding on the spoon. It was like watching someone feed a tall, gangly baby and Free wanted to vomit.

'Hey, Free.' A young woman — the accounting teacher — stopped by their table. 'I loved that post you did on your Facebook page about the river. It was really inspiring.'

'Oh! Thanks. Um, my sister wrote the words.'

'No, I mean the photos. You've really dedicated yourself to the river cause. I felt quite emotional, looking through those pictures, and I've only lived in Mount Clair for a couple of months. I love that you're not afraid to stick it to Buildplex. Fight the power!'

The woman made a resist fist and grinned at Free. She didn't even notice Aidan. Clearly, she had no idea he was the Crown Prince of Buildplex.

'Hah. Yeah,' said Free, hoping Aidan wouldn't say anything horrible.

The accounting teacher moved on and Free locked her eyes on her lunch. Within moments, Aidan had launched into conversation with the

311

sports teacher about a cycling meet. They chatted and guffawed about their sport as only self-satisfied alpha males can. Relieved, Free immersed herself in her phone messages. It wasn't until she was finishing her lunch that she caught the word 'eco-Nazis' and realised Aidan's conversation had shifted.

Kent, the sports teacher, was barking his staccato laugh, which always made Free think of a hyena.

'Haven't heard that expression before!' he bawled in the drop-and-give-me-twenty voice that Free was sure all sport teachers possessed. 'Is that anything like a feminazi?'

'All cut from the same cloth.' Aidan shrugged. 'The same unhygienic organic hemp cloth, I'd say.' He joined Kent in another hyena bray, like an inferior male attempting to ingratiate himself into the pack.

Free left the table and, for a few minutes, she understood why peaceful protesters sometimes got violent.

★ ★ ★

On the nights that Finn wasn't working, Free either stayed at his place or he stayed at hers. Max snoozed between their legs, apparently perfectly content now that his two owners had worked out they belonged together. Free missed sleeping with Finn when he had to work a night shift. They exchanged spare keys so he could join her in bed when he got home. She loved waking up to find him next to her.

When their days off coincided, they hung out together — long hours in bed, or treks in a borrowed 4WD to explore a gorge or hunt out remaining waterfalls as the dry season took hold. Sometimes they simply kept one another company in between their own pursuits — for Free, painting, online chats with international friends, and ordering art supplies for her customers; for Finn, jogging, football practice, or doing odd jobs around either of their units. He often cooked dinner for them, since he was better at it, although he claimed to love Free's pasta.

It felt so easy. Every now and then, Free remembered that her contract would end in a couple of months and she would have to go back to Patersons. It would be a ninety-minute drive just to spend a night with Finn. She pushed the thought away. *We'll work it out somehow*, she told herself.

The term break was upon Free before she knew it. She had originally planned to go home to Paterson Downs for the whole two-week break, but she put off her visit until the first Thursday, and even then only stayed for a couple of nights. She missed Finn too much. She longed to see his Kimberley-creek eyes light up and to feel those big, strong arms slip around her waist. She drove back to her unit on the Saturday morning that marked the middle of the holidays. Knowing that Finn had to work until three, Free messaged Beth to see if she wanted to go to Galileo's for a coffee. Late morning, they met at their usual table.

Free had barely even been served a drink when it started.

'Do you think this relationship with Finn will last beyond the end of your lease?' Beth asked, her gaze locked on Free's face. 'You're going back to live at Patersons when your contract ends, right?'

'Yeah, probably.'

'He's only here in Mount Clair temporarily, isn't he?' Beth said. 'He probably won't stay here for too long.'

'He doesn't have plans to leave.' Free couldn't help getting defensive. 'He loves it here.'

'Everyone does, at first.'

Beth's knowing face was too much for Free. 'You've still got it in for him, and yet he's done nothing wrong. Give the guy a break, Beth.'

'He hasn't heard from the ex-girlfriend at all?'

'No!' Free snapped, but then she had to back-pedal. 'I mean, I don't think so. I haven't asked.'

Beth raised her eyebrows. 'You might *want* to ask.'

Free gave such a forceful huff of frustration that it caused her to splash chai latte onto her skirt. 'He's not interested in her. He's interested in *me*. Why's that so hard for you to grasp?'

Beth had the decency to look surprised. 'It's not at all difficult for me to grasp, as a matter of fact. I can see precisely why he's interested in you. I just don't know about his staying power.'

'No-one knows anything about anybody's 'staying power' until they trust them enough to find out,' Free reminded her. She rubbed at the stain on her skirt with a napkin. 'Just give him a chance, Beth.'

'It's just, I know you, and you tend to jump into things without fully thinking them through. I don't want you to jump into living with Finn or anything like that, only to have him up and leave.'

'That's totally unfair!' Free tried to assemble a reasonable argument, but her outrage scrambled her logic.

'I'm only looking out for my little sister,' Beth said mildly. She sipped her black coffee and pushed her slender shoulders back a little. 'How's the residency going?'

Just coincidence, Free thought furiously. It was just a trick of circumstance that Beth should mention looking out for her little sister in one breath, and the residency in the next. She made an effort to switch topics to her work at the school, but Beth's words hovered at the edges of her mind for several days.

When Free went back to school after the holidays, the new clear glaze and the range of coloured underglazes arrived. She brought them in and examined them with pleasure, although Aidan, wandering by, looked as derisive as ever. He even muttered something that sounded like 'waste of resources'. She tried not to be bothered by it.

'Okay, we need to knuckle down and get these designs finalised,' she told her Year Elevens during class. 'Do you reckon you could get final drafts to me by the end of the week? I really want us to have some clay under our fingernails next

Monday. If you can promise me designs by Friday afternoon, I can promise *you* that you'll get to skip all your other classes on Monday — because Ms Lincoln's given me permission to pull you out of class and work on tile-making all day as soon as the designs are ready!'

There was general agreement, although some students were less certain than others. Free couldn't help but stare.

'Are you serious?' she said. 'I would have *killed* for a whole day in the art room when I was in Year Eleven. Literally killed.'

Maybe they were nervous about getting started on their final tiles, she realised. They might need encouragement.

'I know you can do this. I've gotta tell you a story. Listen.' She wriggled up onto a high work table so everyone could see her properly. 'Once, there was this ceramics teacher, right? On the first day of classes, she split her students into two groups. One half was gonna be judged on *quantity*. She said she'd come to class at the end of semester with a set of scales and weigh their pots. They'd get an A for twenty kilograms of pots, a B for ten, a C for five kilos, and so on.'

The kids stared at her in amazement and Free ploughed on, realising this could go either way.

'But the other group, she said she was going to mark them on quality. They had to make one pot. One amazing, perfect, beautiful pot. So what happened? This is going to blow your minds, I swear.' She settled on Tia's face. The girl was watching her through dark eyes full of interest and admiration. It renewed Free's confidence.

'The best-quality pots? They were made by the *quantity* group. They were *stunning*. Amazing. Innovative! And it happened because that group, who were being marked on how many pots they made, they were all churning out stacks of pots and learning from their mistakes, getting better and better without even thinking about it. They were practising. They were *doing*. But the poor old quality group just sat studying the theory, and trying to get one piece of clay perfect. And in the end, none of their work was brilliant, because they didn't gain the technical skills. The quantity group nailed it, because they bloody well got in there and tried. They kept trying and doing, and they created some freakin' good art, in the end. But the quality group just sat and worried about it.'

There was silence. Did the Year Elevens like the story? Were they inspired? Or were they calling bullshit? Free waited, frozen in sudden terror. What the hell was she doing, using this stupid story on a bunch of cynical teenagers?

Cameron broke the silence, a grin spreading across his face. 'Cool story, Miss Patz. I wanna do the Herne River on mine. The cycle of the seasons, y'know? In case it gets stuffed up by the dam.'

'Can I do more than one final tile?' Jorja asked. 'Spares, like the quantity group did? I know what I *want* mine to look like, but I'm not sure I can make it come out the same as what's in my head.'

'Of course,' said Free, starting to breathe again. 'Of *course*.'

There was a buzz in the class during that lesson, and the students put all their effort into finalising their designs. More hands than usual went up for Free to come and help. Jay arrived part way through the lesson and murmured that she was impressed with the way the kids were working. Tia hovered at the end of the session, after Jay had left for lunch and the other students had dispersed. Even Cameron, who always waited for Tia, had given up.

At last the girl packed her pencils into a case and headed for the exit. She stopped just short of the doorway and glanced back at Free.

'That ceramics teacher story. Were you in the quantity or the quality group?'

Free gave Tia an apologetic grimace. 'I'll level with you. I heard that story one night when I was staying in a youth hostel in London, and there was this American dude there who listened to motivational podcasts on speaker every night. Like *every* damn night. No joke. I was ready to steal his iPod and stick a screwdriver in the speaker. But one night, one of the podcasters told that story. I don't even know if it's true, but it stuck with me. I went and visited this ceramics master, Giacoma Pinelli, in Italy last year. She was a genius. I mean a *genius*, Tia. I asked her what her secret was and my friend had to translate my question for me, but Giacoma looked me square in the face and said, '*esercizio*'.'

Tia frowned.

'*Exercise*. Practice,' Free supplied. 'I've always done *esercizio* because . . . well, I don't know why. I just need to. I paint and draw all the time. *You* do it too, I can see it in the way you work. I'm not a great artist, but I honestly believe *esercizio* is the only path to greatness as an artist, and I'll just keep doing it until one day I hopefully get close.'

Tia's face glowed. 'Thanks, Miss Paterson.'

Free sent Tia to lunch and wandered to the staffroom to join the other teachers. She reheated her container of curry leftovers and sat down in her usual spot at Jay's table, steering clear of Aidan where he sat with Kent, his sports teacher friend, comparing the costs of their road cycles.

'Not having crackers today?' Jay asked Free.

'No, my boyfriend is the best at Thai food!' Free stirred it with her fork, inhaling. 'This is a red chicken curry.'

'You're seeing a cop, right?'

Free stared. 'How did you know that?'

'Small town.' Jay winked.

Something murmured about 'women always go feral over men in uniform' from Aidan's end of the table caught Free's attention. *God, he's such a predictable creep.* She endeavoured to ignore him, but now Aidan's lunch had sparked Jay's interest.

'That looks delicious,' she said, craning her neck to see better.

Aidan regarded his food — smoked salmon, capers and cream cheese on some kind of savoury pikelets. 'It's not as fresh as it could be.

It's from Marcel's Deli. They're a bit hit-and-miss.'

In her surprise, Free forgot that she was avoiding direct conversation with Aidan. 'Do you order your lunch from them every single day?'

'Most days,' was the short reply.

'Marcel's?' Jay put in. 'Didn't your family's company buy that café, Aidan?'

Aidan shrugged. 'Yes.'

Free thought back to the afternoon when he'd taken her for coffee at Marcel's. That poor barista who was trying to close the café — Aidan must have pulled rank to get him to keep it open for them.

'It's all about feeding the troops,' he was saying. 'Marcel's does all Buildplex's corporate catering locally and supplies the project office.'

'Makes sense,' said Kent.

Jay gave Free and Max a silent glance, then got up and headed for the urn — but Aidan saw.

'Might as well support the businesses that support us,' he remarked clearly. 'Right, Free?'

Free blinked, bewildered.

'You know,' Aidan elaborated, poking a languishing piece of salmon back onto a pikelet. 'Supporting your art materials distribution business with a nice big order of ceramic glazes for the school.'

It took her several moments to comprehend the slur. Free's face burned, her heart pounding.

'I didn't push for new materials because of the ordering arrangement with Bostons,' she said, going slightly breathless.

He smiled. 'Of course not.'

320

'No, Aidan.' Free's voice had risen, a pitch of desperate injustice breaking through. She attempted to calm herself. 'I wouldn't do that. This is a school. Jay *asked* me to order for the school.'

'I know.' He said it around a mouthful of his lunch. 'It's just a coincidence that you identified problems with materials the school already happened to be well stocked with.'

Max had not lifted his gaze from his sandwich, but Free knew he was listening hard.

'I didn't do that — I wouldn't — would never . . .'

Free lost her words. She almost couldn't believe he would accuse her of this. Was there a misunderstanding? She looked helplessly at Max but the biology teacher kept his eyes down. Free glanced across the room at Jay but she was immersed in a conversation at the hot-water urn.

'I swear,' Free said, but she sounded uncertain even to her own ears.

'Are your students ready for tile production?' Aidan asked, quite casual.

She gulped. 'Um, nearly.'

'Good. Mine are too. We can start on the final tiles next week.'

18

Try as she might, Free couldn't ignore what Aidan had said. The rest of the day passed in a peculiar kind of haze as she dwelled on his insinuation. Was she just being paranoid? Maybe his remarks had been in jest — or maybe she'd misunderstood entirely. It wouldn't be the first time.

But every now and then, a blade of certainty sheared through her doubts. *Of course he bloody meant it.* He'd made a completely unjust accusation against her. She drove towards home and it was there in the car that her emotion spilled out. Angry tears poured down her face, dampening her dress and blocking her nose. Part way to Marlu Street, she took a sudden turn and drove the jagged, winding road to the top of Mount Clair. She climbed out and sat in the lookout shelter, staring over the red and green landscape with the majestic Herne River winding through it. Her eye fell on the russet scar of the dam construction site and Free clutched the edge of the bench.

Aidan's remarks were abhorrent. With every atom of her being, she hated what he'd said. She hadn't added a percentage when ordering new glazes, since this was part of the tile project and funds were tight. Jay had encouraged her to but Free had refused. But it was her word against Aidan's. If she weren't quite so devastated, the irony of it would have made her laugh. Aidan Hamilton, who'd suggested their public artwork should celebrate the ecological destruction being wreaked by his family's corporation, was accusing *her* of lacking integrity!

This unfair, awful moment had tainted the entire thing. The job. The contract, the residency, the role as teacher, her part in coordinating a public artwork. Once or twice, she even questioned herself. Had she pushed for the replacement glazes without enough consideration for the school's finances? Had Jay's encouragement made her overconfident — made her overstep the mark?

Screw that, she thought. She wasn't *that* person. Surely she knew herself well enough to be sure of that.

It was an hour before she was calm enough to get back into her car for the drive to her unit. Max was waiting for her on the porch, but Finn didn't appear to be home. Free went inside and threw her gear onto the bed. She was heading for the studio to attempt to forget about her day when Finn's door banged. Free changed direction. Just before she reached the front door, she stopped.

Finn was singing. She needed to hear it.

She went into her bedroom and, flicking the last skerrick of water out of the glass from her bedside table, held it up to the wall. Her heart warmed and the turmoil eased. What was it about Finn's singing that made everything feel better? It gave her exactly that feeling of arriving home, the same peace she experienced every time she turned off Herne River Road at the

Paterson Downs sign. She sank to the floor with her ear pressed against the bottom of the glass.

It took her a couple of minutes to realise he'd gone quiet. It was the knock at her front door that shook her back to the present. Free scrambled to her feet and straightened her skirt before dashing to answer it. It was Finn, of course. She managed a smile and stepped into his hug, only relaxing when her face was pressed against his chest, inhaling his warm, clean scent.

Finn flicked the door closed behind him and held her back so he could see her face. His smile faded. 'What's the matter?'

It occurred to her in an instant that Finn's bad days at work consisted of fights, road fatalities and separating abused children from their parents. Hers consisted of some idiot's unfounded sniping and having the crappiest lunch in the staffroom.

She forced another smile. 'Nothing. Just a full-on day. Come in.'

'Are you sure you're okay?'

'Of course. Can I get you a drink? I was thinking I might have a glass of wine.'

Finn wasn't going to let it go. 'I can see something's wrong. Tell me what's happened.'

Before she knew it, Free had poured out the story about Aidan Hamilton and his insinuations. When she'd finished, Finn was silent, frowning slightly, and she felt ashamed of how petty it all was.

'I mean, I know it's a first-world problem, but it bugged me.' She crossed the room to drop onto the couch.

He came to sit beside her and pulled her close. 'Don't say it's a first-world problem. It's serious. That's bloody harsh, what Hamilton said. And — shit, it's even defamatory, Free.' He shook his head. 'Unbelievable. He's probably insecure because he knows he's in a compromised position himself, if it was his mother pulling strings that got *him* the job.'

'How do you know about that?'

'It's come up in conversation down the pub once or twice.'

'Wow, really?' Free thought about it. 'Has anything else come up? About people pulling strings?'

Perhaps something had been hinted about Beth helping *her* get the job. Finn seemed oblivious to her meaning.

'There's a lot being said about Amanda Hamilton's habit of buying any local business that Buildplex is likely to spend money with. Not to mention the way she fudges her people into important roles, that sort of thing. And the protests are causing Buildplex major headaches. There was even some damage to one of their machines yesterday.'

Her heart sank. 'Oh no. Really? That wouldn't have been the protesters, would it?'

'It looks that way. We're having to spend more and more time at the construction site, checking on things, answering call-outs from the workers. The project office is installing extra CCTV and employing more security guards.'

'God, why do people have to do that crap?' Free sighed and slumped back against the couch

325

cushions. 'It ruins the integrity of the protest.'

Finn chuckled. 'I don't know anyone else who talks like you.'

'It's serious, Finn!' A sudden thought hit her and she eyed him in horror. 'I'd assumed you were *against* the dam . . . '

'I am, you cheeky bugger!' He pretended to clip her ear. 'Now you're questioning *my* integrity?'

Free puffed in relief. 'Sorry. I just thought for a moment you might not be against it, with what you said about the protesters.'

'Well, they're going about their protest the wrong way, in my opinion.'

'Yeah. I agree.' She bit her thumbnail. 'Do you want to come to the next protest with me?'

He pulled a face. 'I'll probably be there, no matter what.'

Free caught her breath. 'Do you mean as a *cop*?' Finn nodded. 'Oh, Finn! Oh no. You'll be on the wrong side!'

'The wrong side? I won't be on any side, except the side of the law.'

'But how can you be there, knowing what you know about the dam and what it's doing to the river — and *protecting* the project from the protesters?'

Finn's eyebrows were knitting slowly. 'Uh, because it's my job.'

'But — '

'Free, I'm against the dam. There are threatened species in danger, and possible environmental issues that haven't been managed properly. But it's happening, and protesters are causing criminal damage to the machinery. It's my job to stop that.'

Free twisted her fingers together. Max jumped up on the coffee table and meowed at them accusingly.

'It's okay, Maxie. We're not fighting.' She looked at Finn. 'It's just . . . it's just, not *all* the protesters are doing things like that.'

'I know. But if some of them start, it can have a knock-on effect when emotions are running high. Others get involved, and things get out of control. Then we're obliged to clear everyone out. That's what happened yesterday.'

'You cleared everyone out?' Free's heart plummeted. '*All* of the protesters, just because some of them were doing the wrong thing?'

Finn nodded. 'It's the best way to stop things getting out of control.'

She thought it over, picking at a nail. 'Yes . . . yes, I suppose so. I guess, with people caring so passionately about the river, they might do things that are out of character. But if you got rid of the ones doing the vandalising, I'm sure everyone else would settle down.'

Finn stared at her, then broke into a laugh.

'What?' she demanded.

'I can never quite believe how . . . well, how *pure* your heart is. You can always find the good in people.'

'Are you calling me naive?'

'Maybe a tiny bit . . . idealistic. I bet you even think Aidan Hamilton is simply misguided and misunderstood.'

'Of course not! Although he might be stressed

out about the problems at his mum's project site
. . . ' she started, but Finn was laughing so hard
by now that she rethought it and realised she *was*
being too generous this time.

Her cheeks warmed but she couldn't resent
Finn's smile. Good Lord, she loved those eyes,
shining with dappled colours that mesmerised
her. He squeezed her close and Free snuggled
into him, their legs crisscrossed on the coffee
table.

'It's amazing, the way the universe works,' she
said. 'I mean, maybe your family brought you to
live in Australia purely so we could meet.
Otherwise, we might not have found each other.'
He chuckled and Free poked him. 'I mean it.
How else did this happen? *Us?*'

'I pulled you over for littering the road with
willy-shaped drinking straws, as I recall.'

Free sank into helpless giggles. 'I'm so glad
you didn't judge me on that moment.'

'I did judge you. I decided you were funny,
beautiful and trusting, and I instantly wanted to
know you better.'

She fixed her eyes on his. 'It's just amazing
how you're living here, in the unit attached to
mine in Mount Clair. Sharing my cat.'

'*My* cat,' he said, but the adoration was plain
in his eyes, trained on her face.

Her heart felt so full she would have confessed
she was in love with him, but Free's voice failed
her. Instead, she rested her head on his shoulder
and waited until she could speak.

'Finn, will you sing me a song?'

He made a surprised noise. 'What?'

'Sing for me. A ballad or a pub song. 'Dirty Old Town'. Or any of your songs.'

Finn tensed beneath her. 'What . . . ' He paused. 'What do you mean *my* songs?'

'I can hear you when you sing.'

'Oh no,' he groaned.

'No, I love it! I heard you the very first day I moved in. Were you in the school choir or something? You know so many songs.'

'My family sings a lot,' he said. 'Whenever we get together. I guess it's an Irish thing.'

'I don't recognise most of the songs but I *feel* like I do, you know? Even before I actually knew you, I *knew* you — because of your singing.' He didn't speak for so long that she eventually looked up at him again, a little apprehensive. 'Finn? Will you sing to me?'

There was another long silence, but at last Finn shifted slightly and cleared his throat. When he started, his voice was tight and unnatural, and Free's heart sank a little. But just a couple of lines in to the song he sounded like Finn again, deep and mellow, singing her a traditional ballad in that warm Irish tone.

Free settled herself against him and sighed with deep, peaceful happiness, all her stress momentarily forgotten.

★   ★   ★

At work the next day, Free wanted to explain yesterday's conversation to Max, but the science teacher appeared to be avoiding her. At lunch, he even sat away from their regular table. Being

Tuesday, it was one of Aidan's days off, so Free could only assume *she* was the reason Max had chosen to sit across the staffroom. He probably didn't want to associate with the dodgy, profit-skimming fraud Aidan had made Free out to be.

Even Jay was strangely distant. The head of art was nodding her curly head, deep in conversation with the health teacher — all but ignoring Free. Was Jay aware of what was being said? Did *she* suspect Free of pushing for the new ceramics materials so she could profit? Maybe Jay had forgotten that Free never took a commission on the *Born and Bred* supplies. Free tried to shake off Aidan's accusation, holding her head high. *She* knew she'd done the right thing, even if other people doubted her integrity.

The after-school session with her class rescued her day from being too miserable. Her students were still buzzing with motivation from Free's speech about quality and quantity, and settled in to their work with enthusiasm.

'Hey, Miss Patz,' Cameron said, pausing in shading his design. 'Are you going to the next Herne River dam protest?'

'Probably,' she said. 'Have they set a date?'

'There's one in a couple of weeks. They're talking about getting some music and big names out there.'

'Yeah,' said Jorja. 'Sacred Days and some didjeridu players, and a dance group. I'm going.'

'Wow, that sounds amazing,' said Free. 'I'll definitely go to that. It sounds really positive.'

Cameron looked a little put-out. 'That's what I reckon. Except Mum says I can't go.'

'Why not?'

He rolled his eyes. 'She reckons there's been mischief at the protests and I might get mixed up in it. I wouldn't, though. It's just her thing about me not getting into trouble, y'know. Not going to jail.'

'Oh, of course.' Free watched him with sympathy. His mother shouldn't tar Cameron with the same brush as his brothers. He was a good kid. 'What a shame.'

'I'm sick of the government fu — ' Cameron stopped himself. 'Stuffing up the country. *Oh, look, there's not enough water because we used it all and oh, look, we messed up the climate so the seasons are screwy — hey, I know, let's make a dam to irrigate, then we can farm the shit out of the region and stuff it up even more.*' He held his hand up and gave himself a goofy imaginary high five.

Free burst out laughing. 'Nailed it. My sister and her husband, they're transforming their cattle stations to sustainable farming. It's awesome, all the stuff they're doing out there. They're training the cows to eat native weeds so they don't have to order in as much stockfeed, they're resting pastures to prevent erosion, things like that. And not using pesticides or antibiotics, so the river can get healthy again.'

'That's so cool,' said Petra. 'I wish my family would do that. It's only the younger generation that cares about the environment.'

'Hey,' Free protested. 'I care. My sisters care.

I've been on board with saving the Herne River since day one.'

'*Pfft.* You count as one of us,' Petra informed her.

'Some younger people care but they don't always do something about it, for whatever reason,' Tia said in her soft voice.

'You've got to act, if you care,' Free said.

'Hey, can't you sneak out to the protest, Cam?' Jorja asked him.

He considered it. 'Maybe.'

'You shouldn't,' Tia said, her tone low. 'Your mum will kill you.'

'He should be allowed to go to the protest if he thinks the dam is wrong,' Jorja said.

Free silently agreed with Jorja but she thought she'd better not encourage Cameron to break his mother's rules.

'What if someone sees you there and tells your mum?' Tia said.

Cameron turned to Free. 'You wouldn't do that, would you, Miss Patz? If you saw me at the protest?'

Free pretended innocence. 'Saw who?'

Cameron grinned and Jorja giggled with Petra. Tia bent over her work but Free could see a little crease on the girl's forehead.

Too bad. Free wasn't about to take it back. She could and would stay true to her values, no matter what Aidan Hamilton or anybody else said.

★ ★ ★

Friday felt so much brighter than the earlier part of the week. Free arrived at the school in a good mood, and even the sight of Aidan's pale, serious face and sharp nose couldn't bring her down. Every single one of her students had responded to her exhortation and completed at least one tile design. Midway through her lesson, Free realised what this meant. Tears came to her eyes.

'You guys.' She didn't even try to hide her emotion. 'You *guys*. You are freaking amazing. We're ready!'

'Have you got hay fever, Miss?' Cameron asked, frowning at her.

'No! I'm just super proud!'

Her reaction set the kids giggling, with several of the girls jumping out of their seats to come forward and hug her. Even some of the boys had the sensitivity to look worried. Tia was too shy to come forward but she smiled at Free from the edge of the class.

Free rubbed her tears away. 'I cannot *wait* to create these tiles next week. Monday, we'll work with clay all day. Your pottery skills are epic, and I don't think we'll have any major problems. And if we do, if anyone really has a disaster, we can do catch-up work after school or whatever, okay? No panicking allowed. This is a panic-free zone.'

The students departed on a high and Free headed for the staff-room. Max sat with her and Jay again this lunchtime. In fact, Max was being totally cool — not at all suspicious or doubtful. Jay asked Free to do an art order for yet another friend. Could she have been reading into things

333

too much on Tuesday? Maybe they hadn't taken Aidan's slurs to heart after all.

She didn't speak to Aidan, but since he was sitting at the same table, Free couldn't help but overhear his conversation. Talk turned to the machinery vandalism at the dam construction site and Free tuned in, curious.

'They've rebuilt the fence a few times,' said Kent, the hyena sports teacher. 'It's getting higher every week, I think! But they're still getting in.'

'What about the security cameras?' Max asked. 'Haven't they caught anything?'

The sports teacher shook his head. 'The protesters wear masks and hoodies pulled down low, wait until the security guards are on another part of the site, then jump the fence and smash whatever they can. It's cost Buildplex tens of thousands already.'

'Tricky,' said Jay. 'I can understand their passion, but they've gone too far.'

Aidan sat listening in disgusted silence. Free was saddened by the protester tale, and was also trying not to stare too enviously at Aidan's spinach and ricotta filo triangles. *Oh my God. Was that a pine nut pesto?* She glanced at her own lunch — peanut butter Cruskits again — and repressed a sigh.

Jay's eyes were on Aidan's food too. 'I think I might start going to Marcel's for my lunches,' she said.

'It does look good,' said Free.

Aidan shrugged and took a bite.

'You're anti-dam, aren't you, Free?' Kent

asked her. 'What do you reckon about the vandalism?'

'I'm really bummed that protesters are breaking machinery at Aidan's mum's dam,' she said. 'They should be sticking to peaceful ways to protest. Always.'

Aidan assumed an expression of cool disdain. 'It's not my *mum's* dam. It's the *region's* dam. My family simply happens to be a shareholder in the construction company.'

'Oh!' Free was genuinely surprised. 'I thought your mum owned the Buildplex company.'

The other teachers at the table looked on with interest. Jay's face had gone slightly pink and she appeared to be holding in her mirth. Aidan gave Free a look of undisguised loathing.

'It's not quite that simple. Hamilton Holdings is a major shareholder. Amanda sits on the board. It's not like my mother is down at the construction site in a hard hat every morning.'

His comment elicited a bray of amusement from Kent and an uneasy smile from Max. Weird, how he'd called his own mother by her first name. Free opened her mouth to admit she didn't understand much about how shareholdings worked when Aidan glanced her way and picked up one of his filo triangles.

'Here.' He flicked it into a spin so it slid across the table towards her. 'I don't want you to starve. It's got to be better than what you've got there.'

Free froze. The action was so derogatory, so impeccably contemptuous, that even Max sat with his mouth hanging open in shock. Aidan might have been tossing a scrap to a dog. Every last vestige of Free's sympathy for the guy fell away in an instant. She straightened her shoulders and stopped the filo triangle from spinning, and then slid it delicately back across the table.

'No, thanks. I'm happy with what I've got.'

He shrugged again but there was a malicious pleasure in his face. He picked up the triangle and dropped it into his lunch box before tossing a banana peel on top. Face burning and too angry to look at him, Free dropped her eyes to her own food and kept them there while Aidan chatted to Kent about their next cycling meet.

19

Free varnished the Talbot Gorge painting and gave it to Finn that weekend. She felt awkward as she handed it over. She would never get used to that uncomfortable sensation that she was imposing on the person to whom she gave a painting. She didn't like creating an expectation that someone display her art. But Finn wasted no time. He immediately removed the photo of his family from a wall hook in the lounge room and replaced it with the painted canvas.

'You can't do that,' Free protested. 'That's your *family*.'

He shot her a cynical look. 'What are they going to do, come over and see it, and get offended? They're in another country, Free.'

'But you had that picture on your wall, pride of place. And now you've just ditched it for the painting.'

'I haven't ditched it.' Finn balanced the photo frame on the television cabinet. 'I've just demoted it.'

'But — '

Finn grabbed her around the waist and dipped his head to look into her eyes. 'I bloody love this painting. That photo was only on the hook because I had nothing better to put there. Now I do.'

He said it in a way that meant *no arguments*, and Free gave up. It did look pretty good up there, as it happened. The colours created a contrast in his lounge room, whereas the photo, nice though it was, had a bland frame and neutral tones. Somehow, Finn made her feel good about giving him this artwork — as though she had done him a favour, rather than the other way around.

At school that week, Free was proud to see her students achieve breathtakingly good results with their ceramics work. They had consolidated their skills to an impressive level, and they all produced high-quality clay tiles that Free felt confident would survive the drying and bisquing processes. As soon as the square slabs of clay of their final tiles were partially dry, they worked on the relief, adding dimension and texture to the tile faces. Jorja was working on a sugar-cane-inspired design, Ethan was creating a tall ship and Cameron was working on three different tiles representing the Herne River, using traditional Jamadji styles. He said he would choose his favourite at the end and give the others to his nanna. Tia's oyster shell with semi-formed pearl looked phenomenal, and Petra, whose family was also in cattle farming, was sculpting the big, soft, close-up eye of a cow.

The Year Tens in Aidan's class hadn't had such good results. His kids were younger, she reminded herself — and maybe she was biased towards her own students. But when she examined the Year Tens' tiles, drying on metal racks in the wet area, she sighed. They lacked something intangible — creativity, or perhaps passion? The technical skill wasn't there, either.

Some of the tiles looked downright amateurish, and one or two might not even survive firing. What the hell had Aidan been teaching them? His students had complained about the number of theory slide shows he put them through, and she'd heard his voice droning away in there more than once. It was very possible that Aidan had spent too much time on theory and not enough on practice.

Free had offered to make the remaining tiles required for the wall, which were to be plain squares in solid colours. She stayed after work on Friday to make a start, and had produced fifteen uniform tiles before she was ready to go home. Inga helped Free place the gyprock boards of tiles on a bench and covered them in plastic for the night. Free would have to come back on Saturday afternoon to transfer them to the metal racks. She washed up and headed for her car, waving to the cleaners as she departed.

At home, Finn came out of his house before she'd even rolled down the garage door. He was grinning, his eyes alight.

'Hello,' she called. 'What's going on?'

'Donald and I have been busy,' he said, rubbing Max's ears where the cat was balanced on the porch railing. 'We've made you a surprise.'

Green curry, she thought hopefully. 'Can I have the surprise now?'

'You sure can.' He came down his steps and met her on her porch.

'What are you doing?'

'It's in your place.'

She raised her eyebrows. 'You cooked at my place?'

Finn chuckled. 'It's not dinner, although I can probably stretch to that as well. Come on.' He nodded at the door. 'Open up.'

She unlocked it and put her bag on the table, turning to Finn expectantly. He took her hand and pulled her down the hall towards the studio. The door was closed, which was not how she'd left it. She never shut the door. Finn put his hand on the doorknob and turned to check her face.

'You ready?'

She gave him a blank stare in reply. He swung open the door.

It was like stepping into a different room. Free's mouth fell open as she gazed around herself. The lino mat was still on the floor but there was a big open space in the middle of the room where before the card table had stood, covered in debris. Long tables now sat against two walls, with chairs and stools pushed up underneath them — like a classroom. Two small desk easels were arranged on the tables — her own, and another one she hadn't seen before. Against the third wall, freestanding brackets were arranged in a row of three, all of them holding shallow tubs tipped at a convenient angle for fossicking.

She approached and peered into the tubs one by one. Her acrylics were in one, oils in another, miscellaneous paint pots in the third. Then there were clay tools and chemicals; brushes and sponges; palettes and pencils; rags

340

and newspaper; her assortment of sketch-pads; pastels, chalk and crayons — all meticulously organised. In a daze, she turned and saw the last wall, the one with the doorway. Her big easel was set up there alongside her set of roller drawers, on top of which was clipped a work light with a magnifier. It was bent at its elbow, pointing towards the canvas on her easel — her work-in-progress of horsehair on barbed wire. And hanging on the wall was a timber board covered with screws and nails, some of which had brushes or tools hanging on them. It even had a little shelf at the bottom, where her jars of turpentine rested in holes cut in the wood.

'Where did you get all this stuff?' Free's mouth had gone dry.

'I picked up most of it from the verge collection.'

'What verge collection?'

Finn laughed. 'The verge collection that's been going on for the past fortnight. You didn't notice? We got a flyer in the mail a week or so ago, too.'

'I never read the junk mail,' she said. 'You can't have got everything for free. How much did it cost?'

'I bought some things,' he admitted. 'The timber and screws for the hanging rack, the tubs. But everything else was free.'

'What about that easel?' She pointed.

'It was in a box, in one of your tubs. Never been opened.'

Could that be true — that she had another desk easel she didn't even know about? It was possible. She had so much stuff in her plastic tubs. Well, she had formerly, anyway. Free looked around at all the new furniture again and doubted him. He must have spent more — must be fudging the truth. This stuff looked too good for people to throw away. She met his eye.

'Finn, where did you really get it all?'

'God's honest truth, Free. I picked it up in the kerbside collection. I've been collecting it all week, hiding it at my place, waiting for today so I could set it up while you were at work. What — do you reckon I've been out robbing furniture stores?' He pointed at the brackets. 'They were outside the stockfeed shop. They used to hold worm treatments for horses. That's what the bloke told me when I asked if I could take them. The two trestle tables are from the Girl Guide hall. They got a lotto grant to replace their old ones. The magnifying work light was from Briggsy. Kate gave him a better one for Christmas. And the chairs and stools were from all over town.'

She scanned the room again.

'I didn't throw anything of yours away,' Finn added. 'The tubs and boxes are all in the cupboard there. The tubs are kind of broken, though.'

'I know.'

'I thought it would be easier for you to work with the kids like this.' Finn sounded uncertain now. 'There's room for everyone to have their own desk space and chair. You won't need to use the wobbly card table any more. But there's still lots of room for *you*, and I made sure your easel is positioned so you'll get natural light through the window. I didn't throw anything away, I swear, Free. I just organised it for you. Are you . . . ' He paused, studying her face. 'Are you okay with this?'

She tried not to cry and failed. 'Why did you do this?'

'Because you told me about Olly's set-up and said you wished you had a space like that. I went and checked it out. I've been planning this ever since — but I wasn't sure how to do it without being able to nail stuff to your walls. We're not supposed to put nails in the walls, so I had to rack my brains to come up with an alternative way to set up shelves and benches, and a place for you to hang your tools and brushes. Then when I came across those freestanding brackets at the stockfeed store, I finally knew how to make it work.' He dug in his pocket for a tissue and handed it to her. 'I did it because you said you wanted it.'

Finn waited while she blew her nose, then stepped closer and stroked some hair behind her ear. 'Free, if you don't like what I've done to your studio, I will put it all back to exactly how it was.'

'Put it back?' Free almost choked. 'No! No, definitely not.'

She broke loose and wiped her eyes so she could marvel at this wonderful work space he'd created for her. Then she wiped them again because they were filling as fast as she could wipe them. She saw herself at the easel, a bunch of students working at the tables, everyone with plenty of room and the equipment all easy to find. She could even put little containers inside the paint tubs to divide up the colours. That would make it easier when she was setting up a palette, and she could see what needed reordering more readily.

The damn tears wouldn't stop. Finn was still watching her, worry darkening his eyes.

'It's perfect,' she told him. *You're perfect*, she added in her head.

Finn's brow cleared and his smile returned at last.

★   ★   ★

The Year Elevens' tiles were dry and looking fantastic, so Free moved them onto the colouring stage. She ran through instructions for underglazing again: a quick cram session on borders and textures. Her students worked hard for the whole session and only three of them declared themselves finished and went to lunch afterwards. The remaining Year Elevens stayed, heads bent over their tiles, working silently through lunch.

When the bell for afternoon classes rang, Free ushered them out. 'Make sure you eat on the way to class,' she called. 'I'll look after your tiles. Meet back here after school if you want to keep working.'

All but one returned. 'Petra had to catch the bus out to her farm,' said Leith. 'She asked if you would pack up her tile for her, so she can finish it tomorrow.'

'Gotcha,' said Free.

She covered Petra's work and carried it to the storeroom. The kids barely needed her, so deeply focused were they on their work. One by one, they finished and departed until Tia was the final student remaining. The sun dropped low in the sky and the cleaning staff finished work.

'I think we have to go now, Tia,' Free said, touching the girl gently on the shoulder.

'Oh, right.' Tia stared at her tile and dabbed a little more underglaze onto it. 'I just don't feel like I've got the colours right.'

'There's tomorrow after school. And I think you'll find that the clear glaze will give it the glossy effect you're after.'

'I hope so. I want it to have all those iridescent pearl colours, and it's hard working with these underglazes. They're so matte.'

'You might prefer to try oxides, going forward.' Free slid Tia's piece of gyprock off the bench and carried it to the storeroom. 'In some ways they're harder to control, but they give you more scope for that beautiful, lit-up glow you're trying for. I think you'd get a kick out of them.'

'Do you use them?'

'I do. I use both. Underglazes when I want a soft, natural effect — they're great for botanical designs or traditional patterns. And oxides when I want something more startling, or to emphasise form over decoration.'

She emerged from the storeroom, opening her mouth to say goodbye to Tia, but found the girl right in front of her, staring at Free with an anxious expression.

'I wish you didn't have to leave,' Tia said in a rush.

Free was too surprised to reply. Tia shouldered her bag and scurried out of the classroom and Free's heart twinged. What a beautiful soul Tia had — so private and introverted, and yet so talented and driven. She was incredibly grateful for the amazing bunch of kids she'd been working with. She would miss them when her contract was up. Maybe Jay would let her come back and run a couple of workshops in second semester.

At home, Finn had his front door ajar and the light on, waiting for her. She could see him moving around the kitchen through his screen door. Smells of garlic, ginger and chicken were wafting through the air. Max quacked at her from Finn's porch and Free didn't even bother to go home first; she went straight to Finn's place and, dropping her bag on the bench near the door, met him in the kitchen.

'Home at last,' she said, stretching up for a kiss.

He raised his eyebrows. '*Home?*'

She caught her breath. 'I mean, I didn't mean — '

'I liked the sound of it.' His lips curved up in a grin, eyes sparkling, and Free gave a giggle that was part joy and part nerves.

They ate teriyaki chicken together, discussed their workdays and planned their next off-road journey for the coming weekend. Free fed Max, and after dinner they flopped onto the couch to watch television. One of Free's favourite reality series was starting up again — the new season of a talent program she'd been watching since its inception six years ago. Finn scoffed for the first few minutes, but before long he was immersed in the drama of it as well. She smiled inwardly. Yep, she'd have a viewing buddy for the rest of the season. Legs stretched out before him, Free's feet in his lap, Finn gazed at the show. He rubbed her feet almost absently. Could he get any more perfect?

'That guy's a weak link,' he said, nodding at the screen. 'He'll be out on the next round.' Finn checked Free's face. 'What do you reckon?'

If Free had been the sort to pray, she would have sent up fervent thanks for Finn in that moment.

★   ★   ★

Free put the final tiles through bisquing. She held her breath along with all the students when she opened the kiln to check the first batch, but every tile except for one had fired perfectly — and that one had only suffered a minor injury. Ethan studied his tile and the piece of rigging that had broken off its sailing ship relief.

'I think it still works,' was his verdict, and Free relaxed.

These kids were amazing. So resilient and chilled. She wasn't sure she would have been that calm if one of *her* pieces had cracked during firing when she was in Year Eleven.

The next phase was a breeze compared to the underglazing, since the kids had learned how to use an airbrush to apply clear liquid glazing suspension the year before.

'The dam protest is this Sunday, Miss,' Jorja called to Free as she helped Ethan sieve the glaze. 'You coming?'

'Hell yeah!' Free called back. 'What time?'

'Three, I think. This one is going to be amazing. Sacred Days are definitely coming, and you know the dude from that garden rescue program?'

Free gasped. '*Backyard Revamp?*'

'That's the one.'

'Jared Collins. Oh my God. It was so beautiful when he rescued that woman's backyard — the one with the little boy in a wheelchair. I cried so hard.'

'He's a total environmentalist,' said Jorja. 'He's going to be there too.'

Free shook the sieve into the trough and rinsed it. 'That's awesome. He'll get loads of media attention — the right kind.'

'It's at three o'clock?' Cameron checked with Jorja, and she nodded.

'Did your mum say you could go?' Tia asked him.

He shrugged, not meeting her eye. Tia kept her gaze locked on Cameron.

'You coming, Tia?' Jorja asked.

'I don't think so. I don't think my parents would be okay with it.'

'You need to stand up for what you believe,' Cameron told her, and silently, Free cheered him on.

Tia bent her head over her work again,

Cameron's eyes locked on her. Was something deeper going on there? Free watched them. Tia, for all her dedication, could stand to learn that everyone needed to raise their voice sometimes.

'I'm done,' Ethan announced, busting in on her thoughts. 'Does it look even?'

Free checked. 'Absolutely,' she told him. 'Okay, who's next with the airbrush?'

She supervised the rest of her students through the glazing process and laid out the tiles on racks to dry over the weekend before heading home. She phoned Willow as soon as she got inside the unit.

'Are you coming to the protest this Sunday?' she asked as she dropped cat biscuits into Max's dish.

'I'm still thinking about it,' Willow answered. 'Have you been reading the comments in the group? They're hinting something big is being planned.'

'Yeah, it is! Sacred Days and Jared Collins are going to be there!'

'Yes, I know about that,' said Willow. 'I mean something else.'

Hearing a car, Free checked out the window. Finn was being dropped off by a colleague. He went inside his unit.

'Something else? Like what?' Free wriggled out of her pants and top and into a light dress, manoeuvring her phone through the straps.

'I'm not sure. I just got a weird vibe.'

'Willow, this is what Buildplex wants. They want us to be scared. Intimidation tactics.'

'Maybe,' said Willow. 'I'm just not sure if I'll go yet.'

'Hey, I've gotta run. Finn just got home. Let me know what you decide, okay?'

'I will. Talk soon.'

Free grabbed a bottle of wine, locked her door and hopped over the divider rail with Max, going straight inside Finn's unit.

'Friday drinks!' she called, and Finn chuckled from his bedroom.

'You want to go out?' he called back.

'No, let's stay in. I'll get you a cider.'

'Thanks.'

Finn emerged from his room in shorts and a T-shirt, and she handed him his drink with a kiss.

'Are you working Sunday afternoon?' she asked. 'The dam protest is happening and it looks fantastic. Want to come with me?'

He made a face. 'I'm working. We're *all* rostered on, because there's trouble anticipated.' Finn watched as she cracked open her wine bottle and fetched a glass, rolling his cider bottle between his hands. 'How would you feel about *not* going?'

'Not going?' Free stopped mid-pour. 'What are you talking about?'

'I'm concerned. I don't want you to get hurt.'

'*Hurt?*' She clunked the bottle onto the bench and gave him her full attention. 'What have you heard?'

'Nothing specific. Just that an unruly element could possibly be going along, and they've caused trouble before. Fighting and damage.'

'*You're* going,' she said. 'Why shouldn't I?'

'I'm going because I've been rostered on,' he said. 'You've got a choice.'

So Finn could go but she couldn't? Even though she was passionate about the cause? Free finished fixing her drink in silence.

'Free?' he said.

'I'll stay away from any 'unruly elements',' she said. 'Some of my students are going, and I'd like to be there too. A couple of people have said something's being planned, but why does that necessarily mean something bad? It could be something spectacular. You know — a confetti cannon or a flash mob.'

'Or a brawl.' Finn had his eyebrows raised. 'With tear gas and tasers.'

Free shook her head, her temper firing. 'Jesus, are we living under some kind of fascist regime? There's absolutely no need for the cops to get all heavy-handed — just because they don't want people to stand against the government for what we believe.'

Surprise flickered in Finn's eyes but he kept his composure. 'The trouble is, some people have lost sight of the issue. This used to be an environmental issue, but now it seems to be more about bad blood between corporations and people.'

'Most protesters only care about the river,' she said. 'We're in the majority.'

He shrugged. 'Maybe.'

Maybe?

'Honestly,' Free snapped, 'I don't know how you can do it. How can you stand there at the protests, against your own beliefs, ready to arrest protesters while Buildplex and the government destroy a critical natural watercourse?'

Finn drew a sharp breath. 'That's not very fair.'

Somewhere inside, she also knew it wasn't fair. But she had to get those nagging misgivings about his choices out in the open, or she'd never be able to look him in the eye. She had to know who Finn was.

'You could have asked to be excused from working tomorrow afternoon,' she said. 'It looks like you're on the dam's side if you stand against the protesters.'

He kept his eyes on her face. 'Free, I told you before, I'm not on the dam's side. I'm on the law's side. It's my job to make sure people and property don't get hurt. I can't ask for a day off because I happen to disagree with the project we're attending. The decision about whether the dam went ahead wasn't up to me — it was up to the government. And once the government gave approval — '

'So if the government gave approval for someone to be executed, would you make sure it happened?' she cried. 'If they approved a nuclear bomb test, would you stop people from protesting?'

Finn fell silent.

'Because what you're saying sounds dogmatic,' she went on. 'How can you stand up for your beliefs, or even *have* your own beliefs, if you have to do what the law or the government says?'

He spoke quietly. 'We live in a society with fair

— mostly fair — laws. If someone breaks the law, they should get a hearing before serving a punishment. But none of our justice processes will work if we don't apprehend people who are breaking laws in the first place. I don't decide what's law and what's not, Free. All I do is try to prevent people from breaking laws, or stop them when they do.'

'I just don't know how you can live with integrity, when everything has to be black and white.'

By now, part of Free wished she could take back the whole argument, because she felt like she'd got into a logical tangle. In fact, she half saw Finn's point. But she'd said it now, and she had to face the fallout. She dropped her gaze away from the hurt and bewilderment in his face. Finn stood up and went outside to sit on the front porch. Max gave her a resentful look and followed. Tears jumped to Free's eyes. *Shit.*

She went after him. 'Finn, I'm sorry. I didn't mean to sound so horrible. I'm just frustrated.'

'With me?'

She hesitated. 'With the whole thing. The dam, the river. Not enough people are taking it seriously.'

'Including me, right?'

Tears threatened again. Finn looked up and his eyes softened. He reached for her and Free scrambled thankfully into his arms.

'Please listen. I *am* for saving the river,' he said. 'But I'm a cop, and that's important to me, too.'

'I know. I'm sorry.'

Finn kissed her hair. 'All good.'

Max quacked his approval from the porch rail and some of Free's fears slipped away.

Only a little prickle of uneasiness remained.

★ ★ ★

Apprehensive about causing another argument, Free didn't speak to Finn about the protest again. But when he'd left for work after lunch on Sunday, she pulled out a piece of stiff posterboard and painted a placard that unambiguously stated her position: *SAVE OUR RIVER.* Then she photographed it and posted it on her social media profiles. While she was online, she noticed other protest statements and placards being shared. *BUILDPLEX = NO CONSCIENCE!* And *SMASH THE CORPORATIONS!* Another depicted Amanda Hamilton as Ursula the sea witch on machinery tracks. Free experienced a pang of worry. Maybe Finn was right and the protest was going to degenerate?

She squared her shoulders. If people like her didn't attend, then it would only be the misguided contingent at the protest. She got dressed, took her placard and drove out to the construction site.

Free was completely unprepared for the sight that met her eyes. Cars were crowded along the roads for almost a kilometre away from the worksite, and some people with four-wheel drives were ignoring the roads altogether, going up into the scrub and dirt to park closer. She could hear the noise of the band playing as she walked towards the site, and beneath the music, people chanting and shouting.

Holy crap! Free hadn't even realised there were this many people in Mount Clair. It was bigger than a Muster Festival. She checked everywhere for Tom or Willow's vehicles but didn't see them. Maybe they'd decided not to come after all. Free sent Willow a quick text message to ask, and wove her way through the heaving crowd towards the stage, where Sacred Days was playing. She caught sight of celebrity Jared Collins in the distance, talking animatedly with the woman who ran the anti-dam movement.

The vibe here was positive, buzzing with energy. Warm relief radiated through her. This was incredible. Finn had been wrong. *This* was what could happen when people who cared came together to stand against a wrong. Maybe he would see what true integrity looked like and realise why she had questioned his. She looked around for a police uniform and spotted a couple of cops standing beside their patrol car watching the proceedings, but she couldn't see Finn anywhere.

Someone in the crowd was waving at her. Jorja — and Cameron. She made her way through the throng with difficulty and joined them near the stage.

'Hey, Miss Patz!' Cameron was grinning in a white T-shirt decorated with the words *Jamadjis for the River* in black marker.

'Hi, guys!' she greeted them. 'What a crowd, huh?'

355

'It's huge,' said Jorja. 'Cam snuck out and my big sister gave us a lift here.'

'La-la-la.' Free held her hands over her ears. 'I didn't hear that.'

Cameron and Jorja cracked up laughing.

'You're cool, Miss Patz,' Cameron informed her, which was a high honour for Free. She'd never been *cool* before.

During a break in the band's performance, Jared Collins took the stage and talked about the impact of over-farming on soil salinity and erosion, people cheering every time he paused for breath. He had a *Backyard Revamp* T-shirt on, which Free thought was in slightly poor taste. It made him look like he was promoting his show. He even made a joke about 'revamping' the dam project to make it more sustainable. Free groaned inwardly. *Sleazy move, Jared*, she thought, but everyone else was clapping and laughing. The band started to play again and Free danced with her placard and her students until she noticed Cameron had vanished.

'Where's Cam?' she shouted at Jorja over the noise.

'Dunno.' Jorja was peering across the crowd, her eyes bright with interest.

Free followed her gaze. A different set of noises had started behind them — shouting, banging. People turned around to check out what was going on and the police officers pulled out their batons, heading into the fray. Suddenly, the ringlock gates into the worksite swung open and the crowd surged through. A pair of boltcutters was held triumphantly in the air above the heads of those spilling into the machinery yard.

'They busted through the gate!' Jorja exclaimed.

Free watched in horror as protesters swarmed over the machines, smashing windows with hammers and crowbars, and emptying plastic bags of something slimy into the cabins and gears.

No.

She had to get Jorja to safety and find Cameron. As she had the thought, she spotted Cameron being swept into the machinery yard with the other protesters. More police appeared, seemingly out of nowhere, grabbing people and thrusting them aside in an effort to get to the vandals.

'Stay here!' Free cried to Jorja, and ran after Cameron.

It seemed to take forever to get to the open gate. Someone grabbed her around the waist and she shrieked, fighting against the arm holding her. She turned to find Finn's eyes gazing urgently into hers.

'Get out of here, Free!'

'I can't! Cameron's caught up in it.'

'What?' He couldn't hear her over the noise.

'I need help here!' shouted one of his colleagues.

'Get out of here now!' Finn ordered, releasing Free and moving to help on the front line.

There was so much authority in his voice that she obeyed. But as Free turned to run, she caught another glimpse of Cameron. He was

357

standing beside a machine with a smashed window, staring at a hammer in his hand.

What the hell?

'Cameron!' she shouted, just as Finn clamped a big hand on the boy's shoulder and dragged him away from the machine.

'No!' Free cried. 'No, no, no!'

Someone shoved something into her hand and she looked down to see another hammer.

'Go smash something!' the guy said as he raced into the yard.

Free stared at it stupidly. She was holding a hammer. A metal bar whirred past her line of sight and hit a female officer on the back. The woman cried out in pain. Free lost the ability to make a decision and stared at the scene before her helplessly.

A hand grabbed her arm. 'Drop the hammer. Drop it now!'

She dropped the hammer.

20

Free didn't remember much of the trip to the station, crowded into the rear of a troopy with four other protesters. They were talking, even making jokes. One of them made a crack about 'pig hunting' with hammers and high-fived everyone in the wagon. Free ignored his hand waiting for hers.

All she could think about was Cameron. This was her fault. She should never have encouraged him to sneak out and come to the protest. The vision of him staring at the hammer in his hand twisted her stomach with horror. Where the hell had he got it? Was there any possibility he'd got caught up in the hysteria of the protest and actually damaged the machine? No. *No way.* Cameron must, like her, have simply been handed a hammer and urged to 'smash something'.

The memory of Finn grabbing Cameron and leading him to be handcuffed made her want to be sick.

She was pulled out of the wagon with the other protesters and taken into the station to give her details and await questioning. Briggsy was there. He frowned when he saw her, and Free dropped her gaze. When she checked on him a minute later, he had his phone up — texting Tom or Willow, no doubt, to say that Free was in the lockup on suspicion of criminal damage. Her stomach lurched again and she looked around for something to vomit into. There was nothing, so she took some breaths and willed her stomach to stay where it was.

Finn appeared at her side and bent down to speak in her ear.

'Don't stress. I've told them you weren't involved. You'll be able to go home shortly.'

'I'm okay,' she mumbled.

She couldn't look him in the eye.

Free sat on a bench in the lockup with several other protesters. One by one, they were taken for interviews. After around two hours, it was Free's turn. She was collected by her case officer, a woman who introduced herself as Senior Constable Daphne Laverton. They walked past the outer office on the way to the interview room and Free got a jolt to see Beth sitting there, reading something on her phone. Good Lord, could this get any worse? Briggsy was in the interview room, waiting in a chair at a round table. The woman indicated a chair for Free.

'Miss Freya Paterson.' Briggsy's dark eyes were unreadable. 'What have you got yourself into this time?'

She didn't have an answer.

'Senior Constable Laverton is going to ask you a few questions,' he went on. 'Hopefully, we can work out what went on today.'

The officer ran through some formalities with Free, ensuring she understood she wasn't under arrest and that the interview would be video-recorded, then double-checking her address and personal details. Then she sat with her sharp eyes trained on Free.

'So, you went to the dam protest this afternoon. Tell me what happened when you arrived.'

'Please release Cameron,' Free burst out. 'He's a good kid, never been in trouble! Finn should *not* have arrested him. He wouldn't have even been there except I encouraged him to go. His mum said he couldn't because she thought there might be trouble, and he's got these brothers — only, I didn't believe there would be, so when someone suggested he sneak out, I said I wouldn't dob him in. I should have said I'd tell his mum, then he wouldn't have gone, but I had no idea people would start smashing stuff and Finn would arrest him!'

'Hold on,' Briggsy interrupted. 'Who's Cameron?'

'Cameron Wirra. He's in my art class at the high school.'

'A juvenile apprehended by Kelly,' Senior Constable Laverton murmured.

'He's only sixteen, and he's a really nice boy.' Free stumbled over her words in her haste to convince them. 'I swear, he wouldn't do anything like smash a machine. He never intended to do anything. He only had that hammer because . . . because I gave it to him!'

Briggsy blinked, then covered a smirk. 'Is that right, Free? *You.* You brought along a hammer, stuffed in your handbag, yeah? Because *you* wanted to smash up some earthmovers. Then *you* gave it to a juvenile, encouraging him to

361

inflict criminal damage. *You* did all that. Is that the truth?' He looked straight into her eyes, and although Free attempted to stare bravely back, she crumbled within moments.

'Okay, no — but Cam didn't bring it. I don't know where it came from. Someone gave *me* one, too. Cam didn't have it before, when I was dancing to the band with him and another student. Briggsy, please, please let him go.'

'We need to process young Cameron just like we're processing everyone else,' he told her. 'All you need to do right now, Free, is answer Laverton's questions and tell us what happened. *We'll* worry about Cameron.'

Her panic rose but she did as Briggsy said, trying to explain the afternoon's events in a way that made sense. All the while, she grew more and more agitated over Cameron. Would his mother have been notified yet? Of course she would. He was under eighteen. She was probably already here at the station, her heart breaking over her youngest son, the one she'd hoped to protect. Free didn't even notice she had tears pouring down her face until the case officer pushed a tissue box towards her.

At last it was over. Briggsy ushered her out of the interview room, putting a hand on her shoulder.

'You're in a bit of shock, I'd say. Kelly told me what happened. You were in the wrong place at the wrong time, Free. We won't be charging you. It shouldn't be much longer and you'll be released. Beth's here to take you home.'

'But Cam — '

'We'll see what he's got to say for himself, but you'd be surprised what even the best people are capable of in peer pressure situations.'

'No, Briggsy! Finn didn't see what happened. He just *assumed* Cam smashed something. I was watching Cam the whole time, running towards him to get him out of there.'

'The *whole* time?'

She faltered. 'Almost.'

He nodded. 'Don't fret. We'll get to the bottom of it.'

Briggsy led her back to the lockup, ignoring her pleas to listen, and left her there with the dwindling group of protesters. He was right. Within half an hour, the case officer came back to release Free. Her belongings were returned and she was taken to the outer office to face Beth.

Free expected a torrent of questions but Beth simply hugged her for a long moment.

'You okay?' she asked in a soft voice.

Free nodded, not trusting herself to speak. Finn was in the outer office as well, she realised, talking to a woman who Free instinctively knew was Cameron's mother. She broke from Beth's hold and dashed over.

'Mrs Wirra?' The woman frowned and nodded, and Free rushed on. 'I'm so sorry! Cam's only here because of me. I knew you didn't want him to go to the protest, but I didn't see the harm so I encouraged him when he said he might sneak out.' The woman's eyes opened wide. 'I'm sorry, so sorry! He didn't mean to get caught up in the vandalism. Someone gave him that hammer — he didn't have it earlier — '

'Free,' Finn interrupted, placing a hand on her arm, 'I'm trying to go through Cameron's situation with his mum. Maybe save this discussion for another time, okay?'

Free shook him off. 'How *could* you?' she hissed before she stopped to think. 'You *knew* about him!'

Finn blinked as though she'd slapped him. Beth caught Free under the elbow and pulled her away, heading for the exit.

'Don't,' she said when Free protested. 'You're making a scene, and you'll just make things worse.'

Free gave up trying to stay composed once she was in the Beast. She wailed and ranted, sobbed and remonstrated.

'How could he do that? He knew Cam's circumstances! He knew about his brothers, his uncle — and why it was so important to his mum that Cam stayed out of trouble. But he arrested him anyway!'

'Who are we talking about?' Beth asked, pulling out onto the main road.

'Finn! He arrested Cam!'

'And Cam is your student?'

Free groaned and, amid her tears, explained it all again. Beth listened as they drove towards Marlu Street.

'Wow,' she said at last. 'I feel for Finn. That was a tough call.'

Free wanted to scream. '*No*, Beth! Cam's mum has spent his whole life trying to keep him out of the sort of trouble her other sons got into.

Her own brother died in custody. Cam's a really good kid, too, but now Finn's broken all that! He arrested Cam, and he knew his situation and everything. He *knew* he was a good kid!' She sucked in a breath. 'I'm so bloody angry right now.'

Beth turned into Free's driveway. 'All Finn did was what he had to do, and you're blaming the guy for everything that went wrong. Is that fair? What else could he do — ignore the fact that the boy was standing there with a hammer next to a smashed-up machine?'

'I was standing there with a hammer, too! But I'm a white woman who happens to be a cop's girlfriend, so I got off. Cameron's an Aboriginal teenage boy and he's still in jail. How's that *fair*, Beth?'

Beth tipped her head. 'Okay, point taken. But from what you've said, Finn saw you weren't involved, whereas he didn't see the same thing with your student. Hopefully, someone else saw what really happened.'

Free's heart hammered inside her chest. What if *no-one* had seen what really happened?

Oh God. Had she ruined Cameron's whole future with one stupid decision?

Beth stayed for over two hours, making cup after cup of tea, but Free couldn't calm down. In the end she told Beth to go, claiming tiredness. It was as though her brain was running in fifteen different directions — most of which led back to self-reproach. She messaged Jorja to check she was all right — she was — then tried to contact Cameron. He wasn't answering.

She tried Briggsy. *Has Cameron Wirra been released yet?*

He replied within minutes. *Not yet. We've got a few more checks to do.*

Briggsy, he did nothing!

Stop stressing.

How can you say that? Is his mum okay? Oh my God, this is such a mess. Briggsy, Cameron did NOTHING.

Not talking about this any more. Have a beer. Get some sleep. Kelly will be home soon.

She sent several more messages but Briggsy meant it. He'd finished. He meant it about Finn, too — Free heard him arrive home within twenty minutes. When his front door banged, Free froze where she sat at her table, searching the photos on the Save the River group's page for anything that might exonerate Cameron. She listened hard. The vision of Finn grabbing Cameron wouldn't leave her head. Finn had gone inside his unit, but just minutes later he was out again and coming up her porch steps. He knocked.

Free sat still. Max looked at her expectantly.

Finn knocked again, then tried the locked door. 'Free,' he called.

Max's green-eyed glare became stern.

'Free. I know you're in there. Can we talk?'

She wanted to get up, throw open the door and fall into his arms, but it was as if her body wouldn't respond. She had no idea what to say to him. She dropped her head and laced her fingers at the back of her neck, using her forearms to block out the sound of his voice. Max stood at the door and yowled his cracked

366

meow, aghast at her inertia.

'Free, please. You're giving up on me over this?'

This is important, she wanted to shout back. Pain and disillusionment burnt in her throat like an infection, her eyes and nose dripping onto the table. *No, no, no.* The word ran through her head on a loop. At last, after another minute or so of waiting in silence, Finn went back down her porch steps and up his own. His door closed, then there was quiet.

★ ★ ★

Free left a message for Briggsy as soon as she woke up in the morning, demanding to know about Cameron. The sergeant didn't reply. She went to school and threw herself into work just to pass the time. The kiln had been programmed to start up well before school opened, since the tile-firing schedule would take over twenty-four hours. Almost all of the students' tiles fitted inside, and the remaining few could go in for a second round of firing alongside Free's plain tiles.

There was a memo from the principal in her inbox, sent to all the teachers.

Dear staff,

Some of our students were at a diversion dam protest yesterday, and one of the Year Elevens, Cameron Wirra, was detained for questioning over property damage on the construction site. Please discourage the students from gossip and hearsay so we can best ensure Cameron has a fair trial. If any of your students tells you they know something, please urge them strongly to visit me or contact the police. In the meantime, we hope Cameron is back here with us soon and support him as innocent until proven otherwise. If any student shows distress over the situation, we can offer counselling support through the usual channels.

Jorja didn't say anything in class, but the kids clearly knew what had gone down at the protest. The mood was subdued and there was some quiet muttering about Cameron. No-one asked Free about how she had been apprehended or released. They must all know she was released because she was dating a cop, whereas poor Cameron still mouldered in the lockup. Free forced these thoughts from her mind.

'The first tiles are firing,' she told Jay in the staffroom at lunch.

'Fantastic!' said Jay. 'I'm so happy with what they've produced with you, Free. Hey.' She leaned closer, dropping her voice. 'Did you see the expression of interest request come through for someone to paint a mural at the primary school in Broome? On the education department tenders site?'

'No. When did it come through?'

'Yesterday. It's for Term Four. You should go for it. I can write you a letter of support.'

'Thank you so much,' Free said, but it felt

mechanical and obviously sounded that way too, because Jay frowned at her.

'I heard you got dragged into the cop shop after the protest yesterday. What happened?'

'I got mixed up in the wrong group at the protest. I don't really want to talk about it, though.'

Jay made a face. 'Fair enough. Definitely go for the Broome thing, Free, yeah? I'll forward you the email. Just don't mention it to Lord Muck over there.' Jay nodded towards Aidan, who'd just entered the room. 'Hi, Aidan,' she said to him when he approached. 'Free was just saying the first batch of tiles is firing.'

He sat down and unpacked a number of arancini balls. 'Good to hear.'

'We're well ahead of schedule, which is fantastic.' Jay gave them both a smile. 'Well done, guys. It's going to look great for us that we've achieved this so efficiently. YouthArts and the shire will be more likely to want to work with us again on this kind of project, which is excellent for the school.'

'Nice one,' Max called from his spot further along the table. 'Looking forward to seeing the wall finished.'

Free made an effort to engage in the conversation. 'I'll get the remaining tiles glazed and fired tomorrow. We should have more than enough to finish the wall. We'll need bubble wrap for transporting the tiles — lots of it.'

'Yes. And as soon as the shire finishes fixing the tiles to the wall, we'll get ready for the opening ceremony,' Jay said. 'Some of the

Jamadji nation kids are wanting to be part of a welcome to country, and one of them had a brainwave — multicultural *hors d'oeuvres*, including bush tucker.'

Free nodded. 'Great idea.'

'Very *culturally sensitive*,' Aidan remarked with his superior smile.

Jay appeared to restrain a retort. 'We'll invite all the local dignitaries.'

'Like the shire councillors and the mayor?' asked Free.

Jay nodded. 'Anyone who contributed to the project. The local YouthArts rep. The project committee members. The students' families. The Chamber of Commerce committee.'

'And the other teachers,' added Free. 'And Olly — my gallery friend who showed the kids indigenous art techniques.'

'The dam project management and board should be invited.' Aidan managed to drop that in so casually that Jay was almost nodding before she fully noticed what he'd said.

For Free, it was a step too far.

'Hang on,' she said. 'What have they got to do with the *Born and Bred* project?'

He didn't even look at her. 'The dam is regenerating the region — creating jobs and money. Building the local economy. It's a strategic move to invite them. It might bring more funding the school's way.'

'That's not appropriate.' Free's heart started to race. Everyone must know about her shameful involvement in yesterday's protest, but she ʌldn't let this slide. 'I mean, they had nothing

370

to do with the *Born and Bred* project.'

He raised his eyebrows. 'You'd be surprised what the dam's management has done quietly in the background to grease the wheels of this public art project.'

'You mean getting you into the residency?'

The words fell out before Free could stop them. As soon as she realised what she'd said, her hand flew to her mouth — but it was too late. Jay choked on her tea and Max dropped his phone onto the table. Aidan didn't speak for a few moments, his pale-blue eyes glacially cold. Then he gave an elaborate shrug.

'I don't see how it's any different to inviting the Chamber of Commerce, then. I believe your doctor sister is very *influential* in the chamber — is that right, Free?'

Free couldn't conceal a gasp of horror.

'Now that's enough.' Jay had recovered, her tone as authoritative as though she were defusing a fistfight between a couple of Year Eight boys. 'This is unprofessional and unproductive. I'm in charge of the invitations to the opening, anyway. I don't want to hear any more slurs or speculations from either of you.'

Aidan looked completely unconcerned, giving another of those laconic shrugs, but Free's face was on fire. She stared down at her uneaten lunch for several moments before coming to the conclusion that she had to get away.

Right now.

She closed her lunch box and attempted an unobtrusive departure. Outside, Free wandered the noisy school grounds, her dismay growing with every step she took.

It was true, then. Beth *had* pulled strings to get her the job at the school. But how could Aidan even know about that? She grew hopeful for a moment — there was no way, surely, that Aidan could know whether Beth had influenced the decision or not. But then, she recalled, he moved in those circles. His mother was close with the Chamber of Commerce. Hell, Amanda Hamilton was close with *everyone* in high places.

Free attempted logic. Would Beth honestly go this far? She was protective, Free knew, and didn't think much of Free's ability to cope in the world. Her heart dropped. She could absolutely see Beth doing something like this — something well-meaning that would promote Free's chances of success. Beth would have no idea how devastating it could feel to have a moment of triumph swept away by the realisation that she didn't get there on her own. This had Beth written all over it. Her always-right, always-capable, always-successful older sister who had connived the artist's residency for Free through her business connections.

She couldn't even cry.

First Finn, pulling strings to get her out of trouble while he let a vulnerable boy sit in jail. And now Beth, meddling to smooth the path for Free to win a highly competitive contract at the school. Did neither of them think she was capable of achieving or solving anything on her own? Or was this simply how the world ran — on schmoozing, privilege and nepotism?

She fumbled for her phone. She would call

Beth. She had to ask her, straight up. Maybe Aidan was full of shit. Free was pretty sure she'd be able to detect whether Beth was lying. She sat on an empty bench in a quiet corner of the schoolyard and hit Beth's name on her contact list.

The call went to voicemail. Free swore under her breath and hung up. She called her sister's clinic.

'Mount Clair Medical, this is Dani,' came the bright voice of Beth's receptionist.

'Hi, Dani, it's Free.'

'Oh, hey, Free! How are you?'

'Good. Is Beth available?'

'No, sorry. She's in a consultation. Do you need to see a doctor? Beth's all booked up, but we've got Dr Lavigne available this afternoon, or Dr Shen in the morning.'

'No, it's okay.' Free sighed. 'I just wanted to talk to Beth. Could you ask her to call me?'

'Sure, no problem. See ya, Free.'

She returned to the art room. To her relief, Aidan had vanished, so she didn't have to face him again, but Free longed to be at home where she could find some privacy to cry the tears that threatened to burst out at any moment. When the school day was finally at an end, she dashed for her car.

At home, she didn't know what to do. Finn didn't appear to be in his unit, so she'd escaped that confrontation for the time being. Free dug some chips out of the pantry and crunched her way through them. Next was ice-cream. She repeatedly checked her phone in case Beth had returned her call.

Nothing.

Free scowled. No doubt Beth was busy curing a child of some dreadful disease. Freakin' perfect Beth and her habit of doing good in the world. Well, this time her *good* was not so damn good.

At last, Free went to paint. It was the only thing that could stop her from thinking about Beth and Finn's actions for more than a few moments at a time. By 9 p.m., her eyes were sore and bleary. She checked her phone. Still nothing from Beth, but Finn had sent her a message.

Cameron spent a night in the lockup but he's home now. Can we please talk?

Free wanted to scream at the thought of Cameron in the lockup for the night. Dear Lord, what was Finn thinking? Cameron was just a child! His poor mother — how she must have suffered through that long night. She wrote and deleted about six replies, ranging from pleading with Finn to repent, right through to raging at him for arresting Cameron in the first place. None of them made the cut. It was half an hour before she settled on a message to send back.

I need some time to think. I'll contact you soon.

Free showered and climbed into bed, rolling onto her side so she could stare at the dent in the pillow where Finn's head normally rested. Her heart yearned for him but she couldn't shake the anger that leapt like a searing blue flame in her gut. Finn had disregarded everything he knew about a vulnerable young boy — sold out his own spirit of kindness and understanding.

374

He wasn't the man she thought she knew.

As for Beth . . .

Max curled up against her shoulder blades, purring deeply, and exhaustion crashed through her worries for the first time since Aidan's spiteful remark. Free closed her eyes.

21

Free woke at seven-thirty, dragged herself up and contemplated breakfast. She hadn't eaten dinner after her junk-food binge the night before, but the whirlpool of stress in her stomach told her food might not be such a good idea this morning. The anger at Beth still flared, but overnight her feelings towards Finn had transformed into deep sorrow. She still loved him, she realised. Even though he'd shown her he was the one thing she couldn't tolerate — dishonourable.

And she had no idea what to do about it.

She dressed and made a cup of tea, prolonging the time she stayed at home. It was going to be a horrible day, facing Beth and Finn after work. During the drive to school, she contemplated what she would say to Beth. She'd never pushed back against her sister before — not properly — and the thought filled her with fear. But she couldn't let this one slide. Her mind jumped back to when Beth had pretended their father wasn't seriously ill while Free was in Italy. No. *Not cool*. No matter how well-meaning Beth was when she made these shitty decisions, it had to stop. Free couldn't allow this resentment to keep growing inside her — or let Beth continue to be a puppeteer in her life.

She couldn't even think about how she would

confront Finn. Maybe he wouldn't understand her reaction.

Did this mean they were done?

Oh God — how will I ever get over him?

She parked and headed straight for the art block. Although it was Aidan's day off, Free worried that she would see him. If it were Free, she wouldn't be able to resist coming in to see the results of the tile-firing. There was no way she could look at his stretched, superior face after what they'd said to one another yesterday. But Aidan, thank the saints, was not about. Free went into the wet area to see if Jay had pulled out the students' tiles yet.

Jay was there with a number of students from both Year Eleven and Year Ten, who must have dropped in to check out the results of their work. Their tiles were out of the kiln, all laid out on the bench under the bright art-room lights. But something was off. She could hear arguments and accusations flying around. Free pushed forward to get a look at the tiles.

No. Oh no.

A number of the tiles were broken. Several others had crazing through the glaze layer — obvious and ugly. Jay lifted her face and saw her.

'We've had a less than ideal result.' Her dark eyes were full of disappointment.

Free's skin went hot and then cold. She picked up one of the damaged tiles and examined it closely. She'd never seen anything like it — had never had a result so awful. The tile's surface was like a dry riverbed, cracked and discoloured.

There was no way they could use these for an outdoor public artwork, even if they wanted to. These tiles wouldn't survive a single Mount Clair wet season.

'What on earth happened?' Free's voice wavered. 'Did the kiln door get opened after I left, or something? Did anyone mess with the settings yesterday?'

'The kiln was supervised all day,' said Jay. 'It's part of our safety procedures. Inga was here.'

Inga was beyond reproach. The hardworking assistant would never mess with the kiln settings. She always asked if she wasn't sure — even when it was just about moving a piece of artwork. Free's thoughts skipped to the glaze she'd ordered and her chest felt constricted.

'I guess the glaze didn't match the clay like you thought it would,' Jay said, as though she could read Free's mind.

'But I researched it,' Free said. 'The glaze *was* the right fit for the clay.'

'What about the underglazes?' asked Jay. 'Was it the right fit for those?'

Oh shit. Had she checked that? She thought she had, but maybe . . .

Jay saw Free's doubt and sighed. 'Well, anyone whose tile got broken will have to remake it. Sorry, guys. We'd better use different glazes next time. I'll apply to the committee for extra funding. Maybe they will take pity on us. Otherwise, we can do some fundraising.'

Tia was there, watching Free anxiously.

'I'll pay for it,' Free said in a rush. 'It's my screw-up. I'll cover it.'

Tia opened her mouth, closed it and opened it again. 'Maybe it wasn't your fault, Miss Paterson.' Her voice was barely a murmur.

'It was a poor choice of glaze for the clay,' Jay told Tia, her face stony.

'I'm afraid it *is* my fault, Tia,' Free said, lips trembling.

'But it's only the Year Tens' tiles that got broken,' the girl answered.

Jay whipped her head around to inspect the tiles again. There was a brief silence. 'Put your hand up if your tile is one of the damaged ones,' she said to the group.

Every Year Ten there lifted a hand. None of the Year Elevens did. Jay's eyebrows rose and she looked at Free.

'That's weird,' she said.

'It *is* weird,' said Free. 'I suppose it might just be a coincidence . . . '

'Maybe it was something to do with the production process,' said Jay. 'We'll have to speak to Aidan.'

Tia opened her mouth again, but instead of speaking, she looked around the group and slunk quietly away. The bell rang and the students dispersed, but Free and Jay stayed where they were, gazing at the botched tiles.

'I really did think it was the right match.' Free prayed Jay wouldn't shout at her.

Jay heaved a sigh and pushed her glasses up into her curls. 'I know. Something went wrong, that's for sure. It's just so bloody strange that only the Year Tens' tiles copped it. Aidan didn't produce very good work with the Year Tens, but I

379

thought they looked structurally sound, more or less. If we'd fired them in different batches, I'd say something went wrong with the kiln, but they were all in together.'

'Should I call Aidan?' Free asked.

'God, no,' said Jay. 'Not after yesterday's stoush with him. I'll call him myself. I'll do it now.'

Jay went into the art office to make her call and Free waited, stomach churning. The call went on for almost ten minutes before Jay came back, her puzzled frown no less puzzled.

'Well, I don't have any answers for you,' she told Free. 'Aidan's coming in to have a look later on, but he blames the glaze you wanted.'

He would. 'I'll go online and do more research,' said Free. 'I might try emailing the manufacturer, or maybe I'll ask in this pottery forum I'm on.'

Jay pulled off her glasses and sucked on one of the arms. 'Don't worry about that, Free. I think I'll take charge of research and product selection from now on.' She must have seen Free's cheeks colour because Jay grimaced. 'Sorry. I don't want to hurt your feelings, but I'm in charge of this whole project, and I can't let any more mistakes happen.'

Free wanted to hide under the nearest table. 'Okay. I understand. I'm sorry.'

'Maybe you could sort these tiles for me,' Jay said. 'Put the intact ones somewhere safe and the broken pieces in a box or something.'

'No worries.'

Free did as Jay had asked, then sat in an empty

classroom to work on lesson plans. The loss of Jay's trust smarted like a slap. It made sense, in the context of what had happened — and what Aidan had revealed about Free's fudged selection for the residency. What a gigantic disaster. She would have loved to go home — preferably all the way home to Paterson Downs — to lick her wounds and comfort-snack. Or simply to paint, so she didn't have to think about this mess. Free sighed and stayed where she was, planning lessons until there wasn't an ounce of lesson planning left to do. Then, despite Jay's words, she sneaked in a bit of research on glazes and clays. It made no sense. The products she'd selected should have been good together. She snapped a photo of one of the damaged tiles and emailed the manufacturer to ask if they'd ever seen this problem before.

The day dragged until it was finally time for her after-school session. Everyone was there, just as usual. Heartened by the resilience of her students, Free took a breath and got started — then Jay turned up. Free lost her train of thought as the head of art came into the room and sat in a corner, opening her laptop. She nodded at Free to indicate she should continue.

What the hell?

Jay hadn't sat in on Free's classes since the third week of the semester — and now she trusted Free so little that she was going to start supervising her again? Free couldn't recover the sentence she'd been saying. She changed tack, trying to pretend Jay wasn't there, and got the students working on a basic portrait exercise.

These kids weren't stupid. They knew Ms Lincoln was there because Miss Paterson had screwed up, and they saw how flustered that made Free. They were especially polite to her and tried extra hard, which was touching but didn't diminish her mortification. Tia seemed deeply disturbed by the situation. Her eyes kept creeping up to Free's face and across to Jay, who worked silently on her laptop in the corner. Even worse, Aidan arrived. Free saw him peer into her classroom from the wet area before he retreated into the office.

Normally the hour flew by, but today it felt like a week. At last it was four o'clock and the kids packed up to go home. There were none of the usual high-spirited calls of farewell, either. Just a few subdued 'Bye, Miss Patz'. Free tidied up wordlessly once they'd left, and Jay tapped at her laptop. The classroom door swung open and Tia appeared, panting slightly.

'Oh, hiya,' said Free. 'Did you forget something?'

'I — I need to tell Ms Lincoln something.'

Jay waited. Tia, pink-cheeked, attempted to catch her breath.

'I don't want to accuse anyone of anything, but I saw something a bit weird, and I thought I should tell you.'

'Tell us?' Jay prompted.

'I was in here during lunch last week, working on my oil painting. It was after Mr Hamilton's class. I saw the old glaze — the container — out in the wet area. The Year Tens' tiles had just been sprayed and I thought maybe they'd accidentally used the wrong glaze.' Jay's face changed. 'I should have said something,' Tia added in a rush. 'But I didn't think it was my business.'

Jay's mouth fell open.

'And my neighbour, Callie — '

Tia stopped because Aidan himself appeared, wearing bright cycling colours. The girl's face blanched and she made a move to leave.

'It's okay,' Free told her, catching her arm. 'Wait a minute.'

Aidan observed the three of them. 'So, where are these tiles? Let's see if they can be salvaged.'

Jay slid off her stool and snatched up the box of broken tiles. She thrust it under his nose.

'What do you think, Aidan?' she challenged him. 'Can these be salvaged?'

Tia slipped behind Free. Aidan looked into the box and shot Jay a wary look.

'Probably not.'

Next, Jay strode to the storeroom. She emerged with the tin of older glazing suspension, smacking it down onto the bench. She levered the lid off. Free edged nearer and stood on her tiptoes to peep in from a distance.

'Oh no,' she said, unable to stay silent. 'They did use it. There's hardly any left.'

Jay's mouth had become in a thin, angry line. 'You slimy prick,' she hissed at Aidan.

He blinked. 'What the hell?'

'You deliberately used the old glaze, even after Free warned us what it might do to the kids' tiles.'

He scoffed and denied it but the weight of evidence against him was overwhelming. 'All

383

right,' he said. 'I *may* have *accidentally* used the wrong glaze. An honest mistake.'

'You thought Free was wrong,' Jay fired at him. 'You were trying to prove a point.'

For once, Free didn't demur. As soon as Jay said it, she knew it to be true. That was exactly the kind of thing Aidan would do. He would love to expose Free's foolish extravagance in insisting on the new glazes.

'I wouldn't jeopardise the students' work like that,' Aidan said, putting on a good performance of injured innocence.

Tia was once again making a move towards the door but Jay beckoned her back to the bench.

'What were you going to say about Callie?' she asked.

Tia stared at the floor. Free held her breath during the long silence. She'd just about given up hope when Tia spoke.

'Um, my neighbour, Callie, she's in Year Ten art with Mr Hamilton. Callie reckons he's been saying stuff in class, that the new glaze Miss Paterson ordered is a waste of money and they should just use the old one. And that's why I noticed when he did use the old one.'

'Bullshit,' Aidan snapped. 'What a load of utter bullshit. I never said anything like that. You've been coaching her,' he accused Free.

'You've had it in for Free since she first made the suggestion,' Jay returned. 'And you're so bloody convinced of your own superiority that I'd bet you have never once imagined you might be wrong. You know what? Get the hell out of my art department, you arsehole. I should have known you'd be dodgy,' she added. 'The apple never falls far from the tree.'

His tight face had somehow become tighter. He shot a hate-filled glare at Free, then Tia. Free put a protective arm around the girl and stared back at him, daring him silently to say a word. He gave them his most dignified eyeroll and turned, choosing to stride away through the wet area rather than pass them to exit through the classroom door.

Jay and Free exchanged a long look, Free's heart hammering in her chest. Jay transferred her gaze to the trembling girl.

'Good on you, Tia,' she said. 'I know you don't like to speak out of turn, but it was important that you did this time, and you recognised that. Thank you.'

'It's okay.' Tia almost whispered the words.

'He might still deny it,' Free said.

'I don't care,' Jay said. 'As far as I'm concerned, he's out the door.'

'I hope he doesn't try to claim unfair dismissal.' Free sighed.

'I'll tell what I saw,' Tia offered. 'If anyone asks me.'

'That's so brave!' Free hugged Tia. 'You're amazing!'

A tiny smile broke on Tia's lips. 'I'd better go home.'

'Yes, off you go.' Jay watched as Tia departed. She brought her eyes back to Free. 'Well. Drink?'

They removed to the art office to decompress.

'What a frigging nightmare.' Jay sighed. She

pulled down a fat dictionary of modern art to reveal a little bottle of whisky and poured them both a shot in their coffee mugs.

Free sipped tentatively, and used one of her father's favourite expressions. 'You couldn't make it up.'

Jay chuckled and clinked her cup against Free's, her gaze warm. 'I should have known it was Aidan's screw-up, not yours. You know your stuff — always have.' She shook her black curls. 'I'll be glad to be rid of him. I'll make an official phone call shortly, and if he tries to show his ugly mug here for his next class, I'll be pointing him towards the door.'

'Surely he wouldn't dare,' Free said.

She shrugged. 'He's got arrogance in spades. I never could stand the little prick.' Jay relaxed back in her chair. 'Well, I guess it's just you and me now. We've got a bit of a job ahead of us, getting the Year Tens to remake all their tiles. You up for the challenge?'

'Definitely.'

'Good stuff. You're a keeper, Free.'

A keeper! Free floated towards home on the back of the compliment. She parked near the bridge over the Herne and hopped out, tracking back to the walkway so she could look down into the river. Water trickled down a concrete wall into the main catchment, known as Freshwater Lake. The lake stretched out before her, quiet, green and still in the dying afternoon light. She should take a photo. But she just stood and took it in instead, breathing in the soft, warm scent of a dry-season afternoon, tinged with an earthy

386

edge of wetland life.

A message from Beth came through on her phone.

Saw your missed call yesterday and figured you'd call back if it was important. But Dani just told me you rang the clinic for me, too. Everything okay?

No. Free replied. *We need to talk.*

?? Beth answered, and a moment later, *I'm finished for the day. Can I come over? I've got something for you from Willow.*

Free replied in the affirmative and got back into her car.

22

When Free pulled into her garage, Beth's Beast was already parked on the verge. She parked and came around the side of the house to find Beth on her porch. They eyed one another for a long moment.

'I know what you did,' Free said at last. She climbed the steps to unlock her door. 'In fact, everyone knows. It doesn't help me, you know, when you do stuff like this. It undermines me.'

'What are you talking about?' said Beth, following her inside.

Free switched on the kettle. 'You and the chamber.'

She stopped to give Beth a pointed look, but Beth simply knitted her eyebrows as though she were completely innocent and dropped her bag on the table.

'I don't understand.'

Free huffed a frustrated sigh. 'Look, I can handle you thinking I'm a monumental screw-up. I guess I caused it, in a way, by running to you whenever I had a problem. I should have kept my mouth shut and tried to solve my problems by myself. But the residency. Beth, that was wrong. *Really* wrong. If I couldn't get it on my own merit, I didn't want it.' She studied Beth's face. 'Maybe I'm not successful like you. Maybe I don't have a medical degree and my own business, and maybe I'm just a struggling artist who still lives at home with her dad, but at least you could show me the respect of letting me find my own way. I don't want to ride on your coat-tails. I want to have my occasional little successes *honestly*, not because my big sister greased the wheels for me.' Free sat down opposite her sister and reached across the table to seize her hand. 'Please. Promise me you'll never do that again. Please, Beth.'

Beth had turned a little pale, and her dark eyes were growing rounder by the moment. '*Me?* What the hell? I never greased any wheels!'

Free squinted, trying to work out if she could believe her. Beth snatched her hand away.

'Fine, I'll admit I worry about you. Finn, for example. He hurt you when he was dating that Phoebe girl, and in my experience, that means he'll hurt you again.' Free opened her mouth to argue, but Beth barged on. 'But I never, *ever* interfered in your career, Freya Paterson. I don't even know what you're talking about. Who would I grease the wheels *with*? I don't know anyone who would have any influence in the selection process. Wasn't it all decided by some government agency or something?'

'YouthArts,' said Free, her mind spinning. 'And the shire.'

'The shire? I've got nothing to do with the shire!'

'You're in the Chamber of Commerce,' Free mumbled.

Beth scoffed. 'I'm a member, that's all — like most businesses in Mount Clair. And the chamber isn't the same thing as the shire, anyway. Okay, there are a few members who sit on both, but I've never discussed you or your career with any of them, as far as I can remember. Free, I am entirely innocent of interfering in your contract!' Beth's voice had gone a little shrill with indignation and Free couldn't doubt her sincerity any longer.

She held up her hands in a gesture of surrender. 'Okay! I'm sorry. I guess I got that wrong. Aidan Hamilton implied that was how I got the job, and I got paranoid.'

'That guy you work with?' Beth wrinkled her nose. 'What would he know? He probably had an axe to grind with you for some reason of his own. Let me guess — he asked you out and you knocked him back?' Free's face must have told the story because Beth nodded. 'Yep. Pissed off at being rejected so he undermines your work. Classic workplace sexual harassment.'

'Huh?' Free paused. 'Yeah, actually, you might be right. But are you sure you didn't, you know, somehow inadvertently put in a good word for me?'

Something between exasperation and amusement crossed Beth's face. 'Why in hell would I even need to? You're perfectly capable of impressing people. You've got loads of talent and a natural way of putting people at ease. I wasn't at all surprised when you got selected.'

'Oh!'

Beth dropped her gaze to the scratched table and there was a long silence.

'Okay,' she said at last. 'I'm sorry for being disrespectful. I'll try harder. I never meant to make you feel small or inadequate. I love you and Willow more than anything in the world, and I'm so proud of you — both of you. Making you feel like this — it's totally not what I wanted.' She gave a shaky sigh. 'All I ever wanted was for you two to be safe and happy. Maybe it's turned me into a control freak.'

Free was speechless. She studied her sister for signs of insincerity, but there were none. Beth truly meant it. She was still looking at the table as if she couldn't meet Free's eyes.

'Everyone said, when Mum died, how lucky it was that you and Willow had a big sister to look after you. But I didn't know a thing about looking after you. I tried, but I did a dismal job. I worried so much about you both — especially you, Free. But nothing I said to you seemed to stick. Fact was, you didn't even need me — you just went off on your own trajectory, shooting like a star through the cosmos, talented and passionate and *real*. I just tried to keep up.'

Beth's cheeks were wet with tears now and Free's own eyes filled, watching her beautiful sister with her face down, dark hair brushing the table. She had never seen Beth like this before. Free jumped up and dashed around the table to grasp her sister in a hug.

'Oh God, Beth — I'm sorry! Thank you for trying to look after me. I bet I made it super hard. I didn't know you were trying to protect me — I had no idea. I just thought you were being a pain in the arse.'

Beth sobbed out a laugh. 'Thanks, Free.' She hugged her tight in return. 'I love you so much,'

391

she mumbled into her sister's hair.

They hugged a while longer before eventually drying their eyes, then Free re-boiled the kettle for tea. Mugs in hands, sitting close on the couch, Free told the full story of Aidan Hamilton's insinuations and the screw-up with his students' tiles. Then Beth told her about a child with a disability who lived out at the remote Jamadji community she attended each month. Beth was so worried about the little girl, it made Free feel ashamed. She'd been self-absorbed, she realised, to assume Beth spent all her time fretting and meddling in Free's business, when Beth had her own set of troubles and passions.

'So,' Beth ventured when their stories were told. 'What's happening with Finn?'

'I'm not sure. I'm still really disappointed about what he did, but I'm ready to talk to him.'

Beth was watching her with a strange expression, her eyes roaming over Free's face.

'What?' said Free.

'You've changed.'

'Huh?'

'You. You've really changed. I've seen it coming for a while but this — this shows me how much.' Beth inspected her for another long moment. 'Please don't take this the wrong way, Free, but two years ago, I wouldn't have believed this of you. You would have been running the other way as soon as something went wrong.' Beth must have seen Free's face change because she grabbed her hand and squeezed it. 'I'm sorry! But it's true. Any time things got hard, you would run. Remember when you and Dad had that big disagreement about refugees, and you booked a flight to Cambodia and left the next day? And remember when you didn't get into the Royal Show Art Exhibition with that painting you were really proud of? The watercolour? So you never painted in watercolours again?'

Free had to concede these memories were accurate. She'd never thought of them this way before, but Beth's words tickled at her conscience.

'Crap, you're right,' she admitted. 'I did that. I used to run.'

'But look at you now. Doing this residency and living here on your own. Taking a stand against the diversion dam. The stuff with Finn — and even today's issues with the tile project. These are some real problems, and you're sorting shit out, facing them head-on like a bloody warrior!'

Beth's pride was completely earnest and Free melted. 'Thanks, Bethie. I'm doing my best. I want to act in a way I can be proud of — always. I won't settle for anything less.' She took a big sip of tea to dispel the thought of Finn, but he stayed in there.

Her sister read her mind. 'You're still upset about the student who got arrested?'

Free nodded, swallowing against the pain in her throat.

Beth picked at the couch. 'I wonder if . . . '

'If what?'

Beth shook her head. 'Nothing. We should have a glass of wine. What a day you've had!'

'Wait — what were you going to say?' Free asked, grabbing Beth's wrist as she went to stand.

Beth sat back down. 'I was just going to say, I wonder if your definition of acting in a way you can be *proud of* differs from Finn's.'

The ache inside redoubled. 'That's pretty obvious.'

'No, that's not what I mean. I mean, I know how much integrity means to you, but maybe Finn's integrity is just different from yours — not *less*. You disagree with the way he acted, but I can't help but think he did the only thing he could do. He's a police officer. They stand between criminals and law-abiding citizens.'

'Cam is *not* a criminal — '

'Wait.' Beth held up a hand. 'I wasn't finished. Cops take the role because they're willing to be the person who stops someone from breaking a law, no matter what they feel. If you were dealing drugs or robbing a bank, would you want Finn to look the other way?'

'Beth, it's completely different!'

'How?'

Free opened her mouth and closed it again. She thought hard. 'Because Cam is innocent — he must be. Finn knew how hard Cam's mum was trying to keep him out of jail, and he grabbed him just because the poor kid was standing next to a damaged machine holding a hammer!'

'And if you were innocent, and I was trying to keep you out of jail, but you were standing outside a recently robbed bank in a balaclava,

394

holding a shotgun, would you want Finn to ignore it?'

'Beth,' Free groaned. 'This isn't fair! There are more nuances to this situation.'

'I agree. It's not clear-cut. So why blame Finn when all he did was the thing he promised to do? He promised to stop people who break the law — or appear to break the law. He kept his promise, even under pressure not to — from a woman he really cares about. *That* takes integrity.'

'Well . . . ' Free stopped. There was truth in Beth's words and she didn't know how to get around it. 'Well, yeah. Okay. But . . . ' She stopped again.

Beth stood. 'Wine?'

Free gave up thinking. 'Yes. Wine.'

'Oh.' Beth paused where her handbag sat on the table and fished in it for a moment. She found a little pink thumb drive and lined up to throw it to Free. 'Willow asked me to give you this.'

Free caught it. 'What's on it?'

'Apparently Dad's had Tom digitising all his VHS movies and Willow found one that belongs to you.'

Free tried to imagine what movie she'd ever owned that might be on video cassette. 'Not likely,' she concluded.

While Beth poured wine, Free went for her laptop. She set it up on the coffee table and flicked open the little device, plugging it in. It only contained one video file.

'It's called *Day with Freya* and it's forty-six

minutes long,' Free called. 'What on earth could it be?'

Beth returned with two glasses of wine. She settled back on the couch and shrugged at Free. 'No idea. Let's watch it.'

Free accepted a glass. She opened the file in her movie viewer and hit play.

★   ★   ★

Robin Paterson frowned as she adjusted the position of the camera in the Paterson Downs lounge room, her dark hair tied back in a loose ponytail.

'There,' she said, brightening. 'I think I've got that set up okay. And look, it's already on. It's on,' she repeated a little louder, glancing at someone out of shot.

'Can I dance?' came a reply in the high-pitched voice of a child.

'One second, I'll just do an intro for you.' Robin addressed the camera. 'It occurred to me a few days ago that this is my last year having one of my babies home with me every day.'

'I'm not a baby,' the squeaky voice interrupted.

'You'll always be my baby,' Robin answered. 'Just like Beth and Willow are my babies.'

Apparently placated, the child was silent.

'Freya turns seven in February — just four months from now,' Robin went on. 'I've kept her home with me as long as I can but she's ready to go to school on the bus with her sisters and start Year Two in the new year. Seeing as this is one of the last times it will be just me and Free at Paterson Downs together, I thought we'd make a video to show what a day at home with Free is like.'

'Can I dance now?'

'Hold on.' Robin kicked a few toys strewn across the green floor rug out of the way. 'Free wishes to begin the day, as she does so often, with a dance. Do you want music?' she asked.

'No, I've got the music in my head.'

'Okay, go.'

Robin moved back and six-year-old Free came into view. She was in a worn homemade fairy dress, blue and purple. She danced around the lounge room with high drama — something between ballet and avant-garde — her arms flapping as she stumbled and leapt. At one point, she came up close to the camera and stared right into the lens, her green eyes wide, unruly strings of golden hair falling over her shoulders.

'What are you doing?' Robin asked.

'I'm showing the person watching me who I am.'

'Maybe you'll watch this yourself one day, when you're much older.'

'Maybe. Hello, old Free,' she intoned to the camera. 'I'm *you*.' She did a deep, wobbly curtsey. 'That's the end of the dance,' she told Robin.

'What's next? Should we make a cake for when the girls come home?'

'Yes!'

★ ★ ★

397

Robin had propped the camera on the kitchen table, aimed at the laminated bench. Free kneeled on a chair pushed up to the bench, still in the fairy dress, and very carefully broke an egg on the lip of a bowl of flour. The shell crumbled and half the yolk oozed down the outside. Free tried to catch it with her fingers, smearing it back up the glass and over the edge into the bowl.

'Oops, I got shell in it,' she said.

'Oh dear,' said Robin. She came to the rescue, picking pieces of shell out of the mixture while Free poked into the bowl with a wooden spoon, attempting to stir around her mother's hands.

'All right, Miss Impatience, now you can stir.' Robin stood back.

'The egg is so orange,' Free remarked. 'Can we make the cake different colours?'

'A marble cake?' her mother asked.

'Yep. Orange and red and yellow. Sunset cake.'

'That sounds like a possibility.' Robin picked another piece of eggshell out of the mixture.

Her patience was commendable during the colour mixing. Six-year-old Free treated the bowls of cake mixture as her palette, blending the colours meticulously. She had a mini tantrum when the orange became too brown, and went to stand in the meals area, facing the wall, arms crossed. Robin tidied spilt flour while she waited for Free to calm down.

'Freya, you can stand over there, love, or you can come back and take another shot. While you stand there, this mixture is going to stay the wrong colour. But if you come back and try to fix it, there's a chance you can make it better.'

Robin waited a few minutes, glancing at the camera every now and then, and at last her persistence paid off. Free came back and allowed her mother to help her rescue the offending mixture with a touch more yellow. Then the marbling commenced, Free armed with a bamboo skewer, dragging it through the mixture to create extravagant loops and swirls of colour.

'It's got to go in the oven now, Free,' her mother said at last. 'We've got schoolwork to do.'

★ ★ ★

They were back in the lounge room, Free perched on the couch with a workbook open on her lap. She was intent on her letter practice, pencil in hand.

'Does Beth do writing at school?' Free asked.

'Yes. She's very good at writing now, so she does other kinds of work that use writing.'

'Why doesn't Beth want to play with me any more?'

Robin paused. 'Beth's growing up. Sometimes people don't play as much as they start to get older.'

'I'm always going to play, even when I'm a hundred and fifty.'

'Good for you.'

'Beth used to play hospitals with me and Willow.'

'I know, love. But she's got a lot of homework now she's in high school. It doesn't mean she loves you any less, you know.'

'If she loves me, she should play with me.' Free's tone was decided. 'She's being mean.'

'I'm not sure about that. Beth shows her love in other ways. People do that. Everyone's different, and they care about different things, but that doesn't mean they're better or worse than us. A lot of the time we're all feeling the same things inside.'

Free didn't answer, eyes on her page.

'I can write now,' she announced after a few more moments, glancing up at her mother.

'I know.'

'Real words.'

'What are you writing?' A piece of fabric flicked out from the side of the shot. Robin was shaking out and folding clean washing as she supervised Free's schoolwork.

Free held up her workbook. There were no letters, but a rather beautiful curlicue of pencil on the dotted line where she ought to have been practising the letter *h*.

'I can't read it,' said Robin.

Free assumed a knowing look. 'Only fairies can. And goblins.'

'Can you read it?' Robin asked.

'Of course. I wrote it.'

'Tell me what it says in human language,' Robin urged her.

Free studied it, her eyebrows knitting. 'I like sunset cake,' she translated. 'We should go and visit Dad in the ute.' Free sneaked a glance up at her mother, who laughed.

★　★　★

400

The ute bumped along the track, the camera shaking violently, pointed at the white-blue of the midday sky through the windscreen.

'Is it too heavy?' Robin asked.

'No, I can hold it,' said Free.

The camera dropped, tumbling into her dress-covered lap, and Free retrieved it hastily. She checked the lens and proceeded to film the rest of the drive upside down. When the ute stopped, she passed the camcorder to her mother and scrambled out. Robin righted the camera, using it to follow Free as she ran in her dusty farm boots and fairy dress to the bore where her father was working.

'Hello, you two,' Barry called, pausing in his task of cranking a manual pump handle.

'How's it going, love?' Robin called back as she climbed out of the ute.

'Bloody thing.' He kicked the bore pipe and glanced at the camera. 'What's this all about?'

'I'm filming a day with Free.'

He grinned. 'A day in fairyland, eh?' He gave the pump handle a few more cranks.

'Can I do it?' Free asked, bouncing up and down on the spot.

'Of course, sweetheart. Have a go.' Barry lifted her into position as though she weighed nothing.

She put all her weight behind it but couldn't get the pump handle to move more than an inch or two.

'You gotta work on your muscles,' Barry said, taking over.

Free entertained herself by balancing along the edge of a concrete trough. Robin focused the camera on Free, zooming in on her boots as they wobbled along the ledge beneath Free's skinny brown ankles.

'Any idea why it keeps getting blocked?' Robin asked Barry.

'Iron bacteria,' he grunted. 'Like I thought. Clogging up the pipes and pump.' He stood back, hands on hips, and regarded the bore. 'This one's always given me the shits. Pump's too high.'

'Language,' Robin said mildly. 'Might be time to rebuild this pump. Start over.'

'You've gotta sort this shit out, Dad,' Free piped up.

Barry burst into laughter.

'Such a good influence,' Robin said. 'Free, let's move on. Want to go down to the river?'

The boots leapt off the trough. 'Yes!'

'Here's your morning tea,' Robin said to Barry, holding out a paper bag.

His eyes lit up. 'You bewdy.'

The camera was temporarily forgotten while Robin gave Barry a quick kiss goodbye, then Free flew at her father for a tight hug.

'Bye, Dad!'

★ ★ ★

The camera panned along the Herne River where it curled around on itself in the distance like a lazy letter e before straightening into the broad blue stream where they'd parked. Robin brought the shot around to Free, who was standing on a rock on the riverbank, hands on hips like her father, surveying the scene.

'Free and I come down to the river at least once a week, if the track is passable,' Robin said to the camera's microphone. 'It's our tradition.'

'Is the river ours, or the Westons'?' Free called over her shoulder.

'The river doesn't belong to anybody,' Robin said with complete certainty.

'But is it on the Gundergin side or Patersons side?' Free squinted at the fence on the other side of the water. 'It must be ours, because the fence is over there.'

'The river's not ours or theirs. It runs between the properties.'

Free jumped down and wandered towards the water's edge. She crouched, reaching out to turn over a clay dish of sun-baked mud, and poked her finger into the squishy mud underneath. Then the whole hand went in, and the other. She scooped up a handful and used the top of the overturned dried piece as a work tray. Sticks and pebbles became her tools. Robin filmed in silence for a couple of minutes.

'Maybe she'll be an artist,' she said softly.

She approached. 'What's that you've made, Free?'

'It's a boab tree. See? Fat at the bottom and skinny at the top.'

'Oh yes, I see it.'

Free got to her feet, abandoning her sculpture, and examined her muddy hands. She cast her gaze around until she spotted a big, flat river stone, blue-grey in colour. A blank canvas. Free planted her hands back in the mud, loading them up, then ran over to the blue stone to create two perfect red-mud handprints. She looked up at her mother in delight. Robin laughed.

'Beautiful.'

'You do it too, Mum.'

'I might be able to fit one of my hands in between your prints.'

★ ★ ★

Robin ducked down, the camera trembling, and slapped an open palm into the mud. She crossed to the stone and lay her hand carefully between the two little prints her daughter had made, already drying.

'Did you get it on the camera?' Free asked, staring at the handprints. 'The rain might wash them off.'

'Yep. Captured for posterity.'

'For who?'

'Forever, is what I mean.'

Free found a stick and began to scratch a line in the mud on the water's edge. She paused at stones and other debris, drawing circles around them before continuing her long line, connecting and encasing the river with every part of itself. She said something but the microphone didn't quite catch it.

'What was that, love?' her mother called.

'The river doesn't belong to anybody,' Free called back.

★ ★ ★

Gentle bumping along a farm track. The ute was moving at a crawl because Robin was getting the camera into position while she drove, trying to show Free seated in the passenger seat, eyes closed in sleep. Dried mud streaked her cheek and hands, splotches on the fairy dress. The window was open, the breeze tickling her hair, afternoon sunlight illuminating her face.

'I'm going to miss her so much,' came Robin's voice.

*   *   *

The camera blinked its eye open on the stone and wood sign for Paterson Downs on Herne River Road. Free was up on the stone wall, hanging onto the *D* of 'Downs'. She peered along the road.

'I think I can see it,' she called back. She held still and squinted into the distance for a long moment. 'Yep!' She raised her voice to a holler. 'The bus is coming!'

'The daily drive to meet the school bus,' Robin said quietly from her position further back on the driveway.

Free fidgeted and wriggled with impatience until finally the big orange bus pulled to a stop out the front. Two dark-headed children scrambled out. Beth ran straight across the road but Willow paused to call back to Tom, his blond head stuck out the bus window.

'Meet you at the eastern gate in half an hour.'

He gave her a thumbs up. Robin waved to the bus driver as he pulled away. Beth helped Free down from the stone wall and held her hand as they made their way back to Robin, Willow running to catch up.

'I can write almost as good as you now,' Free was boasting to Beth.

'That's amazing.' Beth caught her mother's eye and shot her a little smile.

'And I made you a sunset cake for afternoon tea.'

'Oh, yum!'

'What are you doing, Mum?' Willow asked as she arrived, staring into the camera.

'Just capturing a few special moments.'

'I wouldn't call spending an hour and a half on the stinky school bus a special moment.' Beth was full of healthy teen sarcasm.

'That's a wrap, Free,' Robin called to her youngest daughter. 'Do you want to take a bow?'

Free broke loose of Beth's hand and did a triple twirl, ending in a deep curtsey. She'd made herself dizzy, however, and she wobbled for a few moments before falling over. Her sisters laughed and Free joined in. She lay back on the gravel drive and gazed up at the blue sky, still giggling.

'Yep,' said Robin, laughter in her voice as well. 'That's Free.'

★ ★ ★

The video ended, flicking back to the *play movie* icon on Free's laptop. Beth was clutching her hand tightly. When Free turned, she found her sister was a mess, tears pouring and shoulders shaking. Free herself wasn't crying. Not yet.

406

'That was amazing.' Beth barely managed the words. 'I didn't even know that video existed.'

'Every week,' Free said wonderingly. A hard lump seemed to be forming in her chest — it felt like both sadness and gratitude. 'At least once a week, Mum took me to the river. *That's* why it means so much to me.'

Beth squeezed her close. 'I'm glad you had that special time with her.'

The lump in Free's chest was changing as the moments wore on, until it became warm and shone golden like a nugget of pure truth. She released a slow sigh.

'I've always felt really hard done by. Like we had horrible luck to lose our mum so young, and I was especially unlucky because I had the shortest time with her. But we were lucky — incredibly lucky — to have her as long as we did. Weren't we?'

Beth sobbed again. 'Free, you have the most amazing knack for speaking the truth.'

23

Free stood outside for a few minutes after Beth drove away. Finn's house was dim, as though he still wasn't home. Beth's words about integrity pinged around inside her head. Max gave his cracked meow and Free let him out to do whatever he needed to do, then went into the house. Tiredness hit. She got undressed and climbed into bed to lie still, thinking.

No more delays. She wanted to talk to Finn now — urgently. She reached for her phone and sent him a message asking when she could see him.

He didn't reply. Maybe he wasn't pulling a late shift, after all. Maybe he was avoiding her. Free sighed. She *had* to see him, even if he didn't want to talk any more. She would sit out the front of his house tomorrow and wait until he appeared. It would be tough, but she would face it head-on.

She rolled over in the darkness and gazed at Finn's pillow dent. Even through the worries crowding her head, she was thinking more clearly than she ever had before. Free pressed her lips together, determined.

She had shit to sort out.

★ ★ ★

Free woke to the sound of banging at her front door. She seized her kimono and staggered out to yank open the door, blinking into the morning sunlight.

'Hey, Miss Patz!'

'*Cam!*'

It was him, standing beside Tia, their bikes on the ground at the bottom of her porch steps.

'Oh my God! Cameron, are you okay?'

Cameron wore his usual grin. 'Of course I'm okay. We're on our way to school.'

'Come in, come in!' She held the door open and ushered them inside. 'Have you got time for a drink? Something to eat?'

'I'm all good,' Cameron said, and Tia shook her head with a quick smile.

'What happened, Cam? Have you been in prison all this time?'

'Nah, just one night. The cops checked the CCTV from the protest and it showed I never smashed nothing. I was lucky the cameras were there.'

Relief hit Free, then an instant later she was filled with outrage. 'I just can't believe they kept you in the lockup overnight! It must have been awful. Why didn't they release you like they released me? *So* unfair.'

'No, that was because of Mum. She got them to keep me in overnight to teach me a lesson for sneaking out.'

Free's jaw dropped. 'She — '

'She's bad-ass, my mum,' he said with a tinge of pride.

Free gathered her wits. 'I hope you don't hate the police after being falsely accused.'

'Your boyfriend, you mean?' Cameron shook

his head. 'He's all right. He was the one who found the video showing I did nothin' wrong.'

Free was silenced.

'Sorry we woke you up,' he added. 'Tia wanted to see you. She told me all about what Mr Hamilton did. What a dick.'

Tia finally got a word in. 'I just wanted to tell you. My mum, she works at the airport. She sold Mr Hamilton a one-way ticket to Perth last night.'

Free gaped. 'He's already gone?'

Tia nodded, a slight sparkle in her eye. Cameron stretched his arms above his head, his grin broadening.

'I guess he didn't feel up to coming back for more,' he said. 'Not after Ms Lincoln tore poor little Aidy a new one.'

'Are you going to help the Year Tens redo their tiles now, Miss Paterson?' Tia asked.

'Yes.' *Those poor kids*, she thought. *Victims of Aidan Hamilton's ego.*

'Callie will be happy. She wanted to be in your class all along.' Tia checked her watch. 'Cam, we'd better go or we'll be late for first bell.'

Free waved her students off and looked at Finn's porch. She held her kimono closed so she wouldn't flash her knickers and singlet to the street, and clambered over the divider. She knocked, heart skipping.

No answer.

Her shoulders slumped. Free climbed back over and went inside her unit. Where was he? She headed for her phone to see if he'd answered her message while she was asleep, but a knock behind her made her jump. She dashed back to open the front door.

Finn was there, those Kimberley-creek eyes darkened with weariness. Hope rushed through her and her head emptied of all coherent conversation. Oh good Lord, how she'd missed him. Longed for him. This was a man whose soul spoke to hers. This was fate, goddammit. She had to try.

She prayed to the god of hasty words that he would be willing to listen.

'I heard your knock,' Finn said. 'I was sleeping and couldn't get to the door in time. I only got home at three.'

Free stepped back to let him inside. 'So you've only had a couple of hours' sleep?'

'Yeah.' His voice was low. 'I've got the day off today to catch up. I couldn't get my head straight yesterday so Briggsy told me to take a day.'

'Oh . . . '

Finn kept his eyes on hers while she struggled to find the right words. 'Finn, I need to talk to you.' She crossed to the table to take a seat and checked that he was coming too. He joined her. 'It's been a weird couple of days,' she said. 'The protest and the arrests. Then I had trouble at work. Aidan said something that made me think Beth had manipulated things behind my back to get me the residency. Turned out she hadn't, though. Then we had a firing disaster with the tiles and it looked like my fault. But it wasn't.'

His eyebrows rose. 'What happened?'

'I'll tell you in a minute. First, I want to talk

about what happened on Sunday.'

He nodded. And waited. An anguished yowl rose from somewhere below them, making Free start.

Finn stood. 'What the hell? Was that Donald?'

Free dashed for the door. She scrambled down the steps, Finn right behind her, and peered into the gloom beneath the porch. Max was there, lying curled up in the dirt, eyes half-closed. He twitched his head and eyed them, giving another of those horrible long cries. Finn crouched down and tried to climb in and get him, but it was hopeless. He was far too big. Free dropped to her knees and commando-crawled into the dusty, cobwebbed space under the house, hampered by her kimono. She scooped Max up. He was weak and floppy, utterly unable to hang on to her or support his own weight like he normally did. She held him against herself as best she could, struggling out between the timber stumps.

'What's happened to him?' said Finn.

'I don't know.' Free stumbled up the steps. Did she have a cat carrier? Of course not. A box? A basket — she had a plastic basket in her wardrobe. Cradling Max, she ran for the bedroom and yanked open her wardrobe door. Everything was in the way. She used one arm to haul out a box of photos, then Finn caught on to what she was after and took over. He pulled out her roller suitcase and her sunhats, and finally got to the basket. He dumped its contents — old university papers — onto the carpet and shoved in an abandoned towel to make a soft bed.

Gently, Free lay the limp cat on top.

'Here,' said Finn. He thrust a discarded dress at her and she flapped her arms out of her kimono so she could pull the dress over her head.

They ran for the car and got in, Finn balancing the basket on his lap. Free started the ignition with a trembling hand.

'Hold on, Max, we'll get you some help,' she said. 'The vet will fix you, I promise.'

Finn had his gaze on Max, keeping a hand on the cat, who was silent and still in his basket. Free kept glancing at them until she could stand it no more.

'Is he — '

'No, I think he's still with us,' said Finn.

She pulled in at the vet clinic and peered at Max. His eyes flickered. *Thank goodness!* She raced around the car to help Finn with the door. Grasping the basket, he ran into the clinic, Free right behind him. The receptionist took a quick look, then led them straight through to the examination room.

The grey-haired vet checked Max over. 'It could be baiting, but I suspect a snakebite,' she said, palpating Max's abdomen. 'We'll do some blood tests. I'll need to take him out the back. Do you want to wait, or — ?'

'We'll wait,' said Free.

They returned to the little waiting room and sat on a bench.

'Snakebite.' Finn shook his head, staring at the floor in front of him.

'Excuse me,' said the receptionist. 'While

413

you're waiting, do you mind if I grab some details about your cat?'

'Of course,' Free said.

'Male or female?'

'Male,' Free said.

'Sterilised,' Finn added.

'What's his name?'

'Donald.' Finn said it at the same moment as Free said, 'Max.'

The woman waited. Finn glanced at Free.

'Max,' he said, to Free's surprise.

The woman tapped on the keyboard. 'Last name?'

'Paterson,' he said, but Free interrupted.

'No! *Kelly*. Max Kelly.'

Finn caught her eye and his mouth tugged up on one side.

The receptionist finished taking details and the two of them sat in the waiting area for half an hour, mostly silent. At length, Free scrounged in her handbag for change and bought a pack of Lions mints off the front counter. She offered them to Finn, who shook his head, then she anxiously crunched her way through the whole lot. At last the vet reappeared, beckoning to them. They followed her out the back, where Max was lying in a cage, hooked up to a drip. He gave them a vacant stare, his inner eyelid membranes partially covering his eyes.

'It's almost certainly a snakebite but we're not sure what type of snake at this stage.' The vet opened the cage door so they could pat him. 'I don't want to seem insensitive, but antivenom is expensive. Do you have a limit on how much you can spend on him?'

Free stroked Max's soft little head. 'Huh?'

'What I mean is, if the treatment cost reaches a certain amount, we can call you to check what you want to do before we proceed.'

Free started to say there was no limit, then she remembered she only had a bit of money sitting in the bank. Certainly not enough to say the funds were unlimited. She looked at Finn.

'I could probably manage two thousand, if I use my credit card,' she said.

He nodded. 'I've been trying to put a bit of money away. I can manage about the same. Let us know if it's going higher than that,' he said to the vet.

'Leave him with us and I'll give you a call as soon as we know anything.'

'Do you think he'll survive?' Finn asked the vet.

The vet pressed her lips together. 'It's pretty bad. But cats are quite resistant to venom and poisoning, so we can only hope. You found him under the house, didn't you say? You might want to call in a snake handler to take a look around your backyard, if that's the case. I know a good snake guy. He's a teacher at the local high school. Max Drummond.'

Free couldn't help a choked laugh, and Finn made a sound to match. Free bent over to kiss Max goodbye, her tears dripping onto his fur. Finn reached in his big hand to give the cat's ears a rub.

'It's okay, Dona — Max. Hang in there, little dude, and then you can come home and have an extra serve of pilchard loaf, I promise.'

They left the cat with the vet and returned to the car.

'Poor Max,' Finn said as they drove along the busy Wednesday morning streets of Mount Clair.

Free was silent, tears welling again.

'What a hell of a few days it's been,' Finn added.

She felt him watching her but neither spoke. Free parked near the bridge over the Herne River and climbed out. They needed to talk, and being by the river would give her courage. Finn got out as well, but when she glanced back, Free found him hovering by the car.

'Come for a walk with me,' she said. 'Please.'

He joined her. They crunched over the yellowing grass of the foreshore down to the riverbank. The Herne was a lazy, peaceful flow beneath the bright blue sky, tracts of pungent red mud exposed on both sides. Free came to a halt and turned to face Finn, sick with nerves. He stopped short, his expression mirroring her feelings.

He rubbed the back of his neck with one hand. 'Free, are we . . . ?'

She jumped in. 'Yes. *Yes.* I'm so sorry I judged you.' The light came back into Finn's eyes in an instant and Free's heart leapt. 'Beth said something that made me realise how brave and true you are. I'm glad that you took a stand against me, Finn.'

He burst into laughter. 'You're the weirdest, most gorgeous woman I've ever met.'

But Free was completely serious. 'I was wrong

416

to assume you didn't care about Cameron. I should have known better. Cam told me it was his *mum* who got you to keep him in the lockup over-night. And that you helped by finding a video that showed he was innocent.'

He grimaced. 'Yeah. I waded through eight hours of footage from four different cameras to find those ten seconds of video. Nothing of you. But the CCTV caught a couple of other interesting moments — including Cameron getting shoved through the gates against his will, and some dickhead putting a hammer in his hands. He was just standing there holding it when I grabbed him.'

'He was never going to smash anything.'

'I know,' said Finn. 'I just needed to find proof.'

She blinked. 'How did you know?'

'It would have been out of character for him.' He caught her eye. 'And I trust your judgement.'

'*My* judgement?'

He grinned. 'Mostly.'

Free caught her breath. Had . . . had they done it? Had they managed to work things out? Finn wore a smile and that was reassurance enough for her. She lunged at him, grabbing the sides of his face and dragging him down so she could kiss his lips. *Oh God*, that was good. His smell, his warmth — his *strength*. He slipped his arms around her and pulled her tight against him.

'I love you,' she said when her lips were her own again.

Finn's whole face changed, lighting up with

417

utter joy in the bright daylight. He tugged her even closer.

'I love you so damn much, Free. I've never loved anyone like this and I never will again. I've wanted to tell you for ages but I didn't want to scare you off.'

'Scare me off? No way. You're the one guy I want to hear that from.'

He buried his face in her hair and Free gave in to the giant sob that had been trying to escape.

'Finn, what if Max dies?' The words spilled out.

He held her tight. 'Let's keep hoping. He's a fighter.'

Finn drove them home and made Free sit down while he put together an omelette for their breakfast. Although she swore she wasn't hungry, she ate it and felt better afterwards. She checked the time. It had been over an hour since they'd left Max, so she braced herself and picked up her phone to dial the vet.

'All Creatures, this is Lesley.'

'Hi, it's Freya Paterson here. I just wanted to check on Max.'

'Hold on,' the receptionist answered. 'I'll speak to the vet.'

She waited, heart thumping, her eyes on Finn on the couch beside her.

The vet's voice sounded on the line. 'Freya?'

'Yes?'

'Max is alive, but he's very unwell. We found the bite — it's inside his mouth. We think it might have been a taipan.'

'It bit him inside his mouth?'

418

'He could have been hunting it, or even defending himself — hissing. Whatever the case, it got him just under his top lip. I'm very concerned about him, I'm afraid. I'm not convinced he's going to make it. His vision seems to have gone — he's not responding to light stimuli and his blood tests show a lot of internal bleeding. Taipan venom is haemotoxic, which means it stops the blood from coagulating. Max is passing blood in his urine. That indicates his system has been seriously damaged by the venom.'

Finn's eyes grew worried, watching Free's reaction to the vet's words. She hit the speaker button so he could listen too.

'Is he in pain?' Free asked this with dread. The idea of Max in pain was worse than the thought that he might die.

'He's not showing signs of pain, but he's gone into a bit of a shutdown, I suppose, so his body can try to heal.' The vet paused. 'Look, I don't know how this one's going to go. He's survived the first few hours, which is good, but sometimes when an animal gets bitten by a snake, the worst comes later. If he survives the initial injury, the toxins may still cause serious ongoing damage that will give him poor quality of life. It's okay to stay hopeful, but I urge you to be realistic. If he survives but ends up with long-term damage, it might still be kinder to put him to sleep.'

The woman's gentle words made Free's throat get tight. 'I understand.'

When the call ended, they tidied up the kitchen and sat together on the couch. Free

419

curled up with her head against Finn's chest, half watching the morning news, half focused on her inner thoughts. There was grief for Max, lingering worries over the river and the Year Tens' tiles, but joy — delirious joy — that she and Finn were held together by this love. He bent down to kiss the top of her head and she wound her arm more tightly around his waist.

Things weren't perfect, but they sure felt better while she sat alongside the great big dose of wonderful that was Finn.

* * *

Free could see that Finn badly needed sleep, so she ordered him into her bed and sat down to write a plan for remaking the tiles with the Year Tens. In the afternoon, she heard him waking up, so Free joined him. The two of them lay side by side, waiting for the vet to reopen for evening surgery so they could find out if Max had survived the day. Free took the opportunity to tell Finn all about the misunderstanding with Beth, and Aidan's misadventures with the wrong glaze.

'You had a lot to cope with over the last few days,' he remarked. 'Good thing you're so resourceful.'

They watched the ceiling in companionable silence for a few minutes. She would like to hear him sing. Would he be up to singing for her, under the circumstances? Maybe he was too sad about Max.

She squeezed his hand. 'Hey. I've been

thinking about when my contract's up.'

Finn tensed, just a little. 'Yeah?'

'I don't think I want to go back to live at Patersons. I need another adventure to look forward to.'

He laughed but it sounded wistful. 'Watch out, world, here comes Free. Where will you go?'

'I'll have to move out of 17A. I won't have a steady job, but maybe I could make a go of the art supplies thing with Bostons, and giving private lessons. What's the policy on couples living in these government-subsidised houses?'

Finn lay completely still beside her. 'You want to live with me?'

'Yes.' Although her nerves fluttered, her tone was firm. 'Yes, I want to live with you — quite a lot, actually. And maybe at the end of the year, if we save up our money, and if you have enough leave, we could go see your parents in Ireland for a few weeks. And your sister, and her kinda-average husband. And your little nephew, Henry.' She paused. '*Our* nephew.'

There was a long silence. 'Do you mean that?' he managed at last.

She turned her head and the joy in Finn's eyes threatened to make her own happiness spill over into tears. Again. She took a breath to steady her emotions.

'Yes.'

Finn flipped himself over the top of her and kissed her hard. *Holy shamole.* Free slipped her hands around the back of his big, strong neck and completely forgot that she'd wanted to hear him sing — until they were interrupted by a text message beeping through on her mobile. She grabbed her phone to toss it away from her but, as she did so, caught sight of the words 'All Creatures Clinic'.

She read the message, laughed, and showed it to Finn.

24

July was a wonderful time to spend a weekend at Patersons. The sky was clear, brilliant blue every day and the heat far milder than in the wet season. Free cut cherry tomatoes for a salad and paused to gaze out of the kitchen window, trying to memorise the paling gold where the blue hit the sunset, the river a dark streak in the distance.

Incredible.

One day, somehow, she would capture that blue.

'What are you doing, Beth?' Free was distracted by Willow's voice behind her.

'I'm making a salad dressing,' said Beth.

'We've got several nice dressings in the fridge.'

'No, this one is better. Trust me.'

'Is this your caesar avocado dressing, Beth?' Free asked, turning from the kitchen window.

'Yeah.'

'Oh good Lord, Willow, let her do it. It's freaking amazing.'

Willow backed off. 'You done with those tomatoes, Free?'

'Yep, here you go.'

They assembled the salad together and Barry came in to pour them drinks. 'You doing up a potato salad as well as the green one, sweetheart?' he asked Willow.

'Yes, Dad. The potatoes are here, cooked and ready.' She shot Free a glance and Free grinned back. Barry hated green salads.

'Don't forget the egg,' he advised. 'Your mum always put egg in.'

He departed, calling further instructions. Willow made a disgruntled noise. 'I swear . . . '

'I'll do the potato salad,' Beth told her.

Willow gave a sigh of relief, sinking onto a stool. She grabbed her glass of red wine and raised it to Free's white. 'Here's to a great outcome with the dam. I still can't believe you had to get arrested for the cause, but it was worth it in the end, right, Free?'

'Sure was,' was Free's fervent reply. 'Hopefully, this inquiry will pull together enough evidence to stop it altogether.'

'Another whistleblower from the Department of Planning has come forward, too, did you hear?' Willow said. 'More evidence of a corrupt approval process.'

'Jesus. They'll have to redo the whole application, surely,' said Beth.

Willow shrugged. 'Who knows? I hope so. There's bound to be a more thorough investigation of the issues if they do. Whatever the case, Buildplex is looking at huge fines.'

'Good to see them hitting Amanda Hamilton in the one place it will hurt,' said Beth.

Free agreed and reflected with grim satisfaction that Aidan was unlikely to get any more art commissions from Buildplex for a while. She attempted to banish the uncharitable thought.

Karma! That stuff was amazing.

'And what's happening with the school

424

residency, Free?' Beth asked. 'Are you finished now?'

'No, I've got a short extension,' she replied. She took the chives off the bench to rinse them. 'Because Aidan did such a crappy job teaching ceramics to the Year Tens, we decided to go through the skills and design stages with them again. I'll be there for another month, probably.'

'Are you getting paid for that?' Willow asked.

'Yes. Youth Arts coughed up some more money. I suspect they were able to recoup the loss when Aidan ducked out of his contract.'

Willow raised her eyebrows. 'So he never tried to worm his way back in?'

Free shook her head, returning the chives to Beth's board. 'We literally never saw the guy again. He went straight back to Perth. There's no way Jay would have had him back, anyway.'

Free checked on Max. He was asleep in his basket in the corner of the kitchen. He spent a lot of time sleeping these days, but he was getting braver — venturing out to seek his litter box or sniff out his food bowl. Max was on a special medicated food that he wasn't impressed with, but he hadn't lost any weight for the change. Cats were so damn resilient, she reflected. He still purred all night between her and Finn on the bed, as if he didn't even mind that he was mostly blind. The vet had assured Free that he was comfortable, although his life was likely to be shortened by the snakebite. Finn had scoffed when Free passed on that part of the message.

'You know what Max is like — he loves

surprising people. He'll be with us till he's twenty, just you watch.'

Free certainly hoped so.

'Can you keep your unit for the extra month?' said Willow.

'Technically, I could have kept it, but I gave it up. I've moved in with Finn — just this week, actually.'

Beth's efficient chopping paused for a brief moment, and then resumed.

'Tom heard you were living with Finn now.' Willow avoided Beth's eye as well, as though she expected their older sister to say something stern. 'Finn's not fazed that your income could be a bit unstable?'

'No, he seems fine with it. But I've got quite a few customers for Bostons now, plus the community centre has space for me to run an oils course starting in September. I've got a few sign-ups already.' She looked at Beth, but her sister was still chopping. 'I'm doing private art classes with a couple of students, too. Finn's set up a space in our front room for me to run one-on-one classes and a painting circle.'

'Oh, cool! How many have you got? All those kids who came around to your place when we visited that day? Anyone else?'

'I've got Tia, and there's Ethan and Jacqueline — brother and sister — all taking private lessons. Jorja and Leith come to painting circle, and Cameron sometimes. Cameron doesn't bother so much any more. He told me he was only ever coming along to hang around with Tia. She's agreed to go out with him now, so he's not as desperate to come paint every weekend.' Free grinned.

'And how's it going?' Willow asked. She shot a hasty glance over at Beth, who was now cutting up the cooked potatoes. 'Living with someone, I mean.'

'Good! I mean, we were practically living together anyway. I've met his mum and dad now — on Skype. They're so sweet. I can barely understand his dad, he's so Irish. And his sister's just as bad. I can't wait to meet them in person. Finn and I think we might tour the north of Ireland, but only for a few days, because we want to spend as much time as we can with Finn's family. Henry — the baby — he's so sweet! I'm painting him this wall frieze of Australian animals. It was Finn's idea. It will roll up nice and small for posting, or we can deliver it ourselves when we fly over at Christmas . . . ' Free stopped herself from babbling. What could be going through Beth's head?

Beth looked up at last. 'Have you got any mustard powder, Willow?' Willow fetched it obediently and Beth scraped the diced potatoes into a bowl with the herbs. 'I bet Finn's family love you, Free,' she said. 'They must be relieved he's got someone to anchor him after their sudden move.'

Free relaxed. 'Yeah. I get the vibe his mum's really glad he met me.'

They were only a few more minutes in the kitchen before they had finished putting together the salads, and then they went out to the patio where Tom was cleaning the barbecue. Willow took him a glass of wine and Free sat beside Finn on the old cane couch, which was positioned so the fading sunlight fell half over them. Finn took her hand and lifted it to his lips, kissing it almost absently as he listened to the conversation. It was like his love was as natural as breathing. Free tipped her head back and gazed upwards.

That sky.

Its precise shade still eluded her, but maybe it was meant to be that way. Maybe if she nailed it, there would be nothing left to work for. Nothing to chase — nothing that would push her to keep trying.

Yeah, that made sense. That tantalising blue was wondrous — perfect — yet unattainable.

Perfection had never been Free's thing, anyway.

Acknowledgements

Once again, I need to express my gratitude to the team that assisted in the production of this novel: my agent, Alex Adsett (especially for her suggestions when I was floundering in a sea of plotting problems); my publisher at Penguin Random House, Ali Watts, who gave me the best structural advice I could hope for; designer Louisa Maggio, who created a cover that is a work of art; and the fabulous editorial team that worked on the novel — Fay Helfenbaum, Saskia Adams, Penelope Goodes and Elena Gomez. Thank you also to the terrific publicity people at PRH who do such a great job in getting my books out into the world.

My gratitude goes to Lizzi Phillips, the specialist arts-media teacher at my daughter's high school, for providing her insights on the art and teaching elements of the story; and to my partner, artist Trevor O'Sullivan, who also helped with any arty questions I had (not to mention the usual support with plot struggles and self-doubt). My deep appreciation to Senior Constable Jan Walker for her detailed advice on the police work described in the book. I am also very grateful to Georgia for her encouragement and listening ear, and Kath for prompting me to make Aidan nastier and the Free-and-Finn dynamic just that little bit spicier!

A special vote of thanks to the reviewers and

readers, especially the advance readers, of book one *(Dear Banjo)*. Your kind words motivated me to write the best sequel I could write so that it would live up to the first book. It's been lovely getting to know many of you on social media or even in real life, and being able to cheer some of you along in your own writing careers. It's good to be part of the writing and reading village here in Australia.

And last of all, thank you to the real feline Max, for allowing me to use his name.